Twelve
NIGHTS

Twelve NIGHTS

ANDREW ZURCHER

PUFFIN

PUFFIN BOOKS

UK | USA | Canada | Ireland | Australia
India | New Zealand | South Africa

Puffin Books is part of the Penguin Random House group of companies
whose addresses can be found at global.penguinrandomhouse.com.

www.penguin.co.uk
www.puffin.co.uk
www.ladybird.co.uk

Penguin
Random House
UK

First published 2018

001

Text copyright © Andrew Zurcher, 2018

The moral right of the author has been asserted

Set in 12/19 pt Adobe Garamond Pro
Typeset by Jouve (UK), Milton Keynes
Printed in Great Britain by Clays Ltd, St Ives plc

A CIP catalogue record for this book is available from the British Library

HARDBACK
ISBN: 978–0–141–38554–9

INTERNATIONAL PAPERBACK
ISBN: 978–0–241–33294–8

All correspondence to:
Puffin Books
Penguin Random House Children's
80 Strand, London WC2R ORL

For my children, Aoife, Una and Eamon

Leap, heart, the wind will catch you —

Part One

WARP

I

Removals

The sun set at six minutes to four. Kay lay stretched out on the floor, reading the very small print on the back of the newspaper. Her right eye she had squeezed firmly shut; her left was growing deliriously tired, and the tiny words loomed at her amid the blur of her big sinking lashes. More and more she had to close them both, and relax her stiff cheek. More and more she squinted sidelong up at the world, with her head cocked to the right. But if her game caused her irritation, she also felt a sense of modest triumph: she had resisted the temptation to look straight at life since the moment she woke up that morning – exactly eight hours before, according to her watch. Had anyone asked her why she was still keeping her right eye shut at thirteen minutes past four in the afternoon of Christmas Eve, when her mother was going frantic and her little sister, Eloise, was playing jacks by herself in the back room, she wouldn't have known what to say. Keeping her right eye closed was simply something she had to do today, and she was doing it.

Just opposite her head, against the wall, leaned a large metal-framed mirror. Her father had promised to hang it above the fireplace, but three months later it still stood there, neglected, collecting dust. Kay regarded herself with curiosity in its dull glass. At school the teachers seemed to talk endlessly about character: having it, getting it, showing it and, above all, building it. Kay was sure she had none, or at least none that was visible. She was the person no one ever really noticed.

Her father was still at work – late, as he had been every day this week and every weekend this month. As he had been every month this year: down at the lab or his office, away for a fortnight on a dig, disappearing off to libraries or meetings – she couldn't keep track. This morning Kay's mum had wiped the worktops forcefully after breakfast, then promised her girls a bike ride and a trip to the cinema. But when the sun went down hours later, their winter shoes and coats still lay undisturbed by the door – exactly where they had left them the evening before. Kay could hear the telephone ringing, and she wondered if it was her father calling. He would be late, as usual.

Just as she was beginning to doze off, her head softly crackling on the open newspaper, her mother burst into the front room, her heels stomping like slippered hammers on the wooden boards. 'Get your coat on, Kay, we're going out. Get your sister's coat on.'

Five minutes later, as they sat in the back of the car blowing steam in the freezing air and giggling nervously, the two girls still had no idea where they were going, or why. As the engine turned over from gear to gear, in rhythm with the car's regular surges, their nervousness began to subside. Kay's hand still held the warm ache where her sister had been squeezing it. She put it in her lap. The night outside the window seemed sharp and clear, and the mostly white lights in the houses they passed shone with a direct intensity. Her window, by contrast, kept fogging up with her breathing. She moved her face impatiently around the glass as far as she could reach, but it was no use. As the car jolted through some lights and then curved down the hill, Ell fidgeted with her foot.

'Eloise, stop it. We'll be out of the car in two minutes.'

'But I have something in my boot. It's uncomfortable.'

Kay turned to the window again. She counted the street-lamps as they passed, numbering them by their glows on the silvery ground, still frosty from the night before. Her left eye was now growing ridiculously tired – or maybe it was the funny flatness of seeing with just one eye – because in the centre of the circle of light cast by every lamp she was sure she could make out a little circular shadow on the ground. Maybe it was just the wisps of foggy breath still clinging to the glass. She was tempted to open her other eye to check – but then, she thought, if she did, and the little dark circles were gone, would that prove that they weren't there, or that they were? Sometimes when you looked right at a star, you couldn't see it; but if you squinted or looked away, you could. And stars were there. Otherwise how would you wish on them?

And then, all at once, she knew where they were going, and why her mother hadn't answered her questions. The car pulled up and stopped outside the familiar gate. Kay went rigid in her seat, feeling her spine arch cold against the comfortable scoop of the fabric behind her. For her part, Ell was obviously disappointed. 'I don't want to go to Dad's work,' she whined, and kicked her grumpy and uncomfortable boot for emphasis against the seat in front of her.

A night porter sat on duty behind the window at the gate: an old, solid man, stiff and knotted as a fardel of wood, with a curve to his thick back and a white handlebar moustache hanging over a square-set jaw. Kay had never seen him before, but as he shuffled to his feet she recognized the white shirt, black trousers and waistcoat as the uniform of the university's porters. The gate opened, and he waved them through into the car park, but then hobbled out of his dimly lit room, down the steps and after the car. He seemed to guess where they would park, because Kay saw him making directly for the spot as her mother doubled round a set of spaces and then reversed back in. He moved with a deliberate and stilted pace, but he still got there just as they were opening the doors. It was a soft voice he had; not the sort of rough bark common to university porters. Maybe he had been to a Christmas party, Kay thought. People were always gentler after a Christmas party.

'Can I help you?' he said to Kay's mum. His voice sounded the way a flannel felt – dense, light and warm – and to Kay it was like a kind extended hand. Yet he stood with his hands dug in his pockets, his fingers working slowly within the fabric, as if turning over coins.

Kay's mum was pulling Ell off the booster seat, then checking the little purple boot absent-mindedly. Ell was too old for a child seat now, and far too tall, but her eighth birthday had been a night of tears, and Kay and her mother had afterwards gone from room to room – and even to the car – carefully restoring old and familiar things.

Her mother shook the little boot; a single jack clattered to the ground, which she retrieved and placed in Ell's outstretched hand. 'No, thank you,' she said. 'I'm just here to collect my husband. He's working late.'

'Everyone's gone home, I'm afraid, Mrs . . .' The man trailed off, and Kay watched him arch his bushy left eyebrow, expecting her mother to identify herself.

'Clare.' *That's because she doesn't have Dad's last name,* Kay thought. *She's not Mrs anybody.* 'Clare Worth.'

'Well, Mrs Worth, I'm not telling stories. As I said, I'm afraid everyone has gone home. The only cars still here are mine and old Professor Jackson's who died Tuesday last, God rest him, and I've been round the halls to lock up, and the place is sealed proper and shut down tight, lights off and not even a mouse.'

Kay felt her mother's arm tense where she was touching it lightly with the palm of her left hand. 'I'm sure you're right,' she said, 'but he did come down to work earlier, so I'll go up and have a look all the same.'

'What did you say your husband's name was? Worth?' The old porter sounded soft but insistent, like a wood pigeon maybe. He shuffled his stiff legs quickly to keep his balance. Kay thought for a second that he was almost smiling at the top left corner of his mouth, but then she changed her mind. Or maybe he changed his face.

'More. Dr More. Edward, I mean. More. He's a fellow at St Nicholas'. He's working on the Fragments Project.'

'Well, I can't say as I know the names of the projects,' said the old man. 'They come and go. But I got a pretty good head for the people, and I don't think I recollect seeing a Dr More before.' He drew a short breath, held his hands up to his face and blew hard on the tips of his fingers, trying to warm them. 'But I'm just the night porter around here.'

'Oh, you'll definitely have seen him,' Kay's mum said. 'He's down here almost every evening. Every night.'

The porter told her he had a directory and a telephone, and he would save Kay's mum the trouble by calling up to the office. She started to protest, but he had already hobbled painfully round and was walking back to his lodge. Eventually they trailed after him. Kay's mother's hand was cold in hers, but then it would be, in the middle of winter. They waited outside the steps of the tiny lodge – really just a bricked-in nook between two buttresses on the old archaeology building, with a lean-to roof and a pretty, circular window. The little window had silver stars stuck in it, and Ell pointed at them and started talking about a card she had made at school with stars just the same, and tinsel. She had repeated herself three or four times, to no effect, by the time the porter turned up again in the doorway. Kay tried to ruffle her hair, but it was drawn back over her scalp as tight as ice.

'I'm afraid I can't find Dr More on my list,' he said. 'In fact, I can't find him on the university list either. Edward More, you said? I tried both spellings.'

Kay's mum sighed heavily and, leaving the girls, went in. They were quiet enough under the window ledge to catch a few

8

snatches of conversation from within. The car park, silent and almost empty, had a few bare trees – saplings of four or five years' growth – dotted at regular intervals down two aisles. Kay remembered that there had been grass here once, but now it was almost all paved. The tree branches glistened black in the bright spotlights from the roofs of the archaeology building. The Pitt, they called it. Kay squeezed hard on her left eye, plunging herself into darkness, and gripped Ell's hand more tightly, as if to compensate.

When the door opened, the muted voices suddenly shot out and rebounded around the empty courtyard. Clare Worth was protesting again: '. . . don't understand. I mean, I know you say it's current, but he's definitely here. He's been here for years. I can show you the room.'

Kay heard the porter pick up his ring of keys, then pull the door shut behind them as they descended the three or four steps into the car park. Her eyes were still closed, and maybe that was why she heard the crisp echo in the courtyard so acutely, with its single clear report. Each step her mother took made a crack against the frosty stone and pavement.

'What did you say your name was?' Clare was asking the porter as Kay prised open her left eye again.

'Rex. Just Rex,' he answered with a wince. He stepped with a stiff hip over a low wall running round the inner grass border of the courtyard, and set off for the near corner where Kay's father had his laboratory and office, on the second floor. Her mother shot him a sharp glance, as if he had just loosed a tarantula, but then – with more resignation – pursued him. She seemed to have forgotten all about her daughters. She didn't speak again, but as she passed by, Kay could see that there were a lot of words in her throat; from the side it looked like it was going to burst open. She and Ell fell back and followed the two adults, holding hands and looking down, watching their footprints making tiny depressions in the frost, crunching slightly. Rex had a light step, Kay noticed, because although her mum's new shoes ground visibly into the frozen grass, for all his rough limp and shuffle Rex's feet didn't seem to make any noise, and hardly any marks at all. All she could hear were his keys jangling on the big ring in his right hand. For a second, in the glare from the spotlights, she saw it very clearly, that ring of keys, and noticed that it had an old-fashioned locking mechanism, with a hinge to open it – like something she had seen at her father's college once, hanging in the manuscript library. Only this ring wasn't plain. She caught another view of it as it swung again briefly into the light. She made out two bits of carving or metalwork, one on the hinge and another on the hasp. She watched for it as they walked, and with glimpse after glimpse she pieced together the design. It was the same on both sides: a long and sinuous snake entwined with a sword.

He must have been in the army, she decided. *He had probably been injured: the limp.*

'His room is on the second floor,' her mother was explaining. 'And his name is just here on the board – look . . .' And then her voice trailed off, because, as they could all see – and they were all looking – his name was not on the black painted board, where it had always been for as long as Kay could remember, in its official white lettering, next to the others. Where his name should have been, the board instead said, DR ANDREA LESSING. Her mother pushed through the heavy swinging doors into the stone lobby, and the girls trailed after.

'What's wrong?' Ell whispered to Kay. Her voice was sharp, urgent.

'This is some kind of joke, girls,' said Clare Worth, forcing a smile at them. 'It's a joke, that's all.' She took out her phone and dialled. 'I'll try the office again,' she was saying. 'There was no answer before, but maybe he's back now.' And then her face went white. 'Stay here,' she said, her voice suddenly pinched almost to a whisper. Turning, she practically leaped up the stairs.

Kay looked at the ring of keys. She stared at it, at every small detail, one after another, taking them in.

Rex noticed her staring, smiled, unhooked it from his belt and held it out to her. 'Have a look if you like,' he said with a warm half-chuckle. He passed her the whole set. His hands were big and gnarled, like the rootball of an oak. She observed them as she took the keys: oafish but gentle, and somehow slender, too, and as he stretched out his fingers she thought she smelled something sweet, like soft fruit – maybe blackcurrant. But then she had the ring. It held an amazing collection of keys. Even Ell came over to look, which was unusual because she tended to make a point of being officially uninterested in whatever Kay was doing. Kay handled them one by one. The best was an enormous key that looked like a fork, with sharp tines, and seemed to be made of gold. It had the same snake and sword cut into it as the ring. And there were three silvery keys, each slightly different from the other, but all with the same kind of shape: a long shaft, with a flat bit fixed at the end – one was square, one circular and one triangular. There were three wooden keys, too – but hard wood, almost like stone, with a gorgeous gold-flecked grain in them. And there were others, short and long, stumpy, heavy. There might have been twenty or thirty of them.

'Stupid keys,' said Ell, and she turned towards the full-length mirror that hung against the lobby wall, studying herself. Kay and the porter – Rex – watched her, too. That faint smile was hovering at his cheek again; like Kay, he knew that Ell didn't mean it. Her sister was shorter than Kay by a hand or more. Where Kay was olive-skinned and chestnut-haired, Ell had bright, almost translucent skin, and undulating tresses of a fine, almost golden red. Their father was fond of remarking that their family was composed of four elements. 'Your angel mother is the air, as open as the sky. I am the hard and plodding earth,' he would say, 'but you girls are the quick matter of the world.' Kay, he said, was water: silent, deep, cold perhaps, but quick with life. Ell, by contrast, was fire, hot and unpredictable, both creative and destructive.

Moody, more like, Kay thought. And she smiled, despite herself.

She looked at the grandfatherly porter and thought she should try to be polite. 'What are they all for?' she asked.

He was still watching Ell. 'Nothing of any consequence now,' he answered. 'Just look at that beauty,' he added, almost as if to himself. 'I'll wager she won't need any keys at all.'

Taking the steps two at a time, Ell had begun to jump up the spiral staircase in her fur-edged purple rubber boots. They were a little too big, a hand-me-down gift from Kay which she had not yet quite grown into. They made her seem smaller than she was; clumsy, a little delicate. At the fifth or sixth step she turned round, grinning impishly, her face flushed and radiant after the cold air outside, her full lips pink and puckered. With an air of priestlike gravity, as if she were performing a sacred ritual, she took her hand from her pocket, opening her palm to reveal three of the jacks she had been playing with earlier at home. 'Knucklebones', their father called them; it was that rare thing, a game he approved of, and he always said the same thing – 'a very ancient game of skill – and chance'. Ell was the acknowledged master of anything and everything to do with jacks, and she wore her title with pride. Now she tossed the little stars into the air, flipped her slender hand with a dancer's grace, and caught them neatly upon her knuckles.

Kay smiled. *Show off.*

It is sometimes the case that something exceptionally beautiful happens just before a calamity. The calamity even seems to reach back in time and twiddle the beautiful thing round, making it even more beautiful because of what was about to happen – or anyway, Kay thought a few moments later, that's how it comes to seem.

Ell looked so beautiful standing there, her lips grinning and pursed at once, her eyes dancing in the light from the lantern in the centre of the lobby, her radiant red hair now loosely draped across her shoulders, her whole form alight with daring and mischief. And then she started to take a step in those big, stupid purple boots, and tripped, and fell, and her face hit the floor first. The jacks clattered on to the stones before her outstretched hand.

In the gap before she could cry out, the porter, Rex, jumped to his feet and sprang lightly over to her. He reached down, lithe and strong, and caught her up. The movement was sinuous, the spring and cradle entirely balletic. Kay hardly had time to breathe before he was sitting down again, the whole sobbing form of her sister tightly, snugly nestled in his arms. She watched, at once shocked and mesmerized. For her part, Ell settled into Rex's arms as if he were a hearth.

Slowly he rocked her; slowly the little girl's sobs subsided. Kay noticed she was gripping Rex's keys so hard that her hand had turned white; a piece of sharp iron had made a welt on the edge of her palm. She held them out. The noise shook Rex from something like a reverie, and he looked up at her. Everything seemed to be happening very slowly. Ell sat up on his knee, as if awaking, and she, too, looked at Kay. Rex took the keys. Still he stared. And then Kay saw it: a perfect symmetry between the old man and the little girl – as if cut from a single stone by the same hand, as if painted in the same colours, as if sung by the same singer, they regarded her with their heads at an angle, their eyes at one focus, their mouths equally parted. All was equal. Kay froze.

'Sometimes,' Rex said slowly, somehow at once both fulfilling and breaking the spell, 'something exceptionally beautiful happens just before a calamity.'

Every hair on the back of Kay's neck stood up, but not in fear. His eyes were too kind for that – as if they were the eyes of her own sister. Sometimes, somehow, something.

'I think these are yours,' he said to Ell as he tipped the three spilled jacks from his palm into hers. Ell looked at them, picked one out and presented it to him.

Just then Clare Worth came running two at a time down the spiral stairs. She sprinted past them, out through the double doors and into the courtyard. Rex set Ell on her feet, then, with some deliberateness, put his hands on his knees, pushing himself up. Slipping the jack in his pocket and hooking the keys back on to his belt, he held the girls' hands, and they walked after Clare Worth as quickly as he could. A few minutes later, safely belted in the back seat of the car, both girls turned as their mother – oblivious – pulled out of the Pitt car park. They were still stunned, watching for the old man on his step. He stood there, looking, Kay thought, like a man composed all of sadness, like someone condemned for a crime he did not commit. His hand was raised in farewell.

It was the same at St Nick's. No one seemed to know Edward More there, either; and the college room where Kay had spent her half-term holidays, looking impatiently out of the window at the afternoon activity, had someone else's name over the door. In fact, it had the same name over the door as that on the board in the Pitt: DR ANDREA LESSING. Only this time the light inside was on, and the woman who answered Clare Worth's knocking appeared to be as surprised as they were. She was tall, but also somehow small and delicate, and Kay thought her bones were probably as thin and wispy as her gold hair. She was wrapped up in serpentine coils of scarves and throws.

'I have no idea what you can possibly mean,' she said. 'I've had these rooms for the last fifteen years. I've never had any other rooms for as long as I have been at St Nick's. Have a look round,' she continued, stepping back from the door and gesturing around the room with fine, elegant fingers. Kay thought they looked, each one, like nimble snakes, writhing with venom and muscle. 'These are my books, my things, my work.' Kay's mum had been frantically explaining while two porters hovered nervously on the stairs behind them, unsure whether to intervene. 'I really can't help you,' Dr Andrea Lessing added. 'In fact, I was just about to go home for the holiday.' She started to close the door, but Clare Worth had seen something, and she wedged her foot firmly in the way.

'I don't know you,' she said accusingly. Kay shrank from the menace in her mother's voice.

'I am sorry for that, but I hardly think it's my fault,' replied Dr Andrea Lessing.

'Are you an archaeologist?' Clare Worth's eyes moved more wildly now, ranging around the room, trying to make out the titles of the books just to the left of the door. The light was low. Kay noticed that her own leg was shaking, so she pressed her foot hard into the floor of the staircase. 'I see you have some of

16

the same books my husband has,' she said. '*Many* of the same books, in fact. Do you work on the Fragments Project?'

'Mrs More –'

'My name is Worth.'

'Mrs Worth, really, I'm sorry, I don't have time for this. Yes, I do, but no, I really must ask you to let me close the door and get home to my family.' Dr Andrea Lessing was pushing the door. Kay's mum's foot was sliding back on the wooden boards. Then her heel hit the ridge where the raised lip of the door-frame blocked the draught. Her foot held. There was an awkward silence, and the porters started to shift, leaning forward as if about to intervene. Kay drew a breath and raised her hand to reach out, to touch her mother on the shoulder or at the vulnerable place at the tip of her elbow. She wanted to get her out of this place. Instead, Ell's hand shot out and took hers; her face was fierce and full.

'Do you know about the Bride of Bithynia?' It was her mother's most level, grave, but also, now, desperate tone.

Kay knew it the way she knew how the stone outcrop behind her house felt to her knee when she smashed down upon it with her full weight. She knew it as well as she knew the tread of the stairs to her room, the soft click of the door's latch behind her, and the comforting, lofty quiet of her top bunk. And she knew that the diminutive Dr Andrea Lessing had to be pushing with enormous force, because this door suddenly slammed shut on her mother, knocking her back on to her left foot and very nearly crushing Kay and Ell against the cold and flaking plaster of the stairwell.

Clare Worth looked dazed, her daughters not less so. The porters were clearly distressed and apologetic. For some reason they could not explain or understand, they felt a sympathy for Clare Worth, whom they knew they knew, though they couldn't say the first thing about Edward More. They kept saying so to one another in muted tones as they walked back through Sealing Court. Clare Worth seemed to have given up trying to understand. The porters held the door for the girls as they stepped through the wicket of the Tree Court gate, back into Litter Lane, where they had distractedly ditched the car half an hour before. With gingerly moving fingers the two men ushered the gate closed behind them, as softly as they could, trying not to give the impression, Kay thought, that they were shutting them out. But they *were* shutting them out. And the moment the lock clicked, Kay's mum began to cry. She didn't move from the gate or put her hands to her face. She just looked down. The only sound Kay could hear was a ventilation fan up the alley, pumping steam and the smell of grease out from the college kitchens. Ell shivered at Kay's light touch.

'Mum,' Kay said.

'Yes, Katharine, what?'

'Mum, there was something strange about that porter at the Pitt. Rex.'

'What, Katharine?' She was still crying. Clare Worth didn't sob when she cried, but the tears now came quickly and heavily.

'Well, for one thing, when you were walking up to Dad's office – well, what *should* have been Dad's office – and the courtyard was really quiet, your feet were making a lot of noise on the stone, and you were leaving footprints in the grass. And so were we. I checked.' Ell had been kicking a cobble. Now she stopped.

'Yes, of course, Kay.' Clare was reaching in her pocket to find an old tissue, which she laboriously picked apart and flattened. She sounded annoyed. Kay took and squeezed Ell's hand while she waited, but Ell pulled it away and stared hard at her sister, as if to warn her off, to make her stop. Ell was always telling her not to bother Mum, not to stick her nose into other people's business.

'Well, you know how that old porter had a limp or something? And he walked heavily? But he didn't leave any prints on the grass, and I don't think I could hear his feet on the cobbles at all.'

'Katharine.' Clare Worth exchanged the tissue in her hand for the keys in her pocket and unlocked the car. 'That's the very least of my worries right now. Something horrible is going on, and footprints in the frost don't matter. Not at all.' She stood up and bore down on her daughters with newly hardened eyes. 'Now get in.'

In the back of the car, Ell's face was wearing that fierce look again. 'Told you,' said her eyes.

So Kay didn't mention the other things on her mind: Ell's fall, the strange kindness and familiarity of the porter, and something she thought she'd seen in the room at St Nick's — what should have been her father's room, but was the room of Dr Andrea Lessing. Something she had seen while her mother was being pushed back on to her left foot as the door closed abruptly behind the enormous strength of a very slight woman. Instead the two girls sat quietly and the car moved slowly, almost reluctantly, through the empty, dark streets, past the reaching winter spines of the chestnuts and the hawthorns and the oaks and the beeches and, above all, the countless lime trees, blacker than the visible light of the black night. And she didn't ask about the Bride of Bithynia, and they ate their cold supper where it still sat on the plates Clare Worth had set out in the afternoon. And because of the tears that sometimes drew and dropped down their mother's cheeks, the girls did as they were asked, or expected, and never once thought of their baubled and tinselled tree, unlit, or of the wooden box that contained their stockings, which in the past they had always hung from the mantel on Christmas Eve. And they never once dared open the door of their father's study, for fear of the emptiness Kay was sure (her ear pressed to the door's painted wood) would lie within it – the vacant shelves, the cleared desk, the stacks of papers that would not stand there on the floor where they had always stood before. The girls never once uttered a single word. Instead they brushed their teeth, and they dressed for bed, and they turned off the light. And all the time, without speaking at all, Kay kept her right eye shut, and Ell picked at her hands, and Clare Worth wiped those occasional tears from the bottom of her jaw on the left side, so that they didn't drip on her blouse.

But when Kay climbed up into her bunk bed, she felt something on her pillow. It was a card. She knew at once that she hadn't left a card on her bed. It was small and stiff, about the size of the train tickets they sometimes got when Mum took them to Ely for a summer picnic. Kay held it up. She couldn't read the writing at first; but a light shone from her mother's room, where – uncharacteristically – she was sobbing a little, and a shaft of it, shooting through a crack in the door, caught the card as Kay turned it. Then the silvery letters leaped out, glittering in her hands. It read:

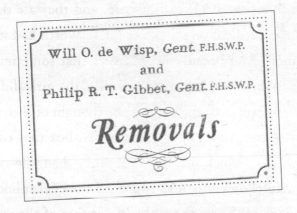

Kay was exhausted, and below her Ell had as usual fallen asleep the moment her head hit the pillow. Listening to her deep breaths made Kay the drowsier, and she looked more and more vacantly at the strange card as it clung to the light in her weakening hand. Just before her left lid finally collapsed, and just as her hand was dropping out of its shaft of light, she might briefly have glimpsed the other side of the card, with its carefully stencilled and embossed silver emblem – the very symbol that, an hour before, she thought she had seen on a book lying on Dr Andrea Lessing's wide wooden desk; a symbol she definitely *had* seen several times that day: the body of a snake entwined with the blade of a sword.

*I*s it done?'
   'Yes.'
'And have they left no trace?'
'Nothing.'
'And the children?'
'The children?'
'Has no one taken order for the children?'
'But –'
'You are a fool.'
'But the order sheet –'
'You are every one of you fools. Did I not use the old words so
that you might understand? Did I not speak them in your ear, as
in the old tales that you love? The snake must strike with the
sword.'
   'It will be done as you say.'
   'They must all be destroyed – the thieving fox and his little
cubs.'
   'As you order it, so it will be.'
   'See that it is.'

2

The Author

Kay was suddenly aware that she had been hearing voices. It was completely dark, so it had still to be night. She turned over very quietly on to her right side, and strained into her ears to hear. At first, still drowsy, she thought it was her mother talking on the phone; but these were low voices, men's voices, and distant – maybe downstairs or in the garden. Then she realized, again at a stroke, that it was dark because her eyes were closed. Though at first slightly afraid to look, she cracked her left eye open imperceptibly. Everything appeared as black as if she had left it shut – until perhaps she saw a flash of light like a headlight sweeping across her window.

She was imagining it. It was nothing but the wind, the moon. Her father said she had *such* an imagination. *Give her a pebble*, he said, *and she will build a castle*.

'Ow!' It was a whisper, or a kind of sharp and hissing breath, but it was loud and unmistakable.

'It's hardly my fault you're so slow. Or that we're gambolling about on gables for the second time in twelve hours.'

'We've been over this already. I couldn't have known she would take it with her. It's not altogether customary to go about town with someone's tooth in your pocket, now, is it? I admit I was wrong in the Habsburg case –'

'You couldn't have been *more* wrong in the Habsburg case –'

'And I said I admit it. But that's quite a different matter. Failing to collect a tooth and omitting – well, omitting a whole body are not, the last time I looked, even on the same page of the code.'

'You didn't just miss the body.'

Kay was more alert now, and her left eye widened. The voices were coming from outside, and there was a light, a light that every so often swept across her window behind the curtain. *It must be a torch*, she thought. There had been a fair amount of grunting and scrabbling, but that stopped now.

'Look, you weren't there. As I testified at the tribunal, it was an honest mistake. The order said, *Archduke Bartolomeo, Prince of Prussia*, and the address was a villa in Vienna. So I went to the place, searched it and identified the subject. I followed procedure and submitted the order sheet. He must have known I was coming. It's not my fault he switched the body – I mean, *his* body – for someone else's. And it looked the same to me; it was right where I'd left it, under a mulberry tree in a courtyard garden, wrapped in a silk kaftan. Still haven't figured out how he knew I was coming.'

'That's hardly the point. You removed the emperor, by the muses!'

'Well, that was a bit on the embarrassing side, I admit. But how was I to know he was the emperor? It's not as if I'd ever seen him up close. Emperor Shmemperor. And like I said, he was just where I'd left the archduke, all wrapped up and dozing under the mulberry tree, as dukishly as you like. Arch as can be. Now what's an emperor doing dozing under a mulberry tree? I ask you.'

'He was wearing the imperial crown, Will.'

'Look, Flip, I'm in removals now. I'm a removals guy. I'm not a herald, I'm not a lawyer and I'm definitely not an emperor. For better or worse – mainly, if truth be told, for worse – I'm in removals. I remove.'

'By the stones, Will, you may be my best friend, but you're still half idiot. Ow!'

Then the grunting started again, and Kay heard a scraping noise – the tiles, the tiles on the lower part of the roof. She flinched; these voices were close.

'Anyway, this is hardly comparable. We'll just pop in, find the tooth and get out again. Nothing simpler.'

'When it comes to working with you, Will, nothing is ever simple.'

The light outside the curtain was bright now, and Kay reckoned they were just on the other side of the window. Something was sounding a note in her head like the muffled bell of a broken alarm clock. *A tooth?* What were they talking about?

Kay tried to sit up straight, but the blood rushed from her head and the world spun giddily around her. And then she remembered the card that had been on her pillow – the card that was now under her pillow. She pulled it out and looked at it again. There at the bottom, in large letters, it clearly read, **Removals**. So these were the removers, Will O. de Wisp and Philip R. T. Gibbet. But who were they here to remove?

Like a wave it broke on her: they were talking about her father's tooth – his wisdom tooth, which he had had removed last year and had given her (reluctantly) because she had asked him for it. Begged him for it, in fact. To remember. She kept it in the left pocket of her cardigan, which was hanging – where? – on the near post of her bed. The cardigan she had been wearing on Christmas Eve. Today. Yesterday.

They were very close now, close to the window, probably shoved up against the ledge. All the scrabbling and scraping against the roof tiles, so clear in the dark stillness of the house, had stopped. In the silence she could hear the latch turning. As quickly as she could, she reached out her hand, stretched down until the blood screamed in her head, felt her way into the pocket of her cardigan and retrieved the tooth. She put it in the palm of her right hand, which she clenched into a fist under her pillow. Then she closed her open eye and, pressing her head with great purpose into the soft down, pretended to be asleep.

Every space has its own noise, like a fingerprint. Most of the time no one notices this noise, of course – it might be a hum, or in some seasons an occasional creak, a draught, the skittering of birds or maybe mice or hedgehogs in the garden. In the winter, for the girls' room, this ambient noise was the quiet

26

voice of the tall evergreens two or three metres outside their window, swaying in the wind or scraping against the corner of the house when disturbed by some night-foraging animal. As Kay lay in her bed with her eyes tightly closed (too tightly? – she relaxed them) and her right hand clutching her father's tooth beneath her pillow, that familiar noise changed completely – opened up as a draught swept in past the curtain. The two men were in the room.

Kay's heart stamped.

'Ow!' One of them tripped off the sill, crashed through the curtain and landed heavily on the floor. Kay held her breath, certain that her mother would have heard it, or that Ell at least would wake up.

'Sshhh,' said a voice from the window. And then, 'Is this tooth really necessary? What happens if we just leave it?'

'Flip, if you want to go back and submit the order sheet to Ghast without all the movables accounted for, that's up to you.' Will sounded like he was sitting up as he whispered, 'To be perfectly frank with you, after the whole Habsburg business I don't mind if I never see Ghast's dirty little nostrils widen at me again . . . Hmm. I think I may develop a bruise.'

'Well, I hope so,' said Flip. 'There'd be no fun left in pushing you if you didn't get hurt once in a while.'

At this Kay dared to crack her left eye open again. Between the fuzz of her parting lashes she saw the light of the torch held in the hand emerging from behind the curtain. It was pointing at the wall opposite her – or, rather, panning the wall as Flip began searching for the tooth.

'Where do you reckon she keeps it?' Flip said, the top of his head curling round the heavy curtain to look down at Will, who was still rubbing his shin.

In the dim light Kay could see almost nothing about them, except that they both seemed very tall, almost stretched or elongated – like the thinned and distorted shadows of normal shapes cast by a light lying on the ground.

'And would you mind getting up to help me, please?' said Flip as an impossibly endless leg (*like a spider's*, Kay thought) came swinging over the sill and under the curtain. The rest of him followed lankily into the cramped room. Flip turned immediately back to the far wall – to the bookcase, the chest of drawers and the small pile of toys still tumbled in the corner where Ell had left them that morning. Which was lucky, because what Will said next made Kay, for only the tiniest second, open her eye very wide indeed – and had Flip been looking in her direction, he could not have missed it.

'The order sheet,' said Will noisily as he unfolded a crumpled piece of paper retrieved from his coat, 'says it will be in the left pocket of her cardigan. Or, with a very low probability, in her right hand.'

'Cardigan?' asked Flip.

'Bedpost,' Will shot back. And then the light swung round, and Flip's body followed it, leaving Kay a split second to squeeze her eye shut again. She held her breath and concentrated on not moving her right fist, with its now precious prize, even a millimetre. But for all her heroic self-control, for all her theatrical stillness, it was already too late. Over the top of

28

his paper, even as he spoke, Will's eyes had settled directly upon her.

Kay felt everything change in the room around her.

Everything.

'Flip,' breathed Will, staring at Kay in a way that she could feel all over her face, despite the fact that her eyes were jammed shut. 'Flip, we have a problem.'

Kay's heart beat a path right out of her chest and into her throat. It was suddenly so tight in her head that she could hardly hear them as they carried on talking.

'Will, you *are* a problem,' answered Flip. 'What now?'

For an instant there was complete silence, and Kay was dimly aware of the sound of the fir tree outside scraping against the gutter.

'We've been witnessed,' Will said in the same low and measured voice. 'It's all right, little girl, you can open your eye,' he said. 'We won't bite.'

'But I read the order sheet. The order sheet doesn't say anything about her being a witness,' Flip whispered hard, like a hawk plummeting to strike, as he stepped over to Will and took the papers. He hauled Will to his feet and then began to scan them. 'Nope,' he said, running his finger down the page. 'No, no, no, no. No powers, no history, no prophecy, no witness. She's entirely clean. No bio on her whatsoever. She can't see us. She can't see us for what we really are.'

'She can see us all right,' said Will, peering at Kay. He was so tall that his head, slightly bowed under the pitch of the sloping ceiling, was level with her own as she lay on the top bunk. He cocked it to one side to look straight at her. 'Hello,' he said in a friendly voice, cracking a smile. 'Hello, little witness. Let's have a look at you.'

Kay huddled back against the wall as his gathering hands suddenly loomed out of the darkness towards her, but it was no use resisting – he was as strong as he was tall, and despite the wadded blankets he had her sitting up in a second. She buried her right hand behind her, almost sitting on it under a lump of duvet.

'Ah. I think we've located the tooth,' Will said over his shoulder. 'In her hand, just as the sheet says.'

Kay had a good stare at him in the indirect light from the torch, which Flip had trained on the pages of the order sheet as he raced hurriedly through them. Will was broad and tall but, on more careful consideration, strangely skinny. The light almost seemed to shine through his shoulders. His neck also appeared normal enough until you looked right at it, when it would suddenly seem to stretch, or twist, or narrow – or something. She couldn't put her finger on it. He was dressed in a long robe or cloak like a housecoat, with a thick rope belt around his waist. The cuffs of his sleeves flared like trumpets, but his wrists were as bony and wraith-like as everything else about him, seeming to disappear into the cavity of his clothing. But he had been so strong, she thought, lifting her up and sitting her back on the bed as if she were almost weightless. And, she noticed suddenly as she searched again for his face, he had a strange way of looking at you with only one of his eyes at a time, or perhaps with both eyes but differently. And with his left eye he was by now studying her very closely. He leaned forward, putting his chin on the edge of her mattress, his elegantly fingered hands tucked up beneath it.

'So,' he said in a very soft and winning voice, 'are you going to give us the tooth? Because I for one would like to go home and get some rest.'

Kay shook her head slowly, then a bit faster.

Will's smile dissipated, and he frowned comically at her from beneath furrowed brows. 'You're not?' he asked. He frumped, sticking out his lower lip.

Kay shook her head again.

'She says she's not going to give us the tooth,' said Will over his shoulder.

Flip was still running his finger down page after page of the order sheet, and seemed not to be able to hear anything but his own murmuring.

Will turned back to the bed. 'Why? Don't you want me to get some rest?' He tried smiling again.

Kay stared at him. She wasn't sure she could speak even if she wanted to. Her throat felt as if it had suddenly been transformed into a brown paper bag.

'It's just that that tooth is extremely important to my career prospects,' Will said, nodding. 'If I don't bring it back to my boss, I might get, you know, laid off.' He shook his head. 'And then what would I do? Freelance fabling? Not a good line of work,' he went on, pausing with two very angular, narrow eyebrows raised. 'Ethically very dubious.'

'Will.' Flip looked up from his papers with a desperate blankness. 'They're not all here. The papers. The order sheet.

There's another page. Look – here, at the bottom . . . it says, page eighteen of nineteen, and then that's it, that's the last sheet. So there's another one. Where is the last sheet, Will? Will, tell me you have the last sheet.' Flip had moved quickly over to the bed, and in a frenzied haste was digging his hands on either side into Will's cloak pockets.

Will, who had stood up slightly stiffly with a sort of doomed but resigned look on a face that now looked lined and haggard, was shoving his own hands deep into other pockets. Kay could hear the chink of metal and the rustle of paper, and many other strange noises besides as the four hands groped around inside more pockets than she could keep track of; pockets that seemed to dive well beyond the depth of a standard lining.

Flip was in up to his elbows when Will suddenly brightened. 'Here, I think I've got it.'

It was a piece of paper folded up very bulkily into a small square. In the dim light Will began gingerly to unpick it from its various tucks and creases.

'Oh, yes, I remember now,' he said as he undid the last fold and tried to flatten it out against the side of Kay's bed, gently stretching along the creases. 'I had a terrible sneezing fit just as Ghast gave me the order, and –'

'I'll have that,' Flip broke in as he swiped the paper impatiently from Will's hand and began to read.

Will made a face at Kay that seemed to say, *Yuck*. She almost giggled.

'Oh no. No – for the love of all that follows, no. Will, you really are a walking disaster.'

32

With a quick snatch of her left hand Kay grabbed the corner of her duvet and drew it up over her knees and around her shoulders. The air in the room had become uncomfortably cold, and the curtain continued to flutter with the light breeze outside. She huddled in the top corner of her bed and flexed her right fist behind her, feeling the edges of her father's tooth in her palm. That hand was clammily hot; the rest of her body, by contrast, was freezing. The cold would be sure to wake Ell, she thought, for Ell was a light sleeper at the best of times. Will had gone back to watching her intently – or, rather, watching intently that part of her right arm that disappeared behind her back – while Flip kept up his agitated reading and muttering.

'You're not going to believe this,' Flip said with a sigh, looking up. Kay saw the same angular face, the same high brows, the same strange gaze. 'I'd better read it to you in full.'

'If it means Ghast is going to dazzle me with his nasal musculature, I'd really rather you didn't.' Will laid his right cheek gently on the mattress and closed his left eye. Kay noticed how, although his brows were black, his hair shone a silvery white in the low light from Flip's torch.

'No, I'm afraid you have to hear this. It's an order proviso, double-underlined, at the foot of the inventory. It's in Ghast's own hand. *Note*, it says. *Domestic removal must be performed while the subject's family is off the premises. Under no circumstances attempt to capture subject or movables in their presence. Do not approach them, even in their sleep.* Did you hear that, Will? We're not even supposed to be here. Oh, for the love of the nine sisters, I can't believe this.' He paused and took a deep breath. 'But there's more. This is the best bit. You're going to love this,' he said, looking up with an expression that seemed to suggest anything but love, and stared at Will's hunched back. '*Subject's daughter is an author*. She's not a witness, you unplottable oaf, she's an *author*.'

Only then, when he stopped speaking, did Kay realize that Will had begun quietly humming to himself – a quick, zippy sort of song. But he stopped at those last words, and there was total silence in the room. Not even the garden's evergreen boughs stirred in this void.

'An *author*,' Flip repeated quietly, and his arm fell to his side, and the torch drooped until its beam shone directly, and very brightly, on the tiny patch of carpet in front of his left knee. Kay was relieved to find herself back in the anonymity of near darkness. Her heart had stopped racing now, and the violent trembling that had made her gather up her duvet had subsided. She thought, as she suddenly found herself swallowing easily and clearing the lump in her throat, that she could speak. So she did.

'Excuse me,' she said. And, more timidly, 'Who are you?'

Will propped his chin back up on the mattress and opened his eye, staring directly into her face from the gloom. His iris looked a deep and inexhaustible grey, and in this light the crow's feet opening into his cheeks seemed to gape like cracks.

Those cracks. Kay was scared she might fall into one of them. 'And what do you mean, I'm an author, please?'

'We're going to have to tell her everything,' Will said to Flip as he continued to regard her carefully but kindly. And then, after a pause, very softly, he said, 'An author. I never thought I would see another author.'

Flip, who had been kneeling bowed on the floor, stood up slowly, as if he were extraordinarily tired. He lifted the torch, throwing light again around the room, and Kay watched him carefully as he turned and, though still slightly stooped, lifted his shoulders to their full height. He passed the torch to his right hand, came up beside Will, put his left arm over his shoulder and then lifted the torch up on to the top bunk, resting it on the bottom corner of the duvet, pointing towards the back wall.

'I'm Flip,' he said, 'and this is Will. We're wraiths.'

Kay stared at them, then tried swallowing again.

'I knew that much,' she said. They both started. 'Your names, I mean. It's because I woke up when you were coming up the roof. I heard what you were saying,' she explained. 'But I don't understand what you're doing here, or why you left me this card, or why you want my father's tooth. Or anything. And I wish you would close the window before Ell and I catch cold.' With her left hand she handed Will the card as Flip ducked behind him to pull the window shut.

'Flip, we should do this introduction properly,' Will said. Flip nodded slowly with his lips pursed pensively together. 'It's like this,' Will went on. 'I'm Will O. de Wisp, wraith and removals man, Fellow of the Honourable Society of Wraiths and Phantasms.' He stepped back and bowed. 'This is my friend Flip Gibbet, also of the Honourable Society and, well, also in removals. We've got an order here from the Sergeant of the Honourable Society to remove your father; an order that comes directly from the top. We started the job this morning and finished with the movables this evening, but we neglected to collect one item – the tooth I think you are hiding in your fist back there – so we had to come back before we could submit for completion. Now, normally we wouldn't have had any trouble with this whatsoever, but seeing as you're an author . . .' He stumbled over this again, and for a moment breathed quickly. 'As you're an author,' he repeated, 'you overheard us and woke up and got involved, and, well, now we have to deal with you.'

Kay looked at Flip, who was nodding slightly, his head tilted to his shoulder. Suddenly he seemed to have thought of or remembered something, and he reached quickly into one of his cloak pockets.

'I'm sure I've got one somewhere,' he said. And then he pulled out a black eyepatch like a pirate's, and held it out to her. 'You might be needing this for a short while, just till your eyes get used to it. It could be easier on the cheeks.'

Leaning forward slightly, Kay took it carefully from him, only to draw quickly back again to pin her right arm against the wall. Settled, she looked at the patch in her hand, where it lay like a dark blot in the darker darkness.

'Will,' said Flip. 'Something tells me this one isn't going to need a patch.'

Will hadn't shifted or broken Kay's gaze, but suddenly he seemed to be staring into her eyes as if she were the dawn and he had waited all night to see her rise.

'Yes,' he said. 'Yes. Keep the patch if you like, but for now, try opening your eyes. Just –' and here he folded his arms up and across his chest, then spread them out like a flower blooming, to take in the whole of the dark room around them – 'just try to keep looking at the world *lightly*. Or don't try – just let it happen. See with two eyes as if they were one.'

Kay let her lids fall gently closed, relaxing all the muscles in her face. It was such a relief that it almost hurt. She thought maybe the wraiths might try to steal the tooth while her eyes were shut, that it was all a ruse. For a second she tensed. But the lightness in her face was too great a pleasure to be surrendered. *Lightly*. She opened her eyes.

The wraiths were still there. Kay's lids blinked fast as a butterfly.

'Now you're practically one of us,' said Will. And then, his face changing, he added hurriedly, 'Ma'am.'

Kay stared stupidly back at them, not sure what to say. Her mother was always telling her to be frank, and never to use two words where she could make herself understood with one. She cut to the chase.

'What do you mean, you have to deal with me? Why do you want my tooth? Where have you put my father?'

Flip answered this time. 'Well – ma'am,' he said, looking quickly – and was it questioningly? – at Will, 'it's as my colleague says. We had an order to remove your father, and we did; and when you remove someone, you also have to take all the movables, the things, associated with that person, so that no trace of them survives in the place from which they have

37

been removed. Otherwise they go on – well, you just do. And we have a complete inventory of his movables –' here he held up the first eighteen pages of the order sheet he had studied so carefully – 'but my *esteemed* partner here –' and here he turned pointedly, at very close range, to Will, and clownishly stuck out the tip of his tongue – 'managed to miss one item – the tooth – during completion this afternoon. So here we are.'

They were clearly not used to explaining themselves, Kay thought. She noticed that she had relaxed her grip a bit on the duvet and she shifted her weight slightly to make herself more comfortable. She sat up a bit higher.

'It's not every day,' Flip went on, 'that a wraith runs into a witness while on a job, but when it happens – it happened, you know, to my cousin Hinkypunk just last year,' he said, turning to Will, who nodded vigorously and with great compassion. 'Well, when it happens, you have to remove the witness, too. Then the Sergeant settles it.'

Kay looked at them, a bit more nervously now. She still had no idea what was involved in being 'removed' or what an 'author' was, and she was about to ask when Flip suddenly prevented her by adding quickly, 'But of course we can't remove *you*, you being an author and all.' He smiled brightly and looked at Will.

Will looked puzzled. 'We can't?' he said.

'No, we can't,' said Flip with finality.

Kay broke in abruptly. 'But what is –?'

But just then, more abruptly still, from the bunk below, Ell gave a loud yawn, murmured something only partly intelligible, and turned heavily over in her sleep. They had all forgotten her. After a moment of what looked like panic in the two wraiths' faces, only Kay was left in a slight agitation, anxious lest Ell should wake up and get removed herself.

Flip, cool again, seemed to understand her worry before she voiced it. 'It's quite all right. According to the order sheet, which is always correct, neither your mother nor your sister can see us or hear us – I mean, *really* see us for what we are. Had they received our calling card, they wouldn't have noticed it. They'd have thought it a blank scrap. Had they heard our voices, it would have been the wind moaning. If they'd bumped into us, they would have persuaded themselves that we were other people entirely, or perhaps that they had imagined us. It's a trick in the way you look at things, or the way you get others to look at things.' With one long, elegant finger he tapped his temple at the corner of his eye. 'Only witnesses can really see us.'

'And authors, obviously,' Will added.

'Who are you?' Ell asked sleepily from the bunk below.

Now, Kay thought, the wraiths really were stunned. They stood so rigid that they bumped their heads on the ceiling.

'Was this on the order sheet?' Will asked.

Flip shook his head. Very slowly they let their eyes sink to the lower bunk, then inclined their heads and dipped their shoulders; and soon they were both doubled over, staring intensely at Ell. She was rubbing her right eye with her right fist. Her strawberry curls bobbed softly about her round, plump face as she herself bobbed slightly, still waking from a deep sleep. She yawned again, and propped herself up a bit higher on her elbow.

'Are you visiting Mummy?' she asked, looking back and forth from one to the other. 'Is Daddy back? Is Kay here?'

Kay was here; in fact, she was already on the bunk ladder, and it wasn't two seconds before she was beside her little sister, her right hand and the tooth already firmly dug in behind them in a wad of duvet, as before.

'This,' said Flip, 'is unexpected in the very extremest sense.'

'This is downright creepy,' agreed Will.

'If we go with you,' Kay said quickly, 'can we get our father back?'

Flip had already started to shake his head, and was about to explain about the irreversibility of removal, when Will cut him off abruptly.

'That's something you'd have to take up with Sergeant Ghast,' he said. 'But I'm sure he would be only too happy to discuss it with you. And we could have you there very quickly.'

Flip began to protest. 'Will, she's a child, and it's a day's flight, and Ghast –'

'No, Flip. In all our years we've never left an author behind – and this one is something special, or I'm not a phantasm.'

'What's a phantasm,' Kay blurted. It wasn't even a question.

'A wraith. An appearance,' Will said. 'Something or someone that appears. Someone who is both there and not there.'

'So you're not really here?'

'I'm here,' Will answered.

'I'm not,' said Flip with an exasperated shake of his head. 'I'm off.' He strode to the window and levered his long body between the curtains. They heard him slide across the short slope of the roof, then swing down to the ground. His footsteps crunched away across the frosty grass.

'Fine,' said Kay decisively, 'we'll go. But I keep the tooth.'

'What tooth? Go where?' asked Ell. 'Where are we going, Kay?'

'To find Dad,' she replied. Just then the window, off its latch, swung in a gust wildly against the metal frame, then back out into the wide, black, icy night.

'*B*ring him before me.'
   'As you order it.'
'Let him not speak. We shall hear no tales tonight. Tighten the bridle.'
'It is done.'
'See, all of you, what it is to give up your life to fond hopes and foolish dreams. Look how time hangs on him like a ragged cloth. The dirt of it crusts on his skin. And when you cut him – watch, all of you; watch how he bleeds. There is nothing so frail as blood, nothing so delicate. It rises and it falls. Its passions are unpredictable. It deceives the mind with visions. It binds the heart to its wild fantasies. Blood is a weakness.'
'But the wound –'
'It is not mortal. Truss him, you two, and take him to the Imaginary. It will amuse me to think of him lying there, feeble and all but forgotten. If I think of him.'
'As you order it.'
'Let it be an instruction to you.'
'It will be.'

'A moment. Remind me. By what name do our enemies call him?'

'They call him the Builder.'

'So they do. The Builder. Let him build in the Imaginary what castles he can. Bind him tightly.'

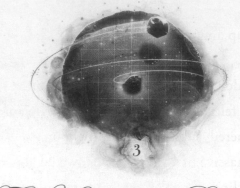

3

The Knights of Bithynia

A few houses down from their own, their little hedged-in lane gave way over a wooden stile to a spread of flat fenland, and Kay and Ell followed the loping strides of the two wraiths on to the frosted stubble. In the slow going of the garden and the tough brake and briars at the end of the lane Kay had been dropping between sleep and wake; now the sharp, frosted air of the fen hit her like a blast, and she looked, hunting and alert, for her sister's hand. Ell was still stumbling a bit, groggy and delicate after nearly tumbling from the low roof outside the back window. Kay dragged her on. Scrambling over a slick stile, she thought she had lost the wraiths completely; but then, ahead, a burst of something caught her eye – a low orange flame, it looked like – and she heard Flip's impatient voice.

'Come on!' he hissed. 'No time! It's almost dawn!'

It only broke on her, as they came in closer and the dark of the sky seemed to engulf them entirely, that they had stepped into the shadow of something enormous.

'Quick – hop up and into the basket,' Will said, putting out a hand.

In another sudden burst of orange flame the entire scene was illuminated. Kay felt a surge of excitement and terror: the two wraiths had tethered a giant hot-air balloon to the frozen ground, and its massive lifting envelope towered above them in the cold and settling damp of the early morning. Kay's eyes were drawn by the burst of flame into the interior of the balloon, into the seemingly endless curve rising into the air. Ell had stopped dead and was pulling back on her arm.

Flip, by contrast, was all motion, scuttling around the balloon and hauling up the stakes that had kept the basket at tether. 'No time, no time,' he was feverishly muttering to himself, punctuated by heaves of effort as he dragged up at the long metal stakes or pushed down on the handle of a complicated-looking contraption he had fetched from its hook on the edge of the basket.

'We really are short on time,' Will said insistently, now from the more-than-darkness left by the extinguishing of the flame. Ell was still dragging backwards. 'We need to make height by dawn, or we'll be noticed. Come on,' he said, now putting both his hands out over the lip of the basket to the two girls, 'and I'll help you up. Plenty of room in here.'

Taking Ell in a warm hug and burying her face in the soft-brushed texture of her fleece, Kay promised that she would take care of her. Then she lifted her up towards Will, climbed easily into the basket herself, and sat down hard on the floor, shutting her eyes against the quickly advancing light that would have shown her – had she turned her head – the end of her lane, the houses pale in the pre-dawn and the streetlights – one, two, three – stepping back to where their mother lay still asleep in her warm bed. Christmas morning – had she turned her head. Kay gritted her teeth. She could hear Ell sobbing, and then felt the weight of her burying into the pit under her right arm. Flip must have been lighting the burner again, because she could feel on her face the heat and light of the huge flame, and hear the rush of the gas. And she could hear him winding winches and tightening the various halyards and straps on what sounded like a thousand cleats. Then, suddenly, there was a jolt, and she heard Flip call out from close by, 'Almost!' And then there was a crash and a lot of grunting as the two wraiths hoisted themselves into position in the basket. Then silence.

For an instant Kay felt nothing but the tension in the whole frame of the balloon – the buoyancy of the bag above, straining to fly free of the cold earth, the hot charged air surging up into its envelope, the creaking in the thick, ancient-looking wooden boards of the basket floor as they seemed to be nearly torn asunder between the cables above and the last taut lines below. Just for an instant.

Kay only noticed that she had been holding her breath when it finally exploded from her – as the balloon broke from its last mooring and sprang into the air. Ell cried out into her side, and shook. Or perhaps that was the shuddering of the basket itself as it throbbed, then leaped into the slack of the cables, then settled again, making the whole balloon lurch sickeningly even as it shot up into the sky. Kay gasped and gasped. She squeezed her eyes tight shut again, braced her leg against something hard and drove herself into the solid wood behind her. And then, after what seemed like a single unbroken and very tense moment, during which they might as well have been falling as rising, she felt something warm covering her lap, and she dared to crack an eye open.

'Here, pull this up to your chins,' said Will as he tucked a heavy blanket round them where they huddled on the boards, under the hang of the basket's rim. The air rushing into their faces, even from their sheltered spot, was well beyond freezing; as cold as the questions that lay chill in Kay's mouth. She quickly drew the blanket up to and over their faces, putting her arm round her sister. Questions could wait.

She found it steadying to watch the two wraiths where they stood, out of reach, talking just beyond her hearing about comfortable things. Neither smiled, but their cheeks carried a composure and their eyes a lift and alertness that made their unheard words dance with welcoming possibility. Ell lay quiet, then asleep in the crook of her arm, and still Kay watched Will and Flip, the former with his lively, lithe limbs and slender, bow-like spring, the latter more solid but spry, a chunk of chestnut to Will's soaring lime. All the while the basket rose, at first quickly, but then, the gas slackening, far more slowly, bobbing into the currents of air that began to throw it eastwards. When the lurch and tumble of the ascent had at last wholly settled, Kay heaved herself into a squat, tucked the blanket around Ell carefully and stood up.

The day was coming on fast, or maybe it had simply become lighter as they climbed in the sky. In any case, the whole of the basket around her seemed suddenly to trip into the dawn. All around it dangled tools of every kind: wrenches, handles, mallets and hammers, tinderboxes and thick metal bars, long stakes and hoops, coils of rope in about twenty different thicknesses, extra hooks and clasps, spare cleats palely gleaming against the intermittent bursts from the wick, buckles and hasps, rings, a collection of keys, buckets of sand, and everywhere – of course – bags of ballast in various sizes. Kay could see the taut ropes running over the sides of the basket where Flip had, in the short time since they had taken off, already thrown out ballast. The thought of the bags swinging freely, then dropping through the air below the basket made her think of the height at which they must be travelling, and she felt suddenly queasy. Home would be vanishing below them, behind them. Christmas. She turned back to the centre, fixing her eye on the floor, and tried to mark out the little things – Flip's sandals with their fine latticing of leather straps; a little wooden capstan with its iron handles at the bottom; and the dense console of instruments suspended from the main ring, hanging before Will in the very middle. Kay could see what looked like dials, which she guessed gave information on their altitude and speed or direction, their position. There were a few levers, and then, beside a long grey tube, the important nozzle that Flip kept adjusting, which must, Kay thought, release the gas into the balloon, taking light from the pilot flame burning on the wick.

So it did, she thought as it burst into orange flame. She would have jumped back, had there been anywhere to jump to. Flip caught her eye and smiled.

'Do you want to see the ocean?' said Will brightly.

In a couple of hesitant, slightly unsteady steps she had joined the two wraiths at the wooden rim, crouching low into her own caution so that only her shoulders cleared the basket. She steadied herself, and then looked out.

Ahead – what was it? – slightly north of east, her father had told her – she could see the sun just about to crest the horizon. She couldn't tell if it was land or sea there, because it began to gleam and glare with its clear light; but there was definitely sea almost directly beneath them, green-grey in the paleness, with a strip of sheer white as it broke against the narrow sands of the Norfolk coast. Around and behind, the dark flats of the fens lay silver in the frost and early mist. Little houses broke up the fields, and every so often a line of streetlamps glowed orange for a while, and then sputtered out. Off to her left Kay could see the lights of a town paling in the onset of dawn, with a bit of coal smoke rising here and there – or at least she imagined it might have been coal smoke.

'Where are we going?' she said after a while. 'Are we going to another world?'

Will stood beside her, hunched over with his elbows spread and his chin resting on the backs of his long fingers. He didn't look at her, but out into the long, level distance to the north-east, watching the sun break from the emerging line of the horizon. He was silent for a long time, but Kay knew that he had heard her so she kept her mouth shut. By the time he answered, Ell was tentatively poking her head under Kay's left arm. The girls listened carefully as the land and ocean resolved and unfurled below them. It roared.

'So far as I know,' Will said, the suspicion of a grin turning up the corners of his mouth, 'this is the only world there is. No,' he continued slowly, as if to himself, 'it's not so much *where* we're going as *how* we are getting there.'

Kay must have appeared baffled by this, because, after glancing down at her face, he tapped his hand thoughtfully and percussively against the rail on the edge of the basket. Kay watched him. He looked out as if at the distance, but also as if he were seeing something; something that hung in the empty space around the balloon. His eye darted in every direction, sometimes pausing for a moment but always moving on with the predictability and pattern (which is to say without either) of a butterfly in a summer garden. His gaze hovered and darted like a bird. It seemed almost to be touching things, so delicately, so deliberately did his pupil swivel, stop, focus and hold its position.

Below them the sea lay ridged and stippled, a booming voice calling silently from the bottom of an enormous well. Ell was silent, but had slipped her arm out of the blanket that still hung draped around her shoulders, and held her sister close by the waist. Kay felt her touch now, still insistent with fear or anxiety, and thought about home slipping away behind them, the glowing streetlights being absorbed into the lesser brilliance of a cold December day, her mother just beginning to turn over in bed, wondering why it was so quiet in the house, so late in the morning. Christmas morning. And all they had left her was a single scribbled note.

'In the old days,' Will said, halfway through a breath, as if just taking up where he had left off, 'we used to travel by sea. Out of Bithynia you could sail nearly anywhere, though of course it took time, more time than now, and naturally that meant we had to be much better organized. These days we rush. We tend to make more mistakes. But then, we have more to do, too.'

From the other side of the basket Flip snorted, still sore, Kay reckoned, over that misplaced final page of the order sheet. Turning, she watched him through the rigging and gear where he paused over the board of meters and dials. He was mothering them, his face and attention completely fixed, his fingertips from time to time lightly brushing them. From the side she noticed his long, childlike lashes, a bloom of red around his cheekbones, his smooth skin, the impatient but somehow amused expression on his face. His crumpled, folded form seemed at one with the complex density of dials and levers positioned around him, as if he were their instrument as much as they were his. Kay thought with pleasure that the balloon was flying him home, and all he was doing was letting it.

'But where are we going? Bithynia? Where's that?'

'No, not to Bithynia,' said Will, shaking his head almost imperceptibly. 'The place we are going, in the mountains, doesn't have a name.' Then he brightened slightly. 'But we're going there in the right way. By the air, through the air.'

'By the air, through the air,' Flip intoned from a couple of metres away. He didn't look up.

'But why not Bithynia?' Kay couldn't let it drop, not after the events of the previous night. Not after Andrea Lessing. She looked directly at Will, holding his gaze. He didn't dare avoid her.

'Because the Bride is gone,' he said simply, and got to his feet, keeping low but shifting quickly over to help Flip, who needed no help. Kay was certain she wasn't going to get any more than that. Nobody ever said more than that, more than those two words – the *Bride*, *Bithynia*, *Bithynia*, the *Bride*. Unbidden but unavoidable, the memory of raised voices in the kitchen, only a week before, clanged in her head. It never *went* anywhere. Bracing her shoulders against the cold air, Kay gritted her teeth and slumped down into the shelter of the blanket to join Ell, who quickly clipped her around the chest, holding her tight. Her eyes closed and, with the gentle swaying of the basket, Kay began to drift into a lightly nauseous doze. It was through this haze, at some distance, that she noticed Will taking up his answer again; groggy and warm, she listened, trying to catch the slow trickle of words.

'The Bride,' he said from somewhere very near her ear – perhaps he was leaning or kneeling above her? – 'of Bithynia. The queen of silk, the mulberry maid, touch to the torch hearts of ten thousand lovers, the only immortal. When I was a boy, before all this, I saw her once, fleetingly, below our house in the valley, in among the plantations, passing on her way to the sea at dusk. Whenever I think of it, of her, I can still feel on my face the damp weight of the air that evening, like a tiny bristling chill on the skin above my lips. Everything that reminds me of her goes through me like a spear.'

There was silence then, or rather a rushing drone like a low howl. Kay felt the spear all right, remembering the sharp, pointed voices of her parents bouncing off the close walls of the little kitchen; the thrusts and parries; the cold, hardened looks. In her mind's eye, as the wind bristled and arched its back, she could see her father slumped where he stood, taking it, taking the criticism, as if he were a victim, as if he were just a misunderstood but patient hero. He had his bag slung over his shoulder, and his coat was on; he stood by the door that led out to the hallway, though he made no move to go. 'She's a Bride, after all – why don't you marry *her*?' There was never anything he could say to that.

But Will was in another world. 'There was a man in my village,' he said; 'an old man, half blind, who had when he was young fought for the Bride in the east, before the trading route was opened, and had lost the use of his legs. He would sit by day on a mat outside his door, in the shade of a massive cedar, and recite the stories he had learned on campaign: of her miraculous delivery out of the foam of the sea, of her Acquisition of the Nine Forms, of the Great Marriage. And he might relate, too, if you waited long enough and listened quietly, the prophecy of her passing.'

Kay nodded heavily, as if she, and not the heavy rocking of the basket in the fore-wind that drove it, were moving her head. Her consciousness seemed to swim sidelong with the motion of her lolling temples, and she thought of opening her eyes. Eye. She couldn't remember how many eyes she had, but then she didn't need to see anyway.

The prophecy of her passing, she thought. Passing.

'Her passing out of this world,' Will said finally and softly; but both girls were fast asleep.

By the time Kay woke, everything was different. For one thing, it was dark again. But the air was dry, too, and bitterly cold, as sharp on her bones as cut glass. Ell had crumpled to one side, and lay lightly snoring; to her other side Kay found the wraiths close, sitting opposite one another as they played some game on a board between them. They stared at little black stones and from time to time, without really taking turns, they moved them.

'Where are we going?' asked Kay abruptly.

Will picked up one of the stones and gripped it in his hand. He seemed startled, then relaxed. 'We're going to see Sergeant Ghast about your father. We're going to do something about all this witnessing.'

'And authoring,' added Flip. He checked a meter and gave the balloon a long pulse of flame.

'But where . . . ?' Kay threw out her hand to take in the black void around the balloon, through which could only dimly be seen a rough, dry expanse of crag and scrub slowly passing beneath them as the wind drove the balloon ever on. 'Where is all this? Where are we now?'

'Everything flows down from the mountains,' said Will. His head lay a little to one side, and he looked at her as if she were an object of great happiness. Every word he said to her he seemed to think a privilege. 'As with water, so it is also with stories. If we want to get to the start of this one, we have to go up and into the mountain.'

Kay could feel her blood rising. 'You're not answering me,' she said. Flat, but not sullen.

'There *is* no answer, really,' said Will. 'Or at least, not the kind of answer you want. At first you may feel disappointed, but in your frustration there is, too, perhaps, a little ground of hope.' He looked down at the board before him, at the shining black stones, and moved first one then another, the first simply and curtly, the second in a long arc. 'There are times when what is most important is glimpsed – *can* be glimpsed – only in the dark. There are times when any mountain will do, when it is important that one goes into *a* mountain rather than *the* mountain, *this particular* mountain. We are going to such a place, in such a way, to see a thing that lies higher than other things.'

Kay wanted to be furious, but with every word Will spoke a little more of her frustration seemed to slip from her. Because he wasn't ignoring her – quite the opposite. His eyes passed back and forth between her and the board on which his hand still rested, almost as if it were a canvas and he were painting her portrait, almost as if he were studying the lines and lights of her face by the raked glow of the lantern.

'I don't understand,' she said. 'I don't understand at all.'

'Good,' said Flip. He was crouching nearer to her, and could reach out his hand and touch her arm. The feel of it, the gentle squeeze near her shoulder – avuncular, delicate strength – buoyed and inflated her. 'Knowing that you don't understand is good. It's usually when people think they understand, when they really think they're sure of themselves, that they're dead wrong.'

'What does Ghast want with my father?'

Will and Flip both stared at the board before them.

'What is he going to do with him?'

'Will,' said Flip, so quietly that Kay could barely hear him. 'She is young, but –'

'She is in danger.'

'She is an *author*. She has come very far already, and very bravely.'

Will sat back a bit, his arms still hugging his knees and pulling them up off the floor of the basket. 'To tell you who Ghast is I need to tell you the story of the knights of Bithynia.'

Bending his head over the board where he and Flip had been playing, Will began to move the small pieces – rounded stones, Kay saw, oblong in shape, of a greyish-blue cast, like the pebbles she sometimes gathered on the Norfolk coast. They swirled in patterns around the board, his long, delicate fingers stirring without pause independently one of the other in continuous curves, loops and eddies. At the end of each finger, at any given moment, one, or two, or a few stones were being gently pushed or pulled, so that Kay could see upon the board a pattern of movement being described in time, the stones collecting together, fanning apart, organizing into groups, trading elements, reconstituting and recombining, then all severing again, constantly changing their distribution across the face of the board. At first this movement bewildered her, and she thought in frustration that she would just turn round, crawl back through the rigging and rejoin Ell beneath the warm blanket. But as she kept watching, she saw that one of the stones was moving differently from the others, and she began to think there might be method to Will's movements: this stone made short, jerky lurches, mostly in straight lines, though it was passed from finger to finger in the process and its motion was not, for that reason, at first obvious to her. As she watched, it was hit repeatedly by the other stones, and she thought that it must be a very sorry stone to be the victim of so many collisions; but it seemed rather that it was drawing these other stones to it – not least because these, after each hit, seemed to lurch away from the encounter with some of its character, interrupting their more graceful arcs around the board with increasingly stilted movements. As Will's fingers continued to weave around the board, Kay began not to notice them at all, and could see only the lives of the stones: the way this one, like a virus, began to infect all the others with its short, jerking stutter, as if it were berating them for their beauty and making them ashamed. Kay's head tightened, and she felt her chin thrusting forward as she tried to swallow a sob.

'Will, stop.'

It was Flip, placing his hand over the board and silencing Will's fingers, who brought Kay back to her senses.

'She can read it,' he said. 'You're shouting at her. Stop it.'

On the board Flip's hand tightened, his knuckles white as if he were pushing against Will's fingers with enormous force.

Kay looked up at Flip, but Will didn't acknowledge him at all; he was speaking in a quiet voice, nearly a whisper, and Kay struggled to hear him above the intense thrill of the wind around them.

'For centuries we were a guild, the thousand and one of us, every wraith an equal voice in the halls of Bithynia, each a knight. The left-wraiths, their hands full of stones, plotted the causes, the effects and the ways of things; while the right-wraiths, with their palms stretched open to the inspiration of the air, of dreams, imagined a universe of ideas. Together we sailed with the wind, weaving up the edges of the earth with our songs. Those were days of power, when the left-wraiths, great bards and tellers of tales, drew from the right-wraiths, from the imaginers and prophets, the matter and grounds for the most magical fables, for epics and romances that sprawled across the continents and encompassed the seven oceans. We lived and turned in a kind of balance then, a poised and perfect motion. The plotters revered the imaginers, and the imaginers in turn deferred to the plotters. We seemed to move in a kind of dance without end –'

'Those days were long ago, old friend,' said Flip. With a gentle gesture, as if he were setting down a delicate, valuable thing upon a precarious surface, he let go of Will's hand where it lay on the board between them.

'We were happy. Maybe we were too innocent. But we were happy.' Kay thought the basket was too small to contain the vast void from which Will spoke. 'But then the balance suddenly seemed to shift, and Ghast, who has forever been as he is now, a voice not so much of story or tale, neither of means nor of motion, no imaginer, no plotter, no visionary or spell-spinner, a force for –'

'Result,' put in Flip quietly. 'From the very beginning, all Ghast has ever wanted has been a result.'

Will nodded. 'Result, yes. He seemed to be clotting around himself more and more of the left-wraiths. It began to appear that they were actually taking orders from him, and not, as formerly, working by the board. We had worked by the board for a thousand years. And they were moving towards Ghast. Over time Ghast attracted more of the left-wraiths, and then, gradually, the right-wraiths, too, and even some phantasms, until there were so many of them that they dared to put the guild to a vote – and we lost it. And Ghast was made Sergeant of the new order, and now we take that order from him.'

'Except when that order happens to be on page nineteen of a sheet you wiped your nose with,' said Flip.

'Yes,' agreed Will, but he wasn't listening.

Flip rolled his eyes merrily at Kay, but she decided that she wasn't listening, either. Flip got to his feet, climbed over Kay to the instruments and began fussing with the ropes and valves, checking his dials and muttering off occasional checklists.

Kay stared hard at the board lying before her; at its irregular, unfinished border, its dark, stained surface that still showed the grain of the tree from which it had been cut, at the sheen that flared from it as the lantern swung unsteadily above. She was quickly spellbound, watching where Will's fingers now continued circulating absent-mindedly, their tips brushing, nudging the stones against the occasional thuds and jolts of the basket in its forward swing. She could see something new in Will's patterns, something strange that she felt should not have been there: two stones at the centre – one almost silent and still, but nudged at regular intervals like the tick of a clock; the other extravagant, sweeping in spontaneous arcs, impulsive, lucky. She felt instinctively that she was the first, that her sister was the second. She knew it as surely as if Will had taken out a brush and colours, and painted their portraits.

Kay looked up to Will. 'What is this board?' she asked. 'What are these stones? Is it a game?'

Will frowned. 'No, not a game. Not exactly a game. There is no contest here, no winner or loser – just movement and reading. It's called a plotting board, and these are plotting stones. No left-wraith will travel without them; they are always with us. It gives us a way to reduce to its simplest elements any story, any situation, any narrative, so that we can see its structure and understand how what is happening now is connected to what has come before, and how what is happening now will lead to other situations and stories in the future.'

'So this is a way of predicting the future? Can you tell me what's going to happen to me? Can you see if we'll find our father?'

'No. That's prophesying. That's different; there are wraiths who do it, but they don't do it with plotting boards. They pluck visions out of the air as the eye does stars on a cold night.

With plotting boards we just look at the shapes of stories and try to understand the way those shapes work. It's about probabilities, patterns, habits, the way things *tend* to fall out. For example, the stone you saw before was Ghast, and the stones around it some of the other wraiths; and I think the interactions between this stone and the others you could see showed the way Ghast came to relate to them, began to exert influence on them, made them into images of himself.'

Kay nodded, wishing that the blackish-bluish stones, now so still but for the occasional nudging, would swirl back again into their finger-driven dance, gliding across the surface of the mottled board.

'And afterwards, that stone was me,' she said, touching it, 'and this one was Ell.'

Will looked at her sharply, as if she had stung him.

'Or not,' she offered. 'Maybe I was wrong.'

'No,' he answered, softening. His fingers danced again on the board. 'There are many ways of seeing any particular movement. And there are many others, of course – countless others. The tension I showed you might also be the relation between order and randomness. Or you might see that movement as the spread of disease, communicating itself between, say, mice in a den or rabbits in a warren, and in time contaminating the whole group. There are as many interpretations of that structure as you have time to evolve them; but I told you it was Ghast, and so you saw Ghast.'

'But is what you do on the board true?' Kay was groping for something, but she wasn't sure what.

'Models, thoughts and stories are always true. What you do with them is a different thing.'

At that moment there was a lurch, and Flip – who had been muttering – began to bark and then to shout. Will leaped to a low squat, his head suddenly, carelessly tangled in the rigging, his long fingers clutching at the air. Everything clashed around them, instruments swinging, tumbling, colliding and breaking as the basket leaped wildly through the sky. It was falling. Before she could register what Flip was saying, Kay was halfway back to the rear of the basket, skirting round towards Ell who, roused with the jolt and the noise, blinked with terror into the grey-black of the night. Will fell down to the floor to haul on a winch, and Flip furiously released gas into the envelope of the balloon – trying, Kay guessed, to create lift in the nauseating plunge of free-fall. For a long while she felt as if she were bouncing, weightless, on the moon. Her arms were around Ell when she finally made sense of the shouting: 'By the *air*, through the *air*.'

Just before they crashed, Kay remembered what, sitting at that plotting board as the commotion began, she had seen: a single, graceful stone still arcing untouched and alone around the margins of the knotted board – slowly, but elegantly, spinning.

'There was a crash.'

They clustered and shifted before him, long and light forms scarcely able to hold their shape against his squat and solid deformity.

'How many dead?'

'None.'

'None yet.'

With sudden decision he strode forward. They parted to let him through, like oil before water, then closed in behind him.

'We must prepare a welcome. See that everything is made ready for them, and for the girl. We must bring our new plans forward.'

The nearest, being the most servile as well as the most ambitious, saw his opportunity.

'We have plotted it on the board, and –'

The rebuke was total, even as the stride unbroken.

'Make no mention of your grandmother's superstitions. Not to me. I will not have your stones and swirling sorceries here.'

They passed in a little group into a large and open hall. Ghast took the centre and spun around slowly. He held his knotted stubs of hands up to the vast reach of the room.

'Call me your master. The master of all this.'

'You are the only master in the mountain.'

'Mine is the only hand that can command. Mine is the only fist. And yet I am not the only master.'

In the hall a hundred lights were lighted.

'Be gentle with the girl. She is a means to my end. And with her sister – however it falls out.' He waved his hand in annoyance. 'But as for the other, spare neither strokes nor speeches. Net him about with lies. He must break, and soon.'

4

Ghast

If the flying had been cold and turbulent, if it had seemed
sometimes difficult and nauseating, the sudden final descent
of the balloon – though short – was far worse. Kay's stomach
heaved into the tips of her fingers, and her throat, dry and
knotted like the gall of an oak, choked her. She almost felt
relief when, after a few seconds, the basket crashed into what
sounded like rocky ground. In a slow havoc it began to drag,
splinter and throb all at once. The envelope of the balloon
continued to deflate, and pulled first rigging then cloth all
around them. Flip must have put out the fire, she thought,
because for the first time since the morning it was pitch-dark.
Time moved so slowly that Kay felt oddly as if she had a lot of
time to think as she gripped Ell to her, groping for air with a
free hand and continuing to wedge herself into the cavity under
the basket's rim. She caught some breath and gradually felt the
terrible forward crushing of the basket ease towards rest. And
then all was quiet.

The pocket of air (she found by a little more groping with
her hand) came from a tear in the balloon fabric. Releasing Ell,

she reached for the tear, pulling it as close as she could amid the folds and tangled mass of the material. Then, latching her sister close, she heaved the two of them up towards it. With some struggling they got their faces free, then out into the night air. She could see almost nothing past a couple of metres. The moon was hidden and there was no sign of Will or Flip.

'Ell, are you okay?' Kay relaxed her arm a little, but the slight body of her sister remained firmly pressed to her side.

The voice might have been muffled, but it come out strong. 'I can't get my legs free.' Eloise sounded as if she were trying to solve a puzzle – rather than extricating herself from the aftermath of a terrifying crash. Kay felt her heart loosen at the simple, courageous statement.

After some pushing and wriggling, Kay disentangled them both from the heavy swaddle of the cloth. They found themselves standing on it, unsteadily attempting to cross its still billowing surface towards the edge, and firmer ground. The thick-draped darkness around them ruffled with the breeze. Under Kay's hand, where the sleeve of her coat had hiked up in the crash, the skin of Ell's arm suddenly broke out in goose pimples.

'Kay,' she said, her little voice still resonant with innocent courage, 'what's happened? I thought we were going to find Dad.'

Even if there had been time to answer, Kay wouldn't have known what to say. She didn't, and there wasn't.

'Jump off. Quickly,' said Will, his face looming out of the darkness, weirdly lit by the raking light of a bright lantern. 'It's not safe. Grab on. Now.'

Kay hauled at Ell and tried to fling her forward. She herself only just had time to lurch and then topple on to Will as a piece of the tackle and rigging sprang airwards, lashing into the place where she had been standing the instant before. At last she saw Flip, with a long knife in his hand, sawing at something. He was cutting a cable.

'We came down on a cliff,' Will said in a low voice. He was just audible over the rising wind. 'I tried to get an anchor in, but it won't hold the basket if the sailcloth goes over and catches the wind. And it is. Going over. Flip's trying to save the basket. What's left of it.'

Flip was moving around the now nearly upended basket, working his way through the ropes and cables, which snapped as he sheared them, and flung away with the tension of the cloth that was still dragging at them. He had four or five to go when he called out to Will, 'Move the girls back in case anything gets fouled.'

Will pulled Kay, and Kay reached out to take Ell's hand. She grasped it and started to pull her towards the shelter of a cluster of large stones. But Ell wasn't coming. Kay tugged.

'Kay,' said the little voice behind her. 'Kay, I think I'm stuck.'

Everything seemed to happen in a slow rush. She turned, and by Will's light immediately saw that her sister's leg had become snagged in a mass of halyards, guy ropes, tethers, sailcloth and other debris from the balloon's crash. But no sooner had she turned than Ell's hand was wrenched from her own, and her tiny form dragged two or three metres across the hard ground. The movement of the fabric in the wind, billowing in places like a sail, twisted and flipped her little body as it dragged her, with each turn, with every metre tangling her further in a tight knot of cords and fabric. She was screaming.

Flip had sprung clear the instant the balloon shifted. At first he was watching only his own feet, keeping himself free, while Kay stood stunned, paralysed, staring into him, willing him to help. And Will – she felt like the three of them were standing deep underwater; for a moment everything seemed so heavy, even thinking.

Then Ell began sliding again.

They all reached her at about the same time – Flip bounding across the dancing ropes like some sort of deranged and acrobatic snake-charmer, Will loping low along the ground, grabbing at the ropes where he could, trying to get purchase on something – anything – to stop the balloon's relentless drag towards the cliff's edge. But Kay had eyes only for Ell, and it was to her outstretched arms that she ran, without any thought that her own feet might become snared as the tackle lashed and swirled around her ankles like so many vicious and venomous jaws.

'Kay, help me! Help!' cried Ell. She was sobbing with frustration, pushing and squirming against the ropes binding her. Kay hooked her fingers around one fragile wrist, then the other. She held, fighting Ell to be quiet, to stay put. Will had his hands on something – a section of fabric – and had dug his heels against the loose stones lying all around; with a heaving effort he was holding back the weight of the cloth, buying the little girl time.

'Just hold it, Will,' called Flip. He was near. He had Ell's leg in his hands. It was wrapped in cords and leather straps. The leg of her trousers had been pulled up and her calf was starting to turn purple. Kay stared at it. There were so many, many knots, so many different strands and threads and turns and twists. Her eyes ached to see it, and the blood in her chest crawled against her ribs like ants.

'Use your knife, Flip – I can't hold it.'

Flip was still staring at Ell's leg, at the mass of knots and tangles. 'I can't – there's too much. I'd cut her. Wait.'

'I can't wait, Flip. If the wind rises –'

Flip dropped Ell's leg and stood up. A mass of fury screamed in Kay's head. *How dare he give up! How dare he walk away!*

'Kay. Kay. Kay.'

Flip's hands were dancing before his face, writhing with his fingers extended, looking intently at Ell, then at his hands, then at Ell. Kay thought at first that he was going to cast some sort of spell, that he thought he was some kind of sorcerer – but that wasn't it. He was moving his hands in the way Will had earlier over the plotting board.

'Three more seconds, Flip,' said Will. He spat every word through a separate surge of exhausted effort.

Flip's hands danced. He seemed mesmerized now, as if he had entranced himself, as if he were watching the most important thing in the world, as if he had become so engaged and enthralled with it that he had fallen out of time, as if he were deep in a kind of intent love with the movement of his hands in the air before him. He seemed as tangled as Ell.

And then, suddenly, he snapped clear of it. With a fluid motion he reached to the knife at his belt, drew it, dropped to his knees and sliced a single cord at the top left of the mass of knots that were still tightening around Ell's knee and thigh. At the same moment Will, exhausted, let slip the cloth from his fists and fell backwards, toppling across Flip's shoulder and knocking him flat on the ground.

But Kay hardly noticed.

She had eyes only for the cords around Ell's leg. They seemed to recoil, as if they were living things, from the place where Flip had cut. Some spun and whipped away; others swirled and untwisted like water pouring down a drain; others again seemed to untie themselves from complex knots and vanish like steam on a breeze – but one way or another, as if a key had turned with a click in its lock, they all sped disentangled off, yawning open, and Ell scrambled to her feet and launched her body into Kay's arms. Kay just held her.

How did he do that?

By the time she opened her eyes again and looked around, the two wraiths had already set about sorting the salvage. Flip was hauling carefully at the basket – upended a few metres away – and, with a tottering crash, had it settled again. Kay scrutinized him over Ell's huddled shoulder. The thought flashed through her mind that he was dangerous; a thought that made her feel guilty when he looked up, catching her in it.

'Sometimes you just need to know which thread to cut,' he said. He held her eyes the space of a long breath, shrugged and then clambered into the basket, checking for damage. 'Not bad!' he called out.

Kay and Ell, after some hesitation and on unsteady legs, followed Will over.

'Instruments? Gear?' Will was asking. 'Can you get our position?'

'The good news,' Flip said, practically beaming, 'is that we're pretty much there. An hour's walk or less, I'd say. And the way the balloon collapsed on to the basket as we fell seems to have kept most of the gear in.'

'Is there bad news?' asked Kay. She felt blank, as stunned as her sister's gaping eyes.

Flip was crouched and clattering in the bottom of the basket. 'The bad news is that we're going to have to carry whatever we want to keep. And if we want to have any hope of . . . that is –'

'We'll run,' said Will. 'Can you girls run?'

Ell was still rubbing her leg where the ropes had strangled it. Of course they were not going to run, Kay thought; but they both nodded.

They each took something: Will and Flip a few brown hessian sacks, which looked heavy; Kay a bag that Flip had filled hastily with a pile of instruments, the plotting board and the stones the girls had found scattered on the floor; and Ell a small pile of blankets. Flip had some flares in the basket, and he lit one immediately, hoping that someone might see it and come for them, but also because, he said, the light it shed as it went up would give them a good sense of the landscape around them. They had fallen on a flat sort of plain high in the mountains; to one side there was a cliff, to the other a gentle slope arcing up towards a high peak. By means of a gentle descent to its left, they could get into a higher valley full of scrub and low trees, Will thought. There the two wraiths figured they might get their bearings. The cloud, too, had started to break up above, and the light of the stars and, before long, the moon gave them surer footing as they carefully picked out a way down. By the time they were properly among the low bushes, they could see each other and the land around them much more easily. Kay held on to Ell at a little distance as Flip put up another flare, and in its showering light they thought they briefly saw movement across the valley.

'That'll be Sprite and Jack –' Will grinned at Flip – 'or I'm not a phantasm.'

Flip went on ahead, bounding in spite of his heavy sack, and Will nudged the girls along. Kay shifted her bag back and forth from her right side to her left, shouldering the burn and the ache of it. She shuffled her feet a little faster so it might seem like she was in fact running. It wasn't long before they could hear animated voices ahead, growing louder, and then, all of a sudden, in an orange glow that popped – like a water-light – from behind a bush, Kay and Ell saw Flip. He was with two other wraiths, like Will tall, gaunt and tapered. They were sharing out the contents of Flip's sack into two others. Will immediately stopped, too, and offered his arm to his friends.

'Sprite,' he said, beaming. The wraith took his arm in a two-handed, crossed grip, and briefly bound it to him hard, like a spar being lashed to a mast. Will turned to the other wraith, who was standing expectantly to greet him. 'Jack of the Lantern,' he cried. 'We'll need your light tonight, my friend.'

Jack took Will's arm in the same curious two-handed hold. All four wraiths then stood quietly, a kind of hum hanging between them, an energy, until they bent again to work. Kay knew that stillness, that taking pleasure in the moment, in silence, before allowing it to pass – for she had longed for it, imagined it, and tried herself to create it so many, many times. Looking at the wraiths, she realized with surprise that it was love.

Will stooped, and began to divide up some of his own load. Kay was thinking how heavy their sacks must have been, and how resolute they had been, carrying them, when she saw what they contained.

'Those are my father's things,' she stated. She was angry, and knew she had been too blunt.

Will's hands stopped moving, and the other wraiths – she could see them very clearly now that they inclined to her, with their round eyes, elegantly angular noses, high cheeks and feathery silvered hair – loomed inquisitively over their sacks.

It was Will who spoke, and he was awkwardly formal. 'I explained to you – ma'am – that we are removers, and we remove. We came to your house with our inventory, and we removed what we were instructed to remove. Down to the last tooth.' He looked up at her slowly, and they both smiled, Kay grudgingly. 'Whether we like it or not – and I promise you that we don't – these days this is our job.'

'Ma'am,' said Flip with a sarcastically exaggerated bow. He rolled his eyes. Will had an impressively long and spiky elbow, and Kay reckoned it probably hurt Flip a lot when it was jabbed into his side.

73

But the others – Will had called them Sprite and Jack – were whispering to each other now, out of the glow of the torch they had brought. Will, like Kay, had seen their curiosity and, holding Kay's gaze, he added loudly, commanding their attention, 'Yes, you heard me. We've got two little girls here who are more than they seem. And one of them –' now suppressing a smile, or a look of pride, beneath the serious, level intensity of the announcement – 'is an author.'

The others were as dumbfounded as Will and Flip had been and, though they said nothing, they shared furtive looks from time to time as Kay and Ell helped distribute the clothes and papers and books, and the other tiny familiar objects from sack to sack. And when they set off, surrounded by the four looming figures, the wraiths kept looking. Ell flagged quickly, and Sprite had to take the blankets over his shoulders, but Kay drew her on, encouraging and cajoling, at times pleading with her, at times roughly dragging at her arm. Once, when her exhausted body had become nothing but a dead and sagging weight, Kay stopped and clasped her sister's pale face to her chest, willing the warmth to flood out of her and into the shivering, tiny form.

'Kay,' said Ell, pushing back with surprising force, 'I thought we were coming to find Dad. Instead all we're doing is helping to get rid of him.' She dropped her last remaining little sack on the ground and began to sob.

It was all Kay could do to calm her sister's tears; after that she had no strength left to try to answer the questions that still whirled in the windy air around them: *What are they doing?*

74

Where is our father? What is all this for? Jack took Ell on his back, and bore her cheerfully enough, but Kay carried on her shoulders only questions.

In less than an hour, having climbed out of the valley, then skidded down a loose scree of heavy rounded rocks and pebbles, they all put down their things outside what seemed to Kay an intolerably forbidding cave.

'Here we are,' said Will, squatting down again to talk to the girls. Seeing Kay's tension, he added, 'Don't be afraid. It's not like any cave you've imagined being in before.'

And it wasn't: as Sprite and Jack breached the opening, their torch held aloft, a thousand other similar staffs fixed to the walls around a broad interior hall began to glow. Nor was it really a cave in anything but name: the walls of the cavernous domed room had been polished to a gleaming, and around it hung tapestries woven of the most extraordinary threads: golds, deep purples, crimsons, blues and yellows as striking as sharp notes, whites more brilliant than the walls themselves. Kay had seen medieval tapestries in old chapels and museums – not only at home, but also in the countless smaller towns and villages through which her father, with his endless itineraries (and notebooks, and cameras), had thought to drag them. Those tapestries had always seemed washed out, mostly a greyish blue or green, and while sometimes of enormous size, invariably they depicted the most boring subjects: victories in forgotten battles, a forest scene, another Madonna and child. But these tapestries were of another kind entirely – luminous, richly vibrant hangings, portraits that fascinated the eye with pictures of passion, danger, suffering, triumph and joy. Kay's eyes roved hungrily. In one scene she saw a hero plunging into a live volcano; next to it two friends lying in a sea of sunflowers; in another three nymphs emerging from a huge and flooding river, chased by porpoises; in others, angry or cheering faces; a choir of boys processing down a yawning Gothic nave; pirates in a slowly capsizing ship; and of course wraiths and gods and dwarfs and fairies, elves, satyrs, giants and monsters. Everywhere Kay looked these almost moving images abutted one on the other, and seemed to create a static dance of texture, of colour, of story, around the walls.

Ell, too, was clearly stirred to wonder by the tapestries. All evidence of her exhaustion had vanished: though her arms hung limp at her sides, her face – angled up to the walls above – danced with excitement, interest and recognition. She turned, and turned. Her eyes floated over the pictures. Kay studied her for a moment, surprised at her concentration and the sudden bravery of her gaze after so much timid clinging through the last day. She stood alone in the long vaulted room, having stepped away from the others – Will and Flip, talking in low excitement with two other wraiths who had just come through from a far door, and Kay herself. Her red hair hung wispily, at last fully unravelled from the tight plait that Kay had woven in her curls the day before. The crash of the balloon had torn the hem of her blue duffel coat, something like grease had stained the leg of her trousers; but otherwise she seemed remarkably unmarked by the day's frenetic events – even her face, seen in profile as she turned, seemed to Kay relaxed, rested. She had an air of composure that Kay had never before seen in her, not even in sleep. It was as if Ell felt for the first time in her life completely at home.

'Kay,' she said, turning, 'I've dreamed about this place, I think. I know these pictures. I know these colours.'

'That's impossible, Ell. You've never been here before, so you couldn't know anything about them.' Kay was surprised to find herself speaking in an impatient tone.

'I know that. But what I mean is, I *feel* like I do.' Ell pointed to a long, low tapestry hanging on the left wall, in which an old man, wizened with age but still brawny and somehow full of majesty, sat enthroned on a ledge. He was looking out on a small group of men who were approaching, bareheaded and in rags, from a shadowy corner in a great grey hall, so dimly lit that Kay thought it looked like granite, like the inside of a mountain. 'I think I know – or I feel, anyway,' Ell said, 'what is happening in that one over there. That old man is a judge, the judge of people's lives, their whole lives, after death. And the men coming to him are people who have just died. And they are going to their life after death, and the judge will tell them where to go – to heaven or else to hell. Kay, they're all like that. They just seem familiar, like they're pictures from a book we have at home. Or like I made them up myself.'

'But, Ell, you know we don't have these pictures in a book.' Something about her sister's urgency and conviction unsettled her; she felt irritated. 'And there are so many of them. Anyway, don't say anything about it just now. Wait till we find Dad.'

Flip must have disappeared through the far door; meanwhile Will was speaking in increasingly animated whispers to the two other wraiths. Kay looked at him critically. In the bright light of the hall he looked even more insubstantial than earlier. Though his features and limbs were every bit as elegant as those of the others, he looked a bit more gaunt, a bit more bent. The others didn't have that tired, if cheerful, wryness to their cheeks. Instead the crescent moon of their faces had a sort of heavy crease, as if, had they been creatures chiselled in stone outside a cathedral, the sculptor had saved the deepest cuts and sharpest lines for their severe brows, their pursed lips, their grave chins. One of them was waving a handful of papers at Will. Kay immediately felt sorry for him – it had to be the inventory, she thought; and, sure enough, in a moment all three wraiths, after a short and evidently tense silence, turned to her. Will came up first and, with his usual stooping grace, dropped to his haunches.

'Kay, I need to ask you for that tooth now. Foliot and Firedrake –' and here he gestured at the others, looming caricatures of officiousness behind him, one of them still clutching the sheaf of inventory instructions – 'they have to clear the removal with Sergeant Ghast, and Ghast doesn't like his officers to keep him waiting.'

Something about the way he said 'officers' – a little hesitation, maybe – made Kay distrust these new wraiths. She avoided looking up at them, instead holding Will's eyes. There she found comfort and, in the face of this new threat which she felt instinctively was dangerous to him as well as to her, resoluteness. 'Tell them, please, that I will take it to Ghast myself.'

Foliot and Firedrake had been listening. Now they tittered mirthlessly and crumpled the papers into a ball just behind Will's head; but he stayed put, and Kay thought she saw another smile at the corner of his eyes. She felt Ell's duffel coat brush up against her, and reached out to hold her, still not breaking Will's gaze. He never looked away. A long moment seemed to open, long enough for Kay to decide – for certain – that whatever he said, she would trust him. Finally he said, 'So. I will go with you, and I will be your guide.' He breathed out and nodded. 'You'll need one.'

There followed a whirl of motion, so brisk and startling that Kay couldn't take it all in. Asking Will to explain was out of the question, as he strode lightly along beside the girls, following Foliot and Firedrake. He was clearly paying close attention to the response of Ghast's emissaries. They must, Kay judged, be Will's superiors: he followed them.

As they passed through the door at the end of the hall, the lights behind them darkened even as the lights before them blazed. Had Kay never dreamed dreams; had her father not carried her on his shoulders through half the cathedrals in England, lifting her as high as he could to see if, just this once, they might touch the fretted, runnelled roof; had she not on summer evenings lain with Ell in the waste field behind their lane, their heads pillowed by a clump of clover, singing songs to put the otherwise lethargic clouds into a dance across the vault of the sky – then she might not have been struck by the room – the cavern – into which the wraiths then led them. But she *had* dreamed, and reached, and sung, and she knew the size of this place, upon which the light of a thousand, or ten thousand, torches suddenly spilled in a concert of discovery. Kay had learned to look up.

It was a library; or, more accurately, a great treasure hall of books. If one were to take the greatest domes, and naves, and halls, and chambers, the grandest throne rooms, and auditoria, and amphitheatres, and stadia, the largest of arenas, and combine them, this colossal cavern would be the result. Had Will not ducked round to follow the girls, urging them on with his brisk tread, Kay would simply have stayed there.

The shelves on which the countless books stood had been carved from the rock of the cave. Along the floor, on carpets woven in wine and violet, long tables had been laid in aisles, on which here and there a plotting board sat, a pile of stones at the edge of each one. She counted four – no, five – aisles. Through the hall, gigantic globes of the earth and moon and stars stood mounted in wooden casings, and low stools were tucked in an orderly way beneath each of the tables – enough for, Kay reckoned, about a thousand wraiths. She couldn't get a close look at any of the books themselves, but she could see plainly that some of them – even, perhaps, most of them – were of a towering, Atlantean size, running to a thousand pages each, or more. Above, the shelves rose towards the vault and the books grew smaller, and as the little group swept out of the hall again, Kay had just time to notice that these upper shelves were stacked with the tiniest ones, hardly larger than her hand. As they exited, the thought struck her hard: there was not a single soul in the whole vast space. It was entirely empty.

After the hall, through another low, thick-walled door arch, the five of them came into a corridor, almost a tunnel. This, unlike the library, unlike the tapestried entrance hall, was not at all empty: wraiths were swarming through it, weaving round and past one another – with grace, yes, but also with worry, pace, determination. Some of them, like Foliot and Firedrake, were frowning, and many of them held papers under their arms. Kay wondered if these were yet more inventories, the lives in catalogue of yet more missing fathers or mothers. Or children. In a sudden panic she nearly collided with Foliot as the two leaders drew up short before a small wooden door. Firedrake raised his fist, hesitated as if listening for something, and then rapped twice, hard. The door swung open.

The halls had been magnificent, and the tapestries engrossing, moving. The room into which this squat door opened was completely unlike those. For one thing, it was dark – so dark that it took her eyes a while to adjust to the light as the wraiths, ducking, ushered them both in. For another, the ceiling was low, and Will had to compensate partly by leaning over, and partly by bending his legs, just to keep his head away from its rough stone surface. But what really made the room unsettling for Kay was that it was filled with short, stumpish wraiths barely taller than herself, and nowhere near as lean or as graceful as Will, or even Foliot and Firedrake. They looked, she decided, positively gnarled, their faces and hands studded with wartlike protuberances, hairy, ruddy and thick-lipped.

Fifteen or so of them sat writing at two large trestle tables on either side of the room, and another five or six carried papers back and forth between the tables and a set of large chests lining the walls. At the far end of the room, up a step and behind a magnificently carved desk, sat a single hunched figure, muttering as he angled his head over several piles of papers. His right hand was on the table before him, bunched into a tense fist, so tight that the individual muscles in his fingers stood out in the low light. At the hush that fell over the room, he looked up.

'Ghast,' said Will, with a whispered emphasis.

'Gross,' murmured Ell, with no emphasis at all.

'At last,' barked Ghast, raising and slamming his fist down upon the table with a crack.

For all her bravado, Ell shuddered next to Kay, and her hand went suddenly clammy. Kay squeezed it hard, willing herself to be strong for the confrontation she had promised herself.

'So,' Ghast went on as he rose from his chair to tower diminutively behind the desk, 'you have really done it this time, you incompetent. I spelled out that inventory in my own hand, you tunnel-scraper, you useless silk-spinning, stone-plotting, muse-loving freak. I should have thrown you out with the poets and that ragtag fantastical scum. And I would have, if it hadn't been a comfort to watch you pulling your guts out of your own backside. You leek, you brainless eel. You're very nearly as incompetent as you are –' he looked Will up and down, then sneered – 'long. How could you *possibly* have mangled this assignment any worse?'

Ghast had started forcefully, but he finished with a roar that, Kay thought, seemed beyond the capacity of his stumpish frame. He stopped, apparently to lick his thick dry lips. Will raised his hand as if about to speak.

'Don't say a word,' Ghast cut him off. 'So these must be the children. Tell me,' he said to Will much more quietly, his eyes never leaving the painfully cramped wraith as, with a prowling excitement, he circled round to the front of the desk and stood at the edge of the step. 'Tell me, you monster, did you ever in your life think you would again be so privileged as to see, to meet or to remove an *author*?' His every word was a snarl of scorn. Kay stood a little prouder as she felt Will's hand lightly on her shoulder.

'By the muses, no,' he said quietly.

'Leave them out of it,' Ghast snapped, again visibly annoyed. 'You know I don't tolerate that kind of talk here.' He paused, and the room was silent, but for the papers rustling at the tables around them as the little troll-like wraiths went about their work. They occasionally snatched furtive glances up at Ghast. 'No, you never thought, did you? Never hoped. And now you've gone and plucked her right out of her childhood, right out of her apprenticeship, as pretty as you like. You might as well have strangled her in her bed.'

At this Kay started at last. Will's hand tightened on her shoulder, and Ell was immediately clinging to her left side.

'You know, it does me good to see a great wraith like yourself, one of the old guard, the oldest, playing your part in our little revolution. It warms me. You have even exceeded the little cameo role I allotted you in your own destruction. What a colossally cack-handed klutz you are.' Ghast smiled, revealing in his square jaw two rows of sharp yellow teeth. *Like a rat's*, Kay thought. He stepped down off the ledge, lower but somehow, as he approached them, still more commanding with every pace he took. Kay's ears throbbed with rushing blood. 'Oh, calm yourselves,' he snapped, looking pointedly at the girls. 'We're not going to hurt you. Though we might have done.' Kay leaned into Will's hand, but she didn't flinch.

Foliot and Firedrake stepped to the left as Ghast approached, Foliot holding out to his master the crumpled sheets of the inventory. Ghast took them and carefully prised them open, smoothing them with his hand, totally engrossed for what seemed like an eternity. Then, still looking down, he confronted Kay, raised his head and, in a voice so authoritative it was almost silent, said slowly and simply, 'The tooth.'

In spite of herself, Kay's right hand came out of her pocket, rose into the air, unclasping around the tooth that sat upright in her palm. Without taking his eyes off hers or moving his steady face an inch, Ghast took it. Every muscle in her body seemed to rebel; and yet every muscle in her body seemed to do exactly what Ghast demanded.

'Thank you,' he said. Sarcasm, not kindness. Wheeling, he strode to one of the long tables, next to which Kay saw the sacks that Flip and Will, Jack and Sprite had lugged back from the balloon, crammed with her father's things. He dropped the tooth into the open fold of the nearest, and then stopped. He did not turn, did not raise his head, but said with the same

84

quiet authority, 'I will want to see this author for myself later. For now take the children to the Quarries, feed them and rest them. Foliot, Firedrake: I will take advice on what to do with them after that. First see these sacks into the cellars. Go.'

The two officious wraiths each hoisted one of the sacks, crossed the room and ducked out through a low door. For a moment there was silence. Ghast had paused by a low mahogany table. His finger absently caressed a stack of papers. He seemed to be lost in a thought.

Kay felt Will turning her with his still strong grasp on her shoulder, trying to lead her back out of the door. She struggled free and took a few steps towards Ghast. Her head spun.

'We came here to find our father. Where is he.' She didn't ask. She simply blurted.

The same ruffling of papers and soft tread of indifferent feet around the room marked the heartbeats as they rushed in Kay's chest. Ghast said nothing for a long time. She watched his knuckles on the table, still tight, then whitening, as if he were growing angry or, she hoped, afraid. She could not see his face, but only the scruff and matt of the tangled hair at the back of his head, and the rough wool collar of his heavy tunic. She waited, knowing he had heard her.

Then Ghast spoke, again quietly; but with the knuckles on the table almost silver now, he spoke with a new, singular menace. 'I have already finished with him. You are too late.'

Will reached out his long arm and dragged Kay from the room.

*G*hast paced around the huddled form where it lay on the stone floor of the Imaginary. It was wrapped in dirty cloths, bound with coarse ropes. Only the head was free of them, though it was matted and caked with sweat, and worse. Two squat wraiths stood to one side, hooded, still muttering and whispering in fervent bursts, maniacal phrases and threats.

'Is he ready?'

One of the wraiths fell silent. He looked up at his master with a pooling, blank stare. In the half-shuttered light his pupils slowly began to acquire focus, as if his gaze were a bird flying in on a tumult of wind from a great way off.

'Nearly.'

'He remembers nothing?'

Just at that moment a breaking groan rose from the huddled body on the stones. It contorted, pushing against the cords that bound it. Ghast was reminded of a beautiful moth or butterfly, struggling fruitlessly in its brittle chrysalis. He had seen one once, in a hot season, writhe against its shell until it was exhausted. When it died.

The shape lay panting. It groaned again.

'My daughters.'

The slight smile drained from Ghast's uneven face.

'He remembers one thing,' said the wraith.

'Then work him harder. Give him no rest. I must have him in the morning, and he must be ready.'

'Yes,' said the wraith, and turned back to his work, hiding his face in the heavy shadow of his hood.

Ghast watched the scene for several minutes. He was careful not to make a sound, even matching his own breaths to the rise and fall of his servants' rhythmic monodies. Their words were not audible to him, but he knew what they were saying. He had designed the technique himself. Again and again they would regale their victim with lies, with false stories, alternative histories, presenting him with a hall of mirrors in which he could not find himself. Their voices would rise and fall, waxing and waning like the drone of locusts eating away at his peace, eating away at his confidence, finally eating away at everything he knew, or thought he knew. He would fall from an irritation into a trance, from a trance into a frenzy, and from a frenzy into a weakness. And in that weakness he would at last relinquish his grip on his own story. He would cease to know himself.

Then he would be ready. When a man reached that state, he was entirely without integrity, without solidity of any kind. He would believe anything, trust anything, and like a man hurtling through a void would grasp at anything at all as if it were solid ground. To that man, every least dream seemed a hard and reliable fact, every flashing fantasy an eternal reality. He would become so hungry for conviction that he would believe anything, so trusting of everything said or done to him, he would become entirely, utterly untrustworthy. In that state, in the very height of his weakness and vulnerability, they would release him. Just like that. Let him fend for himself then, when he could not. Let him tear himself to pieces in his madness. Let him be mocked by children, kicked by passers-by, taken for a vagrant and locked away, or worse.

Ghast smiled. It pleased him to think of the Builder, the great architect of a doomed hope, staggering through the streets of some unfamiliar place, pursued by children and lunatics.

Once, you hunted us, thought Ghast to himself. *But now they will hunt you.*

He smiled again, then turned and stalked from the room.

5

The Quarries

Afterwards Kay could not clearly remember what happened next; she seemed to float through more corridors, tethered listlessly to the others. Sounds – voices, footfalls, the opening and closing of heavy doors – reached her only distantly, as if they were smothered in cotton in an adjacent room. She would recall a sense of downward movement, as if they had descended a long incline, not so much a stairway as a series of extended ledges that seemed to curve ever to the left. Sometimes other wraiths, both short and tall, passed them in pairs or small groups, less often alone. She felt numb and cold and empty; her bones seemed to have drained within her, and were shuddering like hollowed canes in her legs. She had so many questions, and no strength to ask them.

A few times, as they swept ever downwards, she faltered. Each time Will's hand was there to catch her, to prop her up – as if he had read her mind, as if he knew the ache and emptiness in her legs. At first she was grateful, but then she became irritated. She wanted to fall. She wanted to collapse – but he wouldn't let her. He was her friend, she knew, but more and more she felt in his gentle ministrations the arm of a jailer. And then they seemed to swoop through a low arch and into another gloriously cavernous and entirely vacant womb of a hall. This one, unlike the first two, was not at all furnished or lit; but it was much, much bigger. Across the distant ceiling – if it *was* a ceiling – as Kay craned her gaze in wonder, she saw tiny points of light like stars, swirling and cascading in patterns far denser and more ordered than those of the constellations. The soft light they created illuminated very little of what was around them, except to give a general sense of gloomy, cavernous waste. On the cave floor she could at first see nothing particular, but from a number of directions she could hear water moving, as if there were a stream nearby; and a fresh and constant breeze stirred her hair as Will, turning, crouched down to talk to them.

'Now we're in the Quarries. It's not much, but this is where we live. Where the wraiths live, I mean. It's an unspoken rule that we don't speak in the Quarries – well, it *would* be unspoken, wouldn't it?' He smiled. 'Here we are wordless, though in your case I think anyone would make an exception. Still, try to keep your voices down. I'll show you where you can sleep.'

Taking the girls by the hand again, Will led them ever down, this time by a short, steep flight of steps into what felt at first like a pit. When they hit the bottom of the steps and turned through a gash in the wall, they found themselves in another room with a kind of window to one side, and open above to the roof of the cave. Lanterns were hung here and there. Exhausted, Kay slumped to the floor, cradling Ell on her lap. Will pushed a heavy wooden door shut behind them, put his hand to the key in the lock, then hesitated – and, thinking better of it, left it alone. From the table he took a dark loaf of bread, broke it and handed two wedges to the girls. It was the sort of thing that, normally, they would both have refused: brown, almost black, rough, dry. But now Kay ate hungrily. As she chewed, the sound of water, louder here, came to her ears.

'Are we near a river?' she asked.

'Yes, we are, of sorts,' said Will, now taking a stone jug and pouring some water into small clay beakers that he handed to the girls. 'You're drinking it. When we were delving here, centuries ago, we exposed one of the old currents from the glacial melt to the east, tunnelling here through the soft stone of the mountain's lower buttress. We dug it out and quarried around it, which left us with a very useful water supply and a continuous source of beautiful music. This may not be home, but it has its consolations.'

'And the stars?' Kay asked, pointing weakly up.

'We cut shafts directly up through the mountain there to the sunlight. The shafts help to circulate the air, and they are, you have to admit, spectacular.' He smiled broadly. 'Cutting them was my idea.'

Kay thought wearily that it must be day. *How was it day. What were they doing. Where were they.* She was too tired to ask any questions; she felt them sputtering in her throat like wet candles.

'Since coming back into the mountain, we do everything here but our work.' Will pulled over a small table, along with two chairs that had been left by the wall. He put each of the girls on a chair, then sat on the floor, facing them. 'You must have a thousand questions,' he said. 'Let's hear them. Quietly.'

Kay tried to focus. She leaned away into the hard struts of the straight-backed wooden chair, pressing her bones against the ridges. She rubbed them painfully from side to side as she looked about the room, willing herself to be alert. In some places it had been chiselled out of the rock, in others practically gouged. Across the ceiling and floor, the rough strokes of the hammers were sometimes still visible, the surfaces left unfinished, creating dips and rises everywhere. But around the window and the door that stood opposite the gap through which they had come in, it was different. Here with fine tools some workman had carved every edge precisely, patiently cutting out figures in the stone, pillars and fluting; and, though there was no system to it – it seemed to be a haphazard collage – it was beautiful; like opening the door of an old wardrobe, Kay thought, and finding it crammed to bursting with a snowy forest. Now that her eyes had grown accustomed to the low light, she realized that the stone was not exactly the dull grey of granite but a faint blue, like the sky in the east the moment before dusk.

'Why did you quarry here? Where is all *this*?' she asked, lifting her left hand again and gesturing around, beyond the door. The door Will had almost locked. Had he intended to lock someone out? Or was he about to lock them *in*?

Will frowned quickly at her question, as if he had been stung by a wasp, and clasped his arms around his knees, digging in his chin. 'In Bithynia,' he said, his voice almost as hollow, almost as faint, as an echo. His eyes closed, and Kay could tell, as she had on the balloon, that more was coming, if she were only to wait. 'From the Quarries we carved the sky-stone and floated it down the river to the sea. From the mine below the mountain we dug out gold and silver, rich veins with which we threaded the living wood of our halls. Now the Quarries are our home, and the mines –'

But Ell cut in: 'What did he mean, that . . . loud man, when he said he had "finished with him"? Is our dad here?'

Will opened his eyes but did not look up. They were wet with tears. At first Kay wondered if the sorrow was for his home; but then suddenly she felt she knew why he had thought to lock the door, why she had lost her interest in questions. She willed him to stop, not to say the words. Not in front of Ell. She wanted to stand up, to lean over, to clap her hands over his mouth. But instead she sat frozen, the high back of the chair cleaving into the back of her skull.

'No. He isn't here,' Will started, his voice rising – but then he stopped. With a finger of his right hand he followed the ridges of the textured floor of the cave, their ups and downs, their shunts and returns, their half-moons and careening circles. Kay watched this movement closely, aware that its expressive patterning, like the movement of the stones on the plotting board, was rich with significance. Then the finger began to lift, and was soon tapping out random points across the floor, as if mapping raindrops or pecking for grain. 'No,' Will said quietly, his tone softer, 'no, he isn't here.'

'Then where is he?'

The finger went on tapping, tapping. Kay watched it for a while, then looked over at her sister. Although Ell sat a head lower than her on the next chair, her expression was so alert, her eyes so wide and her strawberry hair so electric with her absorption that Kay felt as if she herself were instead looking up at her sister.

'After removal,' Will said quietly, 'dispersal.'

'What does that mean?' Ell asked, not missing a beat. She swivelled towards Kay. 'I don't know what that means.'

Will was silent, but his finger still plucked and dived, though it was slowing. Kay wanted to reach out to Ell: she understood enough of what 'dispersal' meant to know that it sounded bad, horrible, wrong. Too much like 'disposal'. But Ell was still strong and resolute in her defiance.

Will looked up and unfurled his hands over the floor, palms down, as if warming them on the creases and hollows of its rough pattern. 'Let me tell you a story,' he said.

The little girl shot back, 'I don't want a story. I want to get our dad.' She had not even flinched, let alone budged.

'Still, this is a story that is about getting. Sometimes there are truths and comforts and ways *in* stories that are not so apparent *outside* stories. Sometimes stories are answers, or make answers possible. Sometimes they are the mothers of answers.' He was staring hard at Kay now, directly into her eyes. When she met his gaze, she thought his eyes were the calmest, most ice-like blue she had ever seen. She felt as if tears might well out of her fingertips.

'Many hundreds of years ago, before histories were written down in books, great cities and nations told stories about themselves as a way of remembering who they were, where they had come from and what they wanted for themselves and their children. The men and women who told these stories were poets, and because they had to remember huge numbers of facts – names, places, events, in a web of causes and consequences spanning hundreds, even thousands, of years – they had to come up with ways of making their memories stronger. More secure. So they fashioned their stories into rhythms and rhymes, lines and verses, and decorated them with distinctive patterns of language that would help them to put every piece of every story in exactly the right place every time they told it. And they told their stories often: every night, sometimes to one or two children, sometimes to crowds gathered around a great fire or under the stars on a summer evening, they remembered, and they witnessed, and they prophesied.'

As Will spoke and his finger wove across the stone, Kay felt his tone change, and change again. It was like looking through a kaleidoscope, where the colours and shapes shift as it turns, building patterns as delicate as a butterfly's wings. She heard kindness and compassion, brilliance and vision, and beneath it all a music she was sure she knew: the music of her father's voice, reading, reading, reading in the dark of the night. Ell held out her hand and Kay took it; somehow they managed to slip to the floor, and sat clasped together in the shadow of Will's voice.

'Now, turning your story in just such a way that it was most beautiful, most striking, most memorable was a great skill and a gift – something that could be learned, but only by those who were born with a readiness to it. And so famous families of poets arose, men and women with that readiness, who were trained in the mysteries of speaking and who conserved the traditions of the nations, and the cities, and the families. And they competed with one another, and some were considered lesser, others better, and some very few the best.

'Among the best – by far the most celebrated, and indeed the greatest – was the poet Orpheus. He was born the only son of a long line of singers, and the talent ran so rife in him it was said that he himself would never have children, that he gave so much to his tellings, he had nothing left to beget. Stories must be his children. Everywhere he went, he went singing, and in his hands, if there was no harp, still his fingers danced in the air, plucking notes from the breezes, or from the rain, or from shafts of light that dropped at morning and evening between the clouds. As an infant, before even he learned to speak, he learned the rhythms and tones of the ancient modes and melodies, and they were constantly in his throat. And what a throat: like that of a swan for beauty, of a nightingale for song; for strength like that of a wrestler. Beauty and power joined in every syllable, in every line and stanza.'

'Was his father proud of him?' asked Ell. Kay glanced sharply across, annoyed at her for breaking the flow of the tale, annoyed at herself for being annoyed. Ell was sleepy. Her eyelids were sinking.

'Yes, very proud,' said Will. 'For he quickly mastered all the traditional tales on which his father's reputation had been founded. He sang the great battle stories, with their interludes of love, and the fortunes of the famous dynasties descended from the heroes and the gods. As a young man, he was already capable of a depth and range of narrative, memory and passion usually reached by only the best singers in their prime. It had become a speculation on everyone's lips: where would this great artist go next? Where would he find his material? It was the custom in those days for poets to rely on certain tricks of the memory to make the delivery of their songs easier – certain elements of a song would resurface again and again, like bells ringing: four- or five-word phrases, sometimes slightly altered but still roughly the same, returning to the verse like a refrain. This made the poet's load lighter, but also delighted the audience: there is nothing more satisfying than the return of something familiar. There is nothing like ease in the midst of difficulty, nothing like cool water at the height of a hot day. Orpheus, beyond all the other poets of his age, had become adept at this technique, and was famed for the subtle ways in which he could lay down a theme or a motif, let it change or metamorphose and then lie fallow before reviving it, calling it back into the light. Where other poets would make in their poems a web of themes, some of which they caught up again, and others not, it was said that Orpheus never lost a single word. It was said that he could let a word die and go to hell, but he would ransom it back again before the poem was done.'

Kay bristled. *Go to hell*, she thought.

Ell hadn't drifted off. 'No one comes back from hell,' she said.

Will's finger stopped in the air, and he raised his head to look at the girls, each in turn, for a long moment. His eyes seemed full of care for them, as if they were small and helpless. 'Should I keep going?' he asked.

Kay nodded. Will's finger began to move and move. It took him almost a minute to join his voice to it again.

'It was maybe inevitable that so skilled and able a craftsman should fall in love with the Bride. She never comes freely to those who love her. She must be sought, though never directly. One day her lovers find her as they go about their trade. So did Orpheus as he sang beneath a spreading plane tree in a valley in Macedonia. He had been reciting one of the older tales – a history of the making of the world. The best stories pose impossible questions: where was the creation that made this creator? How could he make, and be by that making made? As Orpheus sang, turning and returning to the problem of his art, the nature that fostered it and the art that cultivated that nature, he began to lose control of his tale. Instead, it started to take a purpose and a length of its own, gathering by digressions great folds and skirts, pleated narratives hanging from the main hem. Story after story ribboned from his aching tongue. Searching for one thing, for one great story, he made many. It was far into the night before, in a mood created by his exhaustion and the accelerating rhythm of his invention, he began to see something new, something dazzling. In a voice of sudden thunder he threw it from him like a bolt: the very impossibility of the world was its cause. This is that quality of the Bride which is called her most arcane.

'That night, through a copse at the edge of the village Orpheus glimpsed the Bride for the first time. She wore the same loose-fitting white gown as always, the garment that had first given her her name. She moved silently and at the edge of his vision between the trees. The Bride only ever appeared by means of some other thing, through some other thing, as if she were a light in water or the sudden hues hanging in the air after a storm. Orpheus could feel this, could feel that he must not look at her; and as he looked away with the song running through his mind and his ears, her white gown drifted towards him until he could feel her breath weaving through the hair on the back of his neck. He thought then that, if he lost her, and the touch he knew she was about to bestow, he would never be able to invite her presence again. He was wrong. It was only his first time.'

The Bride, Kay thought. 'The Bride,' she said. 'Who is that? My father works on her.'

Will's finger kept moving, this time dancing over the stone like a feather floating on water. 'No one knows who she is,' he said softly.

'But Orpheus *saw* her. You said he saw her. So what does she look like? Who is she?'

'She is that thing that no one can ever see clearly. The thing you can almost grasp, the thing you can very nearly make out, but then it eludes you – she is what gets away, like a thought or a vision at the moment you start from sleep, like the strand you lose when you look at the twine. Or when you love someone very, very much, and you think you might almost burst – she is the bursting.'

'Oh, oh, oh,' Kay cried, as if she would cry, even though she knew that her heart and her head were clear and dry. 'He can never see her.'

'Never,' agreed Will.

'I can't stand it,' said Kay, tightening her arms around Ell, whose warm, huddled body had sagged into sleep.

'He couldn't stand it, either. The song ended for Orpheus that night, and he did lose the Bride; but she came again and again. He became so practised at invoking the Bride that soon he had only to slip into that familiar mode of thinking or telling, and he would catch sight of her white shift, or hear the light step of her sandals on the grass behind him. It was never the same thoughts, of course – a thought is like the track of a cartwheel in the dirt of a road: the more you think it, the more you run it down the road, the more it wears in, becoming a rut; and a rut slops up and chokes the passage, and that is fatal to the rhythm of the Bride. Always, then, he sought out new stories, new rhythms, new modes in which his thought might tumble over itself, like a wave endlessly reverberating against a shore but never breaking; so that he might live every day in the expectation of a presence, the sense of companionship and witness that he had never before had occasion to feel.

'What the poet had not counted upon, but what others saw in him from the start, was the way this hunger for the Bride was changing him. He was gradually being torn apart from within. As he searched tirelessly for more experiences, more stories, more rhythms, more forms, always after a new means by which he might summon the beautiful, fugitive figure that was almost within his reach, it was true that his art soared, and that he became the greatest poet of all the ages. But his innovations and experimentations, his long nights without sleep and days without rest, the months after months when he stood chanting ever new, ever more complex and moving tales – all this came at a price. The love of the Bride gouged him, scooped at him, quarried him. His eyes sank in his head and his lips paled and cracked; his hair by strands came loose and was shed; his muscles dwindled and his skin grew sallow; his tongue dried; and in his temper and thought, too, he grew always more brittle, less resilient. Finally, one day, coming out of the mountains of Thessalia and taking a seat in a crowded market to tell a variation on the most ancient narrative of the flood, the inevitable occurred. Orpheus' rhythm had become so strong that the Bride, rather than stalking silently behind him, appeared to be running towards him from far off. And as he sang, the faces expectant and full of delight around him, at last he looked up, full into her face as she approached. And at that moment, slowing, she reached out her arm and touched him.'

In the long afterlight cast by the starry holes in the roof of the cave, Will looked slowly down at the faces of the two girls, now slumped against each other on the ground beside him, in one another's arms, the regular, almost silent rise and fall of their breaths indicating how fast asleep they had fallen. He drew with his finger absently on the rock of the cave floor, tracing ellipses.

'Will, what happened when she touched him?'

Kay was awake and murmuring, though her eyelids remained slack and shut, and her arms limp where they draped round Ell's shoulders.

'He came apart, Kay. And he was dispersed.'

'*Bring him.*'

The two hooded wraiths approached the crumpled form, one on either side, stooped, and with the utmost gentleness lifted it to its broken height. The man's head lolled on its neck, spluttering through the filth of mucus and blood that caked its face. Whoever he was, he did not look up. He was ready.

Ghast held wide the oak door to the Imaginary as the wraiths guided the shuffling form between them, and together the four of them descended the sloping stairs of the tower. Their progress was painfully slow.

At the base of the tower Ghast put his hand on the heavy rope and collar where for centuries they had hung on an iron hook. How often had he imagined lifting it, in waking visions as in his dreams! The collar was plain iron, a band of about two inches in width, hammered flat, with a tight hinge to one side and a clasp opposite. The clasp was mounted with a heavy ring, long ago welded to its base with huge slugs of black iron. He knew before he touched it what its weight would be, how its hinge would demand forcing. *Beg for it.* The inch-thick rope had been twined with a thread of steel, then spliced to the ring and the rope ends woven seamlessly back upon the cabling. He drew it slowly from the hook, allowing its mass and heft to shift slowly, coil by coil, into his other palm, each coil a distinct pleasure. To each filament he gave his thumb, but delicately, noticing every ridge and hair as it slipped with its own weight between his hands. It would end too soon, he thought.

It ended too soon.

The head hung before him, its spare remaining tufts of hair clotted with filth. He had no inclination to touch it. He nodded to one of the wraiths, who grasped the hair firmly, lifting the head far enough to expose a band of grey flesh beneath the chin. Ghast broke open the collar with a single sharp tug, then placed it around the neck, as lightly and reverently as if he were crowning a king. In a way, he thought, he was. The reverence was for himself.

As the little group moved through the rough-quarried passages, Ghast always leading, the rope pinched tenderly between the tips of his squat fingers, he thought of the great triumphs of an earlier age, of the generals returning to the imperial city in chariots crowned with golden victories, of the captives paraded in chains, or cages, through the jeering tumults of the streets. He imagined the trumpets, the velvet cushions on which the emperor, seated, would receive with gracious condescension the submission of his enemies. Courtiers lapped up his yawns as cats do milk. With every step he felt the drums pulse up his dwarf calves. He did not need to close his eyes; the vision settled on him waking.

With no haste they gained first the great cavern of the mountain, hung with tapestries, then by a little passage the door to the library.

The lights flared along the walls as Ghast shuffled his prisoner in behind him.

There they stood. They were ready. All he would have to do now, he thought, was wait.

Spiders wait in their webs, but neither, he thought, as patiently nor as silently as he. Soon his daughters would see the great Builder; but the Builder would not see his daughters. For he no longer knew them. To what desperation and recklessness this would drive them, his enemies, Ghast needed not imagine – for he had plotted every step of it already. The girl would break. After that she would do anything to get her father back. And when she learned that only Ghast himself had that power, why, she would give him anything he demanded. She would give him a golden crown.

For now, he would wait.

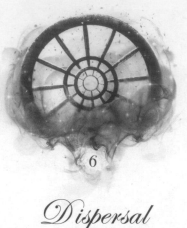

6

Dispersal

Kay woke to hands on her shoulders. *Why?* she thought in the moments before she forced her eyes open.

It was Will. He was crouched above her, arguing with Flip. Kay saw his mouth moving, and understood the metallic clang of his angry tone, understood the hard clamp of his eyes, like a vice, as he volleyed words over her head. But she couldn't make out the meaning.

And he was pinning her down. She pushed against his hands before she found her own. Then she ground them into the stone beneath her, writhing in his grip. Somehow they were up on the floor of the quarry, in the large space, and there was movement – she struggled on to one side, thrashing beneath Will's hands while he pushed her down – and she saw a knot of wraiths moving away across the quarry floor and towards the great stairs.

'I don't care about the thread,' Will was saying. 'He doesn't have the right.' He was hardly paying attention to her as she pushed against him with all her strength.

Ell, she thought. Her eyes rebounded wildly around the huge space, her head lurching from side to side. *Ell. Ell.*

'Right or no right, Will, for the time being he has the voices, and there's nothing you can do about it. We have to make the best of what we can. Don't get too involved with this.' That was Flip. *Where is Eloise?*

'She's only a tiny child. She can't be more than six years old.'

'She's eight,' Kay corrected him. It came out like a howl.

Now, at last, she had Will's full attention. She pushed hard to the right, then rolled immediately to the left. Will's right hand slipped, and Kay sprang on to one foot. She kept low in a crouch, like a dog. A wounded one. About a metre away. She watched Will's hands.

'Where is she?' she said. 'I promised I would stay with her.'

'Foliot came and took her to see Ghast,' said Will. 'And I tried to stop him, and my *friend* Flip here stopped me.' He was steady, and kind, and like always. *But his hands.* 'We thought you would wake up,' he added, almost apologetic. 'And the way we plotted things, we were afraid you might try to go after her.'

Kay glanced quickly at that knot of wraiths still moving across the floor of the Quarries, now very close to the stairs.

'You mean Ghast wanted to see her?' Kay asked. 'I thought Ghast wanted to see *me*. Take me there now.' She didn't move. The wraiths didn't move. They said nothing, but she could sense from their intense silence that there was going to be a problem. The wraiths across the quarry floor reached the stairs, and began to ascend out of sight. In among them as they climbed, Kay caught the flash of Ell's red curls.

Her whole body flinched.

'We can't leave, Kay. Ghast's orders,' Will said finally, softly, and Kay crouched on the ground again, her hands pressed palm down on either side of her, and looked out into the distance, to the other side of the quarry, beyond the stream where it gushed up from below. There were other wraiths coming and going here and there, silently in the shadow. 'The truth is,' Will said, 'they want me to lock you up.'

'The truth is,' said Flip, 'he wants me to lock you both up.'

Kay ignored them. 'What does Ghast want her for?'

'I don't know,' Will said.

Kay turned. 'She's scared. I promised I would stay with her.'

For a long time they just watched one another – or, rather, watched the spaces in between one another. Around them shadows flitted in and among the rocks, and soft footfalls echoed from the tunnels that led out from the cave, so distant and muted that they reminded Kay of the sound of stones settling in the silt of the river when, the summer before, she had gone swimming underwater with her father. Her dispersed father. Ell had been throwing stones from the bank, and Kay had watched them plummet down, making the lightest thud as they half dropped, half settled into the weedy mud. She had decided at the time, as she held her breath and squinted through the murky water, that it was the sound of fairies stamping. She hadn't been far off, she now thought with grim satisfaction; it was the sound of wraiths walking. Kay felt a stiff and brittle rage steel through her shoulders: it was the sound of wraiths walking off with Ell, she thought, while she slept, while Will did nothing. While her mother cried.

Kay stood up. 'Well, I don't care. I'm going to Ghast. You're going to have to stop me.'

She was off and running before they could react. This gave her a few seconds to get ahead. She ducked behind a cleft, darted up through a narrow channel in the rock, then doubled back down some stairs, through one of the quarry pits. They couldn't have seen her go down, she knew, because she was light and low, and had had enough of a start; and at the bottom of the stairs she waited to see if one or both of them would chance it – but they seemed to have gone in the other direction, towards the tunnels. She was now too far down to see them, but there was a glow where the tunnels opened up into the cave, and so she headed in the opposite direction, picking her way as quietly as she could and always looking out for other wraiths. She was hoping that there would be another exit, some way to slip past Will and Flip, get to Ghast and . . . well, at least be with Ell. Even if she couldn't get her out, at least she wouldn't be alone.

Kay found herself at the low, sudden bank of the underground river. It flowed here silently, a bluish-grey column of glass laid in its cut bed like a massive dark jewel. Kay stood watching its apparent motionlessness, looking for some sign – debris, an eddy, a bubble – of its current, knowing that it must be motive and fluid. Mesmerized by its stillness, she crouched down and gingerly stretched out her hand to dip her fingers into the water. The moment of contact came as a shock: it was liquid ice, not water, and from the dead force of it against her fingers she knew that it was moving very fast. After a few seconds, her fingers already numb, she withdrew them and stood up. She backed off and reminded herself of what her mother would say: *If it's that cold on your fingers, Katharine, you certainly don't want to fall in*. Kay smiled; *no, I certainly do not*.

But with the tingling that was beginning in her hand as the cold leached out of her fingers came a thought. She spun round to face upstream, training her eyes along the embankment as far as she could see in the dim light. There was a curve in the course, slightly up and to the right, and some outcroppings that blocked her view; but she thought she could just make out, not too far away, that other tunnel out of the Quarries, a tunnel that had not been carved by wraiths, but scoured by the cold hands of the swift-running river. She ran along the bank, grateful to the wraiths for having left a path clear all the way to the wall. Flip and Will would be watching the quarry entrance, but perhaps she could slip out through the back door.

By the time she reached the gushing, noisy mouth of the stream, she was breathing hard, and had to stop to get her bearings. No one was following her, though it could surely be only a matter of moments before one of them plotted her escape, before one of them saw her hovering. She peered into the dark mouth of the underground watercourse, where it cut its way upwards through soft rock. The wraiths had obviously dug out the channel for some way into the mountainside – but how far? If she went in, would she be able to get out? Kay thought: *The wraiths would probably have taken the trouble to cut the stream's tunnel open only if they were using it for something. You don't delve a dead end directly into a mountain.* She might have heard footsteps. She didn't look back; she dived in.

In the thick chill of the black tunnel she found she had to grope her way along, using her hands against the wall to guide her, and running her toes along the wall, too, with every step. She was terrified of putting a foot wrong and tumbling into the stream to her left. Her fingers remembered its heavy cold. Every step grew more tentative – what would happen if the ledged bank were suddenly to end, and she were to trip or fall into a river of ice? For a moment she stopped completely, too anxious to move forward, too reluctant to turn back. But the thought of Ell alone with Ghast drew her onward again. And someone must be following by now. They would figure it out. They would have lights. Kay forced herself to make progress – slow progress up a slight incline, but progress. The course, she noticed, was slightly inclined, and she felt the air growing cooler and cooler as she bored further and further into the mountainside.

In the darkness Kay suddenly recalled those final words of Will's last story, which she had heard just before drifting off. *He was dispersed*, he had said. Orpheus, the poet, had been dispersed. Kay remembered the myth of Orpheus' death, a story her father had told her a hundred times if he had told her once: how he had descended to Hades to redeem his dead wife, Eurydice; how he had lost her; and how, while singing his songs of lamentation and despair, he had been attacked by frenzied worshippers of the god Bacchus and literally torn to pieces. Dispersed. So this, then, was what Ghast had meant by 'processed'.

In the dark of the tunnel, her arms splayed on the gently sloping rock face, Kay suddenly felt sick, disorientated, vulnerable – and she nearly reeled backwards. It was as if someone had just turned on a very bright, high-beam light right in her face – except that, instead of a light, it was darkness itself they were shining upon her; high-beam darkness, totally unilluminating her. She crouched. After removal, dispersal. And now they had taken Ell. *Why?* She had to go on.

By the time Kay found herself alongside a warm and suddenly very dry section of rock, she was so tired with her fear that she almost failed to notice it. A realization was only just settling in her mind as her hands brushed up against a new texture, one that was definitely neither dry nor wet rock. It felt like wood; and at the centre of it there was a metal knob or handle. The blood in Kay's arms and legs flushed into her chest and neck, and she came up square against the door, the silent river running on behind her. Feeling round the frame of the door, she could tell she was going to have to push. So terrified and exhausted had she become that she hardly paused to wonder what might be on the other side; she just pushed with all her strength.

Nothing happened. She pushed again. Nothing. Her whole head a throbbing mass of despair, she almost cried, and pounded with her fist on the wood.

Unstuck from its seal, the door finally swung open with surprising force, and Kay tumbled into what seemed a blindingly bright room. Her eyes seared by the change in the light, she was able to take in only that the room around her was warm and cluttered, though it was as silent as the passage she had left. She had fallen into someone's arms, and the sleeves and coat up against her face were similarly warm, and smelled strongly of some spice she couldn't precisely place – not mint, but as sharp; not aniseed, but as sweet. She was half on her knees. Another form – a black blur as she had fallen – had rushed across her to close the door, and she felt the draught, at first violently sucking out of the chamber, settle as the door was closed and then – it sounded – locked behind her. For a long moment nothing else happened, and she remained immobile, semi-prostrate, her head buried in the cloth of some stranger's arms. Then he spoke.

'It's all right, Kay. I've got you. You'll be fine.'

It was Will's voice: unmistakably soft, almost a whisper, with that delicate unsureness that made his assurances so believable. She let herself go limp. *But those hands.*

'Will, the thread.'

Kay stiffened a little again. It was Flip. She pushed herself up and tried to open her eyes. 'How did you find me?' she asked. 'I need to find Ell.'

'This will do for both,' said Will, taking something out of his pocket and thrusting it into her hand. It was a small, smooth, cool stone. A plotting stone. 'We plotted your run just now, and we can plot Ghast, too.' Will smiled weakly and held up his hands. *Those hands.* 'It's our one advantage on Ghast – and we reckon we've got about thirty seconds till we lose it. Get up – quickly now.'

Will's arms were around Kay, hauling her up, and then he and Flip practically lifted her in the air as, together, they drew back into the near corner of the small room, behind two tables stacked high with carpets, to rest beside an enormous trunk. To her left, she could see the door through which she had come in. It was flush and seamless with the wall except for a handle which, judging from its shape and size, was exactly like the one on the other side, protruding from its exact centre. She could now see that the handle was in the shape of a plotting stone – oblong, smooth and jet black – but larger.

But to her right . . . To her right, she suddenly realized there was only gloomy air. Over a rail, a kind of balcony, her eye soared out into a chaos of shadows.

'Into the trunk,' said Flip. 'Hurry.'

From a pocket Will produced a ring of keys, holding them up to the light just long enough for Kay to see how similar they were to some she had seen before – where? – and then, selecting one, he undid three separate locks on the battered, banded trunk. When its heavy lid swung open, Kay could see that the blackened interior was almost empty, and easily large enough to take them all. But, helping her in, Will quickly let the lid fall over the two of them, though without quite letting it settle into place. Through a crack Kay could make out Flip, still outside, striding away, the cloth of his cloak whispering urgently as his long legs made for the opposite side of the room.

Away to the right, lights suddenly flared, and she realized that beyond the railing, below and all around, was the great library of the mountain through which they had walked the night before. Everywhere around them were shelves crammed with books, and Kay saw that they were in an alcove perched just above the hall. She shuddered, for no reason that she knew.

Flip bent rigidly over a table; just to his right was a stack of papers, which he was making a show of reading.

'Will . . .' Kay whispered in the dark within the trunk. Her breath rebounded hot against the tight space where they crouched. 'What are we waiting for?'

'We're pretty sure Ghast is coming. And he will have Ell with him, or will know where she is. We worked it out on the plotting board.'

'And that's how you found me?' Kay asked. She recalled, in the Quarries, looking over towards the entrance of the tunnels, and glimpsing a group of wraiths gathering around the light. No wonder they hadn't been searching for her, she thought – or, rather, they *had* been searching for her in their own way. They had just been looking for where she *would be*, rather than where she *was*.

'Yes,' Will said.

'But . . .' Kay paused. 'If you could use the plotting board to find me here, why can't Ghast use it to find the two of us here?'

Will's reply was immediate. 'Ghast and most of his trusted servants are hopeless with plotting boards. They can't use them well. Anyway, your path through the Quarries was unusual, random, unpredictable. That kind of chaotic improvisation makes plotting difficult for anyone but the best.' She could almost feel him winking in the darkness. 'If Ghast tried to plot this now, he would probably think we were still down there. And it's not as if he plots everything.'

'Why can't we just use the plotting board to find out what Ghast is doing with Ell? Why can't we use it to get her back?'

'Too much, too far in advance. A plotting board is excellent for movement, but poor on intentions. It can give us a good idea of where someone will be, especially soon, but it doesn't tell us a lot about what they mean to do. So I was pretty sure – I knew – you would be on the other side of that door, but I didn't know how you would feel about seeing us.'

It was almost like an apology. Or it was an apology. In the trunk Kay took Will's hand and squeezed it. Will seemed almost embarrassed.

'And I am pretty sure Ghast will be here, in the library, in a few seconds. And so we wait.'

'No,' Kay said. The word just flooded out of her. 'No, that's wrong.'

'What is?'

'We're not waiting for him. *He's* waiting for *us*.' All over her head Kay's hair pricked and stood up, like a wave sweeping back from her eyes, across her scalp and down her neck. In her mind, she backed away from herself.

'Kay, what are you –?'

'I think I dreamed it.'

There was just enough light in the trunk for Kay to see Will staring at her, to see his mouth opening in puzzlement – but just then a loud, low hiss came from across the room. Kay's eye shot back up to the crack to find that Flip hadn't moved – he was still hunched over, one arm laid loosely on his pile of papers, apparently hard at work.

'It's time, Kay,' Will said. 'Stay absolutely still.'

There was an abrupt and sharp noise, as of a latch being lifted, that echoed through the library. A confused number of footsteps, heavy and light, sounded around the vast space. Kay could make out very little, save for the dim suggestion of forms moving down below, mere snatches of dark and light shuffling through an opening in the stonework of the balcony.

Flip had got to his feet.

'It's you.' That, she knew with conviction, was Ghast's voice calling. She hadn't forgotten his scornful, raspy bass.

From the edge of the stone balustrade Flip looked down, his silver hair catching the light. 'I'm going through the receipts of dispersals, Sergeant Ghast, as you instructed at our return yesterday. So far everything seems to be in order.'

'I trust you dispatched the papers for the criminal More this morning?'

From below Kay heard the sound of metal scraping on stone, and a low, moaning sort of grunt. She pushed at the heavy lid of the trunk with her shoulder, widening the crack, and tried to peer through the stonework to the right of Flip's leg. Try as she might, she couldn't get an angle – all she could make out was the warty crown of Ghast's head.

'Well?' The head hardly moved, but the voice had hardened in anger.

'I did as I was ordered,' came Flip's curt reply.

'Such a pity you had to lie to the girl. Well, weave the thread, weave the thread,' Ghast said, his tone heavy with sarcasm. 'Foliot will attend to his unravelling. For now, I have another dispersal to enrol. Firedrake.'

Firedrake passed in front of Ghast. His long, limber form towered over his master, and Kay had for a moment a clear view of his sharp, set features. He looked mean, harder and more evil than any wraith she had yet seen. *Remember this*, she told herself. *Whatever happens, he is an enemy – an enemy to anything good.*

Flip looked to his left as Firedrake's footsteps sounded on the tight circular stairs that led up from the library floor. Kay shifted again in the trunk, propping the lid open a little further than before. She felt Will's hand grasp and squeeze her shoulder, though he didn't dare speak. But she would not hold back.

'I think you will find this dispersal, too, has been duly registered,' Ghast said.

Firedrake was now only a few metres away. He stopped. Nothing happened.

'May I ask by what authority this thread is to be cut?' Flip had not taken the piece of paper. It didn't look as if he had even acknowledged Firedrake; instead, his hands were firmly planted on the stone ledge before him. 'As Clerk of Dispersals, I usually expect notification and the customary consultation period before a formal consent can be taken. This is the thread.'

Ghast's reply was immediate, as if he had been waiting for this objection. His tone was suddenly almost jocular. 'Oh, read it. Read it – it will amuse you. I wrote it myself.'

Firedrake stepped forward and handed the piece of paper to Flip. 'Read it aloud,' Ghast said. 'It will give me pleasure.'

Flip took a deep breath and then began.

'*Sergeant Ghast, Steward Controller of the House of Bithynia, Master Extraordinary of the Weave and Chief Clerk of the Bindery, to all wraiths and phantasms, greeting. Whereas it has ever been our confirmed power to act summarily in cases of extreme danger to the Honourable Society, whether present or forecast; and whereas such summary power has been severally exercised in times past by three of our immediate predecessors in the office of Steward Controller, outside the normal course of the thread; and whereas the Steward Controller is bound by oath to defend the Honourable Society from perils present and to come by oath and by duty, regardless of interest or consequence; remembering always both the responsibility of and respect for the office; it is now our grave and careful burden to command the summary dispersal of Eloise Worth-More, author, daughter of the silkrunner and enemy of the Honourable Society, Edward More, called the Builder; whose thread will within these twelve nights by agents deputed be measured, cut and undone in the normal way, and its several remains littered in the corners of the earth. By me this twenty-fifth day, etc.*'

It was all Kay could do to stop herself from screaming as Flip finished intoning the words in a dispassionate, clerk-like voice. Her chest tightened like a limpet on a rock, and her head surged. *Ell. No. No.*

'On what grounds do you invoke the summary power of the office?'

'The child is an author,' Ghast said, 'and the daughter of our greatest enemy these two thousand years. The mere coincidence of danger and power is enough to license my action. Firedrake will carry out the dispersal. You and your disgraced friend will see that the other child is disposed of. She is worth nothing. I do not greatly care where you lose her.'

Despair. Anger. Fear. Sorrow. Shock. Disgust. Bitterness. Kay didn't know what she felt. The pain in her coiled body seemed to be a kind of cavern into which she could cram them all. As she started to stand up – just as the tension and tightness began to flex in her legs – Will gripped her shoulders with both hands. *Those hands, always holding me.* He hardly moved, and she realized that he must have been waiting for this, waiting for her to try to explode. *Always holding me.*

'Not now,' he whispered – so low, so close, that no one could have heard them. Even Firedrake, not three metres away. 'Trust me. You can't do anything for her if he finds you.'

Flip had still said nothing. Kay watched his back, willing him to shout, to defy Ghast, to do anything, to do something.

Firedrake went down the stairs. Below, where Ghast stood with his acolytes, there was no sound.

Don't accept it, Kay thought. *Throw it all back in his face. Tear it up.*

'I will enrol the dispersal,' said Flip.

No. 'No,' she whispered. 'No. No. No.' Thick sobs surged up from her chest, and she choked them back as best she could, whispering 'No' to every tear that ran down her clammy cheek.

'Firedrake. The staff.'

From beneath the lid of the chest Kay saw Firedrake hand Ghast what looked like a long metal rod – the height of a tall man at least, and clearly heavy. Moving stiffly, Ghast seemed to insert it into a hole in the floor, so that it stood erect. He stepped back and paused, regarding it, then placed his hands securely on it, palm over palm, and bowed his head briefly in a gesture that suggested prayer.

'Your little trinket,' he called out to Flip. He was beaming. 'We haven't used this contraption in some time, have we.' It wasn't a question.

'It's the great wheel,' Will whispered. 'From the Shuttle Hall. We used to turn it to mark the nights of the Weave during the revels of the twelve knights. When we left Bithynia, we took it with us and had it set into the floor of the library. Kay, he won't dare – it's sacred . . .' The urgency of Will's whispering simply dissipated, like lingering leaves blasted away by a gale.

Ghast was straining against the rod, pushing it. With an enormous effort he seemed to shift it to the right. A rasp as of metal on stone filled the library, and then a sharp rap or clack echoed its report as the rod settled. Ghast pushed again, and again with great effort shifted the rod, turning something on the floor until it slotted into place with a shudder.

'There,' said Ghast. 'A new kind of festival. One night is already gone. See that the dispersal is properly enrolled. On the twelfth night, it will be performed.'

Down the stairs, the door to the library suddenly opened again. Kay heard footsteps.

'Ah,' said Ghast with cheerful brio. 'Foliot. And our little friend.'

He must have turned. He had turned. Again Kay pushed at the lid of the trunk, which creaked slightly as she wedged it open. She now had an unimpeded view of the little group in the centre of the library, in among the long, lighted tables. Two hooded figures, Firedrake, Ghast – and, on the floor beside Ghast, a kind of huge bundle of rags or cloths. What was that?

'Greet your daughter, silkrunner,' said Ghast, and he hauled with both fists on a rope.

The bundle of rags jerked into life. It raised its head. It said nothing. Kay stared at the head, willing it to turn towards her, willing it to recognize her. And then, as if by a kind of magic, it did: slowly the chin turned on the neck, and the face lifted, and the blank eyes met hers, and she knew that – even concealed, at a height, in the trunk, through the railing – those eyes *saw* her. And yet they did not know her.

There was a scream. The room screamed. It went on; it went on. It deafened her, split her, cut her ears and rived at her heart like an axe. Kay felt herself juddering, felt the trunk juddering with her, felt Will rising, enclosing her huddled and broken form in his arms. *Those hands.*

Her father. That pile of rags. Her father. Those hands. Her sister. Her father. *My father.*

The scream, Ell's scream, went on. Within its awful clamour no one could hear Kay's own sobs, no one noticed the commotion of her spasms or the gentle ministrations of the soothing wraith who held her, whispering to her, 'We will save her. We will save her. I will save her. My dear child, we will save her. We will do everything.'

They must have dragged Ell out of the library, for the rising, hysterical notes faded, the door was shut upon them, and then they disappeared entirely. Kay shook still, but shook silently. Will clasped her as tightly as he could, all pretence of concealment gone. But Ghast wasn't looking up any longer. They were safe.

'That,' said the voice she hated, 'was very satisfactory. Firedrake, see to this dog. And you, Philip,' said Ghast without looking up even as he left the room, 'take care of the rest. Perhaps a cliff would be convenient. I will have more orders for you before long.'

Kay started to rise. Flip thrust out his palm, flat to the ground: *Stop*, it said.

But she wouldn't. She stood. She took the stone balustrade in her hands. She closed her eyes, inclined her head, opened them again – and watched as Firedrake dragged her father from the room by a rope. He scrabbled along the floor like a dog, repeatedly falling to one side, then lurching up again as the wraith jerked at his collar. Had Flip not covered her mouth with his hand, she would have called out to him, or cried, or screamed, or all at once.

The far door closed behind Firedrake. Kay slumped in a chair.

For a long time all three of them sat in silence. Kay kept her eyes closed. She concentrated on her breathing and tried to allow all the other thoughts to fall away, or to settle in the steady rise and fall of her chest. It was hard to let them go: again and again they reared and pinched her – her father, her sister – and again and again she let them fall. At last she opened her eyes.

The others were looking at her. Their eyes were steady, their faces kind.

'So,' she said. 'Is that dispersal? Is what they did to him dispersal? Why would they *do* that to him? What do they want with him? What has he done to them?'

'Yes,' said Flip. 'Dispersal. That is how it begins.'

'And what is this place?'

'It's the Dispersals Room, where the records of all removals and dispersals are kept. We chronicle here a sort of unofficial history of the great creative minds in human history.'

'You mean the most creative people always get removed and dispersed? Like Orpheus?' Kay was silent for a moment. 'Is that why Ghast – my father – because he's *clever*? I don't understand; why do you *do* this?'

'It doesn't make much sense to me, either,' Will replied. 'When I was Clerk of the Bindery, we – well, things were different then. In those days we only removed real criminals; the kind of people whose stories might actually hurt someone.' He sighed. 'Or a lot of people sometimes. But in those days we hardly ever went so far as dispersal. It's much better just to put them in the mines –'

'Will.'

'The mines?' Kay felt suddenly alert, again on edge.

'The river,' Will said, hobbled by Flip's warning. He gestured towards the rear door, the door through which Kay had come in. 'It goes down – where we mined for metals and gems – in the mountain.'

'It's a kind of prison,' finished Flip. 'Only for the worst. Real criminals – not just Ghast's enemies.'

'And my sister?' Kay said. She couldn't even say it. *The author. Ell. The author, Eloise Worth-More.*

'Probably,' answered Flip. He couldn't say it, either. 'Will, we were wrong – about the – Did you hear him?'

'I heard him,' Will said. 'I don't know what to say.'

Kay looked from one face to the other, knowing that both wraiths were evenly balanced between a desire to explain everything and a need to keep her ignorant. This was a balance with which she was growing ever more frustrated. She held her head as high as she could.

'I know I'm not one of you. I know I'm a child. I know I'm not my father.' She looked hard at them, willing them to see her seriousness, her sharpness, her weight and determination. She tried to pinch a furrow in her forehead. 'But you have to tell me what's going on. I heard Ghast say that Ell is an author, like me. You have to tell me what this means. And you lied to me. I need to know how to stop Ell from being dispersed. I heard him say it. Twelve nights. I need to get to her.' *Time is running out.*

Flip stared hard at Will, who was about to speak. He stopped. Flip took over.

'An author is someone born with the ability to receive the highest skills in narrative; it's not a power, but a readiness to acquire a power. An author is the kind of person who somehow already knows all the stories there are – as if they don't even have to make them up, but just remember them. It is rare: neither Will nor I have seen an author in a great many years. Not a real one. This doesn't mean that they don't exist – it's just that we don't always know where they are. They must exist; they always have. We were authors once.' Flip paused, looking into Kay's eyes almost bashfully, apologizing. 'All wraiths were once authors. And we can find new authors with plotting boards, if we have time, a lot of time – but there are so many people in the world, and so much to plot: we'd need centuries to search a single country. More often, in the past, they just appeared, as if by chance; and if we knew about them, it was only after they'd passed away. Sometimes great authors don't become known as such until centuries after their deaths. And so we don't get to them in time.' Flip stopped.

Will started to speak again, but Flip motioned to him to be silent, and then continued himself.

'We thought – on the inventory it said – that the daughter of Edward More was an author. We thought it was you, because you could see us.'

'But we were wrong,' Will cut in. 'It was Eloise.'

Kay suddenly knew that she had been surviving on little more than a hopeful sort of self-importance. Now she felt her expectation collapse like a flimsy box crumpling under the heel of Ghast's boot. Ghast's words rang in her head. *She is worth nothing. I do not greatly care where you lose her.* She gasped for breath, and her head lolled to the left. She stared at the oversize plotting stone that was the handle of the room's rear door. 'So you,' she said, 'you were authors, and now you're you.' Her hands, normally so expressive, dangled limply at her sides. 'Then what am I?'

Will brightened. 'You – you are just something we haven't quite figured out yet.'

'But how can I help her if I – if I can't – can't –' Kay simply came to a stop. Her face was blank.

'You can if I come with you,' Will said.

'Will. Not a good idea.' Flip sat down suddenly at the large table, as if he had just been handed an enormous and insupportable weight. 'Ghast, Foliot, earlier, outside – they were talking about more than just a dispersal. They're going to summon a Weave on Twelfth Night. You need to be here.'

Will did not hesitate. 'There's no point in my being here, Weave or no Weave. I lost the thread a long time ago, and I'm not going to get it back now, Flip, and you know it. If I can do some good here, then, by the muses, I'm going.'

Flip lowered his head into his hands – not, Kay thought, in despair, but in intense concentration. One hand, coming free, danced a little in the air, the fingers picking out rhythms and depths while the head, still bowed, rested motionless. Kay knew he was plotting.

'What is it? What do you see?' Will dragged a chair next to him. 'We need a board.'

'No,' said Flip, looking up, dazed. 'It's something else. Something isn't right. It's as if we were working with the wrong information, as if Ghast were lying – but about what? I can't understand why he would disperse this author, and on Twelfth Night, when we all know – when this Weave is so important. And that gimmick with the wheel – How dare he! He's got to be playing at something.'

'What do you mean? What's a Weave, and who will come to it?'

'The Weave is a grand assembly of all wraiths and phantasms,' Will said, his own fingers now beginning to dance across the table and chair where he sat. 'So, everyone will come – all the wraiths there are. We only call them in extraordinary circumstances; for instance, when the Honourable Society is changing officers. When we're under attack. Or when, as legend has it, we crown a king. Which we have never, ever done. Which is why it's only a legend.'

'Ghast wants to be king?' At first Kay was dumbfounded. But something was niggling at her just as, hours after waking, a half-remembered dream flashes through the mind and is gone, and flashes again, too fast to be handled. 'That's why he took Eloise,' she said. She didn't know why she said it.

Will looked at her sharply.

'Maybe,' Flip said. 'That may well be right. Legend tells us that the crown must be placed upon his head by an author; not by a wraith who was once an author, but by an author. Most of the wraiths still take these matters seriously, and this little detail has kept Ghast in his place for some time.' Flip looked ashen. 'But he may at last have found his opportunity; which is why we're wondering why he would squander it so recklessly, dispersing the very means by which he might at last satisfy his ambition. A king can act outside the Weave. A king can abandon the thread altogether. He himself becomes the thread. It is him; he it. And if that's what he wants, if he really wants to be king, your sister should be just what he has been looking for, for quite some time.'

Will was watching Kay intently. It made her embarrassed. Flip was easier. He continued to rock his head up and down, his fingers tapping it and circling in tight patterns around his ears.

And then, all of a sudden, he slapped his hands down on the table before him, startling them both. 'I just can't see it, Will,' he said – hard, impatient. Kay had never seen him like this, and maybe Will hadn't, either. 'There's something wrong with our plotting, but I can't see what it is. We're going to need help if we're going to stop this.'

Will spoke quietly. 'What do you mean "we", Flip?'

Flip suddenly looked up at Kay. His eyes were as hard and as black as a plotting stone. 'This morning I had to let them take them. Your father, your sister. I had to stand here, in this room, and seal the order, and watch them go through those doors down there. There was nothing I could do.'

Kay stared at him. Hard.

'I am ashamed to say it. I didn't know until – Anyway, I did what I had to do. And now they are both gone.'

Kay's eyes slipped out of focus and she couldn't wrestle them back. 'Gone.' *Why?*

'If I had refused, some other wraith would have been chosen in my place. Some other wraith would have done it. Some other wraith would sit where I sit now, and I would be under guard in the mines.'

'Maybe,' said Kay, hot with anger, 'that would have been a better place for you.'

'No.' And Flip inclined his head to Will, and Kay saw that his eyes were not black at all, but marbled with green and silver. Everything softened. 'No, the best place for us is anywhere on the move. There *is* something wrong with my plotting; I can't figure with a free hand. Every time we move, Ghast has anticipated us. His eyes are everywhere here.'

Flip stood up abruptly, knocking his stool with a clatter against the wall. In a few paces he was at the rear door and had taken the heavy stone in his hand.

'Kay, you were right. We have to run, and we'll have to be sudden. Unpredictable. Spontaneous. Impulsive.'

With a heave he threw open the door, and the room flooded with freezing, dank, mossy air.

'Are we going down to the mines?'

'No,' said Will. 'He'll expect that. We'll never save her like that. Never let someone else plot you like a stone – not even Ghast. Maybe he thinks love makes us simple, easy to predict. Foolish. Maybe he thinks it makes us vulnerable.'

'It does,' said Kay, doubtful. Her heart and thoughts tore to the mines, and she longed to let her feet follow. She fought down the thought of Ell screaming, kicking, frightened; or scared, sullen, locked up in the dark and cold. She would gladly give herself up to hold her sister, to promise her anything –

'Love keeps its promises,' said Will. He held his hand out to Kay, and she stood. 'Love that moves mountains, love that flies through the air, love that dares to imagine anything.'

'Up,' said Flip as they swept through the door, turned right and began to climb through the darkness. 'By the air, through the air.'

'*The fox always runs to his den at last.*'

Ghast leafed absent-mindedly through the papers stacked on his desk. He had no time now to sit down and deal properly with the hundreds of reports, proposals and analyses that his Bindery clerks had prepared for him. A few of them still toiled in the old business, collecting myths and histories, stories, poems, tales and fables — the eternal process of conserving all that is told. There were still a few scouts and wispers who roamed the world beyond the mountain, and from time to time returned bearing trunks filled with papers and scrolls and books of all sizes. These materials had to be enrolled, and copies lodged in the library. Yes, a few clerks still worked on these old tasks; but he had reassigned the rest to his own new project. This was still something of a secret, even in the mountain, for most wraiths would not yet be ready to surrender their plotting stones, or to shut up the doors of the Imaginary forever. But that day was coming. There would be no more need for plotting, or for imagining, when his Bindery clerks had finished their analysis. Very soon he would have an algorithm to create any sort of story he wanted.

For now, it all looked in order. He would have to trust that fear would continue to keep his servants in line.

Ghast surveyed the Bindery. Twenty-three junior left-wraiths, all squat and ugly like himself, hunched over their low tables, writing. To his left stood Foliot, a lean, tall, lithe form, but submissive. Ghast declared, to no one in particular, 'Their love will make them careless.' No one dared to acknowledge his words, though all had heard. He loved to speak to them in this way. To speak to no one at all.

As he crossed the threshold into his private closet, he motioned impatiently for Foliot to remain outside. Ghast closed the door and began to change into his travelling clothes. For many years he had covered and disguised himself carefully whenever he left the mountain – which was not often. One took precautions when one was being hunted, especially by imaginers. Especially by the oldest, most cunning imaginer of them all. Now the imaginers had gone, and his fear was less. Now he could walk freely, and like himself, and he intended to cut an ostentatious figure equal to his status.

He would never be king in the mountain. They underestimated his reach. He would be king in Bithynia, or no king at all. He would not just win the battle. He would not just win the war. He preferred not to destroy but to compel his enemies. They would serve him, even in the sacred precincts of their own temple.

And what could a dog and its two delirious bitch-pups do about that?

7

The Thread

Outside the Dispersals Room Flip's torch punched a hole in the darkness. Kay could see well in both directions – downstream from where, an hour before, she had blindly groped her way up from the Quarries, and upstream along the steeply winding course of the underground river. The water rushed grey and glassily by, about four feet below the ledge, which she could now see was broad, and continued to run uninterrupted along the stream as it rose upwards. Will was moving his hands in the air, his distant gaze absorbed with plotting.

'How far does this path carry on?' she asked, of no one in particular.

Will's hands stopped mid-whirl and he looked directly at her. 'The path goes all the way to the top of the mountain. And I think we should take it.'

Flip, who like Kay had been waiting on Will, staring patiently at the rocky ground, looked sharply up at his friend. His face was all criticism, concern, caution. Kay thought for a moment how much he was like a parent, and Will the child. 'It will be much faster to go through the Quarries and down the mountain. You know where we're heading. You know what we have to do. Going down, we can run. Going up will take hours of climbing – hours we don't have.'

'I know. But, like you said before, there's something wrong with this whole situation. I don't know what it is, either. I can't quite tease it out; but one thing is for certain – they'll be waiting for us in the Quarries.'

Perhaps a cliff would be convenient. Kay was sure she didn't want to run into Ghast or those two skinny vultures, his servants Foliot and Firedrake.

'Say we make it,' said Kay, spinning round. 'Say we make it out of the mountain. Do we go to Bithynia? Where do we go?'

'We go home,' said Flip. 'Your home. Will, we –'

'No,' said Will. 'We keep going. We need help. Nothing scares Ghast now.'

'One thing scares him,' said Kay. She was absolutely sure of it, as sure as anything. The claim poured out of her with a conviction that frightened her, because she had no idea where it came from, or why she was so certain of it. 'Imaginers scare him. We need an imaginer.'

'Yes!' cried Will. 'When plotting doesn't work: imagining!' Immediately he set off to the right, up the steep slope alongside the black glass of the silent water.

In the light of his lantern Flip raised his eyebrows and pursed his lips in disapproval. For a long moment he stood like this, then shrugged and motioned for her to follow. Kay felt like shrugging, too.

What seemed like hours of climbing followed. The walls of the tunnel gradually closed in around them, and the air grew drier and colder. The darkness seemed to close in and bind them as well, until Kay thought the tightness in her chest might suffocate her. At times the path was wet, and in places it was loose with stones and what felt like shards of broken glass under their feet; but always the surface remained clear and almost mathematically regular, and Kay wondered at it: at the skill of the stoneworkers and carvers who had dug out this passage through the mountain. And she wondered, too, as the light from Flip's lantern occasionally swung behind her, its shafts bouncing along the walls, at the carving that adorned them: traceries of complex knotwork that simplified as they climbed and as the passage narrowed until it was just a single, definite channel, waving, then steady along the wall. And then, without warning, it ended.

Will had stopped just ahead in the gloom. He knelt on one knee and ran his open hands across the floor of the tunnel as if over still water.

'Hundreds of years ago,' he said, an intense look of concentration on his face, 'we came to these mountains to quarry their stone. We took it down into Bithynia along the river – down the very same river that had first led us here, up from the fertile valleys and through the foothills to the west. When the river went underground, we followed it, because we had seen in its waters the telltale mineral traces that we knew came from the soft, carvable stone we craved for building. We delved most of this path through the mountain for transport, as far as the Quarries, and further. But this section – the part we have just climbed – was different.'

At that, Will came bolt upright and seemed to tug at something. Kay could see the glint of metal in his hands; it looked like a brass ring.

Flip carried on. 'When the barbarians drove us from Bithynia, we had nowhere to go but here. No one knew these caves like we did; and few knew them at all, or even how to find them. We came up the river, taking only what we needed for our stories: the boards and stones, the books and the tapestries. Our tools we had left here long before, and in time we had transformed this shelled-out waste of caverns into –'

'Not much more than a shelled-out waste of caverns,' said Will, looking up in disgust from the floor, where he continued to heave back on the brass ring.

'In any case, we came here. At first we expected them daily behind us – the warring tribes, hungry men and women who had neither time nor love for stories. They drove us from Bithynia. When they didn't come, we thought they were preparing a siege. We did a lot, then, to make this a fortress, and self-sufficient, but we never grew complacent, and we always knew we might need a way out. Something remote, something unexpected. And that's when we built this part of the tunnel up through the mountain – right here to the very steepest part of its peak. We call it the Needle. From here, like eagles dropping from an eyrie, we might in time of crisis escape. As it happened, our pursuers never came, and we never used the tunnel.'

Will looked up abruptly, and with a grim and pained look on his face said, 'Back – move back.'

Kay and Flip shuffled back down the tunnel as fast as they could, watching Will struggle to his feet with a long chain in his hands, taut as he dragged it with a sort of shuddering, raspy groan from the floor. A sudden tremendous rumble filled the tunnel, and Kay had only a moment to turn before an explosion of gravel and dust shot towards them, pelting then engulfing her. The dust stung her eyes like wasps, and she felt her throat seizing, choking. She held her hands to her face, crying and screaming – and would have gone on trying to scream had Flip not doused her head with water, then firmly pushed her down towards the floor where the air was blissfully clear. She gulped breaths.

'What – what was that?' she begged him, inches away, in a whimper. 'What *is* that?'

'With luck, if the floor held,' answered Flip, 'that's our way out of here.'

At that moment Kay realized that, riding on the cloud of dust and noise, there was light, floods of it, and it only grew now that the dust had begun to thin and recede. She and Flip crawled along the floor, taking metre after metre with agonizing care, until their hands reached what felt like a hole in the tunnel floor. Air was rushing past her in a crisp wind.

She dared to pull her head over the edge and look down –

And might have screamed again – had the view not sucked the air from her lungs. Under the floor was nothing at all: a vast, dizzying void of empty air, yawning for hundreds of metres along a sheer cliff face down to the rocks below.

Perhaps a cliff would be convenient.

Kay froze.

Flip put his hand gently on her shoulder, and then – *mercy* – drew her bodily back on to the solid rock. 'For these last few metres the tunnel is at the top of the cliff, inside a large, single piece of stone jutting out over the valley below. We needed a door that no one would ever find from the outside. The sky *is* above us; but it's also below us. And so there was a real risk that the floor would collapse when Will opened the door.' He smiled. 'But we didn't fall.'

Kay laid her head on the grit, pebble and stone of the floor and closed her eyes as her head swam. *Twelve nights, Ell. He's given me twelve nights to find you, and twelve nights only.*

It took them almost an hour to climb down the hidden handholds that, hundreds of years before, had been driven into the cliff face. Will had gone ahead, but Flip guided Kay's every step from just below, easing her feet slowly down the face of the sheer mountain's side. It was still morning, and though the air was warming, the wind jagged and gusted at them from the north, cold on Kay's ankles; eventually her hands, too, became so chill that she could barely grasp the freezing iron bars. A single glance below her, though, was all she needed to renew her resolve.

'Now, Kay, jump!'

Only three metres or so remained when she leaped free of the rock face and collapsed heavily into the two wraiths' open arms. Firm ground had never been so sure, and she found herself sobbing on to the cracked brown stone where they had finally landed. The tears dropped down her cheeks – like climbers falling from the mountain, she thought – and smashed on the pebbles beneath her. One after another, in their dozens or maybe hundreds, they splashed into oblivion, barely staining the hard earth where they fell.

'Welcome to the Eagle's Nest,' said Will. 'I'll check for company.'

Kay followed him with her eyes as he vaulted on to a ledge just beside them, then scrabbled into a carved niche – a concealed perch from which he could command a view not only of all to the north, but over the ridge to the mountains south and west of them, too. This vantage point had been hidden even during their descent. Before Flip could stop her, Kay had leaped up the ledges to join Will.

'Kay – no – you don't –'

But it was too late. She dug her fingers hard into Will's sleeve to steel herself as the panorama wheeled below her and she wheeled above it. The openness made her feel sick, as if she were somehow flying, high, without wings.

'Don't look down,' Will murmured. There was something fierce, settled in his voice.

Kay shuddered. Far off she could see endless blue, hard and unremitting sun, metals glinting in the sand-coloured mountains, snow. What was below?

It was the river. Its soundless, turbulent current tumbled from the mountain just opposite their perch, then snaked down a steep valley and curved in and out of sight miles away, until it disappeared at the base of a massive hunch of distant stone.

'There are wispers abroad,' Will said quietly, and he pointed to the left, then straight ahead, where up on a slope Kay could see a tiny black form descending. 'Ghast's scouts. Centuries ago they were rangers and pilgrims, the kind you read about in all the old stories, who roamed the world collecting tales, gathering poems, making records of all the new myths and song cycles. In times gone by they used to bring them back to Bithynia for the library. But now they're just common spies working for Ghast. They can hardly tell a joke, let alone spin a yarn. They've lost the thread.'

'Tell me about the thread,' Kay said. 'You keep talking about it.'

'Tell yourself about it,' said Will, gesturing out to the mountains before them. He instantly realized that he had sounded curt, rude, dismissive. 'No, I really mean it. Look at what's in front of you. I think you'll understand.'

He hunched down to mark the wispers. Kay looked out from between two stones. In all the mountains and low hills that stood before her she saw nothing but rock and low scrub. The rock lay brown, in places reddish under the glare of the noon sun, and the scrub looked winter-beaten and dry. It patched and clumped on the slopes as if huddling against the wind and cold. Everywhere the cold had left its marks – not just in small lingering fields of snow on higher and sheltered ground, but in the stains on the cliffs, on the tumbling scree of loose stones and rubble that she knew had been broken and cast down the mountain slopes by ice, freezing and thawing, then freezing again over the years. *Threads.* The landscape before her was entirely uniform, bland almost. Nothing stood out. *Threads.* But for one thing – the river. She watched it from the point where it issued from the rocks of the mountain, pooled, and then flowed downwards, uncoiling among the low slopes.

'It's the river.'

'Yes,' Will answered over his shoulder. 'Tell me what you see. Tell me what the river does.'

Kay stared at it, and saw its bends and turns – like the joints of a long, impossible arm. The more carefully she looked, the more tiny bends and turns she discovered in its course. *It turns at every moment. Of course. Every moment is a turn in the flow of water. Every moment of flow is like a choice. It keeps choosing the best way.* 'It finds the shortest way down,' she said. She thought of the carving on the passage walls earlier, how the carving had comforted her, how it had gone from complex knots to a simpler single course, to a lone line waving, then to a straight channel that ended in the very height. *The thread.* She thought of her mother, back when she was younger, before all the arguments, sitting at the table with a needle in her hand, picking out its course through the threads of a piece of cloth. 'The cloth has its way,' she would say. 'The cloth sews the needle, and not the needle the cloth.'

'The water finds its own way, the best way,' Will agreed. 'It goes the way it always has.'

'That's the thread, then,' said Kay. 'It's the way things work best, the shortest and the easiest way, the way things have always been, the channel they cut, the way things smooth out in time, always growing simpler, growing more definite, straighter, easier. It's the way everyone does it together.'

'Complexity and change can be beautiful,' said Will, 'but, like the river in the mountains, they can sometimes be dangerous. There is sometimes white water. Over time, things settle. The order of things comes into being over time, gets simpler, becomes easier to understand. That's one reason why we honour tradition together, and that's why we prefer to do some things the way we're *expected* to do them. It's a comfort, and it's simple. That's the thread.'

Will went back to observing the wispers. He was clearly watching their patterns as they swept across the mountains, looking for a moment when they might break free unobserved.

But Kay suddenly had no interest in the wispers. Instead her eyes were riveted to the river opposite, and to a barge that was floating – so slowly, so far away below – down its smoother lower waters. From her height it seemed tiny, but she knew that was only the distance, that it was a huge thing, and it seemed to be swarming with wraiths. She tried to count, and reached something like fifty.

'What is that? What are they doing?' she asked.

Flip had climbed up to the lookout to join them. 'They're leaving the mountain,' he answered. His voice was almost a whisper, barely audible over the wind. Kay looked hard at him. He seemed shocked. 'They're taking the river out of the mountain.'

At one end of the barge – its stern – Kay could see a sort of raised area where there was no movement, no scurrying or hurrying forms. But perhaps there was a chair, or several chairs, and at the highest point –

'Ghost is leaving the mountain on a throne,' said Will – to none of them, and to all of them.

'And what is that building at the front?' Kay asked. She was mesmerized by the barge's slow, meandering motion down the silent river, by the rhythmic flow of bodies moving across its deck – rowing or punting their way, perhaps fending off the unseen rocks.

'That's not a building,' said Flip. 'It's a cage.'

When Kay screamed, her shrill and piercing cry shattered the silence of the mountains like the cry of a hawk. The wispers walking on the mountains below knew how to track great birds by their cries; tracking the screams of a girl, a girl they were looking for at that, and to a place they all knew well, was surely too easy.

Before Kay understood what they were doing, Flip and Will were handing her down the ledges on to the little platform where they had landed earlier. Then Flip seemed to vault over another low ledge, and disappeared from view. Following after, as Will practically dragged her behind him, Kay could see him half leaping, half running down a huge sweep of boulders and scree towards the north and east, away from the river, down to a far, narrow plain at the mountain's base.

Kay dug her heels into one of the rocks and stiffened her legs against Will's yanking arm.

'No,' she said. She said it as firmly and as loudly as she could.

Will rounded on her from below. She expected to see anger in his face, but there was only kindness.

'I'm going down the other slope,' she said.

'I am going to tell you something you already know,' Will said. He was speaking almost at a yell, to throw his voice over the blistering gusts of the north wind. 'Something you don't want to hear. You can't do anything for them now. Not one thing. All you can do is join them in that cage. Or worse.'

Kay wanted to cry, but all her tears had already fallen. She yanked her hand loose from Will's and stood facing him for a long moment. The wind buffeted her trousers around her ankles and seared her dry cheeks. She knew he was right. She knew that the courageous thing to do was follow him, and bend, and trust. *Every bone in my body wants to be on that barge.*

'Down there –' he gestured with his thumb over his shoulder – 'Flip has a plane. It's little, but it's solid. He says he hates it, but he's a brilliant pilot. And it's the only plane on the mountain.'

She gave Will her hand again.

He reached out a long arm, gathered her legs into him and hoisted her into an embrace that allowed her to lean against him, looking down and out on the valley of stones below. He held out his other hand, pointing here and there

'You can see them, the wispers, running.'

Kay could see them, from the north and the south, from the west slopes of the two flat hills before them, running. Their paths would converge on the little plain towards which Flip had been loping only moments before.

'We have to get to Flip before they do, or they'll trap us all. And if they do, I can't protect you,' Will said. 'And if I can't protect you, you can't save your sister.'

Or Dad.

'Or your father.'

They ran down the mountain, hurling themselves from boulder to boulder like dancers on a stage, like bees between flowers – barely touching the ground, always looking for the next step, always pitching forward. In what seemed like seconds they had made the plain, and Kay ran behind Will, flagging, losing him, over the dusty, weed-choked flat earth to the south. In the corners of her vision she was sure she could see black shapes moving, but she didn't dare look. She just ran.

Kay barely had time to dodge as Flip drove the little plane bouncing from behind a big boulder. He circled, and Kay heard the propeller start to drone as he opened the throttle into the gust swelling towards him.

'Get in,' said Will. 'Fast.' He wasn't looking at her. He was looking past her, intently. Kay knew what that meant.

Anyway, she needed no prompting. Down the opposite slope a dark-robed wraith was vaulting over the last stones that separated him from the valley floor. It was a matter of seconds before he reached the plane. With Will's help she clambered on to the wing, grabbed a handhold and slung herself over the edge of the rear seat. Flip started to move along the level ground, faster and faster.

Will wasn't in yet. The plane was gathering speed, bumping but starting to race forward. Kay pushed herself low into the warm cushion of the seat, wedging her feet against the wall before her. There was a strap, and she was fumbling with it as a hand suddenly appeared to the side – above her – grappling.

'Flip!' shouted Will. 'Let me climb –'

'No time!' shouted Flip from up ahead, pushing the throttle yet further. 'We have visitors!'

The plane lurched and bumped for what seemed like an hour. Kay grabbed at the straps, forcing herself into them. Against the air rushing at them from the propeller, from their own forward thrust, Will strove with every tendon and sinew of his body. Kay watched in agony as an elbow, a shoulder, then his head appeared. His cheeks and lips were deformed by the rushing wind, and for a moment, as he heaved, he looked like a grotesque, a terrifying gargoyle on some ancient church. Then he sprawled head over heels into the seat on top of Kay, crushing her even as she snapped tight the buckle of her harness.

The plane took off, and suddenly, sickeningly, the jolting stopped.

Will's face seemed to be buried in her shoulder. The plane climbed impossibly fast into the sun-shattered sky.

'That went well, I think,' he said.

*T*he journey west would take ten days. Three of these they would pass in the high, rocky mountains, exposed to sun and wind. Three days they would pass in the high marshes, hidden from the wind by the singing reeds. And three days they would pass in the fertile low valleys of Bithynia, each one lusher than the last, until finally they dropped into the steeply wooded gorge where the wraiths' great hall still stood.

Waiting for its king.

On that last day the barge would rest at the eastern gate. For a wraith who would be king there was but one way to enter the hall at Bithynia, and that was by the Ring. This circuit of the walls, which ascended from the eastern gate by an imperceptible grade to the raised plateau on which the hall stood, was adorned with carved tablets depicting the twelve sources of all story. He knew them as he knew his own face. Soon he would have them chiselled away.

It was said that that old hag they called the Bride had herself taught the first wraiths of the twelve sources. As if she were more than a story herself. In any case, she wouldn't be back, and the guild of wraiths was restless for a leader. A strong leader. One who might give them a sense of purpose again.

Ghast smiled at the smooth current of the course lying between him and the great hall. His preparations had been precise. What is more, his old adversaries — they could hardly still be called that — had underestimated him. They had measured his cunning by their own. It had never occurred to them that he might desire their escape, that he might provoke their hasty flight, that he might have predicted even that which seemed unpredictable — because it was. So heavily did his warts hang upon his cheeks that his deepening smile had the effect of turning down the corners of his mouth. It hardly mattered if the mirror did not find his joy handsome. His satisfaction was his alone, anyway.

He looked with pride at the empty cage where it stood before him on the barge. Set beneath it, just out of sight, was the heavy, forged iron plate of the great wheel. That empty cage, that ancient timepiece — these were better witnesses of his beauty, or his cunning mastery. How he would savour the reports of his wispers, when at length they reached him in the night: how the stones had tumbled from the Needle at the top of the mountain; how the wraiths and the girl had climbed down with laboured caution; how the patient wispers had, as instructed, circled the quarry without closing on them; how the fugitives had watched from the Eagle's Nest, then scrambled suddenly down to the Cut and taken their feeble little plane; how they took off, climbed, banked and flew south. How they thought themselves heroes.

But only he truly knew where they were going. Only he knew what it was all for.

8

Phantastes

K ay woke out of nothing. She hadn't known she was asleep, hadn't noticed falling into it, or even being drowsy. Now it was warm and dark. And loud. She was surprised at the warmth, and then, cracking open her eyes in pain, at the sun all around her lancing off the bright metal of the aircraft's hull, and the long, angelic damsel-fly wings as they strutted and trembled to either side of her. The wind rushed by. In her ears she could feel the plane dropping, losing altitude, and she knew from experience this meant that they would be landing soon. She shuffled herself up a bit and pushed one of the folds of the heavy blanket off to one side. Will, who had been watching intently out of the other side, saw her hand move and waved with a smile, then looked back down at the plotting board he had been neglecting on his lap. He was making plans, Kay thought, and she was awake enough to want to know what they were.

'Where are we?' she asked, wiping with the heel of her hand a crusty piece of sleep from her left eye. Will gave her some dried meat and fruit, and while she chewed slowly, he gathered up the plotting stones, stowing them in his cloak.

'We're about to set down on the beach. It will be warm; we've come a long way south. We're – No, it's better if you don't know for now. You're going to have to keep your face covered, or we may attract attention. You'll need to wear this,' he said, pulling out from beneath the seat a loose cotton robe and passing it over to her. 'See if you can put it on under the straps. We'll be down very soon.' Kay sat upright, and with some inventive contortions got the robe over her head, pulling the hood down the back of her neck and drawing up the ends of the fabric belt to lie ready in her lap. As the plane began its descent, Flip called out for steady, and as they banked slightly she caught sight of a bright sea heaving broadly into the distance to their right. Immediately she swivelled round to the left and peered – as much as she could – over the lip of the seat.

A moment before, looking out the other way, she had been able to see only water and sky. But from this direction the view was very different. A huge city loomed out of the ocean to her left, not so much tall as massive – toppling over with white buildings and green palms, heaped up along avenues that shot back from the sculpted seaside. To the right, a promenaded waterfront stretched for miles to a busy harbour, broken up by sandy bars and beaches where a few people walked – and some of them were pointing at the plane as it dropped.

'We'll have to stow it on the beach,' Will called out merrily, just as Flip cut down in a last swoop to the broad, flat sand and rock left exposed by the tide. 'By the air, through the air!' he whooped, waving his long arm in the sky. The plane was light enough, after a few awkward bounces that made Kay's heart shake, to settle and run itself out, pulling up short and with a sudden exhalation of noise opposite a clapped-up beach house. Kay and Will clambered out and jumped down, and Flip stowed the little plane unobtrusively between a long, crumbling shore-wall and a set of beach shacks. Kay got the sense that the two wraiths had done all this before. *Whatever* this *is*.

They walked up the beach towards the city. Kay's short legs had to work double-time to keep up with Will and Flip, and in the bright sun the white buildings seemed for a long time to hang out of reach. Finally the two wraiths led her off the beach on to a cobbled alleyway that ran down between low houses into a larger square. From that point on, the city became more and more congested with buildings, pedestrians, noise, activity, cars and, above all, smells. Kay could taste alternately the acrid, then sweet, then again acrid waves of bus exhaust against the sweet of street vendors. Ripe garbage rotted in the heat on one corner, and at the next a woman drenched in perfume hailed a taxi. It must be morning, Kay decided, in this new and frenetic place, and she loved it. All the noise and talk, the bustle and haste, the joyful energy of the street absorbed her into its rhythm, and she felt she was bouncing in time with it as they strode through the waking city. *This*, she thought, was what it was to be alive – and not the quiet, sombre fear of the mountain, the subdued flows of murmuring wraiths, the still and empty halls.

But as they walked, she noticed that the wraiths did not seem to love it at all: they walked stiffly, their heads constantly swerving this way and that as they took in the crowds, the motion and, it might be, the threat around them. Kay felt no threat. She had never felt so alive, so glad to be free, to be walking, to be among people and noise and bustle. She caught a flash of herself in a shop window as they passed by and, without even quite meaning to, straightened her back and began to saunter. *Take that, whatever place you are.* She almost giggled – and crashed directly into a woman who had been hurrying past them, a daughter held tightly in each hand.

'Oh, I'm sorry,' Kay said, blushing red and drawing back the hood of her robe.

Will turned, scowling, but the startled woman looked at her uncomprehendingly and said something out of the corner of her mouth that Kay could not understand at all. And then, beneath her brown curls, one of the little girls began to cry. Kay stared at her, and she cried harder. She looked at the mother, then at the girl. *Ell. Mum. What am I doing?*

Will got behind her then, and steered her – gently but firmly. Now she was walking between the two gaunt forms, blocked in from the rush of sometimes inquisitive faces passing them on the pavements. But Kay had stopped noticing. As she looked around for any sign of where they were, what they were doing, her thoughts raced. *Nine days. Nine days to find you.* And then, without warning, Will took her hand and, in the same motion, veered left under a low, dark archway, ducking gracefully and pulling Kay down a dim stone staircase. It was slick with dripping water, and she almost stumbled several times as they went down, and down, and down.

At the bottom, in almost complete darkness, she stopped before a worn, blackened slab of stone, in which a few mysterious words had been cut, their clear capitals still legible against the murk.

ALEXANDRIA WATER COMPANY

Kay turned towards the light of the stair, and Will's black shape against the light behind her.

'Alexandria,' she said. 'That's in –'

'Egypt,' he answered. 'We flew a long way in the night.'

Everything in Kay's body, everything in her heart and on the tip of her tongue, all that she could feel or think dropped like lead shot into her feet; and she stood rooted to the ground as if she were a yew, or a cypress, or some enormous, dark and silent tree.

Will sat lightly on a slick step, and now Kay could see his face, gentle and slightly pained. Flip had gone on ahead; she could hear him knocking or shaking what sounded like a metal door. All the exuberance she had felt up on the street now curdled in her stomach, and she grew dizzy, as if she were sliding slowly into a bottomless hole.

'There's only one way we can get your sister back, Kay, and your father. And the wraith who can help us is here. He left the mountain a long time ago – the last of the imaginers to hold out against Ghast. He hated him. He still hates him. And Ghast still fears him. This, Alexandria, is where he came to hide.' Will paused and looked at his hands, palms down in front of him. 'Ghast wants him dispersed. His wispers are always searching for Phantastes.'

Beside him water trickled down the heavy, square stones of the wall and ran among the outcroppings of furzy moss and slime. Kay watched the little beads gathering head, then running and dispersing, then gathering head again as they raced down the rough dark stone. At the top of the wall the stones were damp, uniformly wet all over; at the bottom, little dropping rivulets fed a whispering current in a gulley running down. Kay looked again and again over the wall, trying to find the place where the dampness became a rivulet. It was right there, but she couldn't see it.

'Phantastes is – well –' and Will stopped for a moment and looked down at Kay seriously. 'When someone has an idea – I mean, a really *new* idea – it has to come into being somehow. You have to create a thing that wasn't there before. From nothing, something. The more you think about it, the more impossible it seems. Now, dispersal – what Ghast did to your father – is absolute. He's gone. It's as if he never was. Where there was something, now there is nothing. Where there was someone, now there is no one at all.'

Kay felt a wail stiffening in her chest. Will put his hand gently on her shoulder, and together they held in the wail.

'It's absolute. But what Phantastes can do – integration – is also absolute. If anyone can find your father, if anyone can help us bring him back, Phantastes can. He's really the only hope we have. And that's exactly why Ghast is afraid of him.'

'And Ell?' said Kay, clenching her fists at her side.

'I don't know. But this is where we can find help, Kay. I know it.'

'In the . . . sewer?'

Will smiled. His eyes smiled. 'Phantastes is still alive because no one knows how to find him; because the only way to reach him is to lose yourself in this maze of dark and ancient tunnels half drowned in water. But if you come down here and you get lost in just the right way, he usually finds you.'

'Usually?' Kay asked.

Flip came running round the corner. 'Five minutes,' he said breathlessly. 'We've got to be very, very fast.'

Kay didn't have a moment even to look confused.

'Come on.' Will grabbed her by the hand and loped after Flip, who had already disappeared back round the corner.

They ran as best they could along the low passages and through several doors that, Kay realized as they swept through each one, Flip had probably just opened. Each one seemed to have a heavy lock, and Flip impatiently clanged each one shut behind them; and then they were off again. The tunnels were hot, and water dripped everywhere around them, so that as they ran Kay began to feel like she was chasing through a greenhouse in the dark, and at any moment she might crash into a bed of orchids or the leaves of some carnivorous swamp plant. In the occasional shafts of light from above she could see moss growing down ancient cobbled walls, and at intervals stone arches just tall enough for her to pass through. And always, beneath her feet, a little water, in places several inches deep, in places only in scattered trickles and puddles.

'Any time now, Will,' Flip muttered under his breath as he raced ahead, ducking under an arch to the next door. He called over his shoulder, 'Two more doors!'

They were through them in a few moments, and as they stood on the far side of the second, in the lowest and darkest of the tunnels yet, Kay could hear a rushing sound.

'It's the flush,' Will said as they spun on their heels and set off again. 'The city sewers flush with river water at periodic intervals during the day.'

The tunnel abruptly ended in a huge, cavernous lake, and Kay, still thinking with forward velocity, nearly tumbled into it. Only with difficulty did she manage to stop and step back from the edge of the pavement. The lake before them looked dark, and it smelled faintly revolting.

'For centuries – since the Romans – Alexandria's cisterns have been fed by canals from the Rosetta Nile, but the canals also supply the major sewers. The waste is flushed into this lake,' Will finished.

Flip was sitting in a small boat that Kay hadn't at first noticed, off to the side of the long landing. He held two oars that were poised in the locks, their blades hanging inches above the fetid water.

'In!' said Will.

Keeping their bodies low, they both scrambled into the boat; the oars dropped, and Flip, sitting opposite Kay, began to pull at them with the strength and regularity of a piston, saying nothing. Kay turned to Will, full of wordless questions about what was happening, and why, and where they were, but he was paying no attention. Instead he was looking back towards the landing; and when she followed his gaze, she saw why.

A metre of foaming green water suddenly began to pour through open grates around that last door, down the passage and into the lake behind them. Kay gasped to think how, if they had been only seconds slower, they might have been caught in its thundering force. It poured and poured, a cataract of colour and motion. As the water flooded through the grilles, and from other doors along the wall of the cavern, a surge began to push into the lake, lifting the boat along as Flip rowed away into the gloom.

Will held his finger to his lips. 'Not one word,' he mouthed with his lips.

Kay looked around as they surged rhythmically across the black, silty lake. Above them a dome of rock hung in shadow, here and there perforated by weak and dusky lights – slipped stones, or drains running from the streets above, Kay thought as she craned her head over her shoulder. Water dripped from the ceiling in places, and as they passed across the surface, the loud plinks fell near and far around the boat in a random pattern.

Now the far shore began to loom out of the grey light. It was much like the one they had left. A long landing perched a couple of metres above the water. Kay couldn't quite pull herself up without help and, as there was no ladder, she was grateful for Will's quick lift. The two wraiths were up in an instant, jumping so lightly from the little skiff that it didn't even rock behind them.

While the wraiths moored the boat, Kay walked on ahead through a low, open archway that led off the landing. Beyond was an ancient passage, bathed in light from above. The door stood unlocked and swung wide, and Kay simply walked through it. No sooner had she stepped across the threshold, turning towards the mossy cobbles of the wall with her hand outstretched, than the heavy iron gate slammed shut behind her. She knew without turning that it was locked. She froze, then spun and grabbed the gate, trying to shake it free. Her stomach heaved into her throat.

Flip was there in three instant bounds. He spoke almost without breathing, in a torrent of exact, unforgettable words. Had Kay had time to think about it, she would have thought it the most urgent thing anyone had ever said to her; but her attention was riveted to every syllable. 'You have between three and four minutes until the next flush. It *will* drown you if you are caught in it. The doors ahead of you are locked. There is no way you can get through them. Don't waste time trying. You are going to have to find another way. Wherever you end up, make noise. A lot of noise. We will find you. Go now.'

Kay stood at the gate, gripping its iron bars as hard as she had gripped anything before in her life. She stared into Flip's eyes, and he into hers. Neither one of them would let go.

'Go!' He was shouting at her. 'Go! Go, go!'

Kay turned and sprinted straight ahead. Before she had gone twenty paces, the abundant light began to fail and she was soon in near-total blackness. She held her hands out in front of her and tried to keep running straight; and for two or three paces she seemed to manage it, slowly, stumblingly. Then, feeling her way along the wall to the right, she advanced more slowly. The tunnel curved, and the stone was rough and wet under her hands. A greyness took shape in front of her, then around her, and she thought she saw light coming through cracks in the high ceiling above. She tried to remember the water she had seen earlier, which had run not much more than a metre deep. If she could just climb clear of it, she could wait it out or get up to those cracks, and – who could say? – maybe she could get out. She put her hands on the wet walls and tried to dig her fingers into the cobbles. She managed to get moss under her nails but couldn't find any purchase. Again, and again, and again she tried, first with her hands, reaching, and then with her feet. Desperation made her foolish, and she scrabbled at the wall to no purpose at all – it was too slick, the stones were too shallowly set, and she hadn't the strength. She began to cry and, as the tears ran, her chest threw up big jerking sobs. Now she couldn't see anything at all, and her arms went suddenly limp. She dropped to the floor and let her head sink against the wall.

I am going to drown.

But her head wasn't leaning against the wall. It had hit something metal, something iron, something very painful. Scrambling round, she found that it was a low grille set into the cobbles, covering a kind of duct or channel.

Of course. The water has to drain out of the passage. Drains.

She crouched and felt her way down the wall, finding more grilles, hoping for a loose one. There were more. She was counting them off, darting from grille to grille, when she realized that the gathering roar around her ears was the flush, already upon her, pouring from up ahead, from above.

Seconds. I have seconds. I have nine nights.

Kay groped furiously, looking for any way out of the tunnel. Her pulse roared in her ears and she felt light – as light as a leaf. 'Here, Kay' – she felt as if someone were speaking to her, leading her from stone to stone. 'Faster,' said the voice, 'Faster.'

Then her hand hit nothing in the darkness – a gap in the wall, large, open. Without a thought she dropped to her knees, kicked out her feet and tipped herself into it. She slid down as if it were coated in butter.

It seemed a long while that she endured the sometimes steep slide, her elbows jarring and knocking against the rough edges of the duct. She didn't dare to open her eyes or take her hands away from her face. The rushing sound had died away, but she knew that the water might engulf her at any time. *Calm before the storm.* She flailed desperately every time her feet got caught up on some obstacle or lip in the stone. Her back felt as if it were being pounded with blunt wooden hammers, and her neck ached as she strove to lift her head just far enough off the duct floor to avoid knocking.

Then, very suddenly, she came to a complete stop. She was level, flat, stuck. With her hand pressed against stone only inches from her face, she knew she was still enclosed in the narrow duct; and now she could hear the water again – higher pitched this time, but rising in volume. She thrust her hands out sideways and grappled for a hold, then pushed herself forward; the floor of the duct was just slick enough to let her continue to slide. On and on, her joints nearly tearing with the strain, she pushed, gasping for breath, until she felt her feet come clear of the ground, no longer beneath her – and then her legs, and then, very nearly, her back. She flipped over on to her stomach, pushed herself out, and hoped that there would be a floor somewhere below. She could see nothing at all, though her eyes gaped open in the rising breeze rushing down the tunnel.

The water was almost upon her. She dropped.

Kay had hoped to hit something and, in that last moment before she let go, had imagined a ledge, another plinth or landing like the one she had seen a few minutes before on the lake shore above. What she hit, only a metre below her dangling legs, surprised her. It felt like earth: a little rocky, but there was a squelch of mud under her shoes, too. Any second now the flush would pour out of the duct. *One. Two. Three.* Then she heard it gushing and – stopping – listened hard. It sounded as if water were pouring out not just here, but all around a very vast space; unlike in the cavern above, here the vault seemed to echo emptily with the draining and dripping of what sounded like a hundred spouts. Slowly, her hands still pressed to the wall, she turned round to face outwards, keeping her feet close, just in case.

To her relief, a grey gloom lit the space in front of her so that she was able to make out the main contours of another great cavern – exactly like the one from which she had just fallen except, judging by the apparent height of the vault, much larger. Behind her, as she clambered away, the drain began to pour with water, and she could hear, if not see, the water streaming down the slope to another great lake. The lake was so wide and the cavern so gloomy that she couldn't see across to the other side; her vision hit the obscurity like a wall. Kay stared for a long time, happy to be on her feet, relieved to have escaped drowning in the flush, but anxious about what this cavern contained, and how she was to get out of it. Flip had said that he and Will would find her, she thought. *He told me to make noise.* She took a deep breath. *Well then, I will make noise.*

She sang. At first she tried songs she had learned at school – quietly, almost under her breath, but occasionally, on the refrains, letting a few bold notes out into the resounding dark. After a few minutes she had begun to find her voice, and the melodies started to soar a little, and even to find out the higher pitches of the cavern's domed ceiling. Having run through all the songs from the school choir, she paused and breathed while she tried to remember the longer and more beautiful songs that her father had taught her. She sang the first phrase that came into her head and, closing her eyes as so often she had done while he lullayed his two daughters to sleep, she let his words well up:

'*The blue light rose like a flower in the night*
when my true love came to me;
she laid her left hand in my right,
and the nightingale sang in the silkworm tree,
to me, when she came to me.

'Had never holy mountain height
nor so dread deep the sea
as the love my true love did me plight
when the nightingale sang in the silkworm tree,
to me, when she came to me.

'Then let the loose leaves laugh with delight
and tremble my love to see
where she rises like morning new, and bright,
and let the nightingale sing in the silkworm tree,
to me, for she comes to me.'

With her chin lifted and eyelids softly set, Kay had drifted while singing into that state perched just over sleep in which, so many nights before, she had listened to those words and heard them in her own head. She didn't know, nor did she worry now, whether she understood the words, or even what they were, so drowsy and warm had she become. She felt as she sang that she followed her voice into all the reaches of the vault, where it flew and bounced and then, rebounding on the water and the walls, bounced again. Well before she came to the last verse she felt that she, like her song, had grown as large as the cavern – or maybe that the cavern itself was singing, and she was only standing in it, a note like any other in its huge, enduring, dark music.

When she reached the end of the song, for a long moment she stood quietly; and in that silence she was suddenly aware of another sound, a sound that was neither the song, nor of the song, and she opened her eyes. It was the whispering swish of a pole in the water, not twenty metres from where she stood on the shore. As she followed it up with her eyes from the surface of the lake, in the gloom, the muscles tightened up her spine, gathering into a compact, rising knot like the fist of a flower: there before her on the lake was a flat boat, and in the boat stood a tall, gaunt old wraith, in his right hand the pole, in his left a large brown book. He was bearded, part brown and part white, and his hair tumbled wispily, too, down over his shoulders. Like the wraiths he wore a hooded grey-black gown, the hood slung low around his shoulders and back, and the front loosely open over his white shirt. He was barefoot, Kay noticed. For a time he did nothing at all; he simply watched her, without staring, as if she were a tree and he were lying in the grass beneath her, looking up through her trembling leaves.

And then, abruptly, he spoke, in a voice so clear and yet so soft that Kay was surprised she could hear him, let alone understand him.

'So you are here at last.' He paused for a long time, still picking out the blue of a spring sky between her breeze-tossed branches. 'Before I was born, that song had already been sung in my family for a thousand years or more. We handed it down from generation to generation, each one teaching the next. My mother sang it to me when I nursed at her breast, and I had it with her milk. When I was a boy, running barefoot through the fertile fields of Assyria, I thought that if I could just run as fast as the wind, I might see the Bride; if I could just burn as hot as fire, she would come to me; if I could just beat upon the rooftops as hard as the autumn rain, she would lull me to sleep in her arms. I wished more than anything to be a storyteller, to become a singer of tales. Well. It took me thirty years to sing that song: an age of man. An age of man to become a man; an age of man to learn that I must sit still to be moved, must close my eyes to see, must give myself up to discover who I am. And yet now, in this age of children, in this time of children who have lost the oldest art, who cannot sit, who cannot close their eyes, who cannot for even a moment surrender their too-cherished selves, in such an age a child now sings this song to me.' He watched her again. Kay had rubbed her nose a moment before, but now, her hands folded loosely across her chest, she stood stock-still. 'Tell me your name,' he said softly.

'Katharine,' said Kay. 'My name is Katharine Worth-More.'

The old man smiled broadly, revealing a thousand furrows in his lean cheeks, above his eyes, and between his mouth and chin. 'Yes. Katharine,' he answered. He shifted his weight on to the pole, and drove the boat slowly in to the shore where she stood. 'And I am Phantastes, the last imaginer,' he said as the front of the long punt began to grate against the rocky soil of the ground before Kay's feet. 'Or very nearly the last.'

Part Two

WEFT

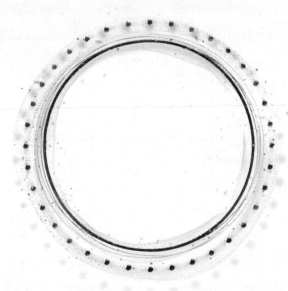

9

Integration

Guiding the punt across the underground lake, Phantastes pulled up alongside a cleft in the rock where water cascaded continuously from a gap very high up. It was a clean, clear stream, diverted, said the old wraith, from a reservoir. Kay doused her hair and washed her hands and face, and then Phantastes pushed the boat back out into the lake and made for the far shore.

Alert now, and shivering, Kay saw a small island – not big enough for five people to stand on, she thought. In the centre stood the massive remains of a giant tree, jagged and broken, thrusting up towards the ceiling.

'What is it?' she asked. 'How did this get here?'

Phantastes continued gently guiding the boat towards the island. 'When this tree first germinated, no more than a seedling, it stood in the middle of a low lagoon, a place where the Nile canals flooded with fresh water a wide area of low-lying marshland. It was only thousands of years later that the silt, constantly collecting around this place, enclosed it and then buried it. Long before that, the great vaulted roof that –'

and here he turned his head upwards, leaning on the long pole and gesturing with his arm to take in the whole cavern – 'you do not see above you was built: one of the grandest, most beautiful temples ever designed, and the crowning architectural achievement of a great society. Of course, no one else now knows that it is here, or that it is of such antiquity. Only I know.'

Kay cocked her head to the left. 'But they *must* know. I came down that duct from the sewage tunnel – someone must have built that.'

The boat made no sound at all as it drew up on the shore of the island. Phantastes held out his hand to help Kay ashore. Their quiet movements felt like reverence.

'Did you think that was a sewer?' the old wraith answered, smiling as he took a seat on one of the gnarled roots of the old trunk. 'No, it was no duct that brought you here. No common sewer. The water that flows into the temple lagoon through that passage is a little purer than that. I dug it out myself, and lined it with grouted stone. It took me many years.' He paused and looked at his withered hands where they rested gently one upon the other on his lap. 'But I'm pleased you thought it was a drain. No one had ever noticed it until you slipped down it.'

Kay looked closely at his face, which was level with her own as she stood a metre or so away, at the edge of the tiny island. The skin beneath his eyes had become cockled over the years, gathering up into the inner corners by his hooked nose and radiating out in loose folds across cheeks that ridged up when he smiled. In this light, the colour of his face hung somewhere between brown and grey. Some of the small hairs around his mouth waved minutely in the air as he breathed. Even when he frowned he seemed kind, as if the frown were a comma between two smiles. 'But all that time you spent digging it out,' she said at last, voicing the question on which she had paused to regard him. 'Why?'

'Because when I arrived here –' and for the second time he straightened, and swung his arm out wide to take in the whole cavern – 'all this was dry. For thousands of years before that this marshland had been kept wet – even under the dome of the great temple – by the flooding of the Nile; but at last the silt, covering over the hidden temple, had cut the water off completely. And when the city above began to leach so much of the water away, and then other cities upstream; and fields, with their irrigation projects, and who knows what else – houses, swimming pools – then the marsh died completely. And if it hadn't been for me –' and he patted the root on which he sat – 'all this would have died, too.'

'But surely it *is* dead,' said Kay. 'It's an old stump.'

At this Phantastes looked up sharply, his mouth suddenly set hard. Then he softened, and his eyes flattened as he smiled again, and he said, rising, 'Come see, come look.'

Just opposite where they had been sitting, out of sight of the boat, a deep gash in the old trunk ran almost to the ground, making a jagged, steep *V*. The brittle husk and shell of the old tree was more than five centimetres deep, and within that Kay thought there was nothing.

'Look inside,' said Phantastes quietly, and he stood back so that she might climb up on to one of the roots and negotiate a passage for her head between the two steeply sloping edges of the trunk. At first it was so dark that she thought she was looking down a well, or into the earth itself; but after a few moments her eyes adjusted to the near-darkness and she could just make out, faintly, five hand-sized, oval leaves that were perhaps green, reaching out from a central stem that was thirty centimetres or more in height. It shot out from a crack in the weathered wood of the centre of the trunk, about a metre in diameter, and grew straight upwards. Kay hastily pulled her head out of the hole, bumping herself painfully on the right ear as she spun round too soon.

'But how is it growing *here*? It's so dark!'

'It is the deepest well that holds the freshest water. Wait a few moments,' Phantastes said, 'and you will see the other little alteration I made to the Great Temple of Osiris.'

Kay stood there, leaning against the side of the cleft trunk, her heart beating fast. Osiris. For years she had heard the stories at bedtime, all of them: Osiris' enmity with his brother, Set; his murder and dismemberment; Isis' long and patient search, with the erection of a thousand temples all over Egypt. Her discovery of her husband's body in a cedar box lying at the centre of a magnificent tree. *But that tree was in –*

'Byblos,' said Phantastes. 'Yes, I know, it was in Byblos. But the priests of Osiris took a cutting from that tree and planted it here, at the very centre of the temple, in the marsh where the goddess later buried his body. And its roots grew down into his flesh, and it towered within the temple, the tips of its branches scraping against the stones of the vault above.'

'But how?' Kay said as a sense of the sanctity of this place began to dawn upon her. 'How did the tree grow inside the temple? Didn't it need light? Doesn't *this* tree need light?' She paused, staring at Phantastes. He said nothing. 'A tree can't grow in a cave, underground.'

'Look,' he said at last, tilting his chin upwards to the vault.

She followed his eyes with her own. For some reason she could not explain, her heart was hammering in her chest. The air was lightening very slightly around the cavern, and for the first time she could see the whole vault above. But she was totally unprepared for what happened next. A narrow beam of light suddenly flared from a hole in the roof, straight down the centre of the shaft of the gigantic old stump, and illuminated the tiny plant growing at its centre. Kay watched in wonder as the beam of light seemed to grow in intensity, transforming the little patch of wood at the centre of the stump from which the sapling sprang into a tiny, brilliant piece of daylight. It went on for about five minutes, during which she tried to stop time, to draw it out, to take in more of the deep, woody greenness of the tiny plant, the delicate hairs bristling under its five fanning leaves, the glistening luminescence of its taut stem.

This is the most beautiful thing I have ever seen.

But then, as abruptly as it had begun, it ended, and the darkness again put out the light. Tears started in Kay's dimmed eyes. The sight of that struggling, tiny stem with its delicate, childlike leaves – bathed in light – cast back into the darkness – it was too much.

'Five minutes a day is all I could manage,' said Phantastes quietly as he put his hand on her head. 'Don't cry. It's enough.'

Kay turned and sat heavily on the upper roots. It hadn't felt like five minutes.

'It took me many years even to get that much. And that was before I knew for sure whether the tree still had life in it. Although I always suspected,' he said, patting the desiccated trunk with his mottled, grey-veined hand, 'that it did. First I had to find a little money – here and there – and then drive some people from their homes, which I did not much enjoy. It was necessary to demolish many buildings while I looked for the right place to dig. And then, after I finally found it, I lost many more years in making mirrors and glasses to focus the light. It doesn't work perfectly even now, and it doesn't last long, but the leaves get a little bit of light every morning. And with the river washing into the temple several times a day now, the conditions are improving. Who knows but, a few years from now, this green stem may grow thick and stout enough to bear its own fruit – the shellfruit of the tree of Byblos, whorled like the shuttle, each one a rife and mysterious trove of tiny seeds, and in every seed the promise of new life, new growth, stems, trunks, a thousand branches, leaves and fruit, harvest on harvest past imagining. All that may be. But for now, it is just enough.'

Kay was crying quietly.

'Daughter,' said the old wraith. 'Even small, even delicate things can sometimes be remarkably resilient.'

For no reason she could name, all Kay's urgency suddenly came striking back into her heart and lungs, pressing down on her chest like heavy stones. The sorrow that had been in her eyes suddenly gripped her heart, and she thought of Ell, remembered her father, remembered her mother at home, sitting at her desk behind the closed door of her room, sobbing quietly the night before they left – the night before Christmas. Where was she now? What had she thought when she woke up the next morning to find her daughters gone? What had she made of Kay's hastily scrawled note? *We are going to find Dad. We will be back soon. We love you*, she had written, crammed in tiny letters on to the back of Will's card, and left in the middle of Ell's neatly made bed. Suddenly Kay felt she couldn't breathe at all. She choked; although the choke sounded more like a sob. 'Why am I here?'

She spoke before she meant to. Her voice echoed for a few moments, and then there was silence.

Phantastes sat down next to her on the stump.

'Kay,' he said, and his tone was much more familiar now, no more the tall and commanding presence he had been. He held out the palm of his right hand, extended before her. It seemed wonderfully still, open and capacious. Her eye was drawn instantly to its centre where the lines crossed, where the contour of finger, sinew, muscle and callus produced a slight cupping or hollow. 'I am not one of those left-wraiths who plots people's movements, as if a man or a woman or a child were no more than a little knot of likelihoods. I am an imaginer. For better or for worse, I see the insides of things. Tell me what is in your heart.'

Kay wanted to tell him what they had lost. She wanted to tell him about sitting at the kitchen table at home, where the lamp swung from the ceiling and gave a warm, golden glow. She wanted to tell him how her parents were seated opposite her, her

175

mother gently stroking the back of her father's hand while he read a book and she, with a pencil, planned a new painting – a big one – sketching out ideas and themes on to page after page of her notebook. She wanted to tell him how Ell liked to pretend that she had homework, too, so that at the end of the evening, when Kay presented her books to her parents, they could disappear upstairs together to play. But it was all so *normal*. Everything they had lost was so *normal*. One by one these things had slipped away: first her parents had begun to quarrel, and no one stroked the back of anyone's hand. The notebook, her mother had lost, or put in a drawer. Then her father – he was always out working late, or away on some trip, and Kay was forever in her room, making lists of things she planned to do, or wanted. And Ell stood in the kitchen, turning the light on and off, over and over, until no one could stand her. *Why did she do that?* Kay wanted to tell Phantastes all this.

'I let her go. I lost her. It was because I wasn't watching. I thought it was all about *me*. I let her go. I let all of them go.'

Phantastes' reply was swift. 'No, Katharine. It's not your fault.'

'But I'm still the only one who can get them back. I'm the only one who can make it right. And I feel like I'll never get to go home again. Not to the home I want.'

'Your father said much the same thing to me once, in this very place.'

Kay looked up sharply, her chin cutting a slicing angle against her neck as she turned to gape at the old wraith. 'How do you –?'

'Do you think I do not know your father?' Kay stared at him in mute unimagining. 'Do you think he and I have not walked in the moonlight on the sands of Alexandria? That he and I have not sailed against the wind off the coast of Anatolia? That he and I have not gathered mulberries in Grecian groves? No, daughter, your father and I are old friends, colleagues and sworn brothers in a struggle far greater than you have yet glimpsed or imagined. A struggle in which Ghast is, has always been, our greatest and most dangerous enemy. And why do you think Ghast wanted your father dispersed, if not because he knew that Ned More was working for me?'

'Working for you?' Kay asked, her mouth hanging open and the words only half pronounced. Her lips, like her eyes, felt numb.

'Among the right-wraiths, your father is known as the Builder. For years he has been excavating around the site of the ancient – and neglected – seat of the Honourable Society of Wraiths and Phantasms in Bithynia –'

Kay nodded with vigour. This was something she recognized. The Fragments Project. 'He's an archaeologist,' she said.

'But not as an archaeologist. No, your father is not studying the place because he wants to understand the past; he is rebuilding it because he wants to shape its future.'

'But Will said –'

'Will does not yet know. It would be too dangerous to tell him because, above all others, Ghast keeps him under constant watch.'

'Watch?' asked Kay. 'Why?'

Phantastes stirred the water at the edge of the little island with the pole, which he had taken up again from where it was leaning against the old trunk. 'Will may fumble sometimes. He may seem a little meek, a little broken. But do not underestimate him. There is no finer wraith in the mountain.'

Then why can't he help me?

'We must help him.'

Kay's whole body stiffened. Even in the low light, Phantastes saw it.

'We will find your sister, Katharine. And your father. We will save him. We will do it together. But to bring the Honourable Society back to Bithynia, to save Will from Ghast – this is what Ned More wants, too. You must help me now to keep Will safe. And you must help me to keep something else safe. It is far too dangerous for me to hold on to it.' Here Phantastes leaned down to the boat and retrieved the book he had been holding before, when Kay first glimpsed him coming out of the darkness of the cavern. Only it could not be a book because, after unhooking a tiny clasp, Phantastes had opened it to reveal a fist-sized, lustrous white object inside. The book was a box, she realized, and it held something very beautiful. In a couple of steps Phantastes was at her side, and he offered it to her.

'Take it,' he said. 'I left the mountain in order to protect this from Ghast. It belongs to Will, but he wouldn't mind.' He smiled, holding out the box again.

Kay took the softly shining, smooth object, but cautiously, afraid it might be brittle like glass and break in her hands; or that it might be slippery, and drop to shatter on the small rocks at her feet. But it was heavy enough, and she could grip it easily. She turned it over in her hands. It was whorled like a shell and bone-smooth, cool to the touch. Here and there it was studded with something that, in the light, might have proved to be a gem or diamond. As she turned it over, she noticed that it was perforated with tiny holes.

'Hold it up to your mouth,' Phantastes said, 'and blow.'

She blew. At first she did not find just the right aperture, but in a moment she could feel the wind forcing a passage into one of the many tiny gaps. A deep, sonorous drone came vibrating out of the stone, and rang in the cavern. The bones in her shoulders shook with the heavy, sugary resonance of the tone; it seemed, as her lungs began to exhaust themselves, that the vibrations were spreading down into her ribs, so that her whole torso began to quiver, and she fought for the note not to end. When at last it did, she suddenly held the glassy stone away from her mouth, scrutinizing it again, then tried a different hole. This time the pitch was higher, and it oscillated like a wave breaking on the shore. Another clashed like swords, high and metallic. Another moaned – the voice of a grieving father at the grave of his only child. She held the stone out in astonishment.

'You want me to keep *this*?' she asked. It was the most beautifully made thing she had ever handled.

'The voice of the shuttle,' said Phantastes quietly. 'And the first note you sounded was that of love. Yes,' he went on. 'I almost think you should be the one to carry it for Will – to bear it, to keep it for him.' He shook his bowed head slowly, and Kay saw a tear drop from the tip of his nose. But he looked up, his eyes shining, and held out the box for her to replace the shuttle. 'Come,' he said more briskly, stowing the box in the punt and taking up the pole again. Kay followed him, fluid with questions, and began asking them the moment she was seated, looking up at the old wraith as he pushed them round the island and towards the near shore behind it.

'Is the shuttle Will's, then?'

'I suppose neither he nor that worthless Philip has told you just who Will is,' said Phantastes, grinning so that the etched lines of his face stretched, soaking in the inky light.

'No,' Kay answered.

'Then we will let him tell you himself, in his own way. Next question.'

'How did you know that Ghast had taken my sister and my father?'

'Not all the wispers are loyal to Ghast – even those he trusts most answer in their quiet ways to me. Despite themselves sometimes. I have been taking regular reports on him, and on you, for quite some time.'

Phantastes grinned at her again, now so widely and impishly that his ears flexed. 'Have a look at the top of the box there –' he gestured down below his feet to where the shuttle lay in its wooden case – 'and I think you might put a few things together.'

Kay looked. Carved into the dark wood of the lid was a shape which she had to trace with her finger before she could resolve it completely: a slender snake entwined with a sword. She knew that symbol. She looked up quickly. 'Rex, the old porter at my father's office!'

'Is that how he hid himself?' Phantastes asked, chuckling. 'Yes, he's one of mine. That was a clever ploy of his, yes. I sent him to recover several vital items, including that shuttle, from your father's study. Next question.'

'Where has Ghast taken my father and my sister? How do we get them back?'

Phantastes didn't answer. They were almost at the shore and, with a wide sweep of the punt pole, he gracefully swung the boat parallel with the long stone plinth on to which they both immediately stepped. Kay turned to him as he secured the punt, and said to his hunched back, 'I mean it. Where are they?'

'First we will have to find Will and Philip,' he answered, neither turning round nor looking up. 'I have a feeling they will be waiting for us in the compound above. I need to know one or two things before we can start making preparations for integration.' He turned on his heel and, squatting, placed his hands on the ground before him. He looked straight into Kay's eyes. 'But we will find them, and we will recover them.'

Kay smiled. If Will gave her hope, Phantastes made her feel safe.

The old wraith rose and set off at pace towards a low door; here a passage led off the landing. Kay followed, almost skipping. Her clothes had almost dried in the warm draughts that stirred the cavern, and as she moved she felt suddenly light. They went up several slightly sloping tunnels, and through one or two open gates.

'The flush –' Kay began.

'Is finished for the day,' Phantastes called over his shoulder. 'Anyway, these passages do not connect to the sewerage system. These are the old corridors of the temple buildings, which I excavated and restored. And in a moment you can see my most ambitious work.'

They went round a few tight corners, and then, without warning, passed through a low door into a huge, open atrium; round the outside a staircase spiralled upwards as far as the eye could see.

'I confess I cheated a bit. We're actually inside an old tower – like everything else, engulfed by the silt – which I dug, or rather flushed, out. Well, dug *and* flushed. All the sediment that used to fill it is back in the lake,' he said, 'where it belongs. The stairs –' which they were already climbing – 'were mostly already here. I made some improvements and repairs. It's a wonderful commute,' he added, laughing over his shoulder at her: she was struggling to keep pace as they rose through the increasingly brighter air towards the top. The atrium seemed to be narrowing as they climbed, until finally it was little more than a circular stone stairwell. Light came from the centre of the roof – very close now – and Kay realized that it was the sun shining through a skylight, and that they had reached ground level again. Just under the skylight, a door stood shut; pulling a ring of keys from the belt beneath his robe, Phantastes quickly opened it. The heavy wood swung wide to reveal an ordinary white-walled room, with sunlight pouring in from two open windows on the left. It dazzled Kay's eyes, and she squinted to see the wooden trestle table standing in the centre, and on it a pile of what looked like dried leaves. Around the walls, tall bookshelves sagged under masses of volumes of every size. The ceiling was painted sky-blue.

'Welcome to my home,' said Phantastes.

He closed the door behind them and locked it. No sooner had he replaced the keys at his belt than a small, balding, wizened wraith scurried in through the door opposite and began to push the dried leaves into a heap, with the same motion setting down two or three heavy books and opening them. Phantastes joined him at the table, peering down at the huge folio volumes as the little man opened them and began, using a small rule, to scan through lines of heavily inked Gothic print.

'Have you found it yet?' said Phantastes quietly, but with authority and urgency.

Kay looked intently at the dark, almost hairless head as it pored over the books. The little wraith said nothing for a moment, but kept running his nimble hands back and forth across the lines of text, mumbling softly to himself. When he looked up at last, he blinked several times in the way someone might clear his throat. And then he cleared his throat.

'Nothing yet. But the maker is still at the fountain, and it may be that I have not remembered all that there is to recall.'

'Keep listening to him,' Phantastes said, setting his hand on the other wraith's slender arm. 'It will come to him in time.'

The old wraith then turned round, indicating Kay with his arm, and said, 'The young man's daughter. The Builder.' The shrunken little wraith bowed with great ceremony. To Kay, Phantastes said, 'Kay, this is our chronicler, Eumnestes. He will remember anything these forty thousand years. And remembering is the first part of integration.'

And then, his duty done, the little wraith bustled out of the room again, the books tucked one under each arm.

'Sit down,' said Phantastes gently, pulling out one of the four high-backed wooden chairs that stood around the table. 'What has Will told you about integration?'

Kay shook her head. 'Nothing. He hasn't told me anything.'

'So you need to know everything from the beginning,' said the wraith. Kay nodded. 'The trouble,' he went on, 'is figuring out where the beginning is. I suppose you have heard of Tantalus.' Kay nodded again. 'His story begins at the beginning in a way, though even by that time it had told itself many times over. Still.'

Phantastes spun round, his finger immediately dancing along the high shelves on the wall opposite. He was looking for something. When he found it and hefted it free, Kay saw that it was a large leather-bound book with gold letters tooled across the spine and the cover. She had no time to look at it, though, because no sooner had he placed it before her than he began to riffle through the ancient yellowed pages, mumbling as he went. Kay saw handwritten English text framing beautiful illustrations in red, purple, blue and gold. Finally Phantastes was satisfied and his hands stopped. 'There,' he said. 'Read that.'

Kay began to read.

'Out loud,' said the wraith.

'*Tantalus was a very pious man, and when he came to be king, his piety, which had always been acknowledged even by those who thought religion a pageant of empty rituals, was heralded the known world over. He had an only son, a beautiful boy called Pelops. Pelops rode poised between childhood and age, full of promise, and that promise was of greatness. Tantalus heard the rumours of his son's goodness, his generosity, his courage, his quick intelligence, and he approved them with his own eyes, observing Pelops whether in the toils of his military exercise down by the stables, or in the less sweaty but no less challenging labours set him by his tutors in arithmetic, composition, music and astronomy. Tantalus was excessively proud of his son, and lamented every day the loss of his wife in a hunting accident, which had left him without the possibility of further children. All his hope and his throne's future was tied up, by her death, in this boy; and he often thought it a marvel, as he watched him in conference with some of his councillors, or running in high spirits with a pack of hounds out of the castle grounds, that his own heart did not burst with pride.*

'*It was with the most painfully anguished regret, then, that he received, and obeyed, the oracle sent him in his son's fourteenth year, that for the good of the nation, and for his own fame and honour, he should make his son a sacrifice to the gods of Olympus. Tantalus sent to the oracle once every year, and had many times in the past received replies that troubled or confused him; but always his piety led him through, and he considered the pain of his many* penances and privations the proper price of good kingship. This time, however, he chewed bitterly over his instruction. Could his piety rise even to this? In the end, after a sleepless night, he resolved that the gods were indeed testing him, and that the sacrifice demanded was so total, so difficult, precisely because the Olympians were prepared to reward his fidelity with equal favour. He drew the knife himself when, the next day, his son's blood was poured into the sacred vessels in the temple of Zeus Thunderer.

'It may well have been a test; what man can know the mind of the gods? For certain we can say only that the outcome was not what he expected: within the year a famine raged in the country, a plague felled one out of every three householders, a terrible whirlwind and a tempest destroyed many of the great public buildings, including the temple of Zeus Thunderer – and Tantalus himself, his faith in the gods not only shaken but entirely consumed, withered and died of grief. His councillors, seeing the better part of the Greek world thrown into civil chaos, sent again to the oracle and received this answer: that there was a young man in Epidaurus, a son of Apollo, who could heal Pelops and return his body to life; and that, unless they brought him to do this, the whole of Lydia, of Greece and of Crete would be plunged into turmoil for a hundred years, and their own names wiped from the records of humanity. This Asclepius – for so he was called – was sent for, and within a few days arrived, disembarking from Tantalus' ship at the head of a convoy of a hundred mules. Every one of these mules was laden with two baskets, and every basket contained a score of snakes, gathered from every variety across the *known world. Many of the most potent venoms in the world are also, under different circumstances, powerful as medicinals and elixirs, and Asclepius beyond all others excelled in this snake lore. Alighting with his snakes at the ruined temple of Zeus, this son of Apollo called for the hewn limbs of Pelops to be brought to him as quickly as possible; thereafter he disappeared from public view, retreating into the deep impenetrability of the sanctum. All the locals could see was that the snakes had been loosed, and they moved freely around the temple in their masses, transforming the place into a horror and convincing many of the citizens that they would escape the compound and infest the city. But they did not; and on the third day Pelops was seen to walk on his own feet out of the temple, through the agora, to his home in the castle. He ruled Lydia, Phrygia, Paphlagonia and most of Greece for sixty years; and Asclepius, travelling with freedom and royal warrant throughout his domains, created a name for himself as the greatest healer the world has ever known. It was in his schools that the great doctor Hippocrates first trained; and it was said that even Apollo, from whom all his arts of healing had been derived, eventually acknowledged Asclepius his better in medicine.'*

The text ended there, with a bold, black, horizontal line. Kay stopped reading and looked up at Phantastes, who had taken a seat opposite her, across the table strewn with dried leaves.

'It was also said, long after,' he continued, 'that Asclepius was finally destroyed by Zeus, who was enraged by his hubris and his skill in the lives and deaths of mortals. But in fact the great healer left Greece to join us in Bithynia, and he was one

of the greatest imaginers among us. For integration – healing –
and imagining go hand in hand, and one cannot make up
a whole without an idea to bind it. And it is in the fate of
Tantalus that perhaps even a child may glimpse the mystery of
integration and its special power. Tantalus was ordered by the
gods to sacrifice his only son, who was his pride, his all in all,
the only joy he had in his life; he was also punished brutally for
his obedience, and some say he is being punished still. But
Tantalus' cruel piety gave us also Asclepius: so the snake
gives fatal venom, but also rebirth; and so too the imaginer
conjures merely dreams, but those dreams – those stories – can
show us a kind of higher truth.'

'Will is always saying that,' said Kay. Phantastes raised his
eyebrows. 'That stories are usually the best answers. Better
than facts.'

'Sometimes,' agreed Phantastes, 'they are. There are some –
like Ghast – who have called us only forgers of lies. And to one
way of thinking, that's just what we are. There was one piece
of Pelops' body that Asclepius could not heal because it had
been eaten by a dog – the shoulder. He made him a new one
out of ivory. But this was a fitting loss, because it is always the
dog, the unbeliever, who cannot be restored by our imaginings,
who is leaden and impervious to the healing of the imagination.

'If we are to recover your father, we will need an imagining –
a great new vision; one that can inspire even a man who has
lost everything, who has lost himself, with new hope, new
purpose, new belief. New *self*. That is why Will has brought
you here to me. Together we can find a story, a vision, that will

help to recover your father. But before I can create that imagining, *if* I can, I need to know the point from which to work – the raw materials, if you will. I can imagine anything, of course, but in order to make an imagining that will mean something to your father, something that will resonate especially and perfectly with him, I will need –'

'A clue,' said Kay.

Brought up short, Phantastes stared at her for a moment without comprehension.

'A thread, so you're not running around blindly in the maze. A scent, like for a dog,' added Kay. 'Dogs can hunt anything. But if they are to hunt the *right* thing, they have to be given the right scent first. To start out with. They have to know what they're looking for.'

Phantastes smiled. 'Exactly.'

'And so your friend, the little bald person –'

'Eumnestes.'

'He is looking for this thing so that you can imagine a new story for my father?'

'Eumnestes reads the chronicles and histories, the stories, the epics and romances of earlier times. He knows all that has ever been done, and all that might have been done, and all that ought to have been done – that, or he knows where to find it. Eumnestes knows all the stories. In one of those stories I hope we can find the right idea. And with the right idea, an imaginer can produce such a vision that your father will not only rouse himself from his stupor, but sing and dance, too. We will find your father, and we will wake him.'

'You won't find anything about him in your books,' said Kay. 'You'll find lots of things, but nothing that will speak to *him*. If you want to speak to *him*, you need *me*.'

'Perhaps,' he said softly. 'Perhaps you are right.'

And then, suddenly, the wraith looked down and scooped up some of the dried leaves, holding them out cupped in two hands for Kay to see. 'You know what these are.'

'From the tree downstairs? But there are so many –'

'Hush,' warned the old wraith. 'None of them know about the temple. I haven't told anyone, so you and I are the only ones in the world. Not even Eumnestes –' and here he paused, looking up through the door at a lithe, athletic and very serious boy pushing a large crate down the hallway beyond – 'or that rascal Anamnestes know about it. Not that I don't trust them, but . . . Well, Ghast is a serious antagonist. If I can turn his acolytes to my service, perhaps he can do the same to me.'

'But the tree is so small, and there are hundreds of leaves here.'

'I gathered these leaves ten thousand years ago,' said the old wraith, almost laughing with a melancholy sigh as he let them fall back to the table. 'When that trunk you saw was no jagged skeletal husk but a huge pillar of wood, and the leaves fell by the cartload every autumn. You had to be quick, of course, because the priests didn't take kindly to anyone stealing into the temple or pilfering bits of their tree; but I came away with stuffed pockets most of the time.'

'Why did you gather them? What are they for? Cooking?'

'Yes, you might say that, yes. We treat it like a herb, and steep it in hot water. But it is not for nourishment. Come, I will show you.'

Phantastes took Kay's suddenly tiny hand and drew her out into the hallway. The scale of the place hit her like a slap: the corridor stretched for hundreds of metres in both directions, with scores of rooms just like the one from which they had come opening in either direction. Everywhere the whitewashed walls gave way to sky-blue ceilings, and at the ends of the hallway it seemed to Kay that she could see a huge floor-to-ceiling mirror that showed the two of them – one towering, gaunt wraith in his flowing, hooded, grey-black gown, and one tired, drooping, scruffy child, with her hair drawn back, in the grey cotton robe that Will had given her on the plane. Standing slightly to one side, in both directions she was able to see multiple – infinite – copies of her mirrored image cascading back at her. She stopped where she was, and waved her arm at it, watching the pattern of repeated movement at one end.

'The mirrors are fascinating, aren't they?' said Phantastes. He waved his own arm behind her head. 'They show us a terrible reality; a reality in which we are trapped forever in repetition, as far as the eye can see. But they also show us something else.' He carefully stepped into the centre of the hallway, and Kay stepped directly before him. Now they occupied all the mirror so completely that they utterly eclipsed the reflection from the other end. 'Sometimes,' he said, 'if you stand in the right place, all the myriads are unified, and then there is only one. Come.' And he strode away straight down the centre of the hall, walking into his own image.

Out through an open door on to a stone terrace, and for the first time since arriving in Alexandria Kay felt the full force of the sun. Immediately she noticed that it was directly overhead rather than off to one side, or even long on the horizon. This sun simply beat down on the scalp, like a continuous falling of heated hammers. Underground, in the temple, the light had seemed gentle, nurturing; here by contrast it felt like an open and boring eye, seeing into all of them with an arid look. Everything around them glared with the light and heat of it: the stone balustrade of the terrace, where she set her hands as she looked down over the rooftops to the sea; the pebbles and sandy grit under her feet; even the water of the large circular fountain in which, to her initial surprise as her eyes adjusted to the light, Will was sitting – with his clothes on.

He looked sleepy – at least his eyelids were heavy and drooping, if not completely closed – and there were beads of sweat sitting proud on his forehead. The water poured out of one side of the fountain, and he sat in the pool up to his knees with his legs crossed before him. His hands hovered over the water, palms open and fingers extended, and seemed to be describing a slow, circular motion across the surface. At first Kay thought he was plotting, but this was something slightly different. And then his hands began to move in other ways, shaping through the air as if he were working with a soft stone or wax and forming, or deforming, the cut of a statue; but still his eyes never stirred, and the lids lay draped across them almost bashfully. His hands moved quickly before his body, now scooping up water from the pool and letting it pour very deliberately through the space before him; now pushing with great force down on some invisible shape being moulded, stamped and pressed.

Eumnestes padded on to the terrace in his cotton slippers. He moved with silence and intent directly to Will's side and, leaning over the wall of the fountain, whispered a few words into his ear. Phantastes let out a low whistle as Eumnestes stood back, watching the effect take hold.

Looking around, Kay realized that several other people were also scrutinizing Will. Flip sat upright and poised on a low chair about three metres away, marking him closely and occasionally moving his own hands – involuntarily, she was sure – in the air at his side. To his right, a little closer to her, another man leaned against the balustrade, almost perched on its top. He was heavier than the two wraiths, and old; the hands gripping the stone behind him were gnarled and slightly empurpled; she felt that she had seen them before, recently, but it was not until she looked at his face that she recognized him as Rex, the porter from the Pitt. Kay tried to catch his eye, but he was watching Will intently and never looked her way, not even when she drew in closer to the little group and sat down on a low stone bench. To Flip's other side, and on the far side of the fountain, someone else was squatting just over the edge of the pool. It was another wraith, a woman, and she had dark and glossy hair, almost purple in the sun, brushed back in tresses over her shoulders. Kay could not see her face well, but could anyway discern that she, too, had at least one eye on Will; and while she looked at her, trying, round the fountain's stem, to get a full view of her face, Kay saw her do something very curious. She slowly reached into her pocket and drew out a dark black stone – no, perhaps a marble, for it was smooth, and gleamed like glass – but not glass, because she squeezed it easily, and it rained a kind of juice into the pool below before she rolled it between her fingers, and dropped it. Her actions were tiny and painfully slow, as if, with everyone's eyes on Will, she were anxious to avoid observation. She squeezed and dropped another, then another; and as Kay craned her neck to see round the fountain, the woman just caught her eye and froze – and broke into a wide smile.

But it was at that second that Will's arms suddenly came to an abrupt halt in the air, his head lifted in a straight and decisive jerk, his eyelids shot up, and he stared straight at Kay. He said only two words, with perfect clarity and intensity, and then fainted, falling to his right into the pool. As he fell, everyone on the terrace scrambled to his side, except Kay; she sat there feeling nothing at all, the words reverberating in her head, the chilling, direct stare burning with a dark blaze into her memory.

'Andrea Lessing.'

No. Not again.

She felt nothing – just a gaping, empty coldness.

Not here. Not again.

Everything seemed to move very slowly, soundlessly, and as if it were at a great distance: the hands pulling Will out of the water; a swarm of unfamiliar wraiths suddenly scaling the terrace from every direction; the body of Eumnestes falling from the second-storey window and crashing, mangled, on the stone before her feet; the cold, cold blade of the knife that, in the middle of that long moment, slid into the soft flesh of her right shoulder. Over the rooftops beyond the terrace, past the swaying tops of two glossy palms, she saw birds circling as she fell forward – circling, circling, but not landing.

*I*t had taken all the skill of forty of the greatest of the left-wraiths. They had plotted for weeks under Ghast's supervision, composing the plan that would destroy his enemies once and for all. It had been a mighty effort; but then, it was the nature of stories, and of the feeble-minded wraiths who still told them, to make the simple look very difficult. From this vantage – that of the present – he considered the problems trivial, and the recent chain of events more or less inevitable. The once-great First Wraith could be relied upon for his incompetence. Having failed everyone around him again and again, he had made failure a kind of habit. He would fall easily into any trap laid for him if the bait were some promise of redemption. His companion Philip was of a subtler temper, but in that subtlety lay his vulnerability: believing himself to be too wise to be duped, he was after a manner duped by his own wisdom. The girl did not bear pondering: give her the slightest nudge, and she would move at a constant speed in whatever direction you chose, until you chose to alter or stop her course. She was so much water; one did but channel her. Ghast frowned. His enemies had proved weaker than he deserved.

Soon his runner would reach the barge with news of his agents' success in Alexandria. Already he had received his first report. Naturally his enemies had fallen like flies into the honey pot, exactly where Ghast had dropped them. With no friends left in the mountain, they sought out – and so betrayed – their last ally. It would be sweet to learn of the old imaginer's death; he had compassed it so often in his imagination he half thought he had become half an imaginer himself.

Now, having played his enemies, he would play his friends. Perhaps that would be more satisfying. In time to come, friend and foe would alike call him master.

'What is it?' he all but spat at his servant, who presumed to interrupt his reverie. The obsequious wraith winced to be acknowledged.

The barge was making slow passage through a wide, mostly rocky mountain valley. It was late in the afternoon. To the right Ghast noticed two of the large vultures that breed in the area, circling low as if about to land on the rough weeds and low shrubs covering the valley floor. He watched them thrust forward and extend their claws as they dropped to the ground. Their wing feathers stood out black against the grey light. Still his minion did not answer.

'I will tell you,' he said, 'what you cannot yourself contrive to say. You come to relay to me the news that the Builder, the man More, has been shaken off and left to beg for food in some ditch or alley at the end of the earth.'

'Yes,' said the terrified eyes of a lesser right-wraith.

'But you have worse news for me, too, and you fear to give it.' He paused and stared hard into the quivering pupils of his victim.

They contracted to terrified pinpricks. 'The runner who came to you passed on this report and vanished, staking not his but your head on his message. And the message is that the little girl, More's daughter, the worthless one, has escaped with her friends. That's it, isn't it?'

The wraith nodded in a way that seemed to offer his head upon an imagined block. But Ghast had no more use for it than an overfed cat for a scrawny mouse. He did not even feel the urge to toy with him.

The barge floated untroubled down this quiet, broad valley. Soon they would put ashore for the night at one of the prepared landings. The girl had escaped by his design, but he would dissemble that; if his enemies were determined to be so hapless, he would have to help them to put up a fight – for only a fight, or the appearance of one, would suit his ends now. Meanwhile he must rouse himself to the performance of a purple fury. Soon the time of ruses would be over.

He longed for the ease of the vulture that never killed for itself.

10

Flip

For what seemed like years Kay lay with her face just beneath the surface of the cold water in the pool on Phantastes' terrace. Beside her lay Will, his eyes turned towards her, unblinking – but not dead, for he smiled from time to time, and his mouth seemed to move in a way that might, out of the water, have been speech. The whole time she lay in the sun-slicing pool, Kay longed to understand these frustrated words, to hear what it was that Will was trying to tell her with his untiring gaze and his kind, slow, exaggerated smiles; but no sound came, and every time she opened her own mouth, the salty water flooded in, thick and viscous, like blood.

Later, with faint surprise, she began to be aware that the world outside the pool was moving, and as time went by she could see it with ever greater clarity. She struggled to lift her head to find out what was going on, but always the exertion brought back the taste of that salt water, and still she could not find her arms or legs, with which she might have braced or pushed herself. Soon she began to hear what seemed to be words, only just beyond her hearing, as if spoken through a thick towel. In time, this drone resolved, and words themselves gradually emerged, then snatches of story, then longer pieces – pieces of knights, and priests, and bankers, and voyages, and precious stones, and unscalable cliffs, of courageous attempts and pitiable losses. Hour after hour she lay in the pool, watching passively as the blurred world above the water shifted by, struggling to hold on to the sense of the slurred words swirling around her ears and keep the taste of the salt at bay.

It never occurred to her to wonder whether, or how, she was breathing. Her breath had poured out of her entirely, and there was only in her lungs and stomach a desperate need to resist the water that engulfed her. But despite her resolve she felt that she was failing, that it was seeping in at the cracks between her lips and at the corners of her mouth, that the pressure was massing at her nose and, when her eyes were open, upon her eyes. Slowly, drop by drop, the pool's thick water forced its inevitable way into her mouth and down her burning throat. With every drop the pain became more severe and she grew more desperate. But in time – how much she never really knew – it became obvious that the water was slowly draining away; or, rather, she began to understand that it was in reality mere air. And as it drained into air, the sound of the voices around her changed from their droning to a more usual tone, and it was clear that the thick drops seeping down her throat were in fact her throat, and that what was forcing its way between her lips and pressing at her nostrils was not choking gulps of water, but essential, rhythmic gasps for breath.

One thing that did not change was the frequent presence of Will's face, less than a metre away, turned towards her. Often he laid his head, unspeaking, on the arm of a chair adjacent to her — she realized that she must also be lying down — but at other times he spoke. The stories, she realized, were — had been — his. When he saw that she was crying, he seemed at first to think it was the pain.

'We're safe now, Kay,' he said. 'You had concussion, and a very shallow wound to your shoulder. It's healing. It will hurt less every day.'

Kay couldn't find her voice, but she managed to shake her head — very slowly, very weakly.

'Do you want me to tell you a story?' Will asked.

Kay tried to shake her head again.

'Do you want to know what's going on?'

She tried with every muscle in her body to push herself up, to speak. *Ell. Dad. How long?* Her eyes shouted at Will to hear her.

'Six nights,' he said. 'Six nights, Kay.' Her body collapsed back into the bed. *Six nights left.* From a great distance she could feel Will squeezing her arm.

'It must have been Ghast. We're not sure how he found Phantastes, the house, the library.' He stopped for a while and turned to look at the ceiling. Then he began again, not looking back at her. She saw that the room they were in had plain white walls and a low ceiling. There must have been a window behind her, because it was very light. 'After Flip and I lost you in the tunnels, we went up a rear chute into the house — it's the way we always go, to avoid being seen on the street. We saw Phantastes, he told us to start the integration – you can guess the rest. I don't know much about what happened once I was in the fountain. After you sit in a pool steeped with leaves, your mind tends to go blank a little – and you probably saw more of me and everything else than I did. But I know that Rex was there, and Flip. And Katalepsis was there. She's a plotter, but one of ours. She used to fly with Flip.

'According to Flip, that's when everything went wrong. There must have been at least four of them – assassins – because someone pushed Eumnestes from the top floor of the library at about the same time as two of them came out on to the terrace. One of them put the knife in your back.' Kay tensed to hear out loud what she had assumed already. 'It's going to be all right, Kay. Phantastes knows a lot of people in Alexandria, and we got you away quickly enough to make sure you were properly looked after. It turned out to be a lot less serious than we'd feared. Flip was hurt a little, too, in the leg. But he's recovering well.' Will looked straight at her and smiled. 'He's in the next room.

'We left Alexandria the next night. Phantastes insisted. It was too dangerous to stay. Rex and Kat had gone on ahead, here, to Greece, and Phantastes hired a ferry for us to follow. We've been holed up in Pylos. It's a nice house, just on the square – you'll like it. The streets outside are all cobbled.' He stopped, and Kay listened to her slow, quiet breathing for a long minute. 'Don't worry: we left Alexandria in the middle of the night, and no one could have followed us. We'll stay here long enough to get you and Flip fit again, while Phantastes tries to figure out what happened and then make new plans for the integration.' Will looked at her again. 'We'll find him, Kay. We'll find both of them.'

She lay there with questions pounding in her head. She wanted to hear about Ell. Did they know where she was? How would they find her? What could she *possibly tell her mother*? How could she explain that she had lost her little sister? Kay felt she could hardly, for weariness, move the muscles in her face, but she sobbed all the same, and huge tears, if they could not run down her cheeks, still they ripped through her body.

Will came and went many times over what seemed like a whole long day. Although there was a shaded window in the room, she thought it had to be overhung by a tree or another building, because Kay couldn't see any direct sunlight – just a grey veil lifting in the morning, becoming slowly but reliably lighter over the day, and then what seemed like a sudden pitch into evening. Kay slept in bursts: sometimes she lay for interminably long hours on the side to which Will had gently rolled her, facing either the window across the floor, or in the other direction the white, immediate surface of the wall running up behind the bed. From beyond the window, which must have been open at least a crack, she thought – though no breeze ever ruffled the curtains – she could hear occasionally a snatch of something that might have been children crying. On the second day, feeling for the first time very alert, she realized that the crying children were gulls.

Will strode into the room and smiled broadly. 'Kay, I think you're well enough to sit up. And if that goes well, we want to take you outside.'

Kay clenched her teeth and put out her arms, feeling the tightness draw back between her shoulder blades and a dull pain in her upper back. 'Will,' she said quietly, 'where is Ell?'

'We're working on that,' he answered as he righted her gradually, shifting the weight on to her waist and reaching for some pillows to put behind her back. Her head swam. 'We've tried to imagine a way out of this mess, and it didn't work. We're going to give plotting another go.'

Shaking her head slightly as if clearing the water from her eyes, Kay tried to think why she didn't know what Will was talking about. She pressed her hands into her lap, painfully. 'I don't understand,' she said slowly.

'Right,' he said, taking a seat by the bed. 'You understand plotting well enough, I take it – how it's done?' Kay nodded, more out of impatience than real understanding. 'Most wraiths can do a little plotting, though some are better than others. There have been a few that had no knack for it at all – like Phantastes. He was never a plotter.' Will looked right into Kay's eyes and said in a whisper, 'He doesn't even have a *board*.' Kay nodded – after her conversation with Phantastes in the Temple of Osiris, this didn't surprise her at all. 'A wraith who can't plot can't plot for one reason, and one reason only. A wraith who can't plot is an imaginer.'

'And Phantastes is the last of the imaginers, or nearly the last,' Kay said quietly.

Will looked up sharply. 'He *is* the last. Did he tell you about the others?'

Kay shook her head.

Though he sat silently enough, Will had suddenly become very agitated, and the silence was as loud as – louder than – the low tolling in her ears.

'There were always three great imaginers, since there were imaginers at all, as far back as anyone could remember: Asclepius, Phantastes and the Siege Vacant. Asclepius was destroyed – his hubris – we do not speak of it, and a lesser right-wraith takes his place on ceremonial occasions – but the Siege Vacant – it has gone by other names –'

'Phantastes told me about Asclepius, but he didn't mention the other, the Siege –'

'That's because it pains him to speak of it. Of her. Unlike the other two imaginers, the Siege Vacant is an open position, filled by one of the lesser right-wraiths when the need arises, but never when the Weave is summoned; there her seat is always left unoccupied. I told you before that the knights are a thousand and one in number, but this isn't strictly true. It is said that the first of the imaginers left the Honourable Society long ago, and hasn't been seen since – the first of the imaginers, gone before my time, and no one knows where or why. Phantastes took the first place among the right-wraiths, leaving his own chair open; it has, ever after, been known as the Siege Vacant – an office never quite filled, because Phantastes believes, somewhere in his heart, that she will return.'

Kay propped herself up a little painfully on one elbow. 'She?'

'She is said to have been the greatest of them,' Will replied. 'It is even said that she built the great loom. She was called Scheherazade.' He vented a long sigh.

Scheherazade, Mother of Stories, called the Breaker of Kings, the Freedom of Kingdoms, Scheherazade of the thousand tales, the healer, the seducer, the bride. Kay's body shook and she sank back on to her pillow, looking up at the empty ceiling.

'Well,' Will went on. 'I suppose Phantastes told you about the tree of Byblos and the Temple of Osiris. It was thousands of years ago, but he still remembers the old places with a kind of reverence, and it was inevitable that he would go back there. You heard me mention the leaves before?' Kay nodded gingerly. 'That tree is – was – very important to the imaginers because its leaves when you chew them put you in a state – of creativity, or epiphany – and the imaginers used to gather them fallen, and sometimes steal into the tree to pick the more potent fresh ones, when it still grew in the Temple of Osiris. One of the three imaginers was pretty much always in Alexandria, for that reason. I don't know if Phantastes explained to you exactly what it is imaginers mostly do, but they often use the leaves for their imaginings, and it is a great good fortune that Phantastes had gathered so very many of them in the years before the temple was destroyed and the tree hacked down – he dried them, and has been using them ever since.

'We should have foreseen, when the armies burned the temple and replaced it with churches to their blind gods, what it would mean for the imaginers. Without the tree, Phantastes had to ration the leaves. Without new leaves, Phantastes and the others would hardly dare imagine; and this weakened them, and their standing with the wraiths. It was during this most difficult time that Ghast, who has always hated imagining, and all the imaginers, first began to attract notice. The lesser left-wraiths started to adhere to him and his ideas, and it wasn't long before his star, in the ascendant, began to eclipse the imaginers completely. Ghast is a plotter – but, to be honest, he is a poor one, and he might never have succeeded in seizing power in the Weave but for one thing. Now, Kay, listen closely. That thing is the House of Razzio in Rome.'

Here Will, who had begun to pause between sentences in order to adjust Kay's pillows and straighten the light sheets in which she was partly wrapped, came to a full stop. His hands fluttered plottily in his lap. He looked troubled.

Kay was feeling stronger, and increasingly more alert and steady as he went on. 'But how could anyone have preferred *him* to *them*? Phantastes is so *kind*.'

'Necessity,' said Will simply, his eyebrows arching as he dropped his head, defeated. 'Razzio is the greatest of all the plotters – to the plotting wraiths what Phantastes is to the imaginers: their spiritual head, if you like. In Rome he has the greatest board in the world – two halls cannot hold it, nor a kingdom purchase the tenth part of its beautiful craftsmanship. It is laid in a floor all studded with gold and silverwork, and above it twists an arbour of branches and vines, with clusters of huge fruit hanging hidden behind the evergreen foliage. Beneath your feet the lines run for what seems like forever. And he doesn't use stones. Two hundred wraiths – he calls them the causes – walk the boards where he calls them to and fro, and he constantly moves among them, trying out patterns, thinking about relationships, working through stories, and coming to know the beginnings and the ends of things. In the huge and sprawling palace that surrounds the board lives Oidos, moving in the silent rooms of the place of pure knowing; to her Razzio resorts to learn the meaning of what he sees plotted on the board. At the centre of the board, upon a raised platform roofed with stone, the other of the two modes, Ontos, dances in silent gyrations. His platform is known as the place of pure being, and while Razzio is on the board, Ontos never leaves it. Working with Oidos and with Ontos, Razzio has become the master of all there is to know about how causes create effects, and effects in turn become new causes. He can show you the million threads that ravel in and unravel out of every event. Everything in the House of the Two Modes comes from something else, and goes to something else. Everything makes sense. It is only there that my hands can truly be still.

'Razzio is a great genius. He has only one flaw. He is very vain. He made up his mind before all time that his way of understanding the world was the right one, and he cannot stand even to be in the same room as Phantastes, or for that matter any of the right-wraiths. Like all the true plotters, he is short, but he is broad and powerful, and it is said that in early times he once bested Phantastes at wrestling – though it is difficult now to conceive of such a thing, both of them being so ancient. But whether that is true or not, it's certainly the case that Phantastes will not tolerate Razzio any more than Razzio will acknowledge Phantastes; and so, when Ghast came to Razzio with a plan that, he said, would drive the great imaginers out of Bithynia for good, of course Razzio jumped at the idea. From his house in Rome he sent an army of his acolytes – all greater left-wraiths – to join with Ghast's left-wraiths. Together the two factions began to dominate and determine all the councils held in our ancient hall.

'When the wraiths were still gathered in Bithynia, once a year – in midwinter, on the twelve days – the twelve knights of Bithynia would return from their journeys, wherever in all the corners and edges of the earth they were, to celebrate the festival of renewal. From Alexandria the three imaginers; from Rome Razzio and the two modes, Oidos and Ontos, the eldest of the left-wraiths; from Lebanon in the east the three youngest of the left-wraiths; from Atlas in the west the three youngest of the right-wraiths. Over the twelve days the twelve knights would mark the festival with storytelling competitions, poetry competitions, song, dance, and of course the feasts – the likes of which I think the world does not elsewhere know: for sumptuousness, for high revelry, for state and for goodness. Oh, Kay, the Shuttle Hall –'

Kay had been looking down at the red hem of the blanket gathered in her lap. Now she stole a glance at Will as his voice faltered, and saw very briefly the tears already collecting on either side of his chin.

I can't bear your tears.

After a few moments and a long breath he began again. 'In the great hall, the Shuttle Hall, where the tiny diamonds in the ceiling, like stars, constellate and shine all night long in the middle of winter, and the mosaics on the floor sweep in foamy tides across shoals of pebbled thought, there did we feast, there sing, there tread the paces of the ancient metres, there create and recreate stories that, had they been told in words out of some forgotten language, still you would have wept for joy, and fear, and joy and fear, only to hear the sound of them. And every wraith in the world came there once a year, and the twelve knights did all this.

'On the last of the twelve days of the festival, when each of the twelve knights had held court for one day, the general synod took place. In the stalls to one side of the hall the left-wraiths took their seats and, opposite them, the right-wraiths. First, before anything else could happen, the great horn was sounded, the Primary Fury – a blast like chaos, like all the clamours of the world gathered into one, shocking the very air and ripping through ears and heart, a cacophony to clear every thought, every fantasy from the minds of its hearers. Then, as the horn's furious note faded, all eyes marked the procession of the twelve knights as they passed down the length of the hall in silence, each wearing the insignia of his or her order, each carrying one of the twelve staves of the Honourable Society – iron rods crowned by a writhing snake and a plotting stone. One by one the knights stowed their staves in the great wheel at the centre of the hall, where the light from the windows dazzles the floor with blue like sapphire; one by one the knights took to their thrones. Then the First Wraith entered, and walked the length of the hall. From the twelve knights he received the shuttle – fashioned from the most luminous, pearlescent stone, whorled and flexed, dimpled and notched to take the pirn – the bobbin – and with it the thread wherewith the weft is worked against the warp, and the web woven. The First Wraith blew upon the shuttle, a call harmonious to answer the great horn, music after fury, choosing a note that would set the tone for the story and the debate to come – love or war, tragedy or quest.

'In that sound, as if in an embrace, as if enclosed and fortified in completeness, the mystery would truly begin. To you, Kay, a wraith must seem a strange sort of thing. We are here and not here, large and real and substantial, but fleeting, evanescent. We come and go like lights in the night. To you perhaps we are like angels, participating in your moment-to-moment, but somehow eternal. You cannot understand. But we are not so strange, if you think about it. What is love? Can you see it? What is justice, or truth? Can you touch them? Can you pour them into a bowl or throw them at the wall? But you know these things *are*. So I am, so Flip is. And so, to us, the Bride is – as ravishing as an epiphany, so beautiful in our thought and trust that she is Beauty itself, a form fleeting and fugitive; but as real, as eternal, as important as the greatest and most certain truths. Most people would do anything for love, for truth, for beauty. These things are absolute and the greatest goods. In just this way wraiths and phantasms live and die by the Bride, for in her, as she touches us and informs us, as she makes us who we are, we all participate in her as the flower does in scent, as the sun does in brightness, as the sky shares in blue and trees in green. In her we are wed to our own being – more, we are wed to being. In her we marry time and space, in her we are joined to truth, in her we are plighted.

'At that sound of the shuttle, if the heart of a wraith is clean, the Bride enters. I cannot describe it to you except to say it is like a star at dawn, and like the dawn, too, something you become aware has been there all along, something that heralds, something that floods. Her presence steals over you like the blue light falling from the windows of the Shuttle Hall, and gathers, as if in a stone, as if in a luminous sapphire that you could hold in the palm of your hand, so real is her presence, so complete her assurance. The moment in that sound has a name: we call it the Bridestone – for what reason no one knows, or it has been long forgotten, but it lasts forever, though it is over in the blink of an eye, though it flies through your heart like a swallow through the hall, in at one window, across a single instant a-flutter and a-dart, and then out the opposite end. And yet an instant is enough, for there, in the presence of the Bride, time sways in its deep and the least of its drops is an eternity.

'In the synods of old, the First Wraith blew upon the shuttle and then sat at the loom, and he wove as the wraiths rose to speak, each one a thread around him, and the day's assembly with all its voices moved the First Wraith's hands, and the tapestry he wove there was the great record and judgement of the assembly, in which, should you read it carefully, you would see every moment of that day and its concerns, alive and speaking in the cloth by colour, texture, pattern, contrast, subject. As you might imagine, we have thousands of them – I think you have seen some of them in the tapestry room in the mountains?'

Kay nodded. She heard the whisper of a light footfall and, following the report with her eye, noticed Flip leaning in the doorway. He smiled faintly, meeting her glance for a moment before looking back at Will who, oblivious to his audience and engrossed, went on.

'The First Wraith was, you might say, the soul of the convocation and its mouth. Through him everything passed and was resolved; through him and through the motion of the shuttle in the threads of the loom. But the voices were those of all the wraiths, speaking if not in harmony then in symphony. We clashed, I don't deny it; but our wars and campaigns found their way into the images we made, and from them flowed back into the stories we told, and spread abroad into the world for everyone to see, and to know, and to tell, to handle. But Ghast – what he did – it is almost unspeakable.

'Because in that year, when Razzio sent his left-wraiths from the house in Rome and they plotted in the mountains the overthrow of the old order, the festival was held as always, and we feasted and revelled for the twelve days and nights, and the Weave assembled, as ever, and the shuttle was placed in the hand of the First Wraith, and he sat at the loom – and there was utter, unspeakable silence.'

Here Flip drew in a sharp breath, and Will spun round violently on his chair, throwing his hands before his face before he realized, just as quickly, who it was. He turned back wearily, breaking.

'A few wraiths spoke – they tried to start the story, the debate, to find the theme, to gather up the threads – but as in weaving you cannot work a warp without a woof, one thread against another, so in debate, in song, no voice can speak alone, no song take flight without its undersong. The loom lurched now and again, and the shuttle clacked within it, but at the end of the day we were left with some straggly and disconnected patches of fabric, without an image, without a border, without any *pattern*. It was as if some huge weight which we thought stable and permanent had suddenly shifted, and because of its weight crashed all around us. We have never held a Weave since, and the festivals slip away, year after year, into memory. I have not heard such a song these two or three hundred years.

'But it did not end there. It had hardly begun. For by the end of that day Ghast had mounted the pedestal, taken the shuttle from the very hand of the First Wraith, and had it cast into the sea. The loom was dismantled and, I was told, fed to the fire. The halls were shut that year, and boarded up, and at Ghast's command we retreated into the mountains, the barbarians at our heels. And we left the mulberry orchards, and we left the plotting gardens with their winding streams, and we left our great library with half our books, and so many other things, all abandoned, all deserted in fear and without hope, without pattern, all haphazard. And the festivals were discontinued, and the twelve knights were sent to the twelve compass points of the earth, Kay.'

'And Ghast set the First Wraith to work doing common removals,' said Flip softly.

214

Kay's eyes shot up to Will's crumpled form where he slumped on the chair, his long legs drawn up to his chin, wrapped in his desperate arms. 'You,' she breathed.

You. It was you.

Will nodded his whole body slowly, without looking at her. It was if he were rocking himself to sleep, and when he carried on talking, his voice was a nightmare lullaby. 'At first Ghast had me imprisoned for misleading the Honourable Society — for making false images. It was clear what his real target was; clear enough. Everyone knew. The old synthesis, Kay, was between the imaginers and the plotters. Always, since time was, the great rift has yawned between these two ways — the warp against the weft — those who create from nothing, and those who believe only in causation. The plotters cannot accept that the imaginers conceive, and the imaginers cannot suffer the sterile mechanics of the plotters. To the plotters, the imaginers are charlatans; to the imaginers, the plotters are machines. This had always been the great divide. All our tapestries represent this conflict in one way or another, because as First Wraith my function was to synthesize and bind these two functions. Ghast wanted to end it; to use his alliance with Razzio to give the plotters the upper hand. He called it "progress". He called it "a new era of efficiency". Kay, he had many of the imaginers dispersed.'

Kay's eye settled on the leather satchel Phantastes had given her, in which she was sure the shuttle still lay, waiting for the touch of its master. It was only at the foot of the bed — she could reach it, give it to Will and change everything, give him a salve for his grief. But something in her didn't dare. Perhaps it was because Phantastes had told her to wait, had warned her, and she trusted him. But there was something deeper, too – it wouldn't be right to put so beautiful a thing into the hands of a wraith who was still so . . . so broken.

All the while he spoke, Will stared over his knees at his hands; they lay there, drained of colour, the knuckles like white peaks in a rough landscape of age and suffering. Kay stared at them, too, and thought of the mountains from which they had flown without Ell, not knowing where she was or how to reach her, how to recover her, how to take her home again. Kay tried to picture in her mind how Ell would be feeling: the emptiness, the fear, but also the wonder, the freedom. Sometimes Ell loved to be lost – at the beach it was sometimes hours before she turned up after lying in the shade of some gorse bushes at the head of a low cliff, playing with the thistle tops. All that time she would watch walkers passing and ships sailing on the sea, and never cry or worry. Perhaps, Kay thought, this time it would be the same. *Maybe she is somewhere calm and quiet. Maybe they have been good to her.* The alternative wasn't . . . It wasn't possible to think about it.

She was still staring at Will's hands when Phantastes barged into the room, all strides and grand gestures.

'Boys, Rex is back from the piers. We need to find Kat. Rex thinks he's seen some wispers shadowing down by the harbour. He doesn't think they've found us yet, but they're definitely in the city. We don't have long. We'll have to move on, probably tonight.'

Will was fully extended and active almost immediately. 'Wait. How could they know we are here? How could they be in Pylos at all? No one could have followed us on that night crossing. And no one could have seen us come in through that storm.' He looked jerkily around at all of them in turn. 'No. This is too close, too fast. They found us here like they found us in Alexandria. This isn't plotting. There's something else going on.'

'Spying?' Phantastes said.

'A leak,' said Will.

'But who?' asked Flip, stepping fully into the now crowded small room and pulling the door shut behind him as he did so. He and Phantastes sat at the end of Kay's bed.

'We need clues,' Will said. 'We need to remember exactly what happened in Alexandria.'

'Will, we've been over this,' Flip said. 'We've been over and over it. There's no new information.'

'And yet,' said Phantastes, 'before we make another move, we must know what's going on. Unless we stay together, there is no hope of recovery.'

'Recovery of what?' interrupted Kay.

'Of Bithynia, of course,' said Phantastes. 'So, again, once more, think back. If they didn't track you through the air and they couldn't have plotted your movement before you left, then how did they find us in Alexandria?'

'But I didn't *see* anything unusual,' Will muttered. 'No suspicious faces. No patterns in the street. No following noises. And there was no one at the house but Flip, Rex, Kat, me – and Kay, of course, and Eumnestes, Anamnestes and you.'

'Kat —' Kay pushed herself up on her elbow — 'she was the one with the beautiful hair?'

Will nodded.

There was a bustle in the room beyond, the door cracked open and Rex leaned in his massy, leathered head, with his tousled white hair bobbing to one side. 'I'm going out to find Kat down at the docks,' he said gruffly. 'I'll take every precaution.'

'See that you do,' Phantastes replied. 'See that you do.'

Kay suddenly had an idea. 'Rex —' she said.

The door had already closed behind him, but he cracked it open and leaned back in. 'Hello, child. Long time no see. I hadn't noticed you were up again.'

'Hi.' Kay felt awkward, but she covered it by speaking quickly. 'Rex, if Kat is coming from the docks and the wispers are down there — well, they'll be following her. She's unmistakable, with that hair.'

'She's right,' said Phantastes. 'Don't come back up here — you'll lead them right to us. Wait till nightfall, at least.'

Rex nodded and was gone again in an instant. Will shifted his seat over to the window and drew the curtain slightly.

Phantastes stood up and took to the door, running his hand absently round the frame as he lost himself in thought. 'Are you sure she's not a plotter?' he said quietly, to no one in particular. But he glanced at Kay, and she knew he was talking about her. 'Details, patterns.' He faced the wall motionlessly for a moment, and then slapped his hand against it. 'I can't plot these situations, Will. Flip, think it through. Find the causes.'

There was silence for a few minutes. Kay was afraid to break it, so deeply and anxiously were they absorbed in their memories and their analysis. Will's and Flip's hands were twitching as they picked through threads of consequence that led to the assassins, to Eumnestes' fall, to the cool steel in Kay's back. She could almost see the webs and branches opening up in the air before her as they thought, and she longed to pick through them with her fingers. *Perhaps I am developing this plotting skill after all.*

Will was the first to break it.

'No, it's just the same. Everything is the same. Up until the fountain I saw and heard nothing that made me in the least suspicious; and after that it was a sealed house – nobody went in or out. Are you sure, Flip,' he said, turning from the window, 'that you haven't forgotten something?'

Flip shook his head. He looked uncertain, Kay thought, but still he shook his head.

Will turned to her. 'And you didn't see anything, Kay? Nothing at the beach, nothing on the streets? Nothing in the sewers? Nothing in the house? Nothing on another terrace maybe? Nobody watching?'

'No.'

'It's so incredibly frustrating,' Will said. 'To be under the leaf at all is bad enough – but that integration was so hard, so painful. I wasn't aware of anything at all except the pain. And then their timing: to come in like that, just at the end, when our concentration was most absorbed, when I was most engrossed and groggy – it was uncanny. It was like they were waiting for a cue or something.'

Something was tapping Kay on the shoulder. She could feel some detail, some half-remembered observation, stirring in her memory. It was something important, she thought.

But if it were something important, wouldn't I remember it?

Then it struck her: Kat. She leaped into the conversation so vigorously that she felt her back twinge.

'Where do you get the leaves for the integration? When do you add them to the fountain?' she asked.

'You know where we get them,' Phantastes said. 'I showed you – on the table. That was my entire store, all that I have left. We add them to the fountain an hour or two before the integration so that the leaves can leach into the water. I readied the fountain as soon as we saw the plane.'

Kay blew out a long breath. 'Then what did I see Kat putting into the fountain while Will was . . . integrating? Is that what you were doing?' She looked from one to the other of them. 'When I first came on to the terrace, I saw her take something from her pocket, and as she dropped it in the pool, she looked right at me. She smiled at me.' Phantastes raised his hand and was about to speak, but Kay cut him off. 'It was small, dark, glassy – like a marble, or a – I don't know. I couldn't see over the edge of the fountain well enough, so I don't know what happened to it, but it looked heavy when she dropped it. It certainly wasn't a leaf.'

Phantastes looked at Will. Will looked up. 'Belladonna,' he said.

'The obvious poison,' agreed Phantastes. He slumped now, but said – to Kay, though he might have been talking to himself, 'The symptoms of belladonna poisoning are almost the same as the effects of the leaves – dilation of the pupils in the eyes, twitching of the hands and feet, lethargy and sleepiness, loss of speech – only it is fatal. We would never have suspected anything. Oh, it all fits: Will complained afterwards – while you were sick – of strange side-effects from the integration. The lethargy, the loss of his voice, the aches in his joints. But more importantly we know that Katalepsis is highly skilled at administering it; unfortunately she has done it for Ghast in the past. We just never thought she would do it to *us*.'

Phantastes spun in front of the door, wedging his arms into the frame, and fixed a look of contempt on Flip, sitting at the foot of Kay's bed. Flip simply dropped his head into his hands and said nothing. But it was Will who spoke – spoke, or groaned with words.

'Flip. I don't understand.' Will held out his hands, together. 'You know Kat was your call, your friend. You've known all along that she was playing us. How could you bring her here, let her do that?' He stopped. Kay thought he was plotting for a moment, but then realized that his hands weren't thinking – they were shaking. His body was sobbing, though his face looked completely clear, empty. 'How much did you know, Flip? The assassins? The wispers? The little girl? Flip, what did you know? Why have you done this to us?' He stared, but was not angry. Full of fear, Kay watched his stoniness and drew back gingerly into the corner of her bed, taking up her knees under the blanket. 'Flip, we could have *died*.'

When Flip raised his head, Kay half expected to see his face covered in tears; but while he seemed rigid, there was no grief in him. He held his face level with Will's and spoke only to him.

'Of course I didn't know what she would do. Of course I didn't know what Ghast would do. I had his word . . .' There he stumbled, and his eyelids dropped momentarily. 'I thought I had his word.'

'But whose word do *we* have, Philip?' Phantastes was angry, almost shouting, boxing at the air with his teeth. 'Whose word for us? What truth is in you? How can we call you friend now?'

'You can't, obviously,' said Flip – evenly, quietly. 'I know that. I knew that. Although you should, now above all. Although I have never been a better friend to you, Will, than I have been in this.' His eyes raised Will's, and the two friends regarded one another impassively. 'You can't know this now, but you will see it later. What I have done – everything – I have done it to protect you. Remember this, Will,' he went on, still staring directly and unblinkingly at him, 'remember that I told you here, now, that you would come to know not just what I have done, but how I have done it. Remember.'

Flip sat rigidly, unmoving. He might have been a stone or a tree trunk. Not even an eye twitched as the two wraiths continued to stare at one another, their hands stilled, their breathing imperceptible, their arms now stiff and straight at their sides. Their friendship was passing between them, Kay thought, but she hardly cared. *Traitor.*

Phantastes took two quick steps, threw back his head, and with a snap of his neck spat at Flip's unflinching brow. 'If you have any friendship in you, you will leave this place and us, and you will never return to the mountains, to Bithynia, to the company of other wraiths. If you have any friendship in you, you will not go to Ghast with this, or with any of our plans. Now get out.'

Flip stood up painfully, as if his limbs ached, as if he were an old man. He drew out the sleeves of his gown and smoothed his front – but he never wiped his face. 'As for you, Phantastes,' he said slowly, 'I have never given you cause to hate me, and I give you no cause now. I will wear this contempt, but not for my own shame. I will wear it for yours.' And with a resolute and even step he let himself out of the white, still room, and the sound of his footsteps quieted and fell away.

Kay sat up suddenly, like a shot, before she was even sure what she would say. She fumbled.

Rex.

'Will. Rex. The square. The window.'

Will turned wearily to her, and all the rigidity and strength of his confrontation with Flip was gone. His mouth laboured words. 'What? Kay?'

She found her thread. 'Kat doesn't know that I'm up, right? If Rex tells Kat that I'm talking, that I'm awake, she'll know she's in danger. She saw that last look I gave her when the knife – He's not safe, Will.'

'She's right,' said Phantastes – but they were all three of them already scrambling to the window. Kay winced and caught her breath, hard, as Will rattled the curtain down its rod. Through the pain she saw the alleyway, three or four storeys down, then the corner of a neighbouring building across the street. Then, beyond that, illuminated in bright sunshine, the central square of the city, with its flagstone pavements and low, rundown buildings. She could see almost the whole square, just as Phantastes had said earlier, and as it came further into focus and her eyes made the adjustment from fever and sleep, she saw people. At first she thought they were dancing, because they all seemed to be skipping to the centre of the square – twenty or thirty people, from all directions.

'By the muses,' Phantastes whispered like a knife.

All those people had stopped in a ring, and within it Kay could just make out, over the top of someone's head, a body lying on the ground, motionless.

Rex.

'She's killed him,' said Will quietly.

As if cued by his words, a single figure pulled out of the crowd, walking without hurry but purposefully towards the far corner of the square. Just before she turned down a lane out of sight, she swept her hand through her mass of black hair.

*A*s he ranted, contorting and squeezing the muscles in his neck and shoulders in order to push every liquid ounce of available blood into his purple face, he wondered for a moment whether he was not in fact frightened. He certainly sounded it. His voice touched a high pitch of fury that could only be explained by fear. He saw that the assembled left-wraiths knew that. He watched them from behind his performance. And he watched his performance. He had practised it, then run it over in his mind for hours while the barge drifted down the river towards nightfall, so often and so thoroughly that it flowed from him now without effort. He was not frightened; but it was a measure of the quality of his performance that even he should doubt himself.

He had killed. He would kill again. In the mines below the mountain, after all, he killed every day. Stories began; why should they not end? To kill was to tell the story of another's end, nothing more. This did not trouble him. What is more, he was ready to accept his own end whenever it should come. He knew the common signs for which he should watch – the foreboding, the dwindling power, his own overreaching – and knew he would recognize them with pleasure when they appeared. That was as it should be. No, neither the thought of his own death nor that of anyone else troubled him.

But improvisation. Improvisation troubled him. What that wild knife of a right-wraith might do. Might have done. Surely by now he was dead.

He removed his thick woollen undercoat, hung it on the peg provided and began to unbutton the long cotton tunic he wore next to the skin of his arms. He always removed his tunic in the same manner, always noted that he did so, and always took pleasure in the observation. There were seven buttons, and thus several thousand distinct patterns in which he might attend to them. He had passed a great deal of time in his childhood experimenting with them until he found a sequence that pleased him. For his own reasons.

The skin of his arms was sacred to him. No hand but his mother's had ever touched it. She had been dead many years, but he still remembered her stroke sweeping over the downy light hairs of his arms, as if to start a story. With a single delicate motion he drew first one sleeve then the other down the length of his shoulder, past his elbow and at last off his forearm. The air in which he stood was freezing, and he watched with pleasure as the taut pores of his skin reacted to the suddenly dry, icy room. He closed his eyes and felt the stroke of cold passing down his arm to his wrist.

No body could refuse that stroke. It made no difference what was in the mind, what vain imaginations frothed there. The body was mechanical, an instrument of cause and effect. Lying, dying on the stone somewhere, his blood leaching out into the earth, draining his corpse of its latest warmth – that was what the great improviser himself would have felt: the slow stroke of a cold hand passing along his arms, touching him lightly at the wrists and letting him go. He could not have resisted it. He did not resist it.

The body was mechanical, an instrument of cause and effect. He smiled. It had taken two hundred wispers, another hundred wraiths, give or take a score, and the combined administrative might of the whole of the Bindery to do it, but he had done it: he had proven, and by experiment, that the much-vaunted imagination of a human child – the very bed and heart of what people naively called 'humanity' – was nothing more than a piece of clockwork. Flood it with sensations, and it would seem to flourish and create, for the play of imagination was nothing but the mechanical decay of past sensation – now remembered imperfectly, like images on a broken mirror, now dispersed, scattered, recombined and, in time, eventually lost. Deprive it of sensation, and the imagination would fail. Twist and batter it with ugliness, and it would grow deformed. Betray it utterly, and it would die, taking the whole body with it. The cold stroke of it, sweeping up the arm, which no one could resist.

The journey down the river from the mountain to the sea was also pleasingly mechanical, and told a story of gathering necessity. Ghast took the heavy blankets one by one from the chest of drawers where they had been laid out for him, and gathered them around his squat frame until he stood like a king in his robes, alone in the centre of the dark room. The bed waited before him, a great carved stead that had borne the weight of countless imaginers, cradle to their fantastic dreams. Grotesques and gargoyle faces, a seemingly endless trailing vine of floral exuberance mingled with human, animal and other forms, caught the scant gleams from the windows. He knew it would be a sacrilege for him to sleep in this place, to defile with his murdering arms a seat of so much fabled power. For a left-wraith to sleep in the bed of dreams.

He climbed into its hold. He knew he would not dream.

II

The Kermes Book

Kay climbed with clumsy, heavy feet into the back of the ancient sedan, squeezing into its spent springs as deeply as she could. She had been woken suddenly after a short, broken sleep, and now she fought her groggy head, trying to bring the whole situation back into focus. She knew it made sense. She knew she could pull it together.

Rex is dead. But Razzio will help us.

At first she couldn't remember why. Surely he had made a pact with Ghast, and would want to stop rather than help them.

But Will said Razzio would help us. To do something. And Razzio is in Rome. And so we will drive to the ferry. But why will Razzio help us, because surely —

At that moment the driver finally succeeded in starting the engine, which coughed and choked its way into a slow and gravelly rumble all around them. Phantastes had hired the car to drive them to Patras, where they could catch a ferry to Brindisi and drive the rest of the way to Rome. Kay put the thoughts together carefully as her vision finally snapped into place. Phantases had assured her that the driver would think the three of them were English tourists. 'It's not that they cannot see us at all,' he had explained; 'it's that they believe the stories we tell them.' The smell of diesel and the violent shaking roar of the engine made Kay wish she really were an English tourist and, like the other tourists, asleep in her bed. Will had almost to shout so that she could hear him. She was surprised to realize she must have been thinking aloud, because Will seemed to be answering her.

'It wasn't long ago, but you would have been absolutely right. Razzio still loathes Phantastes, that's for sure –' Phantastes turned pointedly towards the dark window beside him, and Will rolled his eyes with affectionate theatricality – 'but the partnership with Ghast hasn't quite turned out to be what Razzio expected. For one thing, he thought the festivals were going to continue, only he thought he –'

'He thought he was going to be First Wraith,' snarled Phantastes, turning back suddenly towards them. His hand on the edge of the seat was white with tension. 'Can you imagine? That pompous right-angled miscreant!'

He snorted as he turned back to the window, making a show of peering out into the dark. Will watched him looking through the window at the bare fields and rocky mounds and cliffs that, grey and blue in the near pitch of the night, passed in a nauseating weave. 'But that wasn't it,' he said softly so that only Kay could hear him. 'Razzio would have broken with Ghast anyway. He never intended otherwise.'

Just give me back my sister. That's the only place I want to go.
Kay dug the nails of her right hand into the back of her left.
Five nights.

The journey went on and on; for eight or nine hours Kay
alternately clutched her stomach and braced her aching back as
they swerved and sped up the coast road towards Patras. She
dozed, and when she woke she looked groggily out of her
window for the white road signs looming out of the darkness,
then vanishing behind them: FILIATRA, PYRGOS, AMALIADA.
Every time they turned or came idling to a crossroads, the
sedan rattled so violently that Kay's stomach quivered with the
motion, and she thought that they might see dawn from a
hard shoulder, facing westwards to the sea with a cold wind at
their backs. But then the driver would clap his flat palm
down on the dash and bark a few stern words, and as if in
response the engine would trim up and surge a little, and off
they would lurch again, leaving their stomachs several metres
behind them.

Somehow – after hours of swerving and speeding, rattling
and at times riding on little more than the wind at their backs –
as the long grey light before dawn rose, they pulled up at the
pier in Patras. Cold air rushed all over Kay's skin as she climbed
out of the car. Will said he would go to look for tickets, but
Kay couldn't follow; with the nausea still clutching at her
stomach, she forced herself to walk to the edge of the pier, away
from the waiting cars and buses, and stared at the dark water
where it lapped against the cement. Phantastes had followed

her, and now stood quietly beside her as she let the rhythm of the sea's ripples strike out a music without meaning.

'Kay,' he said. 'This may not be the right time, but there is something I want to ask you before we get to Rome, and to Razzio.'

She stared at the water. She had no appetite for sitting down or focusing her eyes. Phantastes seemed to want her to do both. Beyond the ferry, beyond the breakwater, lay mountains; she couldn't see them, but she knew they were there. The thought of them, of their height and their massy weight on the unseen horizon, gave her a sense of firmness. Her stomach turned, and began to settle.

She sat down on the bench Phantastes had offered her. Behind them lay the soft glow and hum of the small city, but before them a whole scape of darkness, furzed by a little mist off the water, lay thick but scattering, like the cloak a magician might wave over a trick, just before revealing its marvel.

'Look at that,' said Phantastes. 'Have you ever seen anything more beautiful?'

A few lights winked in the darkness beyond the breakwater – how far beyond, it was impossible to tell. At first Kay's eye was drawn to them, puzzling at the flatness of a view that, like a screen, jumbled all its treasures on a single plane. But when she let her gaze drift, she noticed the gathering contours – just suggestions for now, slight intimations of depth and colour – which would, she knew, in time throw forth mountains, oceans, skies, all composed of the widest sailing reaches. It was like seeing the oak in an acorn, or the sky in a drop of water hanging from a leaf.

'No,' Kay whispered in reply. 'It really is wonderful.'

'Sometimes the most compelling images are not the colourful images of great depth and full of matter, but the ones that conceal them. Look at this canvas of black – black-black, blue-black, green-black, star-black, sea-black, cloud-black, tree-black, mountain-black. We know these things are there, that they will shortly awaken, but for now they linger in different qualities of darkness, intense and potent. Before us, all you can see is the effacement of what should be – what will be, as the morning wears on – a gut-clutchingly awesome survey of mountains, forests, precipices, valleys, waves, tides and sky. What you see beyond the harbour now is a much more powerful thing. I look out on this water and see expectation, promise, as great a significance as I have witnessed. My looking, here, is a longing.'

'So the reality isn't as beautiful, then?' For no reason she could name, Kay felt almost annoyed by the way Phantastes was speaking.

'It is – but its beauty is of midday, and it is a beauty that cloys and stales because it is open. The beauty of night never fades because it is a beauty that has not yet shone, a beauty of hope, of expectation, of desire. Your first view of a midday beauty is always in this sense your last: it becomes familiar, commonplace, indifferent, and thus in time neither beautiful nor really a view at all.'

'But then a beautiful thing . . . must always be something you cannot have.' *I want to have it. Give me the day. Give me the day at home.*

Phantastes reached out in the dark and placed his open palm against the night before him, as if it were a windowpane. 'Too dear for our possessing. Yes, perhaps. But, Kay, do you also understand a different kind of beauty? Maybe I have been too hasty. The beauty of the familiar, of the known; the beauty of home and the fullness of light: these are the beauties of knowledge, and although they frighten me like a rock tomb closing in and cutting off my air, even I can see their power. These are the engines that drive plotting and all narrative – always cycling through the ungraspable present towards a possessable *then*, a time in the past or in the future that can be fixed and held, even owned. The left-wraiths, the plotters – there is a place for these beauties, and they hold them dear. But for me – the image, cloudily wrapped in all its potential meaning, the exalted mist of the present –'

He broke off. The water slapped gently against the pier a few feet below them.

'I am saying too much,' said Phantastes. 'I only mean that I was too hasty. Even imagining has its flaws.'

The grey woollen light had shifted while they spoke. It seemed to clear in patches, drawing away like separate veils, first from this swell on the water, then from that ridge of a distant mountain, first dimming that star, then illuminating that cloud. Kay let the illusions and misapprehensions tease her vision as she watched, imagining a grey form to be the near, hulking prow of a ship, only to be shown moments later that it was the far ridge of a hill. The still scene danced with revelations.

'What flaws?' she asked.

'An image cannot be both known and understood, both seen and grasped,' said Phantastes. He spoke slowly, as if carving his thoughts from a block of wood. Kay tried to listen on the edge of his knife. 'In the act of imagination we perceive, and perhaps admire; but to interpret, we must also destroy the image. This process happens in time, and partakes of narrative. And so you may say that the image is vital, that the image is immediate, that the image is present. But you must also say that the image is fleeting, insubstantial, unknown. The image is like the now. When is the present moment? Can you ever say, *It is now*? And yet we know that it is here, and that it means something real to talk about the present. So it is with the image: the moment you begin to be aware of the image, or of the perception, the imagination, it ceases to be that and becomes the interpretation of itself. So the image, along with the faculty of image-making – the imagination – suffers its own flaws.'

Phantastes was quiet for a moment or two, as if he were the surface of a water, and swells were passing through him.

'Child, take this and keep it with you.'

Kay put out her hand and took a little book. The moment it touched her hand, with a shock like electricity recognition seemed to rush along her arm, and in the dim light of the harbour it seemed that she saw and smelled the bright-hued leather, heard the rustling of the ancient pages.

'I know this book,' she said. The words shot out of her like a reflex. The volume Phantastes had handed her was small; almost small enough to fit comfortably into the palm of one hand. Its supple covers were stained a uniform deep red, and within, she knew, the once-white pages had yellowed. She held it in her hand, remembering, and allowed the obscure shadow of the harbour to conjure her memory of that morning the week before. The memory seemed to arise in the book, which was its source and its anchor, to transit through her, and then to issue from her, back into the book. She sat, darkly stunned, both seated on the bench beside Phantastes and not on it – suspended somewhere over that dark water.

'I was reading from it on our journey here, while you slept,' said Phantastes. He reached into one of the pockets of his robe and drew out a small torch. He handed it to her. 'Open it at the page I marked. I think it might interest you.'

Setting down the light for a moment, Kay opened the book carefully, with two hands, stretching with the even pressure of her fingers against the tight binding and the stiff, warped block of paper within. Although she thought she knew what to expect, she was surprised to find that, at the point near the back to which Phantastes' bookmark had directed her, the page – and several pages after it – were thickly covered in her father's cramped, heavily inked hand.

'Why don't you read it aloud, child?' said the wraith.

Kay took up the light and switched it on. Almost at once, as she began to read, she found she did not need it.

'*When Kay reached the top of the stairs and stepped across the threshold of the tiny room that perched above the front of the house, her father would be bent over his notebook, writing. The little desk, too cramped for his long, angular legs, might have*

236

bucked like a startled dog had he ever turned to welcome her, and upset the morning tea she set carefully by his elbow, just far enough away to be sure that no stray splash would blot his work. It wasn't that he was mean or impolite, she thought as she now climbed the stairs; he was just incurably busy, forever absorbed in one thing or another, and recently so much so that he had stopped eating with the rest of the family. Instead he took cold plates of food (when Kay remembered to bring them to him) alone in this makeshift study. Kay knocked gently on the door with her free hand, steadying the mug in her right as she drew slowly to a moment's halt. She pushed the door open.

'The hunched back within the tattered wool of its grey jumper was a greeting she knew well, and one she resented less than her mother did – most of all because she could plainly see, as almost anyone might, just how tense a greeting it was. She put her hand gently on the weary mass of muscle that was her father's right shoulder, and set the steaming tea under the desk lamp, the light of which – against the cold black panes of the window beyond – seemed to drink up its vapour. He said nothing, but then his pen was moving furiously across a line, and without doubt he was in the middle of a thought. For a moment she paused, all her weight poised on her forward knee, and tried to read the titles on the spines of the books piled since the previous night haphazardly across the cluttered workspace. A few of them were in scripts she couldn't recognize, much less read, and a number of others appeared to be the musty old volumes of Transactions of the Royal Archaeological Society that her father often collected from the University Library on his way home for the weekend. But *there was one book, sitting at her father's elbow, that she had never seen before. It was of a brushed and faded rose colour, not especially thick, and obviously very old. No writing at all appeared on the cover. Though it was a tiny book, it seemed nonetheless somehow broad and flat, but between two of the five raised bands that sectioned its spine, in gold capital letters appeared the simple title,* Imagining.

'"Katharine –"'

I can't keep reading this. I can't stop reading this. Dad.

'Kay started as her father looked up from his writing and raised his eyebrows at her. Quizzical, but not unkind. She realized that she was still leaning, now rather heavily, on his shoulder, and pivoted back against the nook created by a battered old filing cabinet that stood hunched against the desk. "Dad, is that a library book – the red one?"*

'Without a glance or a pause her father answered, "Library book – oh. Of a sort. No. I'm borrowing it from an old friend." He stared at her for a few moments from a metre away, apparently watching something that was going on at the back of her head. The way he appeared to look through her made her want to squirm.'*

Dad.

'"It's very beautiful," Kay said, awkwardly stealing a glance back at the book and hoping that she wouldn't have to meet her father's eyes again.*

'"Have you looked inside it, Katharine?" he said. His voice was even, and still very soft.*

'"No, of course not."*

'"Would you like to?"

'The immediacy of his offer almost took Kay's breath away. It was unusual enough for her to get any kind of reaction from her father, above all this early in the morning — so preoccupied, so immersed had he lately become in his study. Any kind of a conversation was extraordinary. But this staring, this genuine interest — she splayed the flats of her fingers uncomfortably against her hips while her father cleared a rough space before him on the desk. Then, with much more care, straightening up in his chair as if to stand, he carefully retrieved the rose-coloured volume. Using both hands, he squared it neatly before him, brushing his long middle fingers along its edges, almost with a flourish or a caress, as he laid it out. Now that the book was closer, Kay could appreciate how deep and rich the brushed red of its cover really was: it had a gathered intensity that made her think of the vital insides of things, and of vulnerability.

'"It's kermes," said her father. He spelled the word for her. "The red colour comes from a dye called kermes, made from the bodies of insects gathered from oak trees. Only the females are red, and only when they are pregnant. They look like tiny berries. Someone would have crushed the dried bodies into a powder, then boiled it in water to produce a dye, then steeped the leather in it. Once it was widely used, not only for binding books but for all kinds of dyeing and pigments. But today it is hardly known."

'Kay leaned over for a closer look, and ran her own finger across the surface of the book's cover, which she found to be much smoother than she had thought, and cool. "It really is beautiful," she said again. "What is the book about?"

'Kay's father leaned back in his creaking chair, took off his glasses and rubbed the back of his knuckles painfully across his wrinkled brow. In the indirect, raking light of the desk lamp the ridges on his face stood out in high relief, like one of the carved, square-set stone faces she sometimes glimpsed on the covers of his books. Replacing his glasses, he sighed and rested the fingertips of both hands upon the edge of the desk before him. He turned his head, looking her full in the face for a second time. His red and haggard eyes glistened even in the low light, and Kay thought suddenly that perhaps he had been sitting at the desk all night.

'"I think I had better show you," he said simply.

'As he prised the book open at its very centre, Kay was immediately surprised to discover that, though it was a delicate and exactly made little volume, bound with stiff leather boards, it was not a book but a manuscript, all written by hand. To the left, the yellow-worn paper was blank except for the faint image of ink bleeding through from the other side; but to the right, nearly the entire page was taken up with an ink drawing. A single unlidded eye stared out at her, drawn freely in heavy black pen, but somehow also with exacting detail. From its sides two brawny, gathering arms extended, each of which concluded in a muscular, outsized hand, the palm spread open. It was framed in a large square, within the enclosed border of which ran a linear pattern of entangled leaves. At the right foot of the page several words were written in the same ink, cursively, and in characters Kay was not certain she recognized.

'"Is this some sort of illustration?" she asked. "But what kind of story would have this in it?"

'"No, it's not a book of stories, Katharine," answered her father. He took up the earlier pages in his left hand and flicked slowly through a sheaf of them, allowing her to see that not just this but every page was covered with similar drawings. "It's a book of emblems – pictures. Each picture is something like a story, except instead of things happening one by one, in a picture like this everything happens at once. In order to understand it, you need to tell its story yourself."

'Kay liked stories, and the weird picture of the staring eye captivated her. "And those words at the bottom of the page – are those the titles of the pictures?" she asked, nearly putting her finger on the writing on the first of the pages, at the centre of the book, beneath the leaf-bordered frame.

'"Of a sort, yes. You won't be able to make out the words because they are in an old form of writing, and anyway not in English. But if I were to translate this one for you, I would say something like 'Seeing without seeing'."

'"I don't understand what that means," Kay said after a pause. "Either you see or you don't. You can't see and not see at the same time, can you?"

'"This particular picture means something, Katharine. Sometimes in order to see what really is, rather than what appears to be, it is necessary to look not with both eyes, but with one eye alone. Looking with two eyes may allow you to see depth and to obtain perspective on the world around you; but it also limits what you may see, precisely by making your view more precise. Sometimes, this picture suggests, you may see more by seeing less, and perhaps you may see in some profounder way by not seeing – in the normal sense – at all."

'"Why does the eye have hands?" Kay asked. "Does that mean something too?"

'"Right. It is with our hands that we make things, so the hands of this eye work as a symbol for a kind of creativity. This kind of seeing, you might say, is generative, creative, making. And the eye has no lid, perhaps because such making-seeing requires focus and concentration – you can never blink."

'Kay studied the shape of the handed eye for a moment. "Are all the drawings like this one?" she asked. "Do they all mean something? Are they all about seeing?"

'"They all mean something, yes, though some of them have meanings I don't understand, or think I don't understand. And no, not all of them are about seeing, though some are. This one –" he turned the page to reveal a drawing of the full moon hanging over a settling ocean – "also represents ways of looking. As the sea becomes still, the water provides a perfect reflection of the moon that illuminates it; the light of the moon is something that the sea beholds, something that the sea itself becomes, and also the very thing by which the two are joined – that is, the light. But it is only in stillness, in concentration, that this union of the watcher, the watched and the watching itself can all become one. And there are deeper meanings to this drawing, but I can only grope at them."

'"Deeper meanings?"

'"I think so. The words at the foot of this drawing I do not understand. They mean something like 'The eye and its double are one'. But there's a pun — that is, the words can mean something else, too, which is more like 'To accuse a friend is to forgive him'."

'The light outside the house was growing paler by the second, so much so that Kay could no longer see her own reflection in the once-black windowpanes before her. In the street a sudden whirring announced the morning's milk delivery. The little truck came to its soft-jolt stop, and sat back on its brakes with a gentle clinking of bottles. Her father stood by the window, looking into the gem-blue of the east. "And the star will show in the morn," he said under his breath. As if to himself.

'"What?"

'"Nothing." He suddenly appeared to have noticed the boy shuffling crates of bottles in the street below. "Is that the time —?" Hurrying to the desk again, he seized the little book of emblems, along with a couple of others, and began to cram them into his ragged rucksack. He fumbled with the straps, tightening them, then turned to Kay and tousled her hair, stuck for a moment, it seemed, for something to say.

'"You forgot your tea," Kay said.

'He smiled, but he didn't have time for tea.

'"Is your mum still angry?"

'"I think she just wants you to stick around for breakfast like other normal dads."

'He was silent for a moment, looking at a book on the desk beside him. He tapped his finger on it, so gently that his finger *didn't make a sound. "Kay, listen," he said. "I wish you didn't always have to be caught in the middle."*

'"I'm not."

'"I'm afraid this time you are."

'The two of them regarded one another for a few seconds. It seemed as long as anything a person might feel or know.

'"Kay, remember what I've shown you here, all right? Remember it as well as you remember anything." And then, as if he had reminded himself of a droll joke, he took up the mug carelessly and sloshed the tea down his throat. Kay almost laughed.

'"I'll see you later," he said. "Love you." He turned to go.

'From the door he turned back. "If you need me, you'll know where to find me. And tell your mother we'll always have Paris. It's a line from an old movie. One she likes."

'"She won't like that," said Kay.

'"No," he agreed. "But tell her anyway."

'And then he was gone. It was the twenty-fourth of December, and the first full day of the winter holiday.'

Kay closed the kermes book and set it on her lap, letting her hands spring away from it a little, as if it were something dangerous or precious. She sat very still and stared at the richly red brushed cover; at the way in which, despite its plainness, it seemed to create rich fields of intensity and depth, regions of hue that gathered and disappeared as quickly.

'Did my father give this book to you?'

'No, he borrowed it from me on the understanding that he would take care of it. It is one of my oldest paper books, and has not felt the touch of a pen in over five hundred years.'

'But he wrote this in it – I mean, this is his handwriting.'

'Yes, I recognized it, too.'

Out in the harbour one of the blinking lights turned out to have been a little boat all along. It didn't seem to be moving.

'This is what happened the morning he left – I mean, the morning he was taken. The morning Ghast took him. It was the last time we saw him at home.' Kay didn't dare to touch the book again. It was all so strange. 'Exactly what happened. It was only last week,' she added.

Phantastes answered instantly, but as if from a distance. 'I thought so. And I wondered then how it was that he could have composed such a history in these words, in this book. For Will recovered it for me from your father's study in your house not five hours later, and gave it to me in Alexandria.'

Kay didn't dare breathe but said instead simply, 'I don't know.' Suddenly she felt very tired again, as if her consciousness were a wave that had run high and splashing over a beach, but then receded into the sea as fast.

'A mystery, then,' Phantastes said. 'But I imagine you will have many powerful mysteries in your life; and so I think you should keep the book. It may be that this story will prove an emblem in its way, and grow to be a great imagining.'

'All right, you lot,' said Will with vigour behind them. 'I've got the tickets. Let's go.' Coming round the front of the bench, he brandished the ferry tickets in the air and smiled – but it was obvious that the smile was an effort, and his eyes seemed to be looking for something, or someone, not there.

Flip.

Will caught sight of the kermes book lying in Kay's lap. For a moment a knot seemed to pull tight across his face; and then he was off again, striding through the rising light, back towards the line of cars and buses that had begun to shift forward on to the gangway.

Kay looked at Phantastes.

'To accuse a friend is to forgive him,' said the old wraith. He didn't look convinced.

Kay shoved the book in her pocket, jumped to her feet and ran after Will.

Will barely spoke the whole journey, neither on the ferry nor, after they docked in Brindisi, when the car ran throttling off the gangway on to the endlessly straight Roman roads slicing across the heel of Italy. Again, Kay mingled dozing with watching the low, stubbled, finished fields, punctuated by the occasional austere majesty of a great pine or the low, leaf-bare olive and walnut groves. And again, as the early afternoon sun began to plummet westwards, she picked out the road signs and, in the failing light, the high towers and battlements of the ancient cities they passed: Taranto, Potenza, Salerno, Caserta. With a bleak attentiveness Will occasionally offered Kay dried fruit and cheese, sips from the large water flask, and something that tasted like very dark, unsweetened chocolate. Phantastes ignored them both, grim and squarely set – probably exhausted, Kay thought, and apprehensive about their destination. At the first signs for ROMA he bristled, and by the time the car was fully engulfed in the lights and activity of the city he was practically panting. He spoke to the driver in rapid, curt bursts, and after some frustrated exclamations and startling near-misses the car pulled through two massive stone pillars, down a wooded lane and, finally, across a wide expanse of perfect grass. The city had quite suddenly melted away, and the car pulled up in front of a massive, stately building all faced in white stone.

'Kay,' said Phantastes. A few minutes had passed, and they were standing on gravel beside an elegant stone staircase that led up to the building's grand entrance. The car had pulled away, crunching then clattering into the chilly evening. Phantastes stood under an orange lantern that lit the creases of his aged face with a rough, unforgiving rake. 'I want to show you something.' He dropped to a squat, holding out his hand. It, too, was etched with deep, crevassing lines; and the further it opened, the more distinct those lines became. The fluid movement of skin and muscle was mesmerizing. 'An open hand can be trusted. Don't forget that,' he said, gripping Kay's shoulder hard and meeting her gaze. 'Don't forget that in there.'

Kay stood with Will at the foot of the steps as Phantastes rang the bell. She looked at the house. The stairs and door were at the centre of a long range of windows across two storeys. She counted twenty-five on one side. Grand, palatial sashes, they all stood dark; their wooden trim, once painted, now cracked and peeled. In places the white stone of the facade had crumbled, and the more intently she peered through the thickening darkness, the more she picked out other occasional flaws: rough boards covering a dormer window in the attic, a gutter cracked and hanging from the eaves, a gap in the black iron railing that ran between the gravel court and the building. Around and above the door where Phantastes stood – growing impatient – an elegant covered porch was supported by dilapidated pillars, bounded by a black wrought-iron railing that ran on either side down the stairs, as much rust as metal. The steps themselves sagged with wear, and here and there weeds had pushed through cracks, though they seemed otherwise intact. After a night and a day of petrol fumes, lurching, swelling seas and nausea, the falling-down edifice looked just about the way Kay felt. *On the verge of hopeless.* She looked at the steps, and thought she might well find it impossible to climb them.

A short, bald, paunchy man in a black waistcoat and crumpled tie opened one side of the black, two-leaved door and wedged himself into the crack. He spoke to Phantastes in a soft Italian that barely carried on the mild air. Even from behind, the old wraith looked grim and set: the lines carved into the skin at the back of his neck seemed to underscore his determination to see this visit as a spiritual trial. Although his hands hung limply at his sides, his shoulders were square and rigid, and his eyes, Kay thought, would be piercing. The other man, by contrast, looked calm and unflappable, languid as if on the verge of sleep, as slow to rouse as the oil that seemed to suffuse his olive complexion, and entirely unconcerned by the sharp interjections fired at him by Phantastes. After one such caustic sally Phantastes simply stared at him; and the fat-cheeked, self-satisfied man – unmoved – refused to answer. He looked up without concern full into Phantastes' angry face, and Kay noticed with some admiration that he didn't blink once. Ten or fifteen seconds passed, after which, like a coil released, Phantastes simultaneously flung up his arm and threw himself at the door, battering it open just enough to sweep into the house behind the waistcoat – the waistcoat who didn't look behind him as the old wraith passed by, but rolled his eyes theatrically.

'*Che brutto*,' he announced, and frowned. Then, putting his hands together before him and inclining his head slightly as if about to pray, he turned to Will and Kay as they reached the top of the stairs, and said, smiling, '*Guglielmo, benvenuto*.' With a flourish he bowed, turned on his heel and strode back into the house, leaving the door, with its flaking paint, standing wide before them.

Dusk was gathering fast in the gravel court that lay before the house, and beneath evergreen trees to one side, pools of darkness among the boughs seemed to ripple outwards. But Kay would have taken any of those trees over the impenetrable gloom that waited beyond the threshold of the house before them. She stood stock-still.

'Kay,' said Will. His voice was soft. 'That book –'

'– is mine,' she said.

'It's strange,' Will offered.

Kay slipped her hand instinctively into her pocket, where the book lay wedged close to her thigh. She thought of her father's wisdom tooth, so many days before, and felt her own teeth set against her friend.

'Look after it,' Will said. 'That's all.' He gave Kay a wink and a twitch of his ears, picked up his sack and skipped lightly over the heavy sill of the doorway, the cares of the last few days lifted by this return, as Kay thought, to a treasured home. She watched him disappear into the dark hallway, and willed herself to pick up her feet and skip as he had done, to take on this new place, this new chance with hope and – what was that word Phantastes had used? *Resilient.*

Maybe this is his home, but it's not mine. Kay looked at the scratches on the backs of her hands. She had made them herself, all through the long night. Each line on her skin was a path to somewhere.

And then she saw that she had made two fists. *An open hand can be trusted.* She crossed the threshold and shut the tall, heavy door quietly behind her.

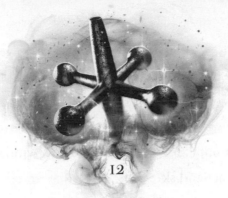

The House of the Two Modes

Kay stood in an ample lobby. Below her feet, stone mosaics in relentlessly geometrical patterns marched, turned and swirled through a muted riot of colour and shape. The walls rose steeply about her, high into a gloom above, from which descended a huge crystal chandelier – unlit and dusty, like the brittle body of a dead spider still dangling from the far corner of a ceiling. The walls Kay at first took to be blank expanses of smooth cream stone, but as her eyes adjusted to the interior light she saw that they, too, threw out texture and shape; etched arcs and circles, eddies and spirals that reminded her of the way Will's hands worked on the board, or in the air, whenever he was plotting.

Will and Phantastes had long since disappeared somewhere into the building beyond her – through one of three doors that led from the room, one in the centre of each of the walls that divided her from the inside of the house. She had stopped in the silent darkness, unsure of which door to take; and in that moment of catching her breath, catching at her own steps, in that moment Kay caught herself, and began to notice the loud and tumbling beauty that seemed to plot the space around her. The patterns on the floor and walls moved with such energy that at first she felt her own voice rising up in her throat, as if they called for an answer or would spur her into song. But then she felt something else instead as she noticed how the flow of movement, as it worked along the edges of the floor, of the walls, of the room, into the corners, held to its line, graced and flirted with the edge but never crossed it. All at once, like a sigh heaving over and coming to its long rest in her thought, Kay's stomach settled and she subsided into calm.

Maybe Will is right. Maybe this is *a kind of home.*

Kay turned to the right and approached the door. From the room behind it, through the cracks that ran around the frame, light was pushing its slender fingers into the lobby. She put her hand to the round brass knob. It turned easily. She pushed.

What lay behind the door immediately surprised her with its size and brilliance. Its scope. Like a grand salon from a fairy tale, it glittered with a luminosity that moments before she could not have imagined; from the high ceiling hung lamps of every kind, from simple round and visored bulbs, to shaded and cupboarded lanterns, to the grandest glass and iron chandeliers, every one shouldering its neighbour, each throwing out its shard or pool or shaft of brilliance, up and down, and all the lights rebounding and shooting around the walls, which were lined on three sides with what seemed like a hundred grand and gaudily grotesqued mirrors. Kay's eyes raced with the light, scattering and glancing from surface to surface, and it was several seconds before she realized that she still had the brass doorknob in her hand, that she was still standing in the entrance. She closed the door behind her, let her feet shuffle back up to it, and leaned against its solid reassurance while she tried to take in what lay before her.

Apart from the mirrors, and the great glass windows that dominated the right-hand wall, the room was nearly empty. An elaborate purple sofa, long and plush, stood in its centre, facing her, and beneath it lay a huge, vibrantly scarlet Persian rug. Elsewhere the floors were wooden. So were the two ornate, gleaming cupboards facing one another from opposite walls at the far end. Nothing moved but the light, and Kay suddenly realized that, for all the warm yellow glow bounding and rebounding in her eyes, the air was extraordinarily cold. Her arms crossed, rubbing her shoulders, she set off straight through the space towards a door in the far wall, and slipped through it.

The next room was much the same in shape: along the right wall a tier of stately windows towered aloft to the ceiling, where a cornice and cast friezes ran in white plaster against the corners; at the distant end of the room another matching door faced her, and in between, in all the inward vastness, there was very little. But this room was only dimly and intermittently lit, by a wood fire that roared in a huge grate to her left, and – beside it – by a tall, elegant standing lamp with three delicate shades shrouding three glowing bulbs. Beside the lamp stood a winged armchair, and to its left a low table, on which there lay a book. Along the walls there were three other tables, none of them very elaborate though all of marble; on one lay another book, on the second stood an earthen pitcher, and on the third was a woven basket full of ripe apples. Kay crossed the twenty paces to the apples, took one and held it up to her nose. It smelled distantly sweet. She bit into it, and found the flesh sharp, crisp and soaking with juice. While she chewed, she pictured this room from the outside of the house, counting down the windows, scaling it against the exterior.

There must be twelve of these rooms on either side of the front door, each alike.

Taking the apple, and neglecting now to close the doors behind her, she strode from room to high-ceilinged room, finding it exactly as she had thought – each the same shape, each decorated, although sparely, in a different way, making an entirely different impression on the senses. In one she found nothing but ten grand paintings hung in ornate gilt frames, and for a moment she thought perhaps she was in a museum. In the next she almost stumbled as she entered, tripping over dice – innumerable dice of every colour and size and material – strewn across the wooden floor in every direction. She picked her way through them, trying to dodge the thousands of paper butterflies strung from the ceiling on lightly elasticated cords, so airy and insubstantial that her very being caused them all to shiver and flutter, and the wind of her breath and her passing sent them gyrating and fluttering in rippling waves of chaos all around her. In the last of the twelve rooms – a corner room – the great windows stood to the right, and again on the far wall; she turned the offered corner, taking a door to her left, and continued resolutely on, passing through space after space, each one different, each one the same.

And then everything changed. As Kay opened the third or fourth door on this new row, the eager and intrepid spirit with which she had raced through the house, the wonder with which she had encountered its novelties and oddities, vanished. Before her, as the chiming of an antique clock tolled in her ears, sat an old wraith on a carved wooden throne – bulky, gnarled, taut; in places twisted, formidable and severe. Her hair, a blend of wax and ash, rushed around her face, drawing in the eye, drawing Kay to her as the door slipped softly on to its latch. Each of her knowing eyes lay nested in a dense tangle of creases and hatchwork, lines texturing her haggard, hard skin, but cutting deeper, too, as if her skin, her lips, her eyes, had been hewn from bone. She wore a simple grey robe that covered her long, folded body. Its hood lay massed behind her broad shoulders, and from its wide sleeves the wraith's tendons, clothed in rough amber skin flecked like a snake's with age, reached to grip the arms of the throne she sat on.

Kay found herself walking towards this wraith, this throne. This throne: the high arms tooled with hammered gold; ridges and veins of wood circled those of gold, and together they arced and darted into the forms of eyes, suns, snakes, arrows and swords. Kay, whose own eye was about level with one of these turned arms, felt her stomach give way a little as she caught sight of a gold sword cutting down through a mass of serpentine carving. Some thought was pressing at the back of her mind, but she had no time to attend to it, because she was too near, because the old woman suddenly leaned forward and, with both knotty but slender hands, took hold of Kay's head.

'Girl, do you know who I am?'

'You are one of the two modes,' Kay answered limply. *Whatever that even means.*

'Do you *know* who I am?' she repeated – only it was not a repetition, because this time Kay heard the question differently, in the same way that, if you lie quietly, listening to your regular heartbeat or a watch tick, you begin to hear a rhythm of stresses. The stresses were screaming in Kay's head.

What am I doing in this place?

'Yes.'

The old woman's eyes, staring down at Kay, never softened, but she let Kay's head drop and returned to her previous posture. With unhurried and deliberate gravity she laid her arms along the arms of the chair. In the long silence Kay shuffled backwards a little, all the while looking closely at those hands resting on the pommels; they reminded her of the hands of someone she had seen recently – but where? As she tried to think back over the confusion of the last days, her eyes drifted to the chair's inlaid carvings, and the two thoughts suddenly merged in her head.

'Oh,' she said aloud. 'Rex. You have the same hands, and the same symbol of a snake entwined with a sword.'

'You did not realize how much you knew,' said the mode. 'How much else do you know, without knowing that you know it?'

'I know a lot about how little I know,' Kay said. 'Especially when it comes to the last few days.'

All I want to know is what I'm supposed to do. All I want to know is how to get my family back. All I want to know is how to go home.

The old wraith said nothing. She was looking, Kay noticed, at her own hands. After a few moments her right hand crossed to her left, and she began, very self-consciously, to rub the large grey-blue veins standing proud behind the angular ridge of her knuckles. Kay thought of the scratches on her own hands, and hid them.

'Rex was my brother,' said the mode. Her voice lay as quiet in the room as a woven mat lies upon the floor, and as still. 'Rex and Oidos, twins in body, twins in thought, two children of the same heart, each the home of the other – till Ghast destroyed him.'

In the afternoon of a searing summer day the heat will sometimes hang thickest and most oppressively long after the sun has reached and passed its height. Here, Kay thought, was pain without glare, a long afternoon of sorrow.

'Has Phantastes been, then, to tell you about what happened?' Kay said, still timid before this enthroned old queen.

Oidos looked up from her hands to Kay's face. Her expression was almost kindly. 'No, child. Ghast destroyed Rex many years ago. What happened in Pylos we all foresaw: the inevitable roll of a distant thunder. But the crack that made that thunder, it is long gone. Ghast is shedding what he thinks is the corrupted blood of a diseased body. He hopes to purify the present by freeing it from the contamination of the past, enlarging it from the prison of its own history.' She stopped, and her right hand seemed to hover and draw like a magnet to cup Kay's cheek. 'I did not think you would be so beautiful, Katharine. Razzio and Ontos promised a pearl, but I think you have more of the diamond about you.'

Kay would have flushed at the praise had she not been so confused. First Will and Flip had thought her what it turned out, in her stead, Ell was – the author. It was Ell who would join the wraiths; *she* could not. But now Oidos was talking as if she mattered; and she wanted to matter, wanted it more than anything else she could think of.

Who am I?

But she didn't dare think about it.

'This is his room, you know.'

'His room?'

'Rex's room. Stand beside me, and see what I see.'

Kay took a place to the left of the high throne, and turned. Looking back towards the door through which she had entered, she saw a wall lined with statues: on the left, standing in the corner, a giant form cut from white marble – goat below, from the torso a rippling, towering man, his great beard parting on a godlike face, its roaring smile breaking like the sun from a storm. Rearing on his hind legs, with the two forward hoofs splayed as if readied for battle, he seemed at once startled, fierce, proud and potent. By his waist in his right hand he gripped a horn, carved with such delicacy and precision that it seemed for a second as if he might lift it to his lips and call them both to the hunt. Kay almost stepped back.

'Sylvanus,' said Oidos. 'The first form taken by the Primary Fury. In the early days of the Honourable Society, when the world was young and the Society's members combined in orgiastic mysteries under the pregnant moon, it was Sylvanus who heralded the beginning of our sacred rites. On his horn he blew the peal that razed the mind and dissolved the limits between us, the eternal dissonance that shivers and erodes all boundaries, flowing like excess itself across thought, feeling, person, perspective. In the hearing of that music, we came together as one; we were unified in a single chorus as elemental as the earth, as potent as the sea, quick as the flame and boundless as the air. Those were the days of blood ritual and sacrifice, when battles raced upon the face of the nations and stories were sung in the war-camps and in the mead-halls, when the bards were kings and their verses spun richer than gold.'

Kay shook, whether from fear or excitement she wasn't sure. The white marble form seemed not blank but imminent, as if it might instantly bloom with colour, burst into motion and plunge them back into its wooded, moonlit, violent world.

'Look again,' said Oidos, extending her right hand to point towards the door through which Kay had come.

Above it – again, carved in white stone – she saw another form, this one a form she knew. Standing not in the porter's uniform of black wool in which she had first met him, but in the long robe that Oidos herself now wore, his arms hanging not limp but ready at his sides, and his face not quite as old as she had known it, but right and still ruddy, square-set and solid like the trunk of a tree, it was Rex. In his right hand he carried a ring from which dangled a collection of keys; keys she recognized, each one a distinct shape — square, circular, triangular, with various tines and edges cut against their several shanks. She tried to study his face, the face in which the sculptor had captured him, but whether it was an effect of the white marble, or something true to his form and likeness, she found her eye incapable of lingering on his cheek, or nose, or mouth, but was drawn inexorably into his gaze, into the blank, white, wide portals of his eyes, as open and encompassing as the level stare into which Oidos had, moments before, also drawn her.

'The Wraith of Keys, my brother, Pyrexis,' murmured Oidos. There was no mistaking the grounded affection in her voice, that soft tenderness with which love reverently handles its beloved. 'Pyrexis, fury, the fever in which the horn is sounded, that like Joshua at the walls of Jericho bursts the doors from their frames and lays open every heart.'

'And the third statue?' Kay pointed to the right corner of the room, where what seemed to be another work in stone stood draped with a heavy white sheet.

'Sylvanus was the first form, Rex the second. The past stands behind and open to us, the present is the door through which we come and go, but the future remains shrouded in its own darkness. Time may or may not reveal what lies beneath that shroud. Rex himself never knew.'

'Did he come here?'

'Yes, my child. Here in the place of pure knowing, in the House of the Two Modes, all wraiths come to find themselves, to read their own story. This is Rex's room, and it was to this room that he often resorted for contemplation and for self-study.'

'And are these his things?' Kay turned, searching the room. In addition to the three statues, she saw – at the room's other end – a tall, elegant, circular table on which stood an hourglass, the sand heaped at its base, and a large but fine-toothed comb, carved perhaps of some kind of bone; beneath their feet a woven carpet covered most of the huge room, its dominant colours purple, blue, red and white, so that it pulsed in rich arteries of hue that burst, here and there, into pools of dense, throbbing intensity. It mesmerized the eye. There was the throne, and beside it a lamp. On the wall hung four large paintings, two to either side of a huge, empty hearth. On the mantel stood several small objects: a gilt book, an empty silver candlestick and a little ball about the size of Kay's fist, covered in a silver netting or lattice, within which, reflecting in the light, was what looked like pure gold.

'Each room in the place of pure knowing contains a collection of twenty objects and elements. Each wing of the house contains –'

'Twenty-five rooms, counting the lobby,' Kay said.

Oidos smiled. 'Very good, child. Very good. But in addition to the front of the house, there is another set of rooms in the rear. There is also another storey following the same plan, and a single room in the eaves.'

'So, for every one of these rooms, there are –' Kay mapped it in her mind, as if she were counting on her fingers – 'four other rooms, behind and above? So,' she said triumphantly, 'Razzio's house has a hundred and twenty-five rooms!'

'I think you turned a corner to reach me?'

Kay paused. She remembered the corner room. But –

'The House of the Two Modes is arranged in a square, child.'

Kay stepped sharply away from the throne, suddenly aware of the vastness of the palace around her.

But that's five hundred rooms. And if each room has twenty objects, then that's –

'Ten thousand things.'

A house of ten thousand things.

'And each one of these ten thousand things has its meaning, and those meanings hold the secret of a wraith's identity, or in most cases the identity of several wraiths – for many things have more than one meaning.'

Kay shook her head as if erasing everything from her mind. 'I didn't count twenty in this room,' she said. *I counted seventeen. Including the carpet.*

Kay met Oidos' eyes, and from within the deep, hard sadness of her face the wraith seemed to smile. She lifted one of her hands off the arm of her throne – Rex's throne – and from within her robe withdrew something and opened her palm.

Upon it were two minutely carved pieces of stone, almost as small as jewellery, but worked with such precision that Kay thought she would never tire of peering at them. Black as obsidian or the night, they gleamed in Oidos' open hand where they caught the light from above. One was a miniature sword, with a slender blade rising from a decorated, two-handed hilt.

The grip had been carved with such care that tiny lozenges reflecting the light seemed to spangle like diamonds, while the blade – though not more than a few centimetres long – bore a tiny cursive inscription. The second piece was a sort of double helix formed of two snakes writhing against one another, their bodies so intricately and flawlessly combined, so exact in every particular, that Kay felt tears start in her eyes. She knew without looking that the blade of the sword would slide easily and completely into the helical void around which the bodies of the snakes turned.

'They're so beautiful,' she said. 'Do they have a meaning?'

'There is nothing in this world that does not have a meaning, because everything in this world is either caused or causing.'

'Then what does it mean?' Kay pushed the sword in Oidos' palm, trying to make out the inscription against the light.

'As I have said, everything is either causing or caused: what you see as the blade of the sword is the space where you do not see the snake, while what you see as the snake is that which is revealed by the blade around which it twines. Both these things exist: the sword that signifies action, and the snake that signifies thought. But we would know nothing of one without the other.'

'So this symbol is about thoughts and actions? It means that you can't have one without the other?'

'It means that you cannot know one without the other. An action is defined by the thoughts that guide it and make sense of it; similarly, a thought is only expressed and made real by an action.'

'Why do only some of the wraiths carry things with this symbol? Rex had it on some keys, and Will and Flip had it when they took my father from his office. That woman in his rooms at St Nick's – she had it, too.'

'They all carry the badge of the left-wraiths because they are all left-wraiths. That is, they are all left-wraiths *now*.'

'You mean Will.'

'Yes, child. He was not always a left-wraith – or, to be more exact, he was not always treated as a left-wraith. Really he is no more a left-wraith than you –' Oidos broke off abruptly. The roots of Kay's hair suddenly burned, as if each of them were an ear straining after a distant voice. The old woman stroked her left hand again purposefully, and then went on. 'But, child, this is beside the point. Ask me the questions you have come to Rome to have answered.'

'I want to know how to find my father and my sister. I want us all to go home. Will you help me?'

Oidos closed her palm tightly over the black stone ornaments and stowed them inside her robe again. She grasped the arms of the throne and turned her head to face the door. Kay thought for a moment that the old wraith might now refuse to speak at all. But her face was not set, and her eyes looked not severe but pensive.

'You must go out into the garden,' said Oidos at last. 'You must be yourself, my daughter, before you can know yourself. Go out into the garden and, when you are ready, return, and I will help you.' With a great effort that was not frailty but, it seemed, exhaustion, she got to her feet and took Kay's hand.

Together they walked through the room, through the door, and another door, and another, until soon they stood in a lobby very like the one through which Kay had first entered the house. Here Oidos turned, leading Kay into the back, to another grand hall that opened through enormous glassed doors into the garden beyond. Kay glimpsed a vast court, paved in places with stone and cobbled paths, in other places covered with vines or grass. Wraiths swarmed everywhere.

'If you return, I will show you what you need to see,' said Oidos, putting her hand to the door that led to the garden. 'For you, too, have a room in the place of pure knowing.'

With those words she opened the door, and a wave of noise and life and exuberance and pleasure flooded into the room, so thick and warm and irresistible that Kay hardly needed Oidos' gentle push, but tumbled over the threshold into the garden, and spun and spun and spun in wonder at the tumult and pace and sudden overwhelming vitality that surrounded her. At first she had simply impressions: a glowing magnolia light, punctuated at swift intervals by a painfully brilliant beam of glaring white; a whirling of outsized motion, as if rhinoceroses were dancing all around her on roller skates; the hot, moist air, like the soggy humidity before a summer storm, billowing upon her face; a carnival noise of horns; and a soft pile beneath her feet which, looking down, she saw was grass.

She was still blinking and dumbfounded when a body slammed into her from the side, sending her stumbling. She might have fallen but for the arms that caught her in their warm embrace – half laughing, half apologetic, it was Will.

'What is this place?' Kay shouted back, drilling her eyes as seriously as she could directly into Will's chin.

He had been grinning like an oaf, and the words seemed to burst through his smile without making any impression on his face at all.

'The House of the Two Modes, Razzio's garden, the largest and most complex plotting board in the world, the place of pure being!' he said.

Kay could barely hear him over the cacophony. A column of trombonists snaking round from his right pushed their way directly between them. She flattened herself against the door and looked about while Will, suddenly transformed again, followed the musicians, shimmying along behind them. He couldn't stop laughing, and Kay found that she couldn't stop smiling, just to see it. Entirely wiped clean, at least for now, were all the hours of anguish and waiting, the long, groggy stretches in the Pylos pension, the everlasting night and day of the journey across Italy, with its weird moonlit shapes and surprising, nauseating bends. She felt the intensity of her conversation with Oidos slipping from her, too, like a shore retreating as her little boat started to toss on Atlantic swells. For a few minutes she drifted without purpose around the huge but inviting open garden, surfing its surges, taking it all in. Here, as a group of animatedly chattering men in long tails strolled out of her path, she happened upon a great oval fountain surrounded by a pool of shimmering water; just beyond it, her fingers still cool from the fountain's water, she nearly collided with a column of waitresses filing across the lawn bearing huge covered platters in hefted hands; yet further, a row of children sat on a row of chairs, gripping jacks in their hands as they watched the game of two older girls; there, further on, in among some bushes, a man reclined on a chaise longue, fantastically exotic birds perched all around him, singing to them in a melody of clicks and warbles. In one place she paused for some minutes just outside a circle of poorly dressed men and women who seemed, as they sat erect on the grass, to be debating some question to do with plotting boards; with delight Kay watched agile and expressive hands describe in the air the perturbations of their thoughts. In another place she found the trombones, no longer snaking but still belting out their brash lines in a huge and deafening horn section, itself only one part of an orchestra, apparently being led by a tall man atop a podium, his hands milling in the air. Will lay sprawled among the trumpets, his feet still tapping out the inescapable rhythms.

Kay crouched at his ear. 'Is that Razzio over there?' She pointed. 'The one leading the orchestra, I mean!'

Will goggled at her, then just shook his head wildly; but, seeing that this was only going to prompt her to further questions, he climbed to his feet and motioned for her to follow. Through the presses of people and the profusion of obstacles – tables, chairs, bushes and trees, more fountains, little grass huts, here and there a canal – Will led her purposefully until, drawing up under the shade of a trellised grape arbour, he ducked gracefully into a corner and sat lightly on a secluded bench. Kay sat beside him, taking in with relief the now muffled fanfares and muted roars of conversation, while she perched in the cool respite of the half-light. Will smiled and stretched out his arms and legs, then let it all flop and threw back his head. He wound in a long, expansive breath, and seemed to hold it for a moment.

'Now *that*,' he said in a gush, 'is what I call *being*.'

'Then what do you call *this*?' Kay asked, almost as a reflex, without consideration.

Will sat up, his eyes bright and alert. 'This?' He gestured around at the vines, the shadowy beams of wood and the cool brick walls. 'This is actual life.' With an arch flick of his eyebrows and the grin that had become, since their arrival, his new feature, he slumped back on to the bench and pulled his hood over his head, and then further over his face, while he began to hum contentedly. 'This is life, life, life,' he said again after a few bars.

Beyond the arbour, over the heads of scores of moving wraiths, Kay could still make out the elevated platform, covered by a sort of arched stone roof surmounted by a steeple, from which the single wraith seemed to be conducting the action of the garden as if, somehow, he controlled it. She watched him for a few moments while Will breathed deeply, inhaling the warm, social air around him. He was jittery, exhilarated, sharp. All of a sudden, Kay thought, he was behaving out of character. She almost didn't trust him. She almost felt abandoned. All around them, in the heavy, wet, cool air, the grapevines coursed up and down the trellises, climbing, hanging, reaching, performing delicate but muscular acts of balance and poise. Kay followed them through the shadow, picking out their interlaced strands and drawing with her eyes the routes from root to fruit again and again, as far as she could see. She braced herself.

'I thought we came here because we were going to try the integration again. You said Razzio had a huge plotting board, the biggest in the world, with wraiths moving instead of stones, and acres of grapevines . . .' Kay's voice trailed off as she suddenly realized where she was. She looked around, then down, expecting to see the lines of the board under her feet, there, in the arbour where they sat. 'Here,' she said, 'and out there, and all those wraiths out there, all of them –'

'Moving on the board!' Will said chirpily.

'But where are the lines?' Kay asked, almost of herself.

'Oh, they're all around you,' Will answered, again chirpily, from beneath his hood. 'But they're very small, and you have to know what you're looking for. Every blade of grass is part of the line, every pebble, every brick – and don't think Razzio's board is flat – no, it runs in every direction. In Razzio's garden, even time is laid on the grid, and every second is part of the line. To understand it, even to glimpse how you might understand it, you have to think of yourself as a spider that spins webs out of choices and hangs them between this, and this.' He held up his right hand, his index finger jammed against his thumb. 'But Razzio has the keenest eyes in the world, and he can't be outplotted.' Will sighed happily, and Kay almost thought he might start humming again. 'Which is why it's so relaxing being here,' he added after a moment. 'One doesn't bother even *trying*.'

Kay thought for a minute, hard. 'So you mean,' she asked, 'that we're on the board right now? And so our movements, and even the time we take to make them, mean something to Razzio?' *So you mean I'm some kind of pawn on a huge chessboard? That Razzio is playing me?*

'Yes.'

'How can that be?' She frowned. 'How can he know what we mean when we don't know ourselves?'

Will sat bolt upright, his eyes so wild that Kay regretted her question.

'That's just it,' he said merrily, spookily. 'That's just it. How else could he know what we meant, except at the moment when we least knew ourselves? Oh, I hadn't realized I was so *tired*!' he said, and settled back into his hooded slouch.

Kay waited another minute as she wondered what Will would do. It was a long, quiet minute, the more painfully silent for the pulsing crescendos of voices, music, and what sounded like footsteps that lapped like the ocean's waves against the shore of the arbour. Will slumped motionless but for the steady rise and fall of his chest. *How do I find them? How do I get home?* 'So you're not going to help me do this? You're not going to help me find Razzio?'

'Find him?' Will objected abruptly. 'We've already found him. He's the one who let you in. Or, I should say, the one who put you on the board.'

'You mean that butler person is Razzio?'

Will whinnied. 'The butler!'

Kay considered this for a while. She found herself slightly annoyed to have her expectations upset. 'Then who is that tall man directing the orchestra?'

Will sat up, pulled back his hood and faced her squarely. 'I'm sorry, Kay. I'm not being helpful. This is Razzio's house because everything that happens here means something to him. He *owns* this place. But that's all he does. You could hardly say he *lives* in it. Maybe if he lived in it, Phantastes wouldn't hate him so much. Everyone else – all the wraiths, all the causes, they *live* here – like us, they're on the board. That is, everyone else but two, and they are Razzio's closest advisers. Inside, somewhere, is Oidos – she –'

'I've met her,' said Kay. Her voice was flat. Will looked sharply at her, as if she had been bitten by a snake; but immediately his face softened.

'Good,' he said. 'Oidos dwells in the place of pure knowing. But in the place of pure being, on the platform just there –' he pointed to the place where Kay had just been watching the conductor – 'that's Ontos, the other of the two modes. He's not on the board. That is, he *is*, but he's fixed. He doesn't move. I don't think he has *ever* moved from that spot, at least not while Razzio was plotting. That is, he moves, but his motion is a reflection of the being that is all around him. It's not only the instruments that follow his lead; everything that is, does.'

'You mean he is conducting us?'

'Yes, exactly. Good. He's conducting us. And everyone else. And everything else. Or maybe they're all conducting him.'

Kay watched Ontos spin and dip, his arms swaying in repeated arcs in a motion contrary to that of his neck. His body undulated like a wave, at the same time rippling like the sudden accelerations that pulse through a murmuration of starlings. His slow dance, rhythmic, silent, was the most beautiful she had ever seen. She could hardly speak.

'It's mesmerizing,' she said.

'It is,' Will agreed. 'It's the purest form of plotting, a complete embodiment of everything we're doing on the board, and a reflection of it. In a way, you could say that everything Oidos knows, Ontos is. She keeps in the place of pure knowing a collection of things that record whatever you could know about the wraiths who walk on Razzio's board. But in the garden Ontos lives out that knowledge as body, as movement.'

Kay thought about this for a second. Her mind gave up.

'What does that mean?'

'He feels who we are,' said Will at last. 'What we're made of, where we're going, what we mean. I guess only he knows what it feels like. But I'm glad someone does.'

He feels what we're made of. Where we're going.

'Can I ask him? What where I'm going feels like?'

'Kay, you can't, it doesn't work like that –'

But Kay had already stood up.

As she approached the platform that bore the gyrating form of Ontos, his lean body reflecting so much sound, heat, light and movement, she could feel the pulse of the garden begin to rise within her own blood. Though it neither knelled nor beat like a sound, it rushed in her ears; it had no taste, but her mouth was full of it; she felt nothing but air against her skin and grass on her feet as she passed towards the dais, and yet that air seemed charged with a new pressure; and she closed her eyes against the smell and held her breath against the light, and, with what seemed like the last awareness in her consciousness, she knew that she had crossed the stretch of grass and was climbing the worn stone steps up to the platform.

After that there was neither after nor that. She had no sense of time, no fears, no regrets. Deep in a trance, she never knew how she stepped into the centre of the dais; she never saw Ontos bow to her, give way to her, withdraw from her and, retreating down the steps, take his place upon the grass; and she never felt the complex contortions through which her body moved as, for three hours and more, she danced to the causes in the garden of the House of the Two Modes, the centre of their being and the author of their movement.

13

War

'Kay. Kay.'

I am not Kay – I am not – I am –

'Kay. Wake up.'

Kay opened her eyes and saw only painful light. She squeezed them shut again and noticed that she had swivelled her head violently to the side.

'Let her sleep, Will.'

Phantastes. Will. What am I doing?

'She's been through an ordeal,' the old imaginer said.

Kay opened her eyes again, determined to see the light.

'Hello in there,' said Will. He was smiling very near her face in an encouraging way. Kay felt grass beneath her hand where it lay beside her, but her head was resting on some sort of cushion or pillow, and there was a blanket drawn close around her shoulders.

You are always with me when I'm lost.

'You gave us a fright,' Will said. Kay recognized that she was lying on the ground, and that Will was lying next to her, looking into her eyes.

How long have I been asleep? How long, how long –

'How long –?'

'Overnight. About nine hours. But you haven't been asleep the whole time.'

'That is an understatement,' said Phantastes. Kay saw that he was sitting at a large stone table a few metres away. He was watching her intently. He looked concerned.

'Do you remember anything at all from . . . before?'

At Will's words a hole seemed to open up in the world and Kay began to fall through miles of air. Her body lurched out of her control and her arm shot out to grab Will's – anything to hold, anything to give her purchase in this world, anything to ground her in the sunlight, on the grass.

Help me.

'It's okay,' he said. He was soothing her. 'I've got you. Maybe don't think too hard about it. Let it in slowly.'

As if she were peering round a corner or blinking against a bright light, Kay allowed herself to glimpse in snatches what she could remember of the preceding night: the conversation with Will in the arbour, the sudden resolution to talk to Ontos, striding across the grass towards the platform, and then – which was strange, like a dream – a feeling of seeing or having seen many things at once – things that didn't so much happen in order, but because of one another. And among it all there was a strong sense of movement, of her own body turning in on itself, like a flower with petals growing and blooming not out towards the sun, but inwards into the stem of herself, as if she were all the light and the bud were opening into its own middle,

275

its own core. And round that corner like planets in a ridiculous jig spun so many perceptions that it tired and dizzied her now to try to see them – the way it hurts deep between the eyes when you try to read the signs on a station platform while the train is passing by at high speed.

'Do you remember anything?' Will asked.

With effort, Kay sat up. 'What happened?'

Will had scrambled to crouch beside her, and with a strong hand placed gently on her left shoulder he kneaded reassurance into it.

'You occupied the place of pure knowing,' he said. 'It's as simple as that.'

'It's as unprecedented as that,' said Phantastes.

'What Phantastes means is, Ontos has never allowed another wraith to take his place on the platform,' said Will. 'To be honest, we didn't think it was possible. We didn't know what would happen. And you – we don't even know who you are, really.'

In the pit of her stomach Kay felt a strange twisting of pride and nausea.

'For three hours, pretty much exactly, you moved on the platform just as Ontos might have done – but it was completely different from Ontos, too. When Ontos moves, everyone and everything moves around him as normal, as if he is just its mirror. But when you stood up there last night – every wraith in the garden, every cause, seemed to turn inwards. No one spoke, no one acknowledged one another. It was as if they had all become entirely engrossed in themselves.'

276

Will was silent. His eyes, which had been on the grass as he traced the blades with his finger, looked up at her. 'Do you know why? What made you fall into a trance? What did it feel like to you? Do you remember?'

Kay breathed in deeply. She closed her eyes and let her head rock back on to her shoulders. *Nothing.* She lifted her face up to the morning sky, feeling the sun pushing bright and warm through her eyelids.

'I remember just one moment,' she said. 'It seemed like a long moment, like a dream. In that moment I looked into Ontos' eyes. It seemed like I was looking into deep, phosphorescing pools. And in the same moment I felt like two hundred arrows being shot from a single bow in two hundred different directions. Two hundred arrows that pierced through two hundred different people, and I was in them all, sticking in them all. It was awful.'

I remember your eyes well enough.

Kay could feel tears, hot ones, starting in the inner corners of her own eyes.

'And all the arrows – every arrow drove right into the stomach, right into the navel of one of the causes. But they weren't arrows. They were shards of something like glass or mirror, and they were cords – something that tied all of us to one another – and I felt this incredible pain tearing out of me, as if everything in me were heaving to get out, as if I were going to be turned inside out, and –'

'Kay,' said Will. His hand tightened on her shoulder. 'You don't have to remember.'

I remember your eyes well enough.

Kay stopped, and opened her eyes, and looked at Will, and at Phantastes. Beyond them, twenty metres away, the causes were milling about in the garden, waking, drifting, chatting. She saw Razzio in his waistcoat standing among them, stealing glances at the three of them at the table. He looked preoccupied and nervous.

'The worst thing about it was that, even though it was a terrible pain, a tearing pain, I wanted it. Even though I hated it. Because it wasn't just pain. It was joy, too. And they were both there, pain and joy, at war inside me.'

Pushing himself towards her, Will leaned in and wrapped her in a warm hug. He swayed them from side to side in a slow pattern like a tall tree in a distant breeze.

'Will, what does it mean?'

Because his head was almost resting on her head, Kay could feel the words in his throat, the deep vibrations that she knew were true. 'You went to Ontos with that question, the question about what you are doing, what you should be doing, what your purpose feels like. You shot that question out in hundreds of different directions last night. Even I felt it. Every cause on the board turned within, as if they were all staring at themselves, as if they were all suddenly intensely curious about their own being. For a long moment, for hours, they all seemed –' he paused, and breathed – 'self-conscious.'

'In a way,' said Phantastes, 'you might say you asked your question of every wraith in the garden. Every one of them mirrored it. Every one of them was tied to you.'

Kay pushed Will's arms away in frustration. 'And what was the answer? What did they do?'

'They slept, Kay, like you. After a while they all lay down wherever they were, and they were silent and still, as if they were dead. And they slept.'

So it was all for nothing. All that pain. All that awful joy. All that pushing and all that connection. All that war for nothing.

And now the tears began to gather in Kay's eyes so fast that she had no time even to sob. And Will rocked her back and forth, his side by her side not so much a comfort but a deep ground and well of sorrow from which she drew bucket after bucket of tears, drawing and pouring, pouring and again drawing, in a continual motion that felt easier than anything she had ever done in her life.

'Whatever is in you, Kay, let it out now,' said Will.

'But what if there is nothing in me at all?'

'What indeed.'

It was a bark like that of a dog: short, peremptory, fierce, the menace before a fight.

It came from Razzio. He stood behind the great stone table at which Phantastes was seated. From where Kay was sitting on the grass, he seemed despite his size to tower above it, and the turret of that tower was contempt. The sneer on his face seemed to bite into her eyes when she looked at him: aggressive, bitter, and yet revolted.

'As if you were the victim,' he said. 'As if any of this concerned you. That you should dare even to think so.' He spat on the table.

'Razzio –' Will put out one of his arms in a vain effort to plot away the old left-wraith's anger, to ward him off with the swirl of his fingers.

Razzio made a fist and held it up before his face. He stared at it as it tightened. He seemed to be striving to crush his own fingers. Kay felt everything in her body and her mind withdrawing from his awful fury – everything but her eyes, which remained fixed, nailed to that tightening fist.

He slammed it down on the stone, making a crunching sound that Kay knew was not the table giving way before skin and bone, but skin and bone compressing and breaking on the unyielding surface of the table. She expected Razzio to shout or cry out, but his face remained stubbornly impassive. He seemed more curious about his hand than pained by it. Like the rest of them, stunned and paralysed, he stood regarding the broken tissue of his fist where it lay before him.

'This is how it should be,' he said quietly – quietly, but his voice was still a thin thread of rage. 'It should be like this. There are bounds. There are impassable limits. A plotter cannot plot without these securities.' Behind him the causes had ceased drifting. Around the garden they stood still and expectant.

Razzio drew himself up to his stout tallest. He held up his right fist then, with his left hand, finger by finger, prised it apart. It was already starting to show a bruise along the inside edge of the palm, and unfolding it seemed to take all his concentration, as if he were meditating on the pain it caused him. Kay felt Will's own hand on her shoulder as a stay against Razzio's fury. Her tears were drying on her face; she could feel them hardening, pursing together the skin of her cheeks in the fresh, cool air of the winter's morning.

Razzio stood still, regarding his hand. He looked at the table before him. With another sudden burst of energy he laid his arm on the edge of the table, then dragged it in an arc right across it. A few plates, several glasses and a candlestick, a book and some clothing fell to the ground, some of it shattering. He seemed neither to notice nor to care. Phantastes had pushed himself back to avoid the sweep of Razzio's arm; now they stared at one another.

'I am angry,' said Razzio.

'We can see that,' said Phantastes.

'I make no apology for my anger.' Razzio took a seat opposite Phantastes, and with his left hand smoothed the creases and crumples in his clothing. 'Sit at the table, all of you,' he said. He did not look at them. Nor did he wait for them to take their places before he began to speak.

'I have watched your approach to the House of the Two Modes. I have watched it with growing disquiet. Ghast had no business interfering with the girl, the author; she ought to have come here, where she might have found her room in the place of pure knowing. Ghast should not have attacked you in Alexandria, and the murder of our brother, Pyrexis, is a crime that will never be blotted from our story. By the stone,' he said, 'that pocky mank-wraith has gone too far. I may not have been a friend to the right-wraiths –' here he looked pointedly at Phantastes – 'indeed, I may never be a friend to the right-wraiths, but even *I* can see that we must return the Society to cohesion, to unity. Had you seen what I have seen on the board many times lately, you might not even have risked coming here.'

Razzio turned to Phantastes and addressed him directly. 'My most ancient antagonist, we have not spoken, even by our seconds, for many centuries. You have suffered a terrible reversal of fortune, caused in no small part by my own ambition for primacy in the assembly. I do not hesitate to acknowledge my part in this. I cannot think what grief it must be to you to be robbed of your temple, to suffer daily the loss of that immortal flower that was the root of your art and function. Had I been deprived of the board, I should surely have lost my mind; though its loss is by its very nature the one chance I cannot, with any kind of plotting, forecast. Indeed, this single blind spot in my art has for many years been the subject of my most intense speculation.' Here he turned, and focused eyes of such deep and penetrating incision on Kay that she almost squirmed beneath them. 'I think you know how Ghast conspired to dissolve the Society of Wraiths and Phantasms and to lead the wraiths out of Bithynia into exile. You may have learned something of my own regrettable part in the swelling of this ulcerous boil that now grows to such a head and crust. But there is one thing you cannot know, one thing that all the stories in the world cannot narrate, that even the dreams of the last imaginer of the timeless temple of Alexandria cannot picture, because even I myself could not see it, and still cannot. All I can see is that it has a great deal to do with you, our new young friend.'

Razzio closed his eyes and folded his hands across his stomach. Kay, by contrast, sat up in her chair, her eyes glistening like those of a cat on the hunt.

'I must tell you what has happened here. I am not a great storyteller. You must bear with me.'

Kay saw the quick glance Will shot Phantastes, but Phantastes, with his eyes closed, took no notice.

'The plots have always changed for as long as the board has been. The wraiths drift and dance about the garden, Ontos conducts them and I gather up from him, from them and from the places of pure knowing an estimation of things. This estimation is never the same, because the world beyond the board is never the same. Sometimes Ontos dances intricately and with the most minute articulations of fingers and eyes; then I must spend hours roaming through the rooms of pure knowing, and Oidos opens a thousand drawers before I can resolve the plot, which is long, difficult and involved. Sometimes, by contrast, the wraiths in the garden slouch and are silent, and Ontos hardly moves at all; then I sit with Oidos on one of the great thrones, and we watch the light drift by hours across the bare walls of a stately room. On other days I must run – I do, I must run – through the places of pure knowing, frantically searching for the signs that will connect and interpret the motions of the wraiths in the garden. Once I sat for a week with a piece of blank paper in my hand, while all the while Ontos slept. But even then a plot emerged from the causes, the dance of forms, the places of pure knowing; a plot *always* emerges.

'Two months ago this changed. I was walking through the garden in the morning, as I always do, taking note of the positions of each of the wraiths – every one of them a cause that plots an entity on the board. You know roughly how it works: instead of stones on a board I read people and things in the garden, setting them in play and then watching their movements day by day. All the things interact in some way with Ontos, even if only by ignoring him and his conducting; and from observing him I can also judge the mode of the movement – is it happy? Sad? Optimistic? Made in fear? In love? Then I know what the movement is, and its mood; taking this in to Oidos, I place the fact and the mode, by certain clues collected in the garden, against one or more of the ten thousand things she preserves in the place of pure knowing. From the union of movement, mood and knowledge, understanding arises; and these understandings present themselves as narratives. Century after century I have studied Ontos in the evening, walked the garden in the morning and passed the afternoon in the house of the ten thousand things. Always the day yields up its journey. Always I take to my bed its insight.

'Two months ago, while walking in the garden, I observed something strange. On the grass near the dais one of the causes lay asleep. This in itself was not unusual – many wraiths sleep in the garden. Some sleep *only* in the garden. But this wraith was sleeping at a time when Ontos himself was writhing with acrobatic intensity. Every other wraith in the garden was surging with unbounded energy. Nor did this wraith awake the day after, or the day after that. Indeed, it was not *just* a sleep, but something deeper. And since that day, another twenty-three causes have, without obvious explanation, slipped into the same coma. Each time I have watched them. Each time I have removed them to a prepared infirmary inside. Each time I have tended them carefully, trying to keep them alive. If one should die – what would that mean for the board? How could I understand the *disappearance of a cause?*'

While Razzio was speaking, one of the causes had put fruit on the table. Will had a grape between the fingers of his right hand. Again and again he was raising it a few centimetres above his plate; again and again he was dropping it. Kay stared at the grape while Razzio gathered his thoughts.

'You must understand the importance of this event. I cannot finish my plotting; instead of reaching an understanding, I am left in ignorance. This is quite unprecedented, quite unlike anything that has ever happened before.'

His eyes still closed and his hands still folded loosely across his stomach, Razzio reclined in silence in his chair. The other two wraiths said nothing. Kay looked back and forth from one face to the other, but they were both blank. She sat up and put her hands on the table.

'Where are these causes going? And why does it matter if –?' She stopped, realizing that what she had been about to say would probably offend Razzio. 'I mean, what will happen if you can't plot?'

What has this to do with me?

No one answered. The three wraiths sat in complete stillness, just as they had before. Nothing happened. Kay reached forward and took some grapes; one by one she plucked them off, put them in her mouth, chewed them and swallowed them. She put her hands in her lap. She put her hands on the edge of the chair behind her back. It was no use. Every moment passed like a sentence beginning with the same word and, no matter what she did, the moment ended and began again, and ended and began again, the same. She didn't notice the tension in her arms and legs until she was almost ready to scream.

'You know what this means,' said Will softly.

'The end of beauty,' Phantastes whispered.

Kay slammed a flat palm down on the stone table. It hardly made a sound. She didn't raise her head, but she knew that they were all looking at her, and that they all knew exactly what she wanted. Will pushed back his chair, and Kay could sense out of the corner of her eye that he was carefully turning to face her. As she waited for him, she noticed that, where her hand had curled on the table, her knuckles had turned white.

I've seen that before. I make no apology for my anger.

'Plotters work with boards, Kay,' he said. 'The boards are of a certain size. We move the stones around the boards, watching the patterns. Our hands think through the narratives of things as they guide and are guided by the stones. But always the stones stay on the board and the narratives are, as we say, conserved. If stones could fall off the board or come on to the board from nowhere, the plotting could not function. For that reason, there is nothing a plotter fears more than the edge of the board; nothing a plotter guards more carefully than the security of the stones. Causes must generate effects, and effects derive from causes; a cause without an effect or an effect without a cause would break the principle of conservation, and would undermine the plot.

286

'The greatest stories flirt with the edge, and become great exactly because of this flirtation. They skirt it, needle it, always toying with the loss of a cause or with the spontaneous effect; but the art of the greatest storytellers lies in the surprise of conservation, in the delight of an expectation dashed, only to be fulfilled. It may be a simple rule, but it is a rule.

'One of our most ancient stories is that of return. A man goes away, then comes back. At home perhaps he leaves a wife and a child. Think that this man goes off to war, and that the war eats up ten years of his life. Think that his journey home is thwarted. Call him Odysseus. Imagine his wife, Penelope, sitting beside their bed every night of those ten years, then another ten, expecting his return. Down the stairs, through two or three strong stone-framed doors, see her child, Telemachus, being carried out of the hall by his nurse. Penelope is followed from the room by the taunts and jeers of a hundred drunken and violent men, her suitors – no better than vultures circling the carcass of her broken marriage, men aspiring to seize the throne of her kingdom in Ithaka, men spending the wealth of Odysseus' royal house. They are impatient. See the snarling, the sharp-toothed smiles behind their grimy beards, when they demand of Penelope every morning, *How long – how long must we wait for your decision? How long until you forget the return of your husband, until you give up your expectation that he will return?* She despairs. By night she lies undreaming and rigid in her bed, wishing that, should she fall asleep, this Odysseus, this man, this cause, would return by morning, would deliver her from her despair. She ruses: she weaves a shroud for her husband's father and promises the suitors that she will choose one among them to be her new husband, that she will forget Odysseus, once the shroud has been completed. By day she weaves this, her forgetting; by night, in place of her anxious despair, she unravels the threads, remembering. Ravel, unravel, ravel, unravel; forget, recall, forget, recall. Meanwhile, on the sea Odysseus is making for home. Always beyond the shore of Ithaka, though he may come to a stall, he never comes to a stop. She may weave and weave; but always she recalls. The edge between forgetting and recalling, between weaving and unravelling, becomes a habit for Penelope; for landlorn Odysseus the edge between hurry and delay becomes a habit and, in the long years of his wandering, his nature. The story begins to look as if it will go on forever, and there is a night, as Penelope cries herself to sleep, when she recognizes this comfort with the edge as despair. She lies along it all night like a knife.'

Kay found herself holding her temples hard, with her eyes squeezed shut. She was thinking of her mother: alone, frightened, anxious. 'Make the story end,' she said weakly. 'Make it end.'

Razzio stood up abruptly, pushing his chair back violently across the cobbles. 'Oh, but it *has* ended, child,' he said. His voice was suddenly as stern as iron once more. 'It ended yesterday when you climbed on to the dais and all twenty-four wraiths woke from their slumbers at a stroke. In a single instant they opened their eyes. In a single motion they rose from their beds and filed into the garden. Behold them now,' he said, gesturing with his bruised hand in a wide arc around him. Looking up, Kay realized with a shock that the twenty-four wraiths had quietly and without ceremony circled the table, and now stood watching them. Their faces were entirely blank. 'I *demand* an explanation,' said Razzio.

Kay was stunned. They all were.

'But there is no explanation that you can give me, because this is not your story. You know as little about it as you know about yourself and, by the stone, that's little enough. This is not your story; it is my story. It is my story, and I will no longer sit idly by and watch Ghast presume to meddle with it.

'I have been working here in my garden for several years on a particular project. It is a great endeavour, the most difficult task I have ever set myself. There are many kinds of story, as we all know. We know their sources, their characteristics. We know how to evolve them. In the Weave, at the Feast of the Twelve Nights, together we composed stories of many kinds – dream visions, great epics, tales of love and friendship, quests, myths, great landscapes of exploration and conquest, stories of battles, of self-discovery, stories of perseverance, hope and survival, stories of despair, loss and defeat. But the methods by which we made our stories were imperfect, and even if they resulted in a great profusion of stories, they never resulted in perfect ones. As long as I have been in the Honourable Society, we have never told the *perfect* story. Always there was room for improvement. Always there was a need to keep going.

'For the last several years I have been toiling almost without rest to create the most perfect stories that can be, one of every type: a story of love, a story of conquest, a story of discovery, and so on. I have set in motion among the causes ideas and actions of such beauty and precision that their every least quirk and oddity has been a revelation. We have discovered and made much in this time. In the last few months I have neared the completion of my goal. To Ghast I sent the fruits of my labours, for we had a bargain. From him I expected advancement – I do not shame to say it. In return for these blueprints, the instruction manuals for building the greatest stories ever to be told, he promised that I should be elevated, that I should be made first among the twelve knights. We have not held a Weave in many years, but now we shall never require one again; I have created a method for composing stories better than any such quarrelsome, noisy congregation could produce.'

Beside her, Will had turned white as a sheet.

'But Ghast did not honour his bargain with me,' said Razzio. 'I sent my writings to the mountain, where I understood he was testing them. This was not my concern. But he did not respect them. He hired *editors*. They *changed* my stories. The jewels I had cut were hammered and smashed. The fine details of my brushwork were scrubbed down and washed away. In that rank and rat-infested rubbish tip he calls the Bindery, these editors dragged thick pens across my genius – for *money*! And to crown his betrayal, having sold my life's work to hucksters for nothing but dirty coin, Ghast, a *clerk* – that squat dwarf with more warts than words – presumed to launch his barge for Bithynia.'

Razzio was now standing before the table, his hands splayed on its surface in a way that, given the purple bruise seeping up towards his wrist, made Kay wince.

'*For Bithynia*. Ghast will not be king in Bithynia. I will not see the mysteries of my art cut into scraps and greased for loose change by a pack of scavenging jackals. This is a war, and I will win it.'

Kay glanced at the twenty-four wraiths that surrounded them. They seemed suddenly menacing, too close, their eyes too blank, the hands at their sides too strong. Beyond them the other causes stood equally immobile and expectant, all eyes – hundreds of eyes – turned towards Razzio. Everyone in the garden except for the three of them – Will, Phantastes and Kay herself – appeared to be *ready* for something.

'What will you do?' Kay asked.

'I will leave the House of the Two Modes for the mountain,' said Razzio. He said it directly to her. 'Ontos, Oidos and all the causes will go with me. We will occupy the mountain, possess it and fortify it. I do not doubt that the left-wraiths will swarm to us. And when the right-wraiths see that I oppose Ghast, well, they will choose any alternative to his ignorant brutality.'

Kay's mind stuttered and whirled.

Ell. Dad. Home.

'You were supposed to help me,' she said. 'I came here so that you could help me.'

'But this was never your story,' Razzio told her. 'It is *my* story. Overnight I issued my instructions. In a few hours the causes will ready a hundred balloons, and we will launch from the garden at dawn tomorrow. You are welcome to return to the mountain with us,' he said to Will and Phantastes.

He looked at Kay. His eyes bored into her heart. 'You are not.'
Will stood up. 'Razzio –'

He hardly needed to make a gesture. Four of the causes stepped forward, two taking up places on either side of Will, and two on either side of Phantastes. Kay sprang out of her chair like a startled cat, expecting to feel hands around her arms, her shoulders, expecting to be lifted or bound. But no one touched her.

'As I say, the First Wraith and the last of the imaginers are both welcome to return with us to the mountain,' said Razzio. 'So welcome that I think I must insist.'

Kay ran. Folding her body low, she threw herself like a rock between the legs of the causes that blocked her way, spinning through their arms, then tearing past the scattered clumps of wraiths who seemed – but too late, arm after arm – to think they should stop her. She ran for the doors, for any door, any way of slipping into the place of pure knowing. Dodging benches, shrubs and water, half flying across the cobbles and the grass, and at last sprinting round the piles of sailcloth and instruments that Razzio's minions had begun to pile by the garden walls, she flew at the nearest of the great glass doors. She turned the handle, with a huge heave forced it open, and crushed herself through the tiny gap. From room to room she sprinted, through door after door, her only thought to lay down as much distance and confusion behind her as she possibly could.

You lied to me. You all lied to me. All of you.

The great empty rooms through which she ran seemed to hold the sound of her cries long after she was gone.

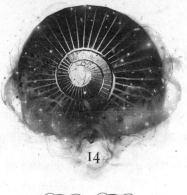

14

The Tomb

K ay had come to rest on a little bed in a garret room, squeezed in under the eaves in a tight wedge where the bed's end met the sloping ceiling. Here she crouched, listening – listening for the sound of a footfall, for the sound of voices, for the sound of any human noise. She longed to be rescued, but felt sure that she would either cower or run if she heard someone coming. Outside, the sky had slid from grey midday into a long and increasingly murky afternoon, and from her corner she now sensed with anxiety the onset of night.

How will I find my way back in the dark?

She thought of the narrow, circular stairwell up which she had raced, taking two stone steps at a time until her thighs burned with the effort. She hadn't seen any lights on the stairs, nor did there appear to be a switch or a bulb anywhere in this room. On one side a dormer window looked out across the green lawns by which they had approached the day before; standing opposite, another dormer window surveyed the garden below. Kay had resisted the urge to look out of this window.

Back to what?

She watched the vague light drift, wondering which of the wraiths called this shabby, dim room home. Apart from the single bed that stood in its corner, all it contained was a long, low table at its very centre on which were laid seventeen large, sharp, fixed-blade knives and a long coil of heavy pitched rope.

From her pocket Kay retrieved the little red book, and read again and again the passage written in her father's hand. She felt she was looking for something, but she wasn't sure what.

When at last she heard footsteps approaching up the stairs several doors down the corridor, she wasn't sure what her nerves were telling her. Maybe it was Will or Phantastes – the tread was light but careful, as of someone looking about him. But maybe it was one of the causes, sent to comb the place of pure knowing until they found and retrieved her. Kay thought about hiding under the bed. With a knife. She pictured herself running.

Instead, she sat up. Oidos stopped at the door, looking at her. Gaunt but strong, her regal figure seemed to occupy the whole frame.

'You have met Katalepsis, I think,' she said. 'Strange that, of all the rooms, you should choose hers. And this is only hers. No other wraith or phantasm comes here.'

'One of the knives is missing,' said Kay, pointing to the table where there was a gap.

'Yes,' said Oidos. 'I noticed it was gone almost at once, last time she was here. That was several years ago. I suppose she wanted me to be prepared. Perhaps she wanted to apologize. As

I told you yesterday, Rex's death was only the distant thunder made by a stroke long past.'

Kay pulled up her knees and put her arms around them.

'Ask me for the answer you most desire,' said Oidos. 'I will tell you.'

'You told me,' said Kay, 'that I, too, had a room in the place of pure knowing. Take me there.'

'Yes, child, I will. I cannot promise that you will like what you find. Follow me.'

Oidos moved with deliberate evenness across the room and out through the far door. Kay waited and waited, listening to her tread pass on and almost out of hearing before she leaped to the floor, jammed the red book back in her pocket and sprinted after her. From room to room she raced, and round one of the corners. Oidos was waiting at the stairwell door.

'We haven't got much time before the light fails completely,' said the old wraith. 'My footing is not what it was. You go first.'

Kay stepped before Oidos into the stairwell and started down. Much of the descent they took in complete darkness; only occasionally did an open door throw a luminous square of light upon the grey stone slabs. Down the centre of the circular staircase a vertical column of stone dropped; the steps followed round in a tight ring, the walls seeming to close ever nearer upon them as they went deeper and deeper into the building. Kay thought she counted three floors, but still they climbed down. The air began to feel wet upon her skin, and the darkness hung impenetrable between her hands and face.

'You noticed yesterday,' said Oidos from above her as they trudged slowly down, 'that something was missing from Rex's room, didn't you?'

Kay said that she had.

'Sometimes,' said Oidos, 'I move things in the place of pure knowing. I have my reasons. It is here, child. There is a sill and a door. Turn to the right and you will find an iron ring.'

Kay felt for the huge iron ring – as wide and heavy as a shackle. She grasped it in both hands and turned it, and the solid door creaked off its latch. Oidos leaned over her and pushed it open with a strong arm, her foot braced on the step behind. The air beyond was as cold as earth, and smelled musty.

'Sometimes I move things. And sometimes, very occasionally, I find it necessary to forget things. There should be a lantern on the other side of the room, child.'

Kay had stepped down off the stone sill into the dark room. She had no idea how large it was, but she could sense the ceiling low above her, and the sound of Oidos' voice seemed to hit near walls, and be absorbed by them. She felt before her face for a table, for a lantern.

What am I, then? What does my room contain? It contains a lantern.

'This is where I bring things that I want to forget,' said Oidos. Kay spun round so fast that she lost her balance. She was falling as she heard the door move. 'I am sorry, child, but now I must forget you.'

The heavy door swung on its hinges, and its latch dropped into place. Kay was on the earthen floor. She could feel dirt under her fingers.

There is no room for me after all.

She knew there was no point in crawling to the door. There would be no handle on this side. She crawled over anyway, and ran her hands up and down the broad oak. There was no handle on this side.

Down on her knees again, Kay turned so that her back was against the door. In the utter darkness she pushed off on to her hands and knees and crawled slowly across the floor.

She said there was a lantern. Let there be a lantern.

After a few minutes of tentative shifting on the damp, gritty surface of the floor, she crushed the tips of her fingers against a stone wall. It had texture, ridges running across it, up it, in arcs and lines. As her hands explored its carved patterns, she tried — and failed — to visualize it. Slowly she rose to her feet, terrified that she might hit something with her head, all the time following the wall with her hands, sweeping them in ever greater circles, taking in the rich pattern and flow of the worked stone.

And then her hands hit a ledge. On the ledge was a lantern. Beside it lay a box of matches.

On her third attempt Kay struck a match. It lasted long enough for her to see the wick of the oil lamp inside a glass dome. In the darkness she removed the glass and set it down. She struggled with the matches, managed to light another, and somehow fumbled the lantern alight. She found that it stood in a little niche carved into the rock wall. She lifted the lantern by its handle and turned round.

She was not in a room at all. Before her, about three metres away, was the oak door through which she had come. It had been shut firmly behind her, and now made a perfect seal with the stone. There was no handle on the inside – not even a keyhole. Kay knew it was pointless to worry at it, pointless to pound on it, pointless to think any further about it. Oidos had forgotten her. She turned to the left.

Before her, as far as her eye could see, stretched a narrow passage. It seemed to slope slightly downwards, but otherwise ran perfectly straight. The walls that bounded it to either side had been roughly carved with geometrical patterns, much like those she had seen the day before on the walls of the place of pure knowing. These carvings started just above the floor and reached well over Kay's head; above them, the passage arched roughly, little more than a hewn tunnel. For the moment Kay avoided thinking about the carvings; first she wanted to know where the passage led. The blood was pounding in her temples and neck. She held the lantern before her face and began to walk.

After about twenty paces she noticed a little recessed alcove on the right. It had been roughly bricked up, using pale, heavy square stones and thick globs of mortar. Kay pushed at the bricks, but they were firm. She kept walking. She passed four more alcoves of the same kind, two to either side, all four bricked up in the same way. Now she could see an end to the passage ahead, where a simple, roughly chiselled wall, all grey stone and dirt, faced her. It was slick with moisture, and as she approached it she began to smell soft earth, the stench of decay. She almost turned back.

Now what?

But as she got closer, she found that the wall was not the tunnel's end but a corner; turning left, she found the ruins of another doorway, this one framed all in stone; hanging to one side on rusted iron hinges, rotten hunks of wood were all that was left of the once-thick door. As Kay picked her way through the gap, something about the smell of the rot touched her with fear, and in the close quiet of the tunnel she suddenly had the sensation that she wasn't alone. Spinning round, she knocked the lantern against the door frame, cracking the glass. The flame sputtered, but kept burning. Kay called out, throwing her voice beyond the near glow of the light, back round the corner, hoping to hear . . . what?

Hoping to hear wraiths scraping their knees on roof tiles.

She took a deep breath. Bringing the lantern close to her chest this time, feeling its heat warm and comfortable on her shirt, she turned back to the only way forward.

No sooner had she done so than she gasped in shock. Her stomach rose into her mouth, and she nearly dropped the lantern. This passage, like the other, was marked at intervals with bricked-up alcoves. But around them both walls, all of white marble almost from floor to ceiling, had been deeply carved in exact relief with incredible intricacy – and the scenes were so lifelike in their animated, flowing shapes that she thought the forms, like straining gargoyles, might rip shrieking out of their stillness into live motion. On one side – the left – human figures processed down the passage, leading animals and, further on, other people bound in chains towards a distant altar. Kay paced down the straight passage, taking it all in, holding the lamp high to catch the full sweep of it: the gravity and seriousness of the cloaked figures, and the terror and anger of the captives and beasts; the columns of people, the swaying trees, the distant hills; and everywhere she looked, no children, no laughter, no lovers, no sign of speech. Notwithstanding the hard, dull grain of the stone, when you looked closely at any one of the shackled faces, you could see the passion cut with minute detail, as if the walls were not walls but the shrunken and petrified remains of a real procession, of real priests and their sacrificial victims. At the end of the passage the carved scenes culminated in a massive altar, stone within stone, supporting the weight of a grim-faced, limb-stiff victim lying sprawled across its surface, awaiting the knife. But then Kay saw something else, as if the stone image before her had flickered, or her eyes had changed depth – and suddenly it was not a victim splayed on an altar but Ontos lolling on his dais, so lifelike that she half expected the form to turn and stare at her; and below him the altar itself, the dais, began to turn and whorl so that it lifted off its base like a great stone flower, and in the unsteady lamplight seemed almost to rise continuously before her eyes.

With a sick heave of her gut Kay thought of the hours she had spent on that platform the night before. *I lay on that altar. I am*

300

going to die here. I am going to die. She reeled, feeling sick, with Phantastes' sceptical warning pounding in her ears – *An open hand can be trusted.* But his eyes were saying, *Don't trust them, Kay; Kay, don't give your heart to a closed fist.* As her head swam, she found herself leaning against the rock at the far end of the passage, breathing hard. Beads of sweat stood out on her forehead, and her body hung from her hands where they gripped the stone. *Why? Why of all the places in the world am I here?* Her mind staggered across the events of the last few days – the balloon, the Quarries, Alexandria, Pylos, Rome – with all the faces and questions, the anger of Ghast, Flip's gentle steel, Will and his childlike, open-handed yearning, the library, the tree of Byblos, Rex's blood silent on stone. And never, no matter where they went, no matter what they did, no matter whom they met, they were never one step closer to Ell, or their father, never one step closer to their mother's lonely tears. *This has all been for nothing. This has all been for nothing. Nothing at all.*

She stared down between her hands. With a start she realized that she had set the lantern on the floor and was leaning on an altar, a real altar, her hands upon the place of sacrifice, dyed with the blood of how many victims she could not imagine. She would have torn her hands away in revulsion had she not been paralysed, turned to very stone herself. Her heart began to spasm, chiselling in her chest with heavy, blunt force.

How many victims – how many times – and I am the last – and this is my tomb –

Like the crack that breaks the dam, that little word released a torrent of recognitions. For suddenly Kay saw that this passage *was* a tomb, and an ancient one, built to the same pattern as the passage tombs to which their father had dragged them, all over Ireland, a few summers before. Low-ceilinged, long, carved – and at what must be the western end, the altar. *Mum. What nightmare is this?* She swayed there, shaking for a long while, squeezing her eyes shut against the tears. At her feet the discarded lamp sputtered again, but again did not quite go out.

When at last she opened her dark eyes, she was almost surprised to find everything still the same. The passage narrowed towards the western end, closing round the back of the altar, and as her vision cleared she found she was barely inches from the north wall – this one immediately different from the one along which she had earlier crawled in fear. The first thing she noticed was that here the lines were softer, and not so acutely chiselled into the stone. As her head cleared, she stepped back, picked up the lamp and began to take in this other scene. The figures it showed were all leaving the temple now, the empty altar behind them free of blood, the heavy cloaks and shackles thrown away somewhere out of sight. With every pace back towards the door, the faces cheered and grew merrier: first the brows lifted and the cheeks bulged and dimpled, then the ears lay back and the corners of the mouths turned up, then the eyes seemed to sparkle and the nostrils flared above rows of gappy white teeth – teeth that caught sparks of mica in the stone and seemed in the lamplight to flash with joy. Hands were joined and raised in the air, arms clapped backs, and one group even formed a ring, circling feverishly as they dunked one of their number with jocund mercilessness in a vat of half-pressed grapes. With a start Kay recognized the long hair and elegant, boned knuckles that gripped the edge of the vat as those of Oidos.

Conservation. Sure. It was all leading up to this. It was all leading up to this, and this is nothing. No Dad, no Mum, no Eloise. And no me.

Kay thought that she had never been truly at the end until now. Of course the others would look for her. Of course they would go to Oidos and to Razzio and press them for answers. But Kay knew how rigid and silent those two wraiths could be; getting answers from them would take time. Kay had always made promises to herself. Her promises generally took a negative form: *I will never . . . I will not . . .* This time, she thought, she would make another kind of promise. *If I get out of this place, if I can just get away, I will go home. I promise myself that I will go home, and I will take my family with me. Nothing will stop me.*

She sat heavily on the floor, sliding down against the wall, scraping what felt like chunks from the skin over her spine. She hardly cared.

I don't need a spine any more anyway.

Her lantern began to flicker. Kay was looking at it and tapping the tank at its base when one of the square stones in the alcove in front of her began to move.

She didn't notice getting to her feet. She noticed being on them, crouching, holding the wall. She noticed the sweat that stood suddenly on her hairline. She noticed the light flickering, and she willed it to be steady, willed it to last.

And she noticed the stone, edging slowly forward, a metre away. She drew a pace closer.

With sudden force the stone lurched forward out of the wall and crunched to the ground beneath. It toppled over, one of its squared corners hitting the carving on the far side of the passage, chipping it. Kay took no notice. She was staring at the black hole left in the bricked wall of the alcove, through which the head of an iron staff had – only for a moment – protruded.

An iron staff topped by a snake writhing to the hilt of a sword.

I've seen that before.

And then the lantern gave out. In the heavy cloth of dark that was left her, Kay began to shout in inarticulate syllables. It felt as if the dark were forcing its way into her mouth in big wads and pads, stifling her attempts to form words. She was terrified, drowning in dark. Her lungs tore at the air, both trying and failing to take it in. After a few seconds, still panting, she clawed at the stone wall, at the grouted alcove, cramming her face against the stones, trying to listen. There was nothing. Every muscle in her body seemed to be wrapped around a nerve, and she was squeezing them all like a fist. She screamed again, this time calling out for help, calling out for rescue. Again she listened, and again she heard only her own breath and, as that faded, silence – that hum just above true silence that she knew was only the noise of her own skin, her own ears.

Why would you do that? Why would you leave me? Who would do such a thing?

In the dark Kay reached for the fallen stone. With both hands she hefted it into her lap where she sat in the void, her back to the stone wall, and cradled it as if it were her child and she its mother.

Hours might have passed. Kay's body grew cold, her joints stiff. Her fingers where she gripped the heavy stone and her leg where its weight pressed into her flesh had long since become numb. She hadn't cried; her cheeks were as dry as her throat. She felt neither hunger nor thirst. She felt nothing so acute as loneliness. All she knew, as the time of emptiness fell on her like a shadow in the night, was her own awareness of a slow loss of sensation.

Eloise. Mum. Dad. Eloise. Mum. Dad. Eloise. Mum. Dad.

The names circled in her head with a rhythm that had become her only time, her only space, her only sensation. She had heard other children talking about how your life passes before your eyes at the moment of your death. *It's not true*, she thought.

What do they know? The names pass over your tongue.

And then only the names were left. *Eloise. Mum. Dad.*

She didn't notice the footsteps when they first approached. She hadn't been listening for them. She hadn't been listening for anything. It was only after they had come and were drawing away again that she suddenly realized – like a body startled out of death – what she had very nearly missed.

The footsteps were passing on the other side of the wall.

Frantic, she scrabbled to her feet, turned and put her face to the aperture, screaming all the while for help, for rescue, for help and rescue, for anything, for those feet to return. She screamed so loudly and for so long that she couldn't hear the voice answering her from beyond the wall. Her wildly working mouth had forced her eyes shut, or she might have seen the glow of another lantern, and might have seen, too – rather than felt – the hand reaching towards her through the gap in the wall.

'Kay,' said the hand. It hadn't tried to grab her. Its flat palm – firm, facing downwards – had called for silence. 'Kay, stand back.'

She stood back. After a few seconds something very hard hit the stones from behind. Then it hit them again, and again. They shook. And again. The mortar between them started to shake loose, and then the stones seemed to buckle. A bulge formed in the wall as, kick upon kick, it started to give way. At last, with a crunching and a crumpling sound, the whole wall tumbled into a heap in the passage before her. Light pooled against the white walls of the passage.

After a few more seconds, a long leg swung out through the gap. Kay rushed to the opening. Attached to the leg was Flip.

And then, at last, at long last, the sobs came.

15

Sacrifice

Flip allowed Kay to cry for a few minutes. They sat beside one another on the pile of stones, Flip holding one of her hands with both his, as if he were holding a butterfly or a breath of air. Kay knew he was eager to get away, to climb back through the hole – but he said nothing at all, only looked at her hand and, when she sobbed, raised his eyebrows at each gasp, as if to acknowledge, as if to honour it.

'Kay,' he said when her sobs had run out, 'we need to go.'

As they climbed back through the rubble of the broken wall, Flip carefully guiding Kay's steps over the loose stones, he tried to explain what had happened to him on that day at Pylos: how he had sat by the sea through the day and night, soaked and shivering, anguished by Phantastes' accusation, worried about Will's safety; how he had wandered back through the square at dawn, and happened as if by chance on the spot where Rex had died; how he had stood there, looking at the stone ground without a thought in his head, until by the first light of day he had noticed something curious.

'With his blood, Kay, Rex had written on the stones. He must have used his finger. Maybe it was the last thing he ever did. The writing wasn't neat, but it was unmistakable. I stared at it for hours, trying to decide what it meant.'

Flip had picked up his lantern. They were walking very slowly down a low, narrow passage. This tunnel had nothing like the ample proportions of the other, nor did it show any decoration at all. Flip nearly had to crouch in order to protect his head and shoulders from the rough rock above. But Kay noticed that he was watching the floor of the passage all the time, studying it as they passed.

'What did it say?'

'He wrote a word in Greek. *Taphoi*. Of course it would be in Greek. Obviously. We were in Greece. But it's also what we call this place.'

'The House of the Two Modes?'

'No. These tunnels. The catacombs. The place of burial.'

'Why do you call them that?'

Flip had stopped before one of the alcoves, and was pressing his fingers along the grooves between the mortared stones. Now he looked at her sharply. 'Don't you know what this place is?'

Kay just looked back at him. Without another word Flip passed her the lantern and crouched on the tunnel floor. In the sand and powder of the passage he drew a square with his finger, and then, through it, a cross, bisecting the sides of the square at their midpoints. Around them both he drew a circle; its circumference touched the corners of the square and the ends of the cross, binding the whole.

'The square is the House of the Two Modes,' said Kay.

'Yes,' said Flip. He looked up. 'And beneath it are the catacombs: two passages at right angles running under the garden, and a huge ring around the whole structure. The catacombs, containing the tombs of the members of the Honourable Society. When wraiths and phantasms die, when they are killed, this is where we bury them.'

Kay almost dropped the lantern. Instead she held it with both hands. It shook. Every tiny hair on her body felt like a worm, and the worms were crawling all over her.

'Can you die?'

Flip put his hand on Kay's elbow as if to steady it. 'Of course. My body can die and, when it does, it will be buried here. But, with luck, Philip R. T. Gibbet, Knight of Bithynia – he will live right on. In some other form, in some other time, some other Philip will arrive at the House of the Two Modes, and find the right room – it's on the first floor, in the northwest corner, where the sun shines on the sundial in the afternoon, and the tables are strewn with dazzling knots. But my body will lie down here, interred and peaceful, until the last story has been told.

'When I saw what Rex had written, at first I thought he wanted me to bring his body here. That is, of course he did – any wraith would have wanted that. *I* would want it. But something made me pause, and I sat there for hours thinking it over. Rex would have known we'd try to bring his body here, anyway. To write that word on the ground at that particular moment – it was for something else. Why did he suddenly need to tell us about this place at the moment of his death? What had he learned? From whom?'

'Kat,' said Kay. 'She was the last wraith he saw.'

'Exactly. Kat must have told him something. And then she drove a knife into him.'

Flip had gone on, and they were walking again – slowly. Kay held the lantern as high as she could while Flip studied the floor of the passage. Minute after minute, they carried their little light through the darkness. To Kay, every footfall seemed like the last, every bit of tunnel face, every stretch of rough pebbled floor the same. To left and right, at intervals, they passed the stone-block alcoves; at each of these Flip paused to touch his fingers to the mortar, shook his head, then moved silently on.

'It's no good,' he said finally, and stopped. 'I've been through this tunnel ten times, and I've not seen a single trace anywhere.'

When he looked at her, Kay held his gaze. In his eyes, in the deep points of his pupils, she saw his focus and intensity; in the bruised and slightly sunken skin below his eyes she read the sleeplessness of the last few days, his lonely journey from Pylos, the desperation of his search.

For what?

'Flip,' said Kay. She said his name slowly. 'What are you looking for?'

He held out his hand, flat as a leaf, palm towards the ground. On the back, between the knuckles, there rested a single jack. Its metal arms caught the yellow light from the lantern, and glistened.

Kay made a sound. It came out of her throat. It was in her mouth. Her tongue made it and her lips shaped it. But it was not a human sound. Her whole body retched. After several seconds she sucked in air, fast, and started speaking words, fast, before she knew what they were.

'That's Ell's jack. She gave it to Rex. In the Pitt. The building – Dad's work. That night. Christmas Eve –'

'It must have been in Rex's hand when he died,' Flip said. His voice was as gentle as his hand was still. 'Kay, I thought you were down here looking for her, too. But you're not, are you? Why are you down here in the catacombs, Kay?'

'Oidos locked me in.'

In a single motion, Flip tossed the jack into the air behind Kay's head, clutched her shoulder with his right hand, snatched the jack with his left, sank to his knees and folded her into an embrace as sure as anything she had ever felt in her life.

'You poor child. I'm sorry,' he said. 'I'm so sorry. I had no idea. I never thought that – I never thought.'

With sudden decision he pushed Kay away. His eyes were lanterns in the lantern light.

'This is very important,' he said. 'What did Oidos say when she brought you down here? Did she say anything at all?'

Kay tried to remember the staircase – how excited she had been, sure that she would find out who she was and what she was meant to do.

She didn't say anything.

'She said I had to go first, because her legs weren't what they were.'

'Kay, think. Nothing else?'

She didn't say anything except –

'She said she had a place where, very occasionally, she brought things she wanted to forget. And she said she would have to forget me. And she shut the door.'

Just saying it made the tears start again in Kay's eyes.

The darkness. The terror.

Flip took no notice. 'I've been so stupid,' he said. 'I've been looking down here, in completely the wrong place. I assumed all along that it was Razzio, that it was Ghast, that they wanted Ell dispersed. Come on, Kay – run!'

Down passage after passage, back the way they had come, Flip led her, doubled over and loping as fast as his strides could take him in the cramped and narrow space. The lantern flickered and swung wildly behind as Kay raced after him, throwing exaggerated shapes along the rough walls as they passed. At the rockfall that led into the white tunnel Flip stopped and leaned for a moment to catch his breath. He set the lantern on the passage floor.

'It was Oidos all along. Don't judge her, Kay – don't judge her for this. The bond between them was so strong. She can't face a future without Rex in it. She can't bring herself to look under that shroud, as I did. As Rex often did.'

Kay's sides were splitting with the strain of the sprint. But her head was clear, and she knew exactly which shroud Flip had in mind. *The shrouded figure standing in the corner. The future that Oidos will not see.* 'Why? What's under the shroud?'

'You mean you didn't look? The third form of the Primary Fury. Eloise Worth-More, the Wraith of Jacks.' Flip picked up the lantern and began to climb through the opening. 'Watch your footing.'

He didn't wait for her. He took the passage with long, urgent strides, the lantern held at arm's length before him. His eyes scrutinized every inch of the ground, and when he drew up alongside the last of the alcoves, hard by the end of the passage with its white stone altar, he whistled between his teeth. As Kay drew up beside him, he was tracing his finger along the carved white stone above the vaulted shape of the stone wall.

'She's added this. Oidos. Look.'

Where his fingers touched the surface Kay saw three asterisks that had been rudely hammered into the stone by an unsteady hand.

'Did she give you a lantern?'

Kay nodded.

'She wanted you to find your sister. I don't think Kat killed Rex that day in Pylos, Kay. Whatever that means. I think Kat told Rex that Eloise was here, in the House of the Two Modes, and then I think Rex sacrificed himself.'

'But why would he do that?'

'Because your sister has a part to play in whatever is coming, and he knew it. It was time for her story.' Now Flip was running his fingers along the wet mortar, looking for a place where the gap was wide enough.

'My fingers are too big,' he said. 'You'll have to do it.'

As fast as she could, Kay thrust her fingers into the narrow gaps between the stones, picking and sliding and dredging out the wet mortar in thick slabs. It fell to the floor as she worked her fingers in and out along each row. Little by little the stones shifted and settled. At length a tiny gap opened at the top. Without waiting to be asked, Flip started working the top stone free, prising and pulling it, straining the tips of his fingers into the space. His face was as hard, as flat as the stone on which he worked. Kay stood back, impatient and desperate.

Flip had shimmied the first stone several centimetres from the wall. Now he dragged it out, allowing it to fall to the floor between his legs.

As he shook the pain from his fingers, still staring at the work to be done, he said, 'Oidos is angry with him. With Rex. For leaving her. But she never wanted to hurt your sister. She wanted you to find her.'

One by one he pulled out the square-cut stones: six, then seven, dragging them out of the wall so that they toppled over one another and away from his legs. Finally the gap was large enough for Kay to peer inside, and with Flip's help she scrambled up and over the wall, to drop into the tight space beside her sister, where she lay on a white stone slab.

Her chest was rising and falling in long, peaceful swells.

She was wrapped in a heavy wool blanket. On her stomach lay a silver horn.

By the time Flip had pulled away the rest of the stones, Kay was sitting next to the stone bed, holding Ell's hand in her lap, caressing it.

'She won't wake up,' she said. 'Why won't she wake up?'

Flip nodded behind him. Kay looked. Across the passage, in the chiselled white stone, the scene showed a sleeping form – a beautiful woman whose heavy tresses, like branches heavy with fruit and possibility, hung down from the stone bed where she lay. On her stomach lay a horn – the image of that still rising and falling with Ell's breath – and above the scene, in a carved panel, had been cut the words of a short verse. Kay read it aloud by the steady light of the lantern.

'The horn will wake the dreamer,
and the dreamer will wind the horn;
leap heart, the wind will catch you,
and the star will show in the morn.'

The words stood proud on the wall in the raking light of the lantern, and Kay read them evenly, as if brushing them like paint on paper, with a steady hand. But something about them troubled her, like a persistent bell ringing at a distance.

'The horn of the Primary Fury,' said Flip. 'The single most sonorous instrument in a world deafened by harmonies. It has gone by many names. The Battle Breaker. The Great Breath of Parnassus. The Pure Noise. The Flower of the Ten Thousand. It has mystical and mathematical properties, of course, but in the end all anyone really needs to understand is its beauty, its power. It is said that the Bride cannot truly be called, can never be commanded. She goes where she will. But in the voice of the horn of the Primary Fury we may, as it were, speak to her in her own language.' And then, in a gentler tone, as if cupping his words in cotton wool, 'It's the partner of the shuttle, whose voice knits up those threads which the horn has scattered to the winds. The one is to the other as sun to moon, as shore to sea, as knowing is to doing.'

He picked up the horn with both hands. It caught the light of the lantern where he had set it on the last course of the wall's rough blocks. Even in this tomb of death it shone.

'It belongs to her,' said Flip, 'as it once did to Rex. I think the time has come to wake the dreamer and give her the horn that is hers.' He handed it to Kay.

Kay put the horn to her lips and closed her eyes. Taking the deepest breath, her lips pursed tightly against the mouthpiece, she blew a peal that seemed to shake the stone around them. The very air as she blew seemed to condense like dew out of itself, and to run down the face of the world in heavy dark drops. In Kay's ears the rupture burst like a dam breaking, and she felt suddenly that all her life she had been waiting to wake at this call, waiting for a summons to break into her with just such an imperious, irresistible, deafening noise.

As her breath gave out and she lowered the horn, Ell sat up, pushing herself up, rising up, her arms up, her face turned up to the ceiling, like a flower thrusting from the grass at dawn, and then she was in Kay's arms, and the two of them in Flip's, and in the centre of the tight embrace Ell shivered and cried, and laughed and was held, and the glow of the light held them together as long as their arms could last, and that was a long time.

To Kay's relief, Ell remembered almost nothing of the long ordeal that had begun in the mountain. Lulled into a trance by murmuring left-wraiths, she could recall since then only snatches of scenes, seen as if through a dream, until the moment Oidos brought her to 'this little room with a hard bed'. There they had shared a cup of chocolate, and Oidos had shown her the horn.

'She promised me that you would come for me, Kay,' said Ell. 'And she told me that the horn would be mine. Is it?'

Kay wrapped it in the wool blanket and gave the parcel to her sister.

'We need to get out of here,' said Flip. He was adjusting the wick on the lantern. 'It will be day soon.'

Dawn. When Razzio will launch his balloons for the mountain.

Kay's heart lurched.

'Flip, before Oidos – before I came down here, we had a kind of council of war. Will and Phantastes brought me here because they said that Razzio could help me find Ell, that he could help me find my father. But that's not what he wants to do. He said he was going back to the mountain. He's taking Will and Phantastes, and Oidos and Ontos, and all the causes. They're going to launch a hundred balloons from the garden at dawn. Razzio is angry with Ghast, and he wants to fight.'

At that last word Flip tangled his fingers in the flame. Swearing a hot oath, he dropped the lantern and it went out. The darkness fell on them instantly, totally.

'Kay,' said Ell. 'I'm scared.'

'Don't be,' she answered, squeezing her sister's hand again. 'Flip, what's wrong?'

'We can't let him launch the balloons. It's a trap. This entire house is surrounded by wispers. It took me the better part of a day to find a way through the cordon and slip into the catacombs – and even then I only got through by a fluke. I didn't understand why they were dug in, but now it's only too obvious: Ghast knows what Razzio means to do, and he intends to stop him. But we can't get out the way I got in – all four exits from the catacombs will be heavily guarded.' Flip was fiddling with the lamp as he spoke, but it was no use – he set it down slowly, with a quiet emphasis that all three of them understood.

'I see a way out,' said Ell. 'Follow the star.'

She was probably pointing, but in the darkness it took Kay a moment to see what she meant. On the wall opposite, out in the passage, a faint patch of light had appeared. It was no bigger than a hand's breadth, and it seemed to be in the shape of a five-pointed star. Flip, in the passage, saw it right away, and immediately got to his feet. He began to walk down towards the near end of the tunnel. The girls, scrambling cautiously over the low wall, weren't far behind.

'This hole wasn't here twenty minutes ago,' he said. He was running his fingers over the edges of a well-defined, star-shaped opening in the thin rock wall above the altar.

'Maybe it was the sound of the horn?' Kay asked. 'It was so loud – it shook powder off the ceiling down the tunnel – I saw it.'

'*The star will show in the morn*,' Flip recited. 'Maybe.'

Kay had frozen. It was there, in the air – she could feel it – *the star – the morn –*

318

Dad. *'Tell your mother we'll always have Paris.'*

But Flip had another idea. Now he swung a leg up on to the stone altar, crouched, and put two or three fingers through the hole, feeling for something. 'There's a door like this in the mountain – it's thousands of years old, and you open it like –'

Whatever had required doing, he did it. Part of the wall behind the altar swung open on a huge pair of iron hinges. Wind rushed through the gap into a little room, where in low light a set of circular steps rose into the ceiling. Flip turned back and held out his hands.

'Leap, hearts,' he said, smiling.

They climbed. Kay's heart felt as if it would hammer a path straight out of her ribs. *Paris.* She felt in her pocket for the little red book. *You'll know where to find me.* At the top of the steps they would have hit a trapdoor, had it not already been open. Ontos was peering down into it, his huge eyes, dark with opiate dilation, surveying the darkness through which they had risen. As they emerged from the stairs into the very centre of his dais, in the middle of the garden, he touched the horn in Ell's arms and, from the distant recesses of his oceanic eyes, he smiled.

He had heard it, too.

Given what was going on around him, Kay quickly realized, this was altogether remarkable. Every one of the hundred rooms running around the interior wall of the garden had a glass door. Before every one of these glass doors a paved square, floored with brick or cobbles, led into the building. On each of these hundred plots the causes had tethered a giant hot-air balloon. Every one of them was the same: a small square basket, capable of holding two or three passengers, all of wicker; a small ring of metal equipment; and a huge, swelling envelope – each one a rich, dark blue, the colour of a sapphire at evening. Around them the causes swarmed, checking the tethers and halyards, loading supplies, making ready to depart – for the sky above was paling, and dawn could not be more than minutes away.

Just then there was a loud cry from one side of the garden. An answering cry rose from the opposite side. Kay searched first for the one and then the other, her eyes rocketing from side to side, even as her arms fixed on her sister and drew her close before her. Dead centre behind the main entrance of the House of the Two Modes, one of the balloons began to lift from the ground. The causes aboard – two – were waving as they rose. Opposite them, in the corresponding place at the back, another balloon was also rising.

'We're too late,' Kay said.

'Perhaps we were wrong,' said Flip. 'Maybe everything will be fine.'

'How can everything be fine when Razzio and all the wraiths in the Society are returning to the mountain?' said Kay. It wasn't really a question. She searched the faces in the garden for any sign of Razzio, of Will, of Phantastes. At last, in one of the corners, she saw all three of them. They were standing together, watching the ascending balloons.

Kay took Ell's hand, and together they ran through the garden. There was no one to block her way this time. She and

Ell dodged the chairs and tables, ran through the complicated plantings of shrubs and small trees, and reached the corner as Razzio was about to turn in through one of the doors.

'Our young friend,' he said to Will and Phantastes. 'I told you she would return when she was hungry.'

Kay made no time for his jibe. 'Razzio,' she said. Her tone was serious enough to make him pause on the threshold. 'Will. Phantastes. Stop. Call the balloons back. It's a trap. Ghast has laid a trap.'

'Kay,' said Will. 'It's not what we want but –'

'*No,*' she insisted. She pulled Ell by the hand, yanking her into view. It was all too fast; they hadn't yet registered.

Now. Pay attention to me now.

They stared at Ell. Kay stared at them.

'Hi,' said Ell. 'I'm back. This is a really giant garden.'

'Ghast knows what you're planning. There are left-wraiths on every side of the house. They're guarding the exits from the catacombs.'

'The cata–' Will was stammering breaths. 'Kay, where have you been?'

'*Call back the balloons!*' She was shouting now. Surely they could hear the fury, the desperation in her voice. Razzio stepped forward off the sill and let go of the door handle. Behind him, Oidos appeared, ashen, at the window. From her expression Kay knew that Flip had stepped up behind her.

'You,' said Will. 'How –?'

'She's right,' said Flip. 'She's telling the truth. I came in through the catacombs, and they're heavily guarded. If someone hadn't knocked out one of the patrols, I'd never have made it myself.'

'He saved Ell,' said Kay. Will was stepping forward towards Flip. As was Phantastes. 'He saved me.'

But there was nothing to fear. The three wraiths fell upon one another in an embrace that testified beyond doubt the affection that they had always had, and would always have, for one another. Their arms were still entangled when the dawn sky burst into flame.

It was the first of the balloons. It had risen four or five hundred metres into the air. Now the two wraiths aboard the basket were waving their arms and screaming. The basket was dropping fast as fire tore through the envelope. The balloon disappeared over the far edge of the building.

Dead.

'Call back the other balloon,' said Kay. She hurled her voice at Razzio, level and commanding. 'Make them land.'

It was too late. A loud shot rang in the silent air over the garden, and the other balloon burst into flame. Two hundred wraiths and more watched as the basket drifted for a moment, suspended in the burning orange air, then plummeted behind the house.

'He *dares*!' shouted Razzio. 'He *dares*!'

'We're not going to the mountain,' said Will. 'Ground the balloons. If we launch them, every cause in the garden will die.'

Oidos had come to the door and opened it. 'There is no other way to escape,' she said. 'Will we live as prisoners in our own house?'

'Would you rather die?' Kay shot back. 'Which future don't you want for us now?'

'If we can find a way past the guards in the catacombs,' said Flip, 'I can get us out.'

Razzio, Phantastes and Will turned towards Flip, as one. Oidos slammed the door and disappeared into the house. Kay knew that Ontos must have been watching intently from his dais in the centre of the garden, because every one of the causes had paused and turned towards Flip.

'It's risky. We'd need a few things from the house to set up a diversion. But we can leave the causes here, for now, and the four of us –'

'The six of us,' said Kay.

'– the six of us could maybe thread through the guards at the southern exit. The tunnel ends near a stand of ash and pine trees there – there's cover.'

'And what would we do once we escaped?' snarled Razzio.

'I know where my father is,' said Kay. 'Take me to Paris. All of you. Take me there. Flip will get us out and I will find my father.'

Kay stepped into the middle of the little group of stunned wraiths, pulling Ell tightly by the hand. She knew that this was her moment, the moment in which she could seize or lose her chance, once and for all. 'This isn't your story, Razzio. It was never your story, and it isn't mine, either. Maybe it doesn't belong to any of us. But I know one thing for certain, and that is, we must never, never, never let it be Ghast's story. I know my father is in Paris. I know it's where they left him, as surely as you know yourselves when you go into your rooms in that house.'

Kay held up her sister's hand, and Flip smiled. He reached into his pocket, took out the jack and placed it there.

Ell almost laughed – an impish, powerful grin – and then she flicked the jack high into the air so that it spun in a circle, and then caught it with a flourish in her coat pocket. She stood up smartly, the horn still tucked in the crook of her other elbow, as if she were reporting for duty.

'This little girl is the third form of the Primary Fury,' said Kay. 'I'd say she's wearing it pretty well. My father is the Builder. I'd say he knows a thing or two about Bithynia. Help me find him. We'll call a Weave. We'll all go to the Shuttle Hall. If Ghast wants a battle, fine, we'll meet him in the field. And we'll beat him.'

'We'll never get past the wispers in the woods,' said Will.

'Never,' agreed Phantastes.

'Yes we will,' said Flip. He had turned towards the garden. His tone was as tired and torn as anything Kay had ever heard in her life.

While she had been speaking, everything across the garden had changed. All ninety-eight blue balloons had slipped their tethers and were rising into the still morning air. Every last one of the causes had boarded a basket and was sailing into the sky.

No.

'Stop! Stop! Stop!' cried Razzio, running towards Ontos. The mode was circling in the place of pure being, his arms extended level from his shoulders, his feet tight together, his head bowed. His palms he had turned up to the sky as he fanned the causes airwards.

'He's sending them to their deaths,' said Will. 'Why would Ontos do that?'

Flip was studying the balloons as they lifted, a ring of blue giants rubbing shoulders as they caught the southerly wind over the house and drifted, always gaining height, into the lightening sky. He looked at the ground before he answered. 'They're all giving their lives for us.' His voice had lost its colour, and was little more than a whisper. 'It's a diversion.'

'It's a sacrifice.' Will and Kay spoke the same words in the same moment.

'And one we must honour,' answered Flip. 'Follow me. Quickly.'

Stuffing food and blankets into loose sacks, they sprinted to the centre of the garden. Every footstep shot through Kay's heart like a knife. Phantastes tackled Razzio along the way, and dragged him to the dais. Within a minute they were all standing on the platform, heaving for breath beside Ontos, shouldering their bags, twitching, nervous – and yet somehow lingering there to watch the slow agony of dawn break like a blue wave over the House of the Two Modes.

'I'm staying another minute,' said Will.

'And I.' Phantastes.

And I. Kay took their hands.

Flip's chest heaved as if he were about to argue. But he didn't.

'Fine.' He took Ell by the shoulders and began to guide her down the stairs. 'But I'm taking this one below. Don't be long.

The south tunnel. You know the route. Stay low, and for the love of the muses, run.'

A few seconds later, the explosions began. This time there was no screaming; even at this distance they could feel the resoluteness, the calm, the steady purpose of nearly two hundred wraiths sailing for the last time off the board. The balloons were still so close to one another that the fire, kindled in several places, seemed to leap from envelope to envelope, and the whole fleet suddenly erupted into a single giant fireball – a huge orange flame of a star blazing across the morning sky.

'By the air, through the air,' whispered Will. He squeezed Kay's hand so hard she thought it might break.

Leap, heart. For the love of the muses.

And they ran.

I gave you strict instructions to wake me.'

Ghast glared up at the tall wraith who stood before him. He had woken to the hard rattle of wooden shutters clacking against their frames, wresting wildly against their hinges. Fumbling into consciousness, he had groped with his eyelids for the light of morning, trying to force them open against the wrong dark. It should have been dawn. Light ought to have been streaming into the old stone room from a thousand cracks and slits. But there was nothing – only a storm of wind and occasional waves of what sounded like pelting rain that swept against the outside walls. He had slowly recognized the truth: that it was still night, that it was darkest night, a raging, merciless night. He had bellowed, not in agony but in command, and the door to the chamber had at last swung open. This fawning servant had come to his bedside, handing him a little lamp, then waiting.

'Will you eat?' the wraith had asked.

A heaviness in his arms, in his head, had perplexed him as he swung his body round to sit on the edge of the bed. He had known then that the lethargy in his limbs, the wrongness of the dark, the

327

meekness of the servant had meaning. He had felt the bedclothes against his skin: wet, matted, sour.

'I gave you strict instructions to wake me.'

'We tried to wake you,' said the wraith. 'You were not yourself.'

Ghast dared not frown. He knew then that he was still not himself, and snatches of what had seemed like an awful nightmare stirred from his memory like monsters surging from a deep ocean. He looked down at a hand that was rising where it seemed he had raised it. It was trembling. He placed it on the lamp, which was hot to the touch. He left it there, burning.

'I will have fruit,' he said. 'Bring it to me, and another light, and a change of clothes.'

The wraith left the room and Ghast waited as his quick steps sounded away down the long hallway outside, merging into the sound of the storm. He took his hand from the lamp, and smelled as he did so the faint stench of burnt skin. He held on to the pain in his hand as if it were a rope pulling him from the deep, from the surging memories of his voice; his voice that had cried out, calling for heads, calling for slaughter, calling for the huddled ruck of settling wings and stabbing beaks of vultures.

Whatever they had seen and heard, it was no matter. Had they been in any doubt before, they would fear him now.

After he had eaten a little plate of fruit and changed into fresh clothes, he draped himself in blankets and sat at a wooden desk in the corner. Two lamps created a pool of steady glowing, and he worked between them. The light and the work staved off the heaves of wind rushing through the valley outside. He had letters to write, business to be transacted in his own hand. Copy after patient copy he drafted and signed, occasionally tearing up imperfect sheets where his grip on the pen had faltered and threatened to soil his authority. Three hours of patient writing. Still the night beat at the shutters; still the light of the lamps steadied him.

'You.'

The unheralded arrival of another tall form, after so much solitude, in such a mix of mind and wind, had surprised him. This one was not meek. A grey dawn hung around his heels, where dripping water, too, gathered on the stone floor.

'Oidos has given them the child. The author. The dreamer.'

'I know who she is,' he spat.

'She has given them the horn.'

'And?'

'And we have crushed the plotter forever.'

'As I instructed you. I expected nothing else.'

'I had expected to meet you downriver, in the marshes –'

'And yet you find me here.'

There was a silence. Ghast knew that something had remained unspoken. He clawed at it with his thought, but his face remained a stone. He would not be drawn to ask what his servant must freely deliver.

'The imaginer is with them.'

So. Not dead. His resolve buckled for a moment, then held. His face never flickered.

'That is nothing now. I have letters summoning the Weave.'

'I will deliver them –'

'In Paris.' Within the hour the barge would be moving downriver again. Many of his company had gone ahead to ready the hall at Bithynia for his landing. 'We will go now at a doubled pace,' he said. 'There is very little time.'

As he held the packet out to Firedrake, Ghast allowed his gaze to rest on the bedstead behind him. And yet he thought he caught in the corner of his eye a fleeting turn of the wraith's mouth, a flicker of disgust. The light was steady; his eye had not deceived him. The girl, then, the dreamer, had power.

It was no matter. He had laced the hive, and the bees would swarm to it.

Part Three

WEB

16

Sparagmos

As the train carriage around her hummed and jostled, Kay fumbled between sleep and wake. She dreamed, and in her dreams images and arguments slid and flowed into one another, all in a turbulent current. She was ahead of herself, looking back with a profound sense of disorientation upon the traumatic events of the early morning. That very day.

Why would he do that? The black smoke rising at dawn.

Her head lolled across field after field, and she murmured intermittent protests. Picking up speed, she felt the train racing north and west, leaving behind Rome and the House of the Two Modes, leaving behind those lawns charred with sacrifice, climbing out of the broad river valleys and back into the mountains and their clear air. Every time the train jolted, Kay woke, felt her speed and remembered where she was. *I am on track for once.*

Escaping from the catacombs had been easier than they expected – easier than they deserved. While descending the staircase from Ontos' dais, Kay had felt strongly that they were captains going gravely below decks on a sinking vessel; but once

333

in the tunnels their pace and their purpose had quickened. Through those halls of death and burial they had blown like the charge of a blast, hurtling through the rock with their torches thrown out ahead, the light striding with them through the darkness. Kay struggled to keep up with the long and loping pace of the wraiths, bent but unbowed as they drove due south to the nearly concealed exit of the tunnels. Here, framed by an ancient stone archway, the dark rock passage gave out on to a little hill; not twenty metres away a tall wood began, now almost stripped of its leaves, but still – in among the evergreen thickets with which it was fringed – offering the promise of cover.

Just inside the archway Flip and Ell had stood waiting. As they approached, he had motioned for them to be quiet and move softly.

'Two wispers.' Kay recalled how he had moved his mouth without making a sound. He had pointed out through the open arch – first left, then almost straight ahead. Peering round the wall, Kay had seen something move in the periphery of her vision, but straight ahead could only see a still form lying in the grass – perhaps just a sack or a coat, for nothing was ever as it seemed in the silvery paling of a very early morning.

Those minutes of waiting had been tense. Flip had made it clear that most of the wispers had moved off, drawn by the flight of the balloons to the north, leaving only these two behind. It was obvious that he, Will, Phantastes and Razzio could overpower them, even if they were armed, but everything depended on what happened in the intervening twenty metres:

would they call for help? If they did, could they run fast enough – could Ell and Kay run fast enough – to slip into the woods without being pursued? Ell had shivered uncontrollably, her muscles after days of sleep sluggish. From his pack Flip had shared out food while the others watched, waited and worried.

And then something inexplicable had happened. An owl had called in the woods – once, then twice, then again. The wisper concealed in the bracken to the left had risen silently and melted into the ravine that ran eastwards around the House of the Two Modes. The other figure lay prone, motionless.

'Now.' Flip had pushed them out. There had been no time to hoist their packs or get their bearings. With their heads low they had raced single-file directly towards the silent form on the grass.

'Not dead,' Will had called back in a volleyed whisper as the girls drew level with Phantastes. 'But whoever struck the blow knew exactly what he was doing.'

The dent in the wraith's temple had looked about three inches long. The bruise forming around it was straight.

'Someone wants us to escape.' Phantastes had crouched by the body to touch his finger to the wound and to gather the wraith's loose robe more tightly around his body. 'I dare say help will come for this one before long.'

Without another word they had all passed into the wood, threading the thorn trees and the dense-growing bushes at its edge, then disappearing into the mists that still lay heavy upon it.

It had taken the whole day to make their way through the trees, across hills and past houses, on buses and down endless streets along the flat brown river into the city. Kay had thought for sure that they would attract attention, but the wraiths in their robes and cloaks seemed to blend perfectly into the surroundings, especially when the little group, moving fast but wearily, Eloise slung across Will's broad back, reached the ancient heart of Rome. Church after church they had passed, and in among them shrines and ancient monuments, decayed, sometimes in ruins, every site swarming with eager faces not sceptical but delighted to see Phantastes' wizened sagacity, Razzio's harrowed despair, Flip's urgent intensity and Will's –

Whatever you are, everyone who sees you loves you.

Kay shifted in her seat. Boarding the train at dusk, the six of them had found a quiet compartment to themselves, and the seats seemed to Kay practically luxurious. After hours of waiting in the station – bleak, lined with shops, thrumming with the passing of footsteps, the sweat and sonorities of countless strangers, the slow and creeping cold that comes of sitting still, waiting – the peace of this enclosed space settled around her exhausted body like a warm bath. To her right, Ell nestled neatly into Will's side, exhausted after a day spent rushing through Rome; opposite her, Phantastes and Razzio and Flip were dozing.

As she turned her face towards the carriage window, looking through her own dim reflection in the glass, Kay started suddenly from her reverie and gasped for air; she had either pulled her coat up over her mouth or sunk down into its folds while she slept. Forms that must have been trees were racing by the train in the pitch of the dark, and for a long waking present Kay observed them, entranced. Also there were larger fields of black void that instantly gave way to the clear, star-shouldering night, and she decided that the train must be among the mountains – the Alps. She peered to discover as much as she could, but there was no moon and she could make out very little. When they did pass roads, they were all uniformly deserted.

And then it happened. The train, in racing by night through so many remote regions, so many ranges and passes of such grandeur and scale, moved at once quickly and – against the huge vistas – very slowly. Anything close to the tracks – buildings, trees, streets and signs, parked cars, platforms, fences, tunnels – came and went in a black blur, punctuated by occasional flashes of bleak light; but the skies full of stars, the mountain slopes and peaks seemed to hang richly inaccessible and constant, shrouded in darkness like – she fumbled – like riddles, mysteries, things that were difficult but true. Kay found herself with her cheek pressed to the glass, staring as intently as she could at everything that passed, with a single eye pushed well in beyond any possibility of being distracted by her own dim reflection – when the train, hurtling out of a tunnel, suddenly broke into a broad-sloped valley, huge in its wheel and almost desolate, therefore pristine. The starlight, faint elsewhere, collected on the high snow that crowned the valley's bowl and its sheer rocks, and from that height poured down illumination on the scene below; like milk in a dish it splashed down on a lone house, a single dark structure steaded firmly in its centre, the focus of all the sleeping splendour that lay about it, like the snug centre of a giant winter rose. And there, for a handful of seconds as they passed through the valley, in lanternly pools where it spilled across the ground, warm, thick, dense, as crammed as amber, Kay saw light, yellow light: the lights of rooms filled with laughter and song, with close-murmuring embraces and long savours, rooms of love, kindness, patience, integrity and respect. It was as if she had glimpsed, for only five or six beats of her own heart, the eternal heart of everything beautiful upon the earth.

Hot tears welled in her eyes, and she sprang back from the glass as if she had been bitten.

'What did you see in the dark?'

It was Will's voice. Careful of Ell's comfort, he hardly dared turn his head; but his eyes were kind, as distant as Kay had ever seen them.

'A home,' she whispered. 'Someone's home.'

And then it passed. Then we went on.

'Do you miss home?'

'No,' Kay said. 'Yes. I think I miss a home we don't have. A home we never had.'

Will was silent. He looked down at Ell's sleeping face where it lay against his heavy cloak. In the darkness Kay fancied she could just see the warm flush on Ell's cheeks.

'I wish that we could be *together*. Everything about that house I just saw was together. It was filled with light.'

'Kay, I'm sorry we took your father away.'

'No.' She spoke with decision. 'Don't be sorry. He was gone long before you took him. For as long as I can remember we've all – all of us – been *apart*.'

Will let a long, slow breath whistle softly between his lips. 'Sometimes people who truly love one another can't bear to come together.'

'Why?'

'Where would you go from there?'

'Where would you need to go?' asked Kay.

'Ask a left-wraith,' said Will. It almost seemed that he might laugh.

Kay turned back to the window. Even in the darkness, she couldn't look at Will and say what she wanted to say.

'Will, that morning before he left, before you took him, before everything went wrong – my father told me that I would know where to find him.'

'And do you?' Will asked.

'No,' said Kay. 'He didn't say that I *did* know. He said I *would*, in the future. That I would *come* to know. I didn't notice at the time – but it was in that little red book –'

'Yes.'

'Why did he say that? How did he know that I would need to find him?'

'Don't you always?'

Kay felt that Will wasn't so much asking questions as leading her forward. She didn't know where they were going.

'Always what?' She traced patterns on the train window with her hand – patterns that weren't there. Patterns that she wished were there.

'Find him. Aren't you always the one who brings him back?'

'Yes,' said Kay. Now she turned back and looked Will full in the eye. 'Yes, I am.'

'How do you feel about that?'

'I'm always the one in the middle,' she answered.

'Like me,' said Will quietly.

'I don't want to be in the middle any more.'

'Do you know what I always say, Kay? The thing I always tell myself when I have to take that long walk down the centre of the Shuttle Hall by myself and leave my friends among the right-wraiths and my friends among the left-wraiths, when I have to pass by the twelve thrones and go to the stiff loom and the hard chair that sits before it, and touch my bruised and blistered fingers to the shuttle, and start to work the warp apart? When the shouts begin and the debate masses like a wave over my head? When the arguments start to flow, laced with taunts and gibes – sometimes merry, sometimes mortal? I bend over my work, alone, knowing that, for the duration of the festival, until the wraiths disperse again into the world as a single fellowship, until the conclave is adjourned and the wispers take up their packs to disappear on the night air, until that moment I am the only thing that binds them. I am their medium. I am their middle.'

'And so long as there is a middle, there is a story,' said Kay.

'So long as there is a middle, there is a story,' agreed Will.

'Will, I'm tired.'

'Do you want to sleep?'

'No, I'm not tired like that. I'm awake. I mean, I'm tired of all this. I want to go home and get into bed.'

'I'm tired, too, Kay.' Will was silent for a little while in the darkness. Beneath them the train rushed reassuringly on.

But to what end?

'This train is travelling very fast,' said Phantastes. He switched on the overhead light, and leaned forward into the little brilliance that it created. His face looked haggard in the night. 'And it makes me wonder what will happen if we find your father, if we make it to Bithynia. It makes me wonder whether we are ready. Ghast has overawed the right-wraiths. Perhaps we will not find even a handful to stand against him.'

The light had woken Razzio, across from Kay.

He added what they all knew: 'I would gladly denounce him now, even before the Weave; but maybe it is too late. The left-wraiths, too, have long been in his power, and now he rules them not with love, but with fear.'

Kay had been staring at the window. In the light cast by the little bulb above Phantastes' head the thick pane seemed to double her face, and she stared at the two overlapping versions of herself.

'I can do it.' She announced it briskly and cheerfully, as if they had asked her the question. Perhaps she had asked it of herself. 'I can find my father. I can bring him back to himself. We can do the integration. I can do it.'

Will protested. They all did. Kay didn't listen. She thought of herself smiling at their disbelief; in the window's altered face she could almost see it.

'Kay.' It was Flip. He had been watching silently. Now he spoke out of the shadows, almost as if he couldn't bear to join the little lighted circle. 'I read the order sheet, the day Ghast enrolled it in the Dispersals Room. The thing is, it wasn't just a dispersal. It was a full sparagmos – irreversible. There's no going back.'

'I don't understand that word,' Kay said. 'Tell me. In Alexandria it was all possible. Tell me what has changed.'

For what seemed like a very long time Phantastes stared at her in the gloom, his eyes anything but soft and merry, as they had been in the subterranean vaults of the Temple of Osiris in Alexandria. He looked abruptly ancient, as if the events of the day before had taken him to the edge of an awful cliff – and he had fallen off. As he began to answer her, Kay noticed that Razzio, beside him, was shuffling stones in a closed fist.

'There are different degrees of dispersal, Kay – even a kind of spectrum. In the insignificant cases it is enough for the removal and dispersal merely to shake a person from her or his path. Here we take up the thread of a life and fray it, shake it, twist it, perhaps splice it. We meddle with the course, but do not stop the flow. In other cases the process is more far-reaching, more substantial. Here we take up the story and we break it, or bind it to a new story, or even cut it off. But even this extreme form – where we snap away and tear off the future of a narrative, and finish it completely – is not the absolute end

342

of that person's thread; because, if you know that thread and you know how to weave a story, you can return to it and start it anew. You can eke it out, graft it together, make it whole again. You have something to work with. But in the case of sparagmos, there the thread is not simply cut and the course impeded. There the bed is dug up. There the thread is burned. Nothing is left. There is no stump from which to coax an afterlife or second beginning. Sparagmos is final. Even Asclepius, in the heady days of the great rebirths, could not remake a full unmaking. There were times when even he sat down and despaired.'

'But Will said –'

'There is one circumstance in which a full sparagmos is thought to be reversible, and one only. If the Bride herself were to gather up the scattered fragments of a life and breathe into it new motion, it is said that she might make something of nothing, and graft being on to absence. So Isis once gathered the parts of Osiris after the god Set had dismembered him and scattered the pieces across the earth. It is said that she remade him. But we simply don't know. It's a story, a belief, a myth, an assumption. But then, who is there who knows the Bride, her ways, her powers? Has anyone sat with her under the spreading plane and learned her mysteries? Has anyone questioned her, as you question me now? Has anyone among us, perished in the endless night of madness, felt the healing power of the Bridestone, or seen the milk-light of its twelve-pointed star? No. You have heard the song, you have sung it – "the star will show in the morn". But the song is all we have. If we know that she can do this, we know it only because we have not had occasion to disprove it.'

'But how does a dispersal take place? How does a sparagmos take place? I want to know.'

The old wraith looked at her sharply. 'It is not a thing that a child should see, even in her imagination.'

'A lot of the things that have happened lately are things I ought not to have seen. I need to know this. Please tell me.'

Kay looked around from face to face. They all seemed about to say something.

'And don't tell stories.'

'When a wraith knows everything there is to know about a person's life, about her mind or his ambitions, about her fears or his weaknesses, about the things she loves and the things he knows – then the wraith knows how to undo them, how to negate them, how to undermine them. In a dispersal, the wraith seizes on one, or many, or all these elements as if they were filaments in the thread of the life, and pulls. They unravel. The mind comes apart.'

'Then my father isn't – You don't mean he's *dead*?'

'He's worse than dead, Kay. He has been tortured beyond his ability to withstand it. He's mad.'

'And he can't get better. You're saying that he can't get better.' Kay's tone was practical, searching. She would press them. Push them.

Make them reach.

'I don't tend to say that things are impossible. But if Foliot and Firedrake performed a full sparagmos, they will have twisted the knife in every corner of his mind, and there will be no part of his being that is not rent and scattered.'

'And in an integration, normally –'

'Well, as you saw in Alexandria. A wraith – and it has to be a skilled one like Will – can meditate, and course back through the motives and causes of a life, as if with plotting stones or the threads in a knot, and find the story that will re-bind or re-graft the thoughts and feelings, the assumptions and first principles that have been broken. Will thought he knew then what they had done to your father, and he was looking for that one clue that would show him which story to tell. Because if we had found your father, then Will might have told him the story that would bring him out of his madness, the way an antidote dispels a poison or soap clears away grime. The way glue sticks. The way a chestnut trees. But Ghast outplotted us, as if they were green novices. Perhaps he had good advice.' Here Phantastes lifted his eyebrow and nodded over to Razzio. 'But let that bygone be a bygone.

'They didn't know they had been followed, of course. But, more importantly, we just don't know how to approach a sparagmos. We were clutching at straws. We are clutching at them now. It's such a serious thing, Kay – almost a sacred thing. It is the destruction not of a life, but of a world. The broken sparagmotic does not keep the madness within, but spreads it, pouring it out into any and all receptive minds. He reels through the world not only broken but breaking. It is almost uncontrollable, a desperate and a dire thing; something that Ghast would never have dared to do in the old days, in

Bithynia. That he has done it now means he believes himself untouchable. And it suggests that he really does want to destroy the world around us – at least, he wants to change it permanently.'

'But the Bride –'

'The Bride, child – what we mean when we talk about summoning the Bride – it's about a feeling, about sharing a feeling, about every wraith in the hall having the same sense of a luminous and overbinding presence, the sense of an enablement. It's about everyone *believing*, all at once. They believe that they are wedded to the world! But you can't *make* people believe. They have to come to it themselves. These things you want, Kay – they are colossal improbabilities. We don't know *how* to do what we want to do.'

'But say we could, just say we could. If we knew where Foliot and Firedrake left him, surely we could find my father through plotting? And then Will could talk to him and tell him stories like that old poet in the myths, and –'

Phantastes shook his head slowly, pressing his long fingers against his knees. His face passed in and out of the light, like a huge pendulum beating out an eternal refusal. 'No, child. Plotting works by reason, and the necessary movement from cause to effect. It follows patterns. Even I know that. But the sparagmotic is no more reasonable than chaos itself. He is borne on a current of madness, as if he were headless, and he chants a melody that is beyond form. Plotting cannot reach after him.'

'Then we do the reverse of plotting. We'll take every step the wrong way. Can't you *imagine* a way out of this?'

'Of course I can imagine. But I wouldn't know what I was imagining. The madness of sparagmos is not the reverse of the pattern; it is *everything but* the pattern – an infinite range of non-being, in every direction, for everything that is. It's not just a shadow but a comprehensive darkness. You can no more predict it than you can explain the cause of all causes. Sparagmos is final.'

'Kay doesn't think asparagus moss is final. And that's final.' No one had noticed that Ell had woken, that she had been watching the conversation with the fascination of a kitten, new eyed.

In the double face of the window, Kay almost thought she was laughing, and because she thought she was, she just about did. The train answered her with a long, stomach-churning curve. She sat up.

That thing Phantastes said – the night isn't all bad. You can look on the night and see expectation, promise, as great a significance as you could ever hope for. At night, looking can be longing. The star will show in the morn – and stars are there.

It took her only a few minutes to convince them. She told them what had happened on the dais, in the place of pure being, when she had seen and felt the power of the cause of all causes. How she had for a moment been not in one but two places, seen not one but two worlds, how she had been at once both far and near, both subject and object of her own regarding.

She told them how she had been and not been at the same time, how she had suffered sparagmos.

I will perform a sparagmos on myself. I will go again into the place of pure being, to the place where everything dissolves and is one, and then I will return. I will know what my father knows. I will know where he is. I will find him there, and I will bring him to himself. And then I will bring him home.

Before long, they were all asleep. The train sped on.

*T*he landing was built of stone quarried in the mountain. The barge came to rest snugly against it, and was still. After the rough passage through the storm, its stillness was to be savoured. Ghast sat, then, at rest in his throne. Soon he would have the title that the throne implied. Then he would destroy this landing, with the quaintly intricate carvings that ran unchecked around its storied walls. From every face of the eastern gate the form of the First Wraith danced. This was unquestionably his place, his temple, the seat of his lost power. If it had been possible to move Ghast to any emotion, he might have felt rage. Instead he felt the foretaste of his final victory. It tasted of steel.

The exhausted wraiths drew their long poles out of the water and, while they still dripped with the river, ran them one to each side through the slots cut into the throne. Two to each end of each pole, they lifted him and bore him on to the landing; river water dripped from the throne as they passed. The light was falling now, and in the shadows antic shapes gathered and recoiled in the carved walls of the eastern gate. Ghast forced himself to watch them as they passed. His servants were now bearing him along the ancient ramp of the Ring, circling the walls as they ascended towards the height. Twice, then three times they passed through the dark interior of the east tower as they turned, and he felt the chill of the dark stone settle on his skin. Shapes, chill, darkness were nothing to him. Let his arms bristle. He was coming as a conqueror, and would soon have his crown; all this – shapes, chill, darkness – would be his kingdom, to wield as he willed.

From the height of the walls, in the last of the evening's red light, he finally looked down on the Shuttle Hall, the library, the Bindery, the Imaginary and the vast dormitories. Beyond lay the overgrown mulberry orchards, long left untended and draped thick with ungathered silk. He felt no affection for these crumbling shells of an antiquated order. Soon he would have them all destroyed. He would erect in their place the more functional offices his clerks had designed. He would require many fewer wraiths than in the past. And their duties would be somewhat lighter. They would operate the machines that made the stories.

He had sent his letters. He thought of them coursing through the air, landing in the hands of their recipients, drawing them back to Bithynia. He thought of the movement of the Weave, and of the shuttle writhing through the warp and weft of the fabric, back and forth, almost faster than the eye could pick it out. His was the hand, his the movement in the *fabric. He looked at his hands, reddish in the light of the setting sun, and for a moment they looked like worms turning in the soil. It disgusted him. But he would be king of this, too.*

17

Leaves

K ay looked out of the window. She thought they must be about to arrive: a sort of grey cast hung over the buildings they passed, and though there was greenery and some open space, its order and symmetry made it obvious that it was the greenery and open space of a city. Kay jostled Ell awake, and the two girls rubbed their eyes and stretched their feet, pushing out the kinks and aches.

'Ell,' Kay said. 'I think we're in Paris. We're going to have to get out and walk again for a while.'

'Okay, oh Kay,' said Ell. *Imp.* It was an old joke. 'Kay,' she said, and she held her older sister's arm where it lay across her own chest. 'Thank you for saving me. I knew you were going to. And I know you're going to get us all home.'

Kay squeezed hard, and the tension wasn't all affection. *If I can.*

The two girls got to their feet and clung somewhere to the cloth between Flip and Phantastes; Razzio and Will had gone on ahead, and were already waiting by the carriage door. The train was slowing, and outside Kay could make out the same frosty pavements and chill, dry air they had left behind in England the week before. The shock of the familiar northern winter caught her unprepared, and she thought instantly and unguardedly of their mother, surely now outside her wits with worry over her husband and daughters. As the train pulled up to the platform, slowing all the time, Kay noticed on the next track a press of people waiting to board another train – little clumps gathered in the frosty morning, expecting the doors to open and give their cheeks some respite. Here and there a family stood close together, clutching satchels and sometimes one another. Kay felt tears standing in her eyes, and looked away at a panel of blinking lights on the rear wall of the carriage. *I know what I have to do*, she told herself. *I only have to find him. I only have to find him.*

The air outside the train rushed in at them as the doors opened. It was every bit as cold as it had looked; even bundled within the hairy anoraks Oidos had rustled up from a well-remembered room, they were only tired, slight children, and they shivered almost uncontrollably. The station around them, barrel-vaulted by huge steel and glass arcs, crawled with trains and their passengers, and the wraiths took trouble to bring the girls safely and quickly through the crowds, up a grand stone staircase and out through an arcade of shops into the street. Flip led with his loping gait, trailing Phantastes and Razzio some way behind, and Will brought up the rear with the girls. Kay noticed that Flip seemed enormously confident in these streets, as if he had walked them many times before, and so knew exactly where to cut a corner, where to look for an oncoming car, where to slow down or stop in order to keep his followers with him. Many of the buildings they passed, she observed, stood forbidding and proud – empty and tenantless at this time of year, and dark; but for all that, they had a kind of human sternness, which made Kay shiver a little harder.

After about twenty minutes of breathless walking the girls crossed a wide but drab square and suddenly found themselves next to a river. 'The Seine,' Will said as he scooped Ell up for a better look over the embankment. 'It's named for Sequana, a nymph or goddess. Thousands of years ago the ancient Gauls used to pray to her for healing.' He pointed to the centre of the river, where the current of the river parted, smooth and heavy, on the foreshore of a spit of island. 'Her temple used to stand over there.'

Kay looked at the rocks and low, leafless trees on the narrow island.

'As nymphs go, she was really nice,' Will said.

When Kay stared hard at him, Will couldn't help but smile. 'Okay, we never met. But watch yourself here – this is where it will get interesting, especially if we're not alone.'

Kay kept moving across the bridge, just to keep warm, and Will and Ell followed. The others were still slightly strung out ahead of them, with Flip well in the lead, already turning a corner and disappearing behind the grand facade of a monumental public building, all of white stone. In sixty steps Kay had reached it, and found herself turning into what looked like an abandoned car park. Towering nearby she could see the buttressed tower of a huge church. 'Is that where we're going?'

she asked, pointing up to it as Will rounded the corner. 'Not today,' he said. 'That's the cathedral. We're just going to the chapel.'

The others were nowhere to be seen. Will took the hands of the two girls and led them on past a parked car and through a low, narrowly arched wooden door in a wall that, for its unremarkably flat grey aspect, Kay had hardly even noticed. Beyond a short course of steps and through another low stone doorway the girls spilled into a dim, damp room with a low ceiling. 'Not here,' said Will simply, and held open another tiny door – so small that Kay hardly thought he would be able to fold himself through it. Ell first, the girls ascended by narrow spiral stairs, all of stone heavily worn at the centre of each sagging step. Kay counted the treads: seventeen to the top.

The tall chapel on to which the stairs gave seemed at first to be built all of coloured light: not only did rich blues and reds cascade over the walls, but the very air seemed impregnated with colour, and glowed in the beams of suddenly warm sunshine all around. The ceiling was very high and the chapel long and narrow. Great stained-glass windows, through which the light poured, ran along every side. The two girls turned and turned in the space, soaking up the warmth and the sumptuously velveted air, their arms limp and gestureless at their sides but their eyes – no longer wind-burned and teary – glazed rather with wonder and admiration. Delicately wrought stone pillars ran up almost like latticework all around the walls and into the vaults of the lofty ceiling; here and there an ornament in the stone or a blemish interrupted the flow, but the overall effect was of agility, elegance and power emanating like impossible exhalations from the strife of light and stone.

'The Sainte-Chapelle,' said Flip, rounding on the girls from the far end of the chapel, where he had been poking his head down another stairwell. 'Normally it's packed with tourists, but now it is empty for the Christmas holidays. It's an old royal chapel, built by the Capetian kings –'

'And it's a very handy, quiet place at midwinter for a sparagmos,' finished Will.

Kay stopped turning. 'Why here?' she asked.

'You don't want to be disturbed during a dispersal,' Will answered. Razzio and Flip spoke in whispers at the far end of the room. Phantastes was rummaging in his sack. 'To work your way back to the first causes of a person's being means un-telling a lot of stories, and the process can take many hours, even for the most skilled unravellers. So privacy is important. But if you can get it, a large space like this always amplifies the impact of any imagining.'

'No,' Kay persisted. 'I mean, why *here*? Why in *Paris*? Why did they bring him *here*? If I'm going to do this – I have to know.'

Will grimaced. 'I haven't thought about much else since yesterday, Kay. Maybe it's random.'

'No. It's not.'

Will looked at her as if he were a child caught stealing sweets. 'I know. I think Ghast may be trying to force us away from the

356

mountain, away from Bithynia. I think he's trying to make it impossible for us to summon a Weave.'

Kay looked at Will blankly. 'Or else he's daring us,' she said.

She let her shoulders slump. *What am I doing?*

'Ready?' he asked.

'Ready,' she replied. *I am not ready.*

'You're not ready, are you?' Will put his hands on her shoulders and smiled at her with such vast compassion that Kay was overwhelmed with a desire to hug him. 'You don't need to do this,' he said, mussing up her hair. 'Maybe it's not a good idea.'

Kay pushed him away and stood apart. 'I'm sure, Will. I know how to lose myself. Being ready has exactly nothing to do with it.'

Phantastes crossed the chapel with a clutch of dried leaves in his hand. Kay looked at the floor. Between their feet, the stone had been painted with a picture of two wolves staring at a nest which contained three eggs. A goose flew overhead.

'You'll need to choose one of these,' said Phantastes softly, all the edge melted from his resonant bass voice. 'I'd choose for you, but only the imaginer can know which leaf will be right for her when the time comes.'

'How am I to know?' Kay asked.

'Look at them and think about what you have to do. Sometimes you won't even know why you know, or what you know. But you'll take one.'

Kay looked at the large, veined, olive-green leaves fanned out in Phantastes' hand. They looked a bit like the bay leaves that grew in a large earthenware pot behind the house at home, but they were larger, more rounded, and even dried were of a much deeper evergreen, and their whitish veins protruded milkily from them – like scurf on the sea, she thought. She needed to find her father, to think his thoughts – but not his thoughts at all. She needed to dream his dreams, and to follow the fever of his frenzy. The veins on the leaves stood out in some places more prominently than others, and Kay could almost see in the milk-white veins the foamy saliva of a ranting madman. She traced her fingers over the proffered leaves, touching the ridges of the veins, and let her touch linger on the nodules where the veins stood out most prominently. Where the spine felt thickest – though not on the largest of the leaves – she pinched and drew it out. She had hardly looked.

'A good choice,' Phantastes said kindly, staring at his hands, where Kay saw his veins, too, standing proudly blue against the skin. In her own hand she turned the leaf – and saw that it was fresh, supple, not dried at all, covered with tiny hairs, bursting with juice.

'But this leaf –'

'I picked it from the tree, in Alexandria – at home – for this –' He had no more words. Every nerve in Kay's body hummed.

'Oh, Phantastes,' she said, and twirled and twirled the supple fabric of the leaf between her thumb and forefinger, dizzy with it, drunk already on its moment.

'Trace the veins back to the stem, Kay. Follow the milk of the leaf.' And then he had slipped away.

Will was sitting beside Ell, talking quietly about the colours of the glass above them. Kay saw that he had the horn in his hand, where he held it unobtrusively just outside their conversation. She knew what it was for, and that Ell would have to blow it when the time came; and, thinking that the time had better come sooner than later, she sat down and thrust the leaf all at once into her mouth, squeezing her eyes shut and sinking down cross-legged on to the floor. She only just had time to place her palms on her knees before a bitter rush of metal spiked beneath her tongue and seemed to course like electricity through her nerves. Her toes throbbed suddenly.

For a few moments Kay swam, just keeping her head above the level and taking in the metal flavour that began to soak first her joints, then her limbs, then her pelvis and abdomen, rising all the time. She didn't know exactly what she had expected, but somehow thought something would happen to her vision, her head; this by contrast was a simple taste, and yet one that she could feel not only in her mouth, but all over her body – as if she were bathing in a sea of cold electric soup and her feet were tongues. She was aware that the others were circling her, watching her, settling down on the floor around her to watch, and speaking in hushed whispers; but they dwindled from her awareness like candles snuffed by dawn, still burning but shedding no light. Instead this sun of metal rose into her throat, burning and beginning to hum, scattering all the clouds and shadows of thought before it, and leaving only a single light of awareness, a single long and resonant peal of equal sound, condensing all causes and effects into that single, lasting, momentous eternity of presence into which all consequence was instantly absorbed.

But even so, Kay found she could think.

In her thought was the image of her father lying on this floor, staring up into the hued shadows of the stone vault above; she walked towards him with her awareness, each step a shudderingly effortful shedding of distance, and stood over him, peering down at his sunken eyes, the grey stubble of his lank and careworn cheeks, the mottle-pored bone of his nose and the slight movement at the inner edges of his pallid lips as he breathed softly in, then out. How. How to see what he saw, to feel what he felt. Feels. Sees. How. As if she were leaping into the air and diving into a hole into the ground all at once, Kay contorted her thought and let it fall, just heavily enough to alight on his vantage. Her eyes widened; she was staring at the ceiling, exhausted with the effort of approach and thinking nothing at all.

Like a balloon balanced on the point of a pin, Kay felt an unimagined, unarticulated dread of any thought, any movement of perception – all ways might lead to catastrophe. Without allowing this awareness to surface into her consciousness, she felt a muffled command: to settle on just the right thought; the thought that would allow her to follow the thread back not to where he had been – she was already there – but to what he had been, just on that precipice of the moment before they had turned him out into the street. She spread herself all over the floor, just knowing its coldness, his coldness, beneath the metallic hum still knifing constantly through her nerves. She sensed herself too warm, too high, still too gathered, too bound. She remembered what Phantastes had said: she should follow the vein, follow the milk of the leaf. With a subdued but sudden sense of surprise she realized that the leaf still lay whole between her tongue and palate; all the silver seeping through her nerves was the taste of its skin. With immediate resolve she chewed it, and felt instantly the pulpy, woody paste of the leaf sap dropping fluidly on to her gums. Its taste was richer, deeper, more of garlic and roots that grow in the ground, and in her mind the current flow opened, as if the metal were running to the wood, and the wood running to the ground. Suddenly there were worms. Fingersful of them. Kay felt her body shudder, her mouth recoiling from the leaf. It was too much, it would be too much. As if from a great distance, she could feel her stomach heave. The worms turned, crawling like reaching fingers up from her abdomen, crawling into her thoughts, pushing with eating mouths into her throat. They were rising red into a red sun. A scream built in her mind. Unlike the scream of a voice, it needed no breath to sustain it, and it went on and on. She swallowed, like a fist pushing down the worms where they climbed. They rose. She swallowed, remembering something – what was it? – but determined not to let the memory reach her.

Here the scream ended. Here where the sap dived into the ground Kay at last felt the cold, like a kind of despair not wrapping but enclosing her sense as it pushed, in fluid beads, between the small stones, the gelid and unyielding grit and clay of the beginning of thoughts – not her thinking, or his thinking, but the possibility of thinking. *Think.* She had been on the surface of the leaf, the leaf like a page, and the page that of a book; then by the margin she had sunk to its stem, gathering in; and now she was burrowing within the opening, down to the threads of the stitching where they looped and tunnelled in the unliving earth, through the binding, and then out, anchoring, diffusing, radical. Here it begins. Here begins. *Here.*

This is it. I realize. In the moment he was – thinking – nothing but this –

Thinking that he had been set apart, cut off, left alone; but thinking also that he had become joined, too, by this unravelling, this unstemming, this unstorying – joined to a cause – joined to a first matter of earth – joined to them all – joined to all. Thinking he was apart, he was together; he was being impossibly far away, right here. On the one hand he was single, alone, himself, cut off and discrete; on the other hand he had become real, timeless, like a wraith, as large and encompassing as an idea, universal. Kay held the singularity and the universality in the two hands of her thought and travelled upwards, back into the stem and trunk of state that joined cause to effect, the accident to its consequence, root to fruit. She knew she had to issue from every vein at once, simultaneously; she had to hold the two currents together, not only through this central shaft, where it was so snug, so compact, so easy to twine them, but out explosively into the branch and leaf and text and texture of every least vein, every least vein that was a moment. With a huge breathing swell she forced her thought out along every available and imagined taste, sound, sight, touch and scent at once. *Come home.*

Just before she felt the sound of the horn goring into her stomach like a tusk, shattering her concentration, she seemed to feel herself coming to herself from a great distance, herself running to herself, a wind running through her running to herself; and she knew the place, the posture, the sense of it. *Muttering, a door dug into an earthen wall; light, but also stench; breeze, but also a heaviness; black pavement below, white stone above; concord.*

With a sigh of exhausted expression she sank upon the surface of the cold floor, feeling its distinct and angled hardness against her side, her leg, her ankle. The leaf was still in her mouth, and before she opened her eyes she spat it out; a little saliva dribbled sideways down her cheek, and she realized she must be lying with her cheek against the floor. Her stiff hand she tightened. She tested her strength against the floor, with the ball of her palm pushing weakly up. There were voices now, and the sound of the horn was a memory, and the voices were pulling her beneath her armpits, each one dragging at her, now here, now there. Or were they hands? She fell into them, and found herself sitting up. She opened her eyes into Ell's.

'Kay, did you hear the horn?' she asked brightly. 'Did you hear me blow it? It worked, didn't it? I did it.'

Kay smiled and thought to put her hand on Ell's cheek; but it only lifted as far as her arm, so Kay rested it there, almost against Ell's elbow, and squeezed. 'You did it.'

The wraiths gave her five or ten minutes, some water and some dried fruit before they began to ask her the questions she was so anxious to answer. Phantastes wanted to know everything she had noticed from the beginning, and although Kay was ready to recount it all, Flip broke in severely and kept the questions short and direct. 'She hasn't got the energy and we haven't got the time. If Ghast, or Kat, or any of them know we're here, they'll know why we're here; and if they know why we're here, they'll be racing to prevent us from finding him. We've been followed before.'

Chastened, Phantastes left the questions to Will and Flip, and instead hovered around Razzio who, plainly revolted by the whole process, sat hard against the far wall, idly tracing patterns in the worn stone floor. Kay dutifully reconstructed her final impression, trying to recall the minute detail of its clarity, like a white light – bright; so bright she almost could not look at it, even now. It struck her like a dream, something she knew inside and out but had no words to describe, something that could only be experienced, and not detailed; but still she struggled to observe it, as if she had been outside rather than within it, and gave them all the details she could.

They were plainly stumped. She had mentioned the stench, as of rotting leaves or maybe sewage; the door framed by rough stone and set into the earthen wall; the two sorts of stone, one perhaps the paving of a road, the other a sculpting stone, almost marble in its smoothness and translucence. She had recalled the little breeze, which perhaps she had not felt, but seen stirring in – what? – newspapers? But also a heaviness in the air, as of pressure. A sense of movement she remembered, but also a presence or a stasis. The wraiths could do nothing with it. Flip became more and more impatient, his hands stretched taut as he sketched fruitlessly in the air. By contrast Will waited quietly, although he, too, was evidently frustrated – wondering if *he* ought to have tried the integration again, Kay thought; wondering if he ought to have let so young a child risk so much and fail them so completely. Kay searched through her memory of that moment of apprehension, and tried as hard as she could to particularize a little more of it – but it was like trying to tear at granite with her fingernails. Though she was sitting still, she felt her lungs heave, and she gasped after air; a weakness eddied in the muscles of her arms and shoulders; and her head hurt. All she could say, as she at last gave up her attempt at recollection and analysis, was the one word she had almost forgotten: *concord*.

The two wraiths both looked up and at her with sudden interest, then at one another. They had heard something in that of which Kay was entirely ignorant, she knew – she could see the excitement and hope on both haggard faces.

'Was that a word you saw or heard during the dismantling, Kay?' Will asked quietly but urgently.

'No – it was more the word that was hovering over all the things I saw and heard and felt and smelled and tasted – as if they all had a theme or a colour to them, and that was it. Concord. It was the last thing I thought before I realized I was hearing the horn.'

Flip had already got to his feet, and with a fluid motion slung Ell by both arms up and on to his back; she looked surprised, but clung on with manifest delight. 'Let's go,' he said – loudly enough that Phantastes and Razzio, ten metres away, heard him and immediately gathered themselves ready to follow. Flip was stooping out through the door and down the near stairs. Kay looked imploringly at Will.

'The Place de la Concorde. It's in the centre of the city, not far. It may make sense of some of the things you said – it's worth a try, anyway. Anything is worth a try.'

'There was something else,' said Kay.

Will hesitated. Flip was gone.

'There were worms. In the leaf. Something I remembered –'

Will placed his hand, his broad hand, like a blanket on her shoulder, as if to say she should not worry. Its warmth radiated down her side like the heat of a fire or the stroke of a healing knife.

Down from the chapel, banging out through the heavy wooden doors, through the court and on to the street Kay trailed after Razzio with Will beside her. Her legs hung from her waist like withered branches, and something vacant had opened up in her stomach during the dispersal – if that's what it was – in the chapel. She counted out the paces again, forcing herself to throw her legs forward on to the pavement, stride after stride. Will must have noticed her struggling, and when he offered her his back, she took it. After that she was able to give more attention to the streets and buildings they were passing: first, row after row of massive white stone piles, even during these quiet holidays guarded by soldiers and non-uniformed sentries; then the river again, which they crossed by an old bridge with an ornamented stone balustrade running down both sides. A few low boats – almost like canal boats – were moving lazily up and down the river, and though it was cold and the doors were shut up fast, Kay could hear the faint sound of music and something like a megaphone. Beyond that, on the far bank, they passed the front of the Louvre – Will stopped for a moment so that Kay could spin her head all around the interior court, where a huge glass pyramid surrounded by a pool of water stood austerely amid the grand ornamentation of the palace walls. But the others were already gone, and Will had to break almost into a canter in order to keep them in sight as they passed through gilt iron gates and into the palace gardens. Pebbles and cold sand crunched underfoot, and the trees stood stark against the crisp, bright sky. A few snow patches lingered in places on the grey-green grass, and clumps of people – tourists and some couples – ambled around the lesser paths and near the huge Ferris wheel that suddenly dominated the garden. Ahead Kay could see a stone obelisk nearing, directly beyond the end of the garden, and something about the colour of the stone, as they neared it, made her sure that this must be where they were headed. It was like recognizing an old familiar taste. Without surprise she noticed that the garden ended in a long flight of steps, and that, to either side, it must meet the street beyond in a sheer wall. Without surprise she observed a thin but constant stream of traffic circulating around the obelisk, which stood serene and stable in its centre. Without surprise, as they went down the steps, she felt a sudden cool, dank heaviness surround her, as if they had descended into the earthy shadow of the long swards of turf they had just crossed. *It would be here*, she thought. *It must be here.* She slipped off Will's back, touching down into the place.

And then, as they rounded the corner beyond the gate at the bottom of the steps, there he was. If Kay hadn't been looking for him, she would have walked by without knowing him. Though it was the middle of winter, his face glared red in the morning sunlight as if it had burned him; his hair, normally combed back, stood up here and there in ragged brown tufts; his clothes, rumpled and dirty, only seemed familiar on closer consideration; but, above all, his expressions and gestures were completely alien, as if he were playing out some sort of exaggerated character inversion. And his face and hands were animated: he sat on a low crate by the wall, surrounded by little piles of windblown debris, speaking to himself in an unhurried but unimpeded monotone, and gesticulating in a kind of parody of plotting. Kay might almost have thought him some kind of crazed and destitute performer, had she not known him for himself. And while she wanted to run to him, to hug him and hold on to him until he became himself again, Kay knew that she was frightened of him, too.

Will and Flip had stopped by her side. Ell, still clasping Flip's shoulders, was craning to look at Ned More. 'Did I look like that?' Kay asked. 'I mean, was I doing those things . . . when . . . before?'

Will placed his hand gently on her shoulder, but didn't take his eye off Edward More. 'No, Kay, of course not. Most of the time you just lay very still. I still think what you were doing wasn't quite the same as dispersal –'

'It was,' Kay said flatly. 'I still felt solid, kind of whole, when Ell blew the horn, but I was glimpsing something else – this place, here – and if I had just loosened for a moment – Will, believe me, it was the same. I just didn't finish it.'

Flip cut in. 'I don't think we should approach him – at least, not quickly, and not all together. I wonder if we should let him see the girls at all. But if we could get Ell and the horn –'

'The horn is useless here,' Will said, flatly but quietly. Flip didn't argue, though Phantastes raised his eyebrows and watched the others intently.

'Then what do you recommend?'

'Flip, I think we need to do things the old-fashioned way, and trust to our strengths. Maybe we can make a miracle happen.'

Flip was impatient. 'We've been through this so many times. There is no way that she –'

'Will.' Phantastes had his bag off his shoulder in a heartbeat, and was rummaging in it as he spoke. Kay knew what he was looking for, and her eyes pooled with tears at the thought of it. 'Will, I have something of yours that you must take back into your keeping now. I have been carrying it around long enough.'

He withdrew from his sack a little satchel, which Kay had almost forgotten about. Now he carefully loosened its buckles, one by one, then took from it a little wooden box she had first seen in a boat on an underground lake in the caverns beneath Alexandria. In the bright midday January sun it seemed so common and trivial a thing that Kay wondered for a second whether her memory was playing tricks on her. Perhaps this wasn't the same wooden box. Perhaps that incredible thing which she had held to her lips, which she had sounded through the ancient caverns beside the tree of Byblos, was all just a false memory, a dream.

'Old friend, now is not the time for –'

'Take it. Now is exactly the time.'

Will took the box. Kay's heart beat huge strokes in her throat. He undid the metal hasp, and with one last quizzical look at the old wraith cracked the two wooden covers apart. Ell's eyes looked ready to pop with absorption, and even Razzio was staring. But no one could have been so surprised, so focused, so overwrought as immediately, the shuttle in his hand, Will had become.

'But . . . but . . .' he stammered. 'Ghast had it thrown into the sea. It should be lying half cased in silt at the bottom of the ocean. I don't understand.'

'Oh, I heard all his boasts: I will break the loom, I will throw this and that into the sea. But before I let you surrender it up, I plugged all the stops with wax,' Phantastes replied. His brow was furrowed with mischief. 'And I hoped desperately. The night after Ghast's barbarisms I took two boats and we rowed the coast off Bithynia with a net. It's a heavy thing, but the hollow chamber within it must have given it just enough buoyancy; we recovered it after only seven hours.'

Kay could see that Will's hand was a natural but also a practised fit for the shuttle. He spun it absently between his thumb and palm as he gawked, sucking air, and then looked at Edward More. A colossal sadness was clearing like a cloud from his features, and he appeared suddenly boyish – blood under his temples, a tip to his ears, hair slightly sparky and a pucker swelling in one of his cheeks. For the first time in days Kay felt an exhilarating surge of unchecked hope.

'Use it, Will. If ever anyone deserved a miracle, that one is you.'

Will looked to Flip for his approval.

'Do it. It's our best chance now.'

Will held the shuttle to his lips as he skirted along the wall towards Kay's father. At first Kay thought he was about to blow it, but after a few steps it became clear that he was whispering to it as he walked. Perhaps, she thought, he was saying a prayer. Flip gently dropped Ell to the ground, and the two girls, with the wraiths in their wake, cautiously followed Will until they were close enough to eavesdrop on what was said. Kay could hear her father talking now, the angry and percussive notes of his monologue punching through the light drone of traffic passing nearby. She couldn't make out individual words, and perhaps there were none to speak of; but the tone and voice, though altered, were his. He gave no sign, as Will sat down a couple of metres away against the wall, that he was aware he had been joined. The girls paced a little way off before themselves cowering into the safety of the wall, almost out of sight. The others settled beside them. And then they all remained completely still for several minutes.

When at last the shuttle sounded, Kay was looking at the obelisk across the road. The note was so thoroughly embedded in the air itself that at first she assumed her mind was playing a trick on her, and she was simply hearing what she had been admiring, seconds before, as the awesome majesty of the obelisk. But this sound, it soon became clear, was of another character: though a single high note, it throbbed with intense overtones that came and went, came and went like a petulant tide. Will's face behind the shuttle and his fists lay still and impassive, but the note ached with expression. Kay found herself paralysed by it, as did her father, whose restive rant came to an abrupt end. He stared about him, as if furtively.

Phantastes leaned over to Kay's ear. 'Good choice!' he whispered. 'I thought he might go for that on a day like today. The note you sounded. Love.' They all settled back and drew their coats over their noses as Will began to speak.

18

The Clue

'When Theseus came to the city of Knossos, he was only a boy of eighteen, but he had been charged with a peril on which the weight of his father's kingdom depended. Athens with all its country had for years been a vassal state to the Cretan king, Minos. Now Minos was a great master of wave and wind. From his island seat he had grown to be judge over many peoples and nations. These he bound to his power through a hard regime of heavy exactions – that is, fines which his subjugate princes paid not only in money, but in human lives. To his palace at Knossos annually the richer cities of Greece sent tribute in oil, fish, pottery and gold. They also sent their children: the foremost among the boys and girls of every city, who entered the gates of Minos' palace in chains, and never departed after. It was said that he loosed them in his legendary labyrinth, a maze of winding tunnels built all of stone, at the centre of which was situated the lair of the Minotaur, a gigantic and fabulous beast with the body of a man and the head of a bull. Perhaps this monster existed. Perhaps this monster devoured the children. At any rate, they never again returned to their homes, to their parents.

'King Aegeus ruled over the richest and most powerful city of the Greek Peloponnese, and the bloody conquest of his Athens was the brightest jewel in Minos' awful crown. The proudest horses are broken only with the cruellest whipping, and so it was with Aegeus: to him and to his city Minos reserved the most terrible of tributes, demanding the yearly surrender of so many goods, so much lustrous metal, so many fired pots and painted vases, that in a short time he beggared the kingdom. All this Athens might have borne. What it could not bear was the annual harvest of its youth: fourteen of the fairest and most promising children of the city, picked out by Minos' lieutenants, shackled in sober rows on his galleys and shipped into the swallowing sea. In five years the city had grown sombre and quiet; after ten years it was little more than a wasteland. The citizens went about their daily business like stick figures in an empty dream. Fishermen lost their catches. Musicians forgot their notes. Buildings began to crumble.

'Aegeus had no hope, but he had a son, and in the twelfth year of the Cretan tyranny this son, Theseus, was selected by Minos' agents to be sent across the sea, sacrificed and fed to the Minotaur. Theseus, too, had no hope, but he had beauty, and when the galleys arrived in Knossos and he was delivered into the hands of Minos' palace officers, it happened that the eye of the young princess, Minos' only daughter, Ariadne, fell upon him. Her eye fell upon him as the pale sky falls upon the morning, when frost lies on the land and no birds sing. The touch of her glance alighted here and there, on this eye and the chiselled turn of that high cheek, upon his dark hair and the new brawn of his arm, on the fullness of his lip and the dusty furze of his thigh. But like the dawn her particular glance sheeted and enveloped him, too; and who can find himself revealed by such a light, and not search for the lamp that made it? She drew him like a thread; suffice that he who was illuminated at last found out the source of that radiance. Their eyes met. Each looked. Each was looked upon. For that moment each was nothing but that look.

'In those days no woman in the Greek world was reputed so fair, so royal as the Cretan princess Ariadne. Poets adorned her with their epithets: she of the white arms, she of the flashing eyes, she of the burnished hair, she with fingers fast as flights of arrows, she with skin clear as the cream of goats. Her circling arms were a king's cradle, her voice his well-tuned lyre, her broad and unclouded brow the fair field of his fortunes. This was cheap poet stuff. In truth her beauty dazzled; but for all her outward speaking ornament, the real ground and substance of her glories was inward, and snaked within in close-seamed veins of rich ore unmined. She knew her worth, but dimly; others grasped clutchingly only at an outward shadow.

'Chief among those who misprized Ariadne was her father. From the first she was to him a jewel, which he was content to wear among the other jewels of his crown, the better to show off his majesty. But as she grew and matured, he doted upon her ever more obsequiously until – when she had become a woman – the services and honour he offered her amounted to nothing less than idolatry. Ariadne was the most precious thing in his life. She was the sum of his cares and achievements, the circle and ambit of his happiness. Without her he could not stir, not even to dine or to pastimes. At affairs of state he was naked unless she stood by his side. When decisions were taken, either she graced the proceedings or they did not proceed. She was his life, his all in all.

'To be cherished so absolutely may seem a blessing. It can be a curse. Ariadne found herself imprisoned in the love of her father, the admiration of his court, the devotion of many nations. Not one man saw her for who she was or – what was worse – for who she might become. In days to come not even Helen of Troy would be so shamefully bound and bent to every man's need, made into the sign and emblem of their honour. Ariadne passed the nights in the darkness of sleep, but she woke into a greater darkness, and more complete. Her life was a maze, a tunnelling, in which she wandered blindly with no hope of escape. It was said that Minos' queen, Pasiphaë, had borne at Ariadne's birth another child, the Minotaur, a monster sired not by her husband but by the bull of Poseidon. To Ariadne, this beast that laired at the centre of the labyrinth, this brother, this terrifying half-god that ate up the beauty of her father's imperial sway, was her double. She felt herself to be imprisoned in the dark tunnels of its mazy monstrousness.

'When Ariadne's look fell upon the beauty of Theseus, she saw in him as in a crushing fall of rock the whole depth of a hopeless ambition. He had an insatiable appetite to prove himself, to survive the Minotaur and to deliver his people from their bondage. But she also saw her own deliverance, a choice that she might make, the chance to be more than an ornament or an icon, the chance to plot. She saw the chance to create her own story.

'On the night before he was to be led into the labyrinth and sacrificed to the Minotaur, Ariadne put into his hands what is known as a clue – a spool of twisted thread, wound tight – and a knife. Theseus knew what to do. Minos' officers came in the morning, before dawn, and roused the young prince not with a kick or a blow to the head, but with a whispered call. The priest poured oil and milk upon his face and loins, and summoned the gods by strange names as he consecrated the victim's flesh and life to their glory. Theseus stood motionless in the paling gloom, saying nothing; for in his mouth he concealed the tightly bound clue, and against the inside of his thigh, beneath his tunic, hung Ariadne's knife. The officers lifted him by the elbows and marched him slowly down the long, straight flight of steps that bowelled below the palace. Before the great bronze door, embossed with the astonishing head of Poseidon's sea-charging bull, they released him, then stepped back to the safety of the flight ascending. The priest chanted from the third step. Theseus knelt only a moment on his knee. The door swung with surprising ease when he pushed it. Within, all was darkness; that darkness closed on him like a tomb as he drove the door shut then dropped the long bolt home. But he walked boldly into the labyrinth, bearing ever towards the centre, unspooling the thread behind him. When he reached the monster, there was no struggle. It awaited him like a lover, panting. After they had embraced, he killed it with a soft upward thrust of his blade; and then he followed the thread – back to Ariadne, back to the light and freedom, back to his father's ship, back to Athens. But Ariadne – hers was not a human thread. The gods claimed her.'

19

The Bride

Kay discovered herself standing before her father. The cold wind that ran along the wall bit at her fingertips, and she felt dizzy, as if she had been turning cartwheels. She couldn't think how she had come to be standing there – here – when all the time, she thought, she had been sitting with Ell by the wall, listening to Will's story. And she remembered it, down to the last syllable – which in itself was strange because, though it seemed impossible to her even as she thought it, she somehow knew that story herself, and had always known it; it was not as if she knew the words to say, but that she knew the threads that would draw forth from her the same words that had come from Will. Every word he had spoken, she thought as she stood blinking into the stinging cold before her father, she had willed him to speak.

So preoccupied was Kay with her thoughts that she startled to hear her father speak as he turned sharply to Will. 'Did you see what I saw?' he demanded, and in his usual voice. Direct, authoritative.

'I don't know what I saw. I don't believe what I saw,' Will immediately replied. His face he had thrust into his palms, and the long tips of his fingers uncurled from his pendent hair, and then, suddenly tensing, dug into his scalp. He sobbed quietly, as Kay had heard her mother sob the week before.

'Please,' Kay said, 'Dad, please, let's go home.' She wanted above all things to throw her arms around him, to bury her face in the warm woollen must of his jacket. *Take us home.*

Edward More was a tall, thickset man, but beneath the brawn his muscles, supple and responsive, were sure. And his body, sitting on an old crate, resisted her approach, gave nothing to her. Instead, his gaze locked into hers across the scant distance that separated them. He eyed her not suspiciously but curiously, as if he were newly appraising her – as if, Kay thought, alarmed, she were no longer his daughter.

'Dad, please –' she began.

'No, Katharine. Don't you understand what has just happened? Can't you feel, can't you remember, what you just did?'

Dad. Won't you just take us home?

Kay looked around. 'I must have stood up while the story . . . I must have walked over, that's all,' she said hesitantly. She was about to point to Ell and Phantastes and Flip and Razzio, but when she turned to them, even as she began to raise her arm, she saw that something was not right. Ell was cowering in the crook of Flip's arm, and Razzio and Phantastes held her gaze with a kind of stupefaction, but only for a moment;

then they turned away. Without looking directly at her, and almost as if feeling self-conscious, Phantastes pushed himself to his feet and crossed silently to where Will and her father sat. He placed his hand very gingerly on Kay's shoulder, as if assuring himself that it was still there, that it was still a shoulder.

Why?

'And Ontos let her on to the dais,' said Phantastes, almost in a whisper. 'We ought to have known then, Will. We ought. We ought to have thought.'

Kay looked down at herself, her sense of time and place still in disarray. Her battered brown shoes carried the scars of frost and ice, and in a few places nicks and gouges from the hard stone of the mountain. On her instep the alluvial mud of the Nile had caked, leaving streaks, now in the cold turned almost white. There was salt here, too, from the spray of the sea off Patras and, on the lower cuff of her trousers, grass stains she had picked up – where? – in the House of the Two Modes. Tucked in around her waist she could feel the light cotton wad of the robe Will had given her in Alexandria – no, in the air, above Alexandria. She had *flown*. On top of that, this heavy anorak Oidos had dug from an old chest of drawers, a garment perhaps as old as memory, stained with the old wraith's tears. She couldn't take it all in. She felt lean, somehow, and under the tough, stained fabric of her trousers her legs looked more sinewy than she had remembered them. She held out her hands; they seemed as ever, though a little cracked and a little scabbed, and red across the knuckles from the cold.

Phantastes, standing just to her left, held out his awkward hands, cupped, as if he would take hers. But he didn't. 'Child, do you recall any of what you just said?'

Kay looked up at him, squinting into the wind, for the first time.

'Katharine,' said her father, 'a moment ago you stood up, walked directly over to me and put your hands on my face. Are you sure you don't remember that?'

'No. I mean, no, I don't remember that.'

Why won't anyone touch me?

Her father turned to look at Will, who lifted his head from his hands to reveal a gaze so drawn, eyes so inky, cheeks so lined that Kay's head rushed with an exhilaration that almost made her giggle. 'Tell her, Will.'

Will held out his hands, palms cupped and facing upwards. 'Kay, there is something I never told you about the Bride, and the old stories about how she appeared to Orpheus. I think I didn't tell you because I hoped it was true, but I feared that it wasn't.' He stopped and closed his hands, looking at them for a long few moments. 'It is said that Orpheus spoke of her whispering, spoke of her mouth moving inscrutably as she darted between trees or slid round corners just out of sight. It is said that the whispering touched him in his dreams, and that, where others saw and felt the visions and movements of their dream-thoughts, he heard them, and saw not things but words weaving into and from him. And it is also said that, when he became practised at inviting the presence of the Bride, and could call her to him almost like a familiar – it is said that he

381

found the words she was whispering to be none other than his own.'

Kay stood shivering in the cold breeze. Her father sat very near her, her sister, too, and she was surrounded by friends she trusted and had come to adore – but instantly she throbbed with a loneliness that coursed through her arms and legs like cold lead pumping from her stomach. She took a step back towards the street and, she remembered, the moving traffic. She hardly cared.

'I don't understand. Why are you telling me this?'

'For the past several minutes, Kay – more; longer – you have been telling the story with me. Using the same words. You weren't repeating what I said – you were just saying the words as I was also saying them. All of them. At the same time. You didn't miss one word. And when I tried to stop the story, to change what I was saying, to lose the thread – it was like you knew that, too, and no matter what I did, you were there with me. It seemed almost as if you knew why I was saying what I was saying. More: it seemed as if you were speaking the words through me.'

'What does that mean?' Kay's whole exhausted body ached for her father to pick her up and take her home. *Somebody tell me what that means.*

'What I think makes no sense,' said Will.

Kay stiffened. 'You mean you think that I –'

'No,' Will said. 'I –'

'Yes,' said Phantastes, with decision. 'Yes I do.'

'As do I,' said Razzio as he got to his feet. 'That was a feat I could not have plotted with all the causes in the world.'

'Nor a dream I might have imagined with all the leaves of the tree of Byblos.'

'It's just . . . maybe at last we know what you are,' said Will.

'I knew you would find me,' said Ned More. 'Now everything is possible.'

Kay stared at her father, at his soiled, matted clothing, his filthy hair, his stubbled and exhausted face, his eyes that were once so playful, so generous, so warm. Now they seemed cold, appraising.

This was all on purpose.

She couldn't go to him.

You set me up. Did you set me up?

She shuddered. *Ariadne.* Her gaze moved without comprehension across each of the rest of them in turn, from Will to Phantastes to Razzio. She lingered there; the old left-wraith's broad smile was as warm as it was unusual, and Kay knew it, and she wanted to smile back, to take his olive hands, and dance, to cry out for joy, and sing, because this was a triumph, theirs was the victory, hers was the quest's end and it had all been for *something*, they had *done it* – but there was a mass of muscle squeezing the top of her neck, and her whole head felt as if it were a fist tightening.

Ariadne. The gods claimed her. Hers was not a human thread.

She couldn't bear to think, and didn't: in a single movement she turned and walked down the street, away from all of them and back towards the river, following the flow of the cars. Had she wondered whether they would follow her, she wouldn't have cared; but as she walked her mind was entirely occupied with other sensations, other feelings: the wind, still on the back of her neck; the firmness of the paving stones beneath her thin soles, and the chill of them; the sharp, acid taste of the car exhaust in the rounded curve of her nostrils as she breathed; and under it all, the thin, frail sense of a body that she had thought her own, but which seemed to be something else completely. She wished that the wind would stop blowing her along, and would simply blow through her. She wished it might carry her into the black profound of the silty river.

She took the corners haphazardly, choosing a way and then, as randomly as she could, striking off in the opposite direction whenever the inkling struck her. She was determined not to be determined, and if they would follow her, then at least she would give them a time of it. Some of the streets, as narrow as cart tracks, almost invited her to perch on their miniature stoops and sills, where the white gloss of the wooden door panelling touched the heavy, foot-sallowed stone, or where the flaking black painted handrails drilled into the discoloured tiles. She might have rested, might have waited for the others who surely trailed not far behind her. She longed to sit on a stoop and cry. Yet she always carried on to just one further corner, or across one further intersection, one further trunk-lined park. To stop would be to admit limit; and so, even though she was growing footsore, even though she often longed to sit, or even to lean up against a wall in the shadow of some wall or tree, she pressed on, out – past the constraint that, until today, she would have called herself. *Myself.*

On a broad and empty avenue, largely deserted but for the occasional taxi with its droning rush hurtling past her, Kay's legs finally gave out and she crumpled at a bus stop. For three or four minutes she enjoyed the stillness and the sense of relief in her fatigued muscles, and listened to her heart play its rhythm across the motion of her breathing as it slowed. For three or four minutes she wished the others might just leave her for three or four more minutes. But no one came; no slight peripheral motion, as of dark coats and hesitant steps, gathered at the edges of her waiting. A small knot of fear wound itself up in her gut as she leaned on the swivel stool in the bus shelter, watching the lines on the street as they ran motionless into her vision and then ran out again. Ten minutes passed. She began to count them. Twenty. When she finally amassed the courage to look around, there was nothing to see but an old drunk staggering down the near side of the street, away from her, with one arm extended and his voice at full rant. A convulsion ran through her upper body like a shock. She dug one set of nails into the back of the other hand, but she didn't know which.

They would not be coming for her. She was alone. And because she had deliberately avoided pattern, avoided paying attention to her choices, avoided even looking around as she walked, she could remember or gather no sense of her path, no guess at a trail that might lead her back to the place from which she had come. She had felt an overwhelming need to escape from the stories Will had been telling, and to evade and avoid all the elements of those stories, and how they might erase her, shadow her, reduce her. But, she thought, by doing that she had lost her father again. She had lost Ell again. Kay began to cry because no one was there to watch her do it.

Hot sobs boiled out of her, and the tears ran down her face. To be alone. To have run. To have lost them all. To be alone. She wiped at her tears. This was not what she wanted. Still she cried. As she held the wet cuff of her robe to her face, feeling its cold pressing on her cheek, she seemed to see something very far away – a dark room, a bewildered awakening, a body wrapped in damp blankets, a lamp at the door – and, with a start like the flood of the leaf on her tongue, she remembered her dreams, night after night of them: dreams of her father and of Ghast; dreams of a journey down the river, of Firedrake, of anger, of pride; dreams of a wicked, cold intensity. Dreams of a red light setting on Bithynia.

What does it mean? What can it all mean?

And then, suddenly, as if still in a dream, an incredible thing happened. Down the empty street a bus loomed and rumbled, and the driver, seeing Kay huddled in the glass shelter, began to apply the squealing brakes. Kay turned from the bus as it stopped and the door swung wide: she had no money, no idea where to go, and above all no French. Facing towards the back of the bus, she tried to give the driver the impression that she was not intending to travel. In the back of the bus two or three people sat in different places – in the far rear, under the lights, an old woman with a white bun and dark red lipstick; on the far side, facing her, a dark-skinned boy in a pressed shirt with starched lapels, clutching a rucksack on his lap; and near her, very near her, facing away, a dark shock of long black hair that must belong to a young woman. Kay was looking at her as the door closed and the bus's engine began to lumber up into motion again. And that's when the woman turned her face.

It was Kat. Their eyes met, and Kat leaped from her seat, but the bus was already picking up speed, and all she could do was to race to the back, fumbling for the bell as she clambered into the rear windows, trying to bring the bus to a halt while, Kay realized, not losing sight of her sudden quarry. Kay's legs recoiled on their exhaustion like springs, and she shot out of the shelter in a panic. At first she simply wanted to get out of sight and to evade that gaze; but as soon as she had thrown herself safely behind the pier of a large office building, she realized she needed to know where and when the bus would make its next stop. As she peered out from behind the stone and watched it slowing, she thought she would turn to run the opposite way, but then it struck her – Kat was a left-wraith, and if she were in Paris, she would be here for one reason only: *she had been on her way to the others*. A stifling gob rose in Kay's throat as she apprehended the danger the others were in, and the complexity of what she would have to do to recover them. The bus had slowed to a stop nearly half a mile down the straight, broad boulevard. Sure enough, only one dark-haired passenger issued on to the pavement and, sure enough, she headed directly back towards Kay, half running and half flying in her haste. *So it will be a game of cat and mouse*, Kay thought. *Hunter-seeker.*

On still weekend days in November, when the fog had settled overnight and hugged the stubbled fields like a damp blanket,

Kay and Ell had played along the edge of the trees, darting in and out of visibility in a game that was not quite catch. Each sought the other; each evaded the other. The rules were simple, but the action quickly became complex: both hunted and both were prey, and, because the game could only end by surprise, both struggled to keep the other within and just out of sight. It was a game of edges. Now Kay played it again, using a logic that had become instinctive. She moved laterally, down the side street just behind her, but making sure first to weave slightly into the boulevard so that Kat would see her turning. It was crucial that Kat should commit to the long stretch of boulevard between the two of them, and not turn before her – Kay wanted her to follow her, and not to intercept her – so she took her time, moving slowly, trying to give the impression that she didn't know that Kat had left the bus, didn't know that Kat was following her. She pretended to be careless, and hoped. Once round the corner and out of sight, she sprinted down the street and then turned left again, doubling back in the direction of the bus, but one block over. So much mist, Kay thought with a little satisfaction, into which she might disappear, and from which she might luringly dart.

The next stage was the slip. This was Kay's favourite part of the game, and the one at which she was most accomplished. In the field behind the Laundry Farm, where she and her sister had most often played the previous autumn, Kay had so fully perfected the slip that she had almost hesitated to use it, knowing how desperately frustrated it made Ell feel. But her tools there were trees, fogs, hedges and the odd ditch, fence or stile, while here she had buildings, crowds and – just at that moment she picked it out in the distance, three blocks ahead, topped by its oval sign and sinuous lettering – a Métro station. Once she saw this, Kay didn't even need to plan. She had pulled Kat back towards the bus route, drawing her – she hoped – in the direction she had been going. Now, if she could just manage to lose her, Kat might well take the bait and revert to her first purpose.

Down the narrowing street, threading through the casual shoppers with their underarm parcels and their steaming breath, Kay resisted the urge to look behind her, trusting that Kat was still pointing to the quarry. She pretended ease, trying to look relaxed, casual, even as her feet moved quickly under her. There was hardly any traffic on the street, so she stole only the most careless-seeming glance behind her as she crossed over, about a block before the station. She thought she glimpsed Kat – perhaps running now, but certainly much closer – about a hundred metres away. Kay paused for a moment before a pâtisserie, pretending for the briefest delay to covet some cakes; in reality she was ticking off the seconds as her heart raced, one second to every two, then three beats, letting Kat close the gap, letting her relax into this little snare. Then Kay wheeled, touched a lamppost with her shaking arm and drove forward, down into the Métro stairs.

The rank, warm smell of rot and urine wafted up as she took the stairs two at a time – now out of sight and again racing a little, making up time to work the slip and listening hard for the sound of a train. The whole art would depend on choosing the right platform – of which, she saw as she came off the stairs, there were four: two pairs on two lines. She had no ticket, but the station was mostly deserted at midday just after the new year, and with a little speed she might clear the stiles (just like in the fields at home) without anyone much taking notice. She hardly thought, but a scramble needs none; and at the small price of a knocked knee, she got away. Now she slowed, still listening hard, trying to pull the sounds of the trains out of their tunnels. There was a faint rumble from somewhere, but which of the two sets of stairs produced it she could not yet tell. Footsteps, however, she did hear – but too plodding, too heavy to be Kat's. And then another set, this one lighter, quicker, not even but syncopated, as if taking the steps in hurls, and then threading around someone else – and Kay held her posture for a second, but only a second – like a bob on a line, just before the fish bites – and then dropped towards the stairs.

The rumble was growing louder, but Kay was still unsure. She would have to guess, and did. As soon as she was out of sight of the turnstiles, she threw herself at the stairs, trying to get to the bottom and round the corner before Kat gained them, half sliding with her hands down the rails to either side. At the bottom she almost froze – the sound of the approaching train had grown fainter, not louder, but she was now committed, with no way back. Ahead the corridor ran straight for about twenty metres; to the right and left smaller passages led to the platforms. Kay heard steps behind her. She walked slowly towards the right-hand tunnel, seeming to check the signs as she ducked into the alcove, as casually as she could. Instantly behind the shadow of the wall she sprang again into full flight. She had about seven seconds on her pursuer, and needed to use every one of them if she were to escape this dead end. The platform itself was almost empty, but the rumbling, strangely, seemed a little louder. Kay scanned the tunnel in both directions, looking for lights, for some kind of departure screen, for expectant passengers.

And then she saw it, just beyond a couple of teenagers holding hands down by the furthest end of the platform: a dark corridor leading on to a small staircase, marked with the colours of the second line. That's where the sound was coming from. She bolted for the passage. As she gained another stairway, she heard the clack of Kat's heeled shoes behind her. Three by three she dropped down these new stairs, shot over the connecting corridor and round a corner, and then down the last flight. The train was just pulling in below her, and there might just be time – and the right vantages – to pull it off. From the connecting corridor Kat would be able to see the platform for a few seconds before, turning the corner and heading down the stairs, she lost sight of it and Kay disappeared for a couple of seconds. If she timed it just so, Kat would see her running and would assume that she had boarded the train. Kay didn't know which way the train would be travelling, but as she flew off the stairs she crossed her fingers. A conductor stood on the platform, and Kay's heart sank – surely he would follow her with his eyes as she peeled off back up the main stairs? – but he nodded for her to board, and then stepped on himself. Kat's heels rang out on the access bridge above the platform. Kay bounded down the side of the train, hoping that her white coat was catching the light. As the footsteps suddenly grew muffled, she leaped into a side passage. Behind her the doors closed and the train began to pull away. Kay stole a glance backwards as she heaved pantingly up the stairs and – *Brilliant!* she thought – saw the train pulling forward, away from the sound of Kat's footsteps, now almost drowned by the roar. Kat wouldn't be able to see the empty carriage as it disappeared into the tunnel, nor – she thought as she yanked herself round another corner at the top of the stairs – the quiet-stepping girl as she vanished into the maze of passageways, heading waywardly back towards the light.

But the hunt was hardly over, and Kay sobered quickly. She had to gather her breath and find a safe, invisible hiding place from which to mark her own prey. As she came back up, Kat would quickly reveal whether she had fallen for the lure: if she took the main corridors, slowly and directly heading for the street, Kay would know that she was safe; but if she took the smaller side passages, listening for footsteps, the slip would have failed.

Kay bounded up the long flight of stairs before her as quietly and quickly as she could, puffing her cheeks strenuously and pushing down on her aching, wobbly thighs with more than a girl's force. *If I am to be the Bride*, Kay thought grimly to herself, *I'll have to get better at disappearing*.

She gained the level. Up here she would have an easier time of it, she thought: columns stood at regular intervals in a few parts of the station lobby, and she need only skulk in a shadow and then play the circling game. The columns were not much thicker than trees, and Kay was a past professional at the childish sport of trunk-shadowing; without crackling leaves underfoot to give her away, it would be even easier than at home. She chose her column and waited for the clack of those telltale heels.

This left her now on the cusp of the last, easiest part of the course: the flip and chase. With a few more thudding heartstrokes and a bit of jittery footwork, Kay was sure it had worked – Kat's footsteps died away as she rounded the corner of the station exit, and Kay could hear them slow as she laboured – now tired – up the final set of stairs. She waited until the sound had just died away, and then sprinted after her. So the hunted became the hunter.

Once again in the sunlight, Kay tried hard to plot her bearings. She had come up a different stairway from the one by which she had entered, and for a moment she spun, terrified, thinking that she had emerged on an entirely different street or forgotten which way she was headed. But then a purple awning a minute's walk away began to shake as the proprietor drew it a bit further out against the sun, and Kay remembered she had noted it for a landmark just before she dashed into the Métro. Kat couldn't have gone far, she decided, and if she wasn't on this street, she would have crossed back to the larger boulevard, perhaps to get the bus again. Kay set off warily, keeping her head moving as she walked, prying with her eyes into every alcove, every storefront, every alley as she passed it. Now that she was the hunter, she must not lose her prey. The street had emptied slightly, or perhaps there were fewer shops along this section, but still there was no sign of Kat moving among the few sparse groups of people. Kay began to panic, and raced to the first corner, hoping to find that Kat had simply turned left.

She hadn't: the tree-lined street, with its two lines of parked cars and its neatly manicured front doors, was completely void of people. Kay spun round, but in the other direction, across the larger road, it was the same. She ran back to the intersection, furious with herself for letting the line slacken, and terrified that Kat would pop out behind her and put the chase back on the other foot. She whirled. A few cars raced past on the street, revving their engines menacingly, and an old man, nearly bumping into Kay as she reeled, stopped short in annoyance, then kept walking. *Down*, she thought – she had to get down, put her head down, keep her advantage. She crashed heavily into a corner beside some newspapers that lay stacked just outside a newsagent's, and huddled there with her back against some aluminium screening. She watched the street frantically.

She couldn't have been luckier. A few doors down, the black hair swept out on to the street from a café, and Kat passed within a metre of Kay, taking the corner to the left from which Kay had just returned. She was carrying a piece of cake wrapped in paper, and taking slow, uneven strides as she ate. Kay counted to twenty, then another ten for good measure, and followed her. The cars would give her cover, she knew, and the emptiness of the street would work to her advantage, now that she was giving chase.

From street to street Kay marked her: on to the boulevard, down a quarter of a mile, left along a park, through a pavilion dominated by weird cube sculptures, and through a maze of tiny back streets, partly cobbled. She made the most of the cover she found, but she hardly needed to worry: Kat had long since given up thinking about Kay, and seemed completely unaware that she was being tracked. When they came out on to the river, and the wraith began to make for a large bridge, Kay's heart sank and soared at once, for just beyond the bridge was the obelisk she had watched earlier in the morning, but the ground between the bridge and the open plaza, where the obelisk stood, was completely open. No place to hide at all. There was no way she could risk following Kat across the water, though she felt sure that her father, Ell and the others could not be far. Instead, she squatted at a corner, half behind a post, and hoped for the best, watching the black duffel coat and glossy hair slowly disappear into the middle distance.

When Kat had almost vanished on to the far side of the plaza, Kay threaded through the traffic of the busy street and struck out for the wall against which they had sat earlier that morning, hoping to hang as much as she could in its shadow. But she couldn't make up the lost ground, and Kat crossed behind some traffic and turned in behind a bus; when the bus pulled away, she had gone. Kay wondered if she had boarded the bus itself, or had slipped behind it down one of two smaller lanes she could just make out from across the road, and she was just about to break into a run when a large arm grabbed her from the right, lifted her fully off the ground and practically hoisted her sideways across the pavement and into the opening door of a parked car.

She might have screamed, but something stiff was shoved up against her mouth. Instead she kicked, and hard, but because she couldn't see, her legs mostly met air, and her knees shook painfully beneath the caps. The car door slammed behind her, and after a severe bout of jostling and stamping she got her head free enough to see, and to scream.

She stopped yelling almost as soon as she started, because the face staring into hers from the front was that of Phantastes himself. The arm still clasped warmly about her middle was Flip's, and he gave her a gentle squeeze. 'You're a lot heavier than your sister, Kay,' he said in a low voice, smiling. 'Now get your heads down. Now!'

Phantastes faced forward and slumped down in his seat. Judging from the sleeve she could see, Razzio sat behind the wheel, with a hood drawn over his head. Flip could hardly make himself as inconspicuous as either of them, but he slid down anyway, with his legs lying across the floor of the car, and hunkered as low as he was able.

'We thought you were gone,' Flip said. 'Just after you walked off we were ambushed from the wall by about ten of Ghast's most loyal acolytes. Somehow they must not have seen you, but they certainly saw us. We thought we might find some left-wraiths skulking about your father, but not in those numbers, and while we were prepared –' he touched his palm to the long knife belted at his side – 'well, we weren't *that* prepared. We scattered. Will took your sister and your father. They ran towards the river. The three of us split up, heading back up the stairs and through the garden. They must have been after Will, because only two of them paid us any attention at all, and between the three of us we lost them. Well, we did more than lose them.'

Kay raised her eyebrows. Flip clearly wanted to say more.

'One of the advantages of being a clever left-wraith,' he said, 'is that a carefully plotted tale is not, in some circumstances, altogether different from a well-orchestrated rumble. They ought to remember very little of our little trap when they wake up from their concussions – eh, Phantastes?'

'Boom,' said Phantastes with a chuckle.

'But Kat –'

'Yes, we saw her. We certainly didn't expect to see you following her, though! How did you find her?'

'I didn't. I just ran into her. Like a dream. At a bus stop. She tried to catch me, but I gave her the slip. Then I followed her back here. I thought she would lead me back to you.'

'Smart. Kat's been in Paris a lot, and knows it better than any of us. I'd guess she's organizing Ghast's wispers here, maybe everywhere – though not closely enough to recognize the car we borrowed from those two unfortunate goons of hers. Anyway, she'll almost definitely have gone to Ghast's Paris hide, up on the hill near Montmartre. I think she probably just wanted to take a little walk-through here to see if the place had been cleared.'

'But why didn't she recognize you, if she was looking for you? If she's a left-wraith, shouldn't she have figured all this out?' Kay wriggled lower in the seat to take the stress off her back.

'Sure – except that there is one thing the left-wraiths *aren't* plotting for, and it's throwing off all their thinking. If I'm right, it will be the reason why Will and your father and Ell got away on the river.'

Kay raised her eyebrows but said nothing. *The river.*

'They would never believe that the Bride has returned,' said Flip, beaming, and he rubbed her head furiously. 'You're going to blow up in their faces like a bomb!'

Razzio coughed from the front seat. 'I might remind you, Flip, that you and I are both left-wraiths.'

Flip's smile broadened, if that were possible. 'Kay, they're going to love it. By the time you're finished with them, Ghast won't have the loyalty of the least tick crawling on that mangy pelt of his. When they find out that the Bride has returned! We'll run him off the mountain. No, we'll seal him in the mountain, and then we'll leave him there. We'll go back to Bithynia.' *Bithynia. A red light over Bithynia.*

'I suppose we'll have to,' said Razzio, sighing.

'*I suppose we'll have to,*' echoed Phantastes, quietly guffawing.

'And how are they going to find out?' said Kay, blushing.

'We'll show them, of course. Razzio, drive.'

*H*e stood in the hall, where the banners had been hung according to his instructions. The hearth had been laid ready for the fire. On the dais at the west end the twelve thrones also stood ready, and before them, like a promise, his own chair of state. Before that, set by his servants into its ancient place in the floor, the iron wheel lay ready for the great consult. Eleven times he had turned it; only one night still remained.

He walked the length of the hall and counted every step. He returned, and did it again. He would not yet sit on the throne, not in this place. The moment would be all.

The other wraiths were sleeping. It was the dead of night. But he would leave nothing to chance, nothing to the improvisation that the imaginers claimed for an art, but which was no more than chance.

There was one throne that would of course remain empty. He looked at it. It was, after all, a plain wooden chair, not broad, the carved arms low, the back gently curved and not high. It was fashioned of a dark wood – mahogany, he supposed – which gleamed in the light of his lamp as he held it close. It had been *empty for as long as he could remember – in fact, one of his earliest memories of the Shuttle Hall was of staring at this chair with a mean eye that he came later to realize had been contempt. It was nothing special, granted; but it had been hers, and she had left it all the same. As a young man, he had stood almost where he stood now, staring at that chair while the others cried out in the throes of story, staring at the loose end, the void, the fault, the little wound.*

It was only later, when he was more mature and experienced, that he came to understand that the absence was only a symbol. The right-wraiths could have filled the place, had they wanted to do so. They did not. They preferred in their arrogance to let the chair sit empty, a goad to the left-wraiths, a breezy performance of their own careless self-assurance. How it had galled him to see the First Wraith kneel before that empty chair at every Twelfth Night and ask for guidance from a deserter!

He turned to the left, walked the twenty-eight paces to the stalls and took his ancient place among the benches of the left-wraiths. He had not sat here for many years. In the gloom of middle night he could see no further than his lamp could show him, but he felt the old presence of the Shuttle Hall around him all the same, complete. He thought of his pride at first joining the Honourable Society, his anger at discovering how little his kind were esteemed within it, the revenge he had sworn when they called him 'scrivener'.

Of the twelve sources of story he knew all there was to know. Within quest, three branches; within love, alike three; within chronicle, three; and one each for discovery, for gain and for loss.

He knew the character of heroes, the trials of lovers, the cunning of politicians and the strategies of generals. He knew the songs of bards and the idle games of shepherds, the laughter of tricksters and the venom of revengers. All forms of poetry he knew, and every kind of prose. Many of the greatest anthologies, the treasure books and mythologies that now stood in the library in the mountain, he had copied. He had seldom blotted a line, and bore the scars of that precision in the dullness of his eye and the thick mass of locked muscle in his neck. What he had done for the Honourable Society. What he had given.

Although a left-wraith by name, he had never cared for the affectations of plotters, for their boards and stones, their talk of the thread and their reverence for their little collection of sacred instruments. He had endured the voice of the shuttle, the braying sandblast of the horn, the clack of the loom. Throughout his youth he had rolled his eyes in private at the talk of snakes and swords. He had said the words, though they almost stuck in his throat. He had tolerated Razzio's hocus-pocus with the two modes. But his patience only went so far.

He placed his hands on the bench beneath him and ran them along the cool grain of the old wood. Its furrows and ridges irritated him, as did the slight concavity where his own body had, over the years, hollowed out his place. These ridges and hollows had nothing to do with his clean copies. His copies had always been exact, and now, locked up in the mountain, they would stay exact forever. He had done everything exactly as he was told. They could never fault him for a single mark out of place.

Ghast took up his lamp and made his way to the vestibule by the entrance. Once behind the curtain, he extinguished his light and stood in the empty silence. It was pure, void and true — untroubled by the ache of hearts, the pounding of fists, the cry of antagonists. It lay as quiet as a grave, ready for the blood that he would spill in it.

20

The Loom

The hall fell as silent as the huge oak beams that spanned it, and to the rhythm of their spanning Kay timed her breathing. She fought back a smile that lingered, aching, just behind her eyes, and counted the wooden stalls lined along the two walls to either side of her, and before them the long benches ranked five deep to the aisle the whole length of the hall – to the right the right-wraiths and to the left the left-wraiths. From one end to the other, Kay guessed, seven hundred or more wraiths sat gathered, murmuring expectantly – agitated, even. But why shouldn't they be? The first Twelfth Night, the first Weave, for three hundred years? Kay threw back her head and, as the hair tressed and bowed over her shoulders, let the smile pour into the tiny diamond lights that studded the ceiling. *To think we have come to Bithynia at last.*

Two days before it hadn't seemed possible. Kay looked vacantly towards the far end where the dais stood with its twelve high thrones, and remembered the tumult of their arrival in Montmartre – how she and Flip and Razzio and Phantastes had tumbled out of the car in a tiny lane on the steep hillside over the city, and she had followed Flip through the low door into a pretty cobbled courtyard, where they heard, faintly, urgent voices – her father's voice among them – passing an argument back and forth like a ticking charge. Up an external stair and into the warm wooden interior she had swept exhaustedly with a kind of bleak hope, dazzled by the thought that she was about to fall into the arms of the wraith who, hours before, had hunted her almost to an end. Her enemy. Their enemy. She had suddenly thought how difficult Flip and Will and Phantastes would find this – to confront, to make truce with, the wraith who had killed Rex.

But perhaps the thrill of the plot had been carrying them, for when they pushed into the low-ceilinged, comfortable room they had found Will and Ned More seated before the hearth fire, drinking hot cider and arguing, if urgently, also animatedly, also respectfully, with Kat.

All that gorgeous black hair. Those gripping eyes.

Murderer, she had thought. Now she thought it again.

Ell had been sitting in a cushioned window seat, ostensibly looking at a huge picture book but actually, over the top of the page, watching Kat intensely. The duffel coat she had shed, but her clothes beneath were black, too, and her hair was there in its piles of luxurious, gorgeous sheen. At once Kay had wanted both to lie in it and tear it out by the clump. All three adults (but not Ell) had looked up as the door opened, but they hadn't paused for a moment in the conversation, and Kay and the others had taken seats where they could find them and had listened intently.

'Ghast can't stand against this – not after that happened in Rome – you know that even Foliot will fall from him at the return of the Bride,' Will had said. 'And with the horn, with the shuttle, with the hall nearly ready – Kat, we have time to hold the Weave *this year* – we can do it in two days.'

'We can,' said Ned.

'Just about,' said Flip.

'Not without the loom,' she had concluded flatly, quietly. *'And only a muse may hew the wood whereof the loom is made –* you know the old saying, Will. An instrument like that –'

'We can do it without the loom, but we can't do it without you.' Kay suddenly realized that her father must have washed and changed his clothes at Kat's house. As he courted Kat's participation in the Weave, he seemed his old self – serious, assured and direct. 'We need you to call in all the wispers. Bring them to Bithynia, Kat.'

Kay had hated her only for that long moment before she answered; but who could hate a voice like hers that dropped like clumps of soft cream into your ears, its accent like a hot wash that burned the throat of your hearing, but so warmly, as if you couldn't hear the words too slowly? 'I don't know,' she had said. And then, 'A few hours ago I would happily have accepted a tidy commendation from Ghast for bringing in that child; and now I'm to forget all that? Now I am to forget that Ghast is my master?'

'Yes,' Ned More had said. 'Forget mastery altogether. Remember, rather, the thread. Take the girl, but take us, too. Call Ghast to Bithynia. Let him bring his armies, his bodyguards, his clerks, his private servants. Let them all come. All we need is an instant. Eloise will blow the horn, and Katharine will answer. The First Wraith will take to the loom, and then all the wraiths and phantasms in the Honourable Society will see what we have seen.' The fire had caught at all her father's sharpest angles as he spoke, and his face had flickered with its flames. Kay shuddered to remember it. *Two nights*, she had thought.

And she shuddered, too, to remember the messenger who had arrived just at that moment – a terrified, obsequious wraith with a letter in his hand, summoning Kat to a Weave on Ghast's own authority, and commanding her to do exactly what Ned More had – only instants before – been urging her to do in defiance of her master – that is, to call the wispers in their hundreds to their ancient seat. How Kat had stared at them in wonder and confusion! How that messenger had looked at them, with fear and distrust! How his eyes had spoken of the horrors that, under Ghast's authority, the whole Society suffered!

But Kat had done it. She had called them all home – century on century of wispers, trailing on their secret paths wheresoever, had answered to their summonings. And from the mountain Ghast, with his armies, his bodyguards, his clerks and his private servants – somehow, beyond hope, they were there. Phantastes had roused the right-wraiths out of hiding – those that could be found – and from Rome Razzio recalled Oidos, Ontos, and the handful of causes who had somehow, miraculously, survived the fire. At the airport Kay and Ell had sat quietly with their father as Flip told a tale or two, and before long the flight crew had made them all at home at the front of a sparsely occupied service to Istanbul. The girls had slept all the way there and, though she'd had a headache as they stepped out into the smoky, dim light of the Turkish airport, Kay hadn't failed to notice the odd tall figure rushing past them, or the odd cloak or robe among the suits and skirts of their fellow passengers. The next day they had rested in the country and made plans – called on favours, arranged for deliveries, and talked and talked as the girls ran wild in a fresh snowfall outside – but on the following morning they had set out again, now by car, for the hall. In a pouch at his waist Will had borne the shuttle. In the sack over his shoulder Phantastes had carried the horn. Flip and Razzio had driven the two cars down the winding, potholed roads. And then they were here.

Here.

There had been no appetite for feasting, no nerves for dancing or for revelry. The command to all had been to assemble, and the wraiths who now sat around the hall – and Kay could see them still trickling in, by the twos and fives – had come to speak, and not to celebrate. Some faces, she saw, looked hopeful, jubilant, expectant – these, she supposed, would be the right-wraiths. Rumours had been passed. Stories had been told. Others seemed more nervous, more fearful, and there were many of them – these, Kay guessed, were Ghast's servants, the left-wraiths and the lesser right-wraiths. Of Ghast there was as yet no sign, though they had set a chair for him in the centre of the lower part of the hall, opposite the dais. Kay sat in the very midst of all, on a tiny stool at the midpoint of the hall's long length, but hard up against the benches of the right-wraiths. Opposite her, on another stool, Ell perched nervously, holding Phantastes' sack with the horn within. When the procession began, she knew her part – to blow one long peal on the horn, and then to wait. She had practised in the car, very nearly driving them from the road and their senses; but Kay thought now, with pleasure, that Ell would pull it off perfectly.

To think, she mused to herself again, *that we have come to Bithynia.*

The hall was mostly unadorned – only a few banners hung to each side – and in many places the water and frost damage was severe, and plainly to be seen. Gouges stood out in some of the walls, and the mosaics of the floor were in places badly cracked or missing. But the ceiling was at last intact, and though the place was draughty, it also felt warm, and no rain or snow or wind seeped in through its massive leaded windows. Under heavy clouds, they were almost dark now; just beyond them the weather had turned ever fouler – cold, gusty and sleet-showered. It hardly mattered. With a handful of students and local men, her father had been at work here, off and on, for almost eight months, and together they had at least made the hall watertight and stopped the rot. In time more banners would hang again from poles anchored in the row of empty wall-slots. In time the floors would be relaid. In time the massive stalls would feel the sharp blades of the master woodcarvers, and the missing diamonds would be re-set in the oak lattice of the ceiling. In time the tapestries would come down from the mountain.

But there was one thing, Kay thought with simple happiness as the great curtain at the lower hall was drawn aside, for which they would not have to wait. Six wraiths on either side now bore it up, set on a pallet hoisted with cross-staves, to the top of the hall and set it down. No one knew who had rebuilt it, or how it had been delivered to the hall. Ned More thought perhaps his foreman – who denied it – had had a hand in it, but others ventured that Ghast himself, to mock them, had caused it to be remade, and left for the right time in the vestibule of the Shuttle Hall. However it had got there, and whoever had carved and built it, as was the tradition, from solid ash, there it now stood: the great loom of the First Wraith, waxed and set with warp and woof, ready for the consult to begin.

The loom bearers removed their staves and then took their own seats. The heavy green and gold embroidered curtain, fifteen feet across and at least as high, again drew back, and with a start Kay realized that the procession had already begun. It was a simple but a solemn movement down the hall, led by Phantastes and, behind him, one of the lesser imaginers whom he had appointed that day from among the exiled right-wraiths. They wore cassocks of green inlaid with silver, and around their collars tiny diamond studs; their heads were bare. After a short gap, next followed Razzio, leading Oidos and Ontos, all in heavy gowns and black cloaks, with buttons of jet and a single ivory stone set into the cuff at either hand. Behind them, again after a small space, the three youngest of the right-wraiths came in blue cassocks, with gold studs set round their collars; and behind them, last of all, the three youngest left-wraiths, in grey gowns and cloaks, with a black plotting stone threaded into the cuff at either hand, as before. Each of them carried a rod of black iron, its tip embellished with a snake writhing to the point, which was capped with a plotting stone. They came, each of them, without other adornment, and no further ceremony but the stately pace at which they measured the hall, and the register of import that lay graved in their twelve faces; even Phantastes, who had almost gibbered with enthusiasm about the Weave just that morning, stared forward with a resolution that shamed Kay for her delight. She looked down as they approached, and crossed her legs with a scowl.

But at the same moment Ell slid to her feet, and when the twelve, led by Phantastes, stopped just shy of her stool, she lifted the horn to her lips and blew the peal for which she had practised all that day. Kay had heard the horn before, but not like this – not in this hall, with its huge resound and the amplifying distortion of its wooden ceiling and stalls. It whined like a siren, roared like a lion and wailed like a child all at once, and well before it ended Kay thought her eardrums might bleed with the singleness of its insistent boring, boring into her awareness. All her thoughts lay down and shrivelled before the noise. She watched the sound explode between her hands.

Then, as suddenly as it had begun, it ended, and as the hum and its after-peal rang in the ears of nearly a thousand wraiths, Phantastes called out to the hall in a resonant bass Kay had never before heard from him.

'Leap, heart!'

Every wraith in the Shuttle Hall answered him as one.

'*The wind will catch you!*'

Then the old imaginer led the procession again on its grave way to the dais. Kay studied them as they passed: Phantastes with his shining scalp, massive temples, broad shoulders and thick protruding veins upon his neck; the older right-wraith with his great eyes like pools, and again the thick blue veins running across his hands and down his necks; Razzio, Oidos and Ontos with their olive skin and different heights and gaits; the younger right-wraiths, again broad and tall, but sallow and sickly after decades – maybe centuries – in penurious hiding; and the younger left-wraiths, again short like Razzio, and one of them very corpulent, but with long, delicate fingers. As these last passed her, Phantastes had already reached the wheel. Without breaking step he advanced to its first position and set his rod into the hole, allowing it to slide heavily through his fingers until with a clang it stood sure; then he turned and took his place before his throne. The right-wraith behind him took the second position and the seat beside his master, and so, each placing a rod and each choosing a seat, they all completed their procession, the imaginers fanning off to the left, the plotters to the right, the right-wraiths to the far left and the left-wraiths to the far right. When they were all at last standing before their thrones, with a single motion they sat together. A murmur went around the hall, and Kay recognized that the consult had now officially begun.

'Call the First Wraith!' came a shout from the benches of the right-wraiths, followed by many others, from both sides, clamouring.

Will appeared from the anteroom, adorned in nothing but his old cloak, and walked quickly, even urgently down the length of his hall with no ceremony at all; he even raised his eyebrows, with a little cock of the cheek, as he passed Kay, though he didn't look up from the floor. First he went to the wheel and, grasping two rods in his outstretched hands, ground the huge iron frame along its circular path into its final position.

Twelve nights.

He stood for a moment, looking at it and seeming to draw his breath in dying waves. At the step, then, before the thrones, on one knee he received from Razzio the shuttle; when he reached the loom, he turned to face the hall and held it up before him. At this there was a greater murmur than before. Will held it to his lips and blew a seven-second note – not this time one of the familiar tones, but a new one: low, jarring, but rising, and finishing in a keen knife-thrust note as bleak and total as the horn of the Primary Fury. Kay stiffened; she needed no interpreter to tell her that this was the note of tragedy. Now the wraiths in the hall no longer murmured but talked openly, and their voices on both sides sounded distressed – why had the First Wraith chosen the note of the old tragedies? What would befall them all tonight?

'Call the antagonist!' shouted a voice from the benches of the left-wraiths, and though not as many voices as before answered it, still the call was taken up until Ghast himself appeared from the anteroom, his short, swart form dwarfed by the grand drape of the hall curtain. No wonder, Kay thought, Ghast had wanted to get away from this place – it was completely the wrong scale for him. Suddenly, across the hall among the left-wraiths, she picked out Flip sitting beside Kat and, catching his eye, smiled at him. He rolled his eyes; he thought he had an idea of what was coming.

But at the sight of Ghast, a knot had gathered in Kay's stomach. She saw him look out over the hall, and she thought suddenly that his gaze looked *practised*.

In a flash she saw him walking the length of the hall alone, lamp held aloft in the darkness. She saw him pace the floor, saw him take the seat just opposite her on the bench among the left-wraiths. She saw his thoughts. *My dream. What have we done?* She knew it was no use trying to hold on to a dream, that it surfaced like bubbles in a pond, no sooner visible than vanished. She knew that she could not hold it even now, that it would slip from her fingers the instant she grasped after it. But it was there, that she knew – and her stomach tightened. Blood spilled on the stone.

'Wraiths and phantasms!' bellowed Ghast. 'Many years ago we held what I thought was to be our last congregation in this hall. At your bidding, then, the instruments of the old ways were broken up and scattered, and a new order was spun for the Weave. Since then much has changed, and changed for the better.' He was spitting out his words slowly and clearly, and though he was positioned at the low and far end of the hall, his eyes were roving over the crowded wraiths, taking in as many gazes as he could. Flickers of recognition played across his features as he spoke, and Kay knew he was consummately playing the politician. She watched the wraiths, picking out the few she knew – Foliot, installed at the high end of the hall among the left-wraiths; Kat beside Flip, and on the other side of her Sprite, by the floor, and Jack, among the stalls at the low end of the right-wraiths. Jack looked worried, Kay thought as Ghast went on.

'For around us, too, the world has changed. Who sits by the fire to drink up the words of the poet? Who pores by weak candlelight over the heavy volumes of the old tales? When was the saga last sung? Who toils through the vedas? What child thinks of Alexander now? Where lie the bones of Gog Magog, or who honours the ashes of the jade queen? These are the lost preoccupations of lesser ages and the dreams of vanished nights. Who knows them now? Scholars!' With theatrical exaggeration Ghast spat profusely on the floor before him. 'Scholars who would sooner own a story than honour it, who would sooner scorn a tale than have skill in it.

'It is the world of women and men that has driven us into the mountain, the world of women and men that has broken the loom, lost the shuttle, crushed the horn and burned the old thread. Some have called me bloody, some ruthless, but the imaginers were not dispersed, nor the right-wraiths scattered by my hand; or if my hand was the instrument, the world of women and men armed me to it.' He paused, letting this improbable logic sink improbably in.

Kay looked at Will, her eyes asking whether this had not gone on too long; but his face was inclined to the floor, his eyes scattered in the grey arcs of stone that washed across the hall between the benches.

414

'The stories have all been written,' Ghast shouted, 'and there is no new thing under the sun! The great tree is dead, and its leaves all are withered! The moors and fens and mountains where once our wispers stalked are farmed, drained and scaled. Why should we walk now by the known ways of the earth, reminding the ungrateful of what they have chosen to forget? We do ourselves dishonour even to think it. There are some who think we must conserve the past and become curators of our vanished glories; but for whose sake shall we rebuild our great library? For whose sake re-hang the huge tapestried hall? Surely not for our own.

'No.' Ghast was striding the hall now, covering the floor between his low-set seat and the midpoint where Kay perched, increasingly worried, upon her stool. Had he come from the mountain for this? Was this the trap that she had dreamed? Will still hung his head, the shuttle moving absently between his fingers as he sat averted from the loom. Kay looked to Flip, but he was – strangely – beaming, as if privy to some joke Kay had not yet fathomed. And where was her father? Beyond the windows the meagre daylight – which was their only illumination – sagged and darkened, as if on Ghast's cue. He was not speaking now but pacing the hall, searching the faces of the wraiths on both sides, challenging his antagonists to refute him. Had they come to Bithynia for the Bride? his eyes demanded. Had they really believed for a moment that such a childish myth could *be*?

'The loom has been rebuilt, they say – but by whom, and for what? Indeed it stands before us, and I am grateful that it should be so, and that we should meet in the shadow of its authority. But what should we make upon its great rack now, except the greater sacrifice of our hands? I have heard the horn has been recovered. I have heard the shuttle has been dredged up from the ocean floor. I have heard of keys, of shellfruits, of blossoms underground – I have heard such whatnots! And to what end? That you should thrall yourselves to the empty ceremonies of a sterile and all-too-fruitful fruitlessness? That you should throw open the doors upon a tomb, and perish in it?'

Suddenly, and with menacing strides, Ghast covered the half-length of the hall, drove directly up to Kay and pointed his stubby, fat finger right in her face. At his height, his eyes were almost level with her own. She recoiled from his curled lip, fearing he would spit even upon her. But instead – and for the first time that evening he lowered his voice – he spoke directly to her. 'You don't believe the hocus-pocus of shellfruits and causes any more than I do. *I* know you. You know what's beneath the House of the Two Modes. You saw the carvings on the walls. You saw the altar. *You* know, as I know, that that house is built on a vast and swallowing grave. It is built on nothing but *death*. And through *that* door –' he spun and shouted now at Will, who sat silently with his head bowed – 'there is *no passage*.' And now he turned back to Kay, and sneered almost down her throat. 'In that night there are no stars, only darkness.'

Kay's throat suddenly ran dry as sand, and her stomach collapsed in sickening knots.

'But we have an alternative. We may *manage* our stories. We may *package* them. We may *sell* them. Let us not go back to the Quarries – fine. Let us not go back to the mountain – good. Let us seal it up – excellent. But this place is no more our home now than those craggy voids, for the world of women and men has forgotten it, has thrown it through the door into the bottomless grave of useless history, and if we stay here – if we stay here like this, I say, then we fall with it!'

Ghast stood very close to Kay and let his words sink in for a moment. Then, in a hushed voice, surely almost inaudible to the wraiths sitting at the far reaches of the stalls, he concluded. 'Some of you may be surprised to see me here. Perhaps you thought I could not be lured by the trifling tale-telling of our right-handed retroverts. Perhaps you thought I would even now be making good my escape. But I have more respect for the Honourable Society than to think it the passive limb of a wasted, withered philosophy. You are something more than the playthings of tired, mad imaginations. And yet I am glad that we stand here once more, assembled in our ancient home, and with the due form of all our ritual toys observed. Let us resolve once and for all to leave this way. Let us create the forms for a new Weave, a better Weave, a more efficient Weave, a more *prosperous* Weave. Let us do so, and close these doors behind us forever.'

Ghast fell silent where he stood, and the whole hall of wraiths on both sides sat speechless, each perhaps waiting for the other to begin. But where the shouts had pealed readily before Ghast's arrival, now Kay thought despairingly that the smiles and bright looks had drooped, and the fixed grimaces of the left-wraiths had hardened. Still Will looked down, and still he turned the shuttle absently in his hands. Meanwhile Ghast walked quietly back to the lower end of the hall. There was a chair there – a plain, everyday chair. Kay wondered that she hadn't noticed it earlier. With one of his meaty hands he took hold of it by the back, then dragged it, scraping the stone floor, until it rested just beyond the lowest, the most humble of the stalls of the left-wraiths. He stood before it.

'I have spoken,' he said at last, and sat.

The walls of stone where, at the ends of the hall, they rose unadorned from the floor to the oak-beamed ceiling were not more silent than the Weave during the long breath that greeted Ghast's conclusion. Kay fought her rising panic as the silence continued and still Will did nothing. Then, suddenly, from a wraith sitting not three metres from her stool, a courage-curdling cry came: 'Let him be king!' Kay's heart flooded furiously in her chest as the cry was taken up, and up, all around the hall – first by two or three, then five, then twenty, until hundreds of wraiths began to chant it in a gradually resolving unison. The sense of horror and alienation Kay experienced as, on her stool, she began to fold under the pressure of the chanting was absolute. For a long moment she dared not raise her eyes from the floor, even to steal a glance at Will or Flip; but when at last she did, she wished she hadn't.

For Flip was no longer smiling, but was himself chanting. Nor was he chanting only, but he began to beat his hands emphatically against the bench before him, in a display of impatience and fury. When Kay sought his gaze, she achieved no recognition; was this, she thought, what it was all for? All the friendship, the betrayals, the reconciliations, the stories, the trust? To bring us to this room, this fate, this event? And still between his hands, almost prostrate, Will turned the shuttle over. With sudden and piercing distress Kay remembered that, though Ghast had before aspired to a kingship over the Honourable Society, he had been prevented by the necessary form of proceeding: he required an author. Ell sat blinking and terrified on her stool, obviously wanting very much to break across the narrow floor to hide in her sister's arms. She had never looked so small to Kay, or so important.

The next few moments seemed to pass very quickly: Ghast stole over the length of the hall with his chair, placing himself opposite the loom and before the twelve knights; Flip slipped off the benches and delivered a velvet bag to Razzio, which Kay by its size and shape knew must contain a crown; the chanting intensified; and the three youngest left-wraiths, in what must have been a carefully orchestrated abduction, descended off the dais and, processing down the hall, suddenly snatched Ell and returned to the loom, bearing her between their hands. Kay's instinct was to give chase and to free Ell from their grasp by any ineffectual means, but the chanting cowed her, and the elongated faces – set, determined – of so many wraiths around the hall.

As if in a dream, and as the chanting continued, the three youngest left-wraiths deposited Ell on the dais before Razzio who, with his hands upon hers, helped her to lift the crown before the assembly. Flip took a place to the right of the loom, and they all – including Will, who at last and too late lifted his haggard head – turned to watch the proceedings. Ten of the knights sat still enthroned on the dais; only Razzio was on his feet, puffed out with the pride Kay had seen in him on their first arrival in Rome the week before, his chin thrust high into the air and his eyelids heavy upon the sights that did not truly concern him. Kay bored into their hearts as she watched how they betrayed themselves, the story of their trials and travels, the friendships and revelations they had sorrowed and suffered for. Now Razzio himself knelt low to the floor and presented his knee to Ell, gesturing for her to stand upon it and, from above, to place the crown upon the head of the seated Ghast. For his part, his face spoke total command: not a line, not a hairy mole was out of place.

As Eloise lifted the shell-ivory crown, with its elaborate ornament of whorl and plotting stone, delicately into place upon Ghast's head, the chanting erupted into a magnificent, feral cheer. The hair on the back of Kay's neck bristled to hear it, and for the first time that day she felt not anger, but real fear. Ghast stood up to cheers and loud halloos from the hall all around, and stood fixed while the wraiths in company continued to salute him – by no means all, Kay thought as she looked tentatively around, but enough to carry the momentum of a cheer. Enough, she thought, to overpower the others.

The greater half of the wraiths in the hall were still cheering as Flip, dragging Ell by her little hand, walked slowly back from the disregarded loom, past where Kay was sitting, towards the back of the hall. As they approached, Kay felt the full force of loss like a knife twisting in her gut. *It has all been for this. All the searching, all the discovery, all the awful losses and recoveries. After all this, and I have lost her anyway. I had twelve nights to save you all, and on the twelfth, I failed.*

And for a moment she didn't care.

I am too tired.

As Flip neared her, she saw his face. And, from nothing, her heart ignited in a rage. He still wore the same merry but deranged expression, intent and unhinged, but now he stared full in Kay's face as he passed, taking her eyes in a hold that for an instant she thought she couldn't sustain. Everything in her steeled and went cold, and her head felt flattened within by an overwhelming drone that she knew was nothing but the blood surging like ice through her veins.

But then, suddenly, and so quickly that Kay instantly fretted that she had not seen it at all, she thought he winked. Kay's thoughts spun. She sat dumb and unmoving – betrayed, reprieved, betrayed again, reprieved again, uncertain whether to collapse in defeat or throw back her shoulders in triumph.

In a moment Flip had disappeared from the hall, and Ell with him, and the cheering began to fall just a little, and then, as if dragged down under its own weight, it died completely. Ghast seemed about to speak; but just as he raised his right hand and took a deep, ponderous breath, the curtain behind Kay was drawn and into the hall strode, very purposefully, her father.

Within fifty long paces, all measured by a shocked silence, he had covered the length of the hall and stood before the loom and the newly crowned king. Without flourish, he sank to one knee, and in a direct address to Ghast requested, without ceremony or form, that the king would upon the festival of his coronation grant him a boon.

Kay could see clearly Ghast's discomfort: he still stood immediately next to the loom, where Will sat, indifferent; the eleven knights still sat enthroned behind him, where Razzio had retaken his seat; and it was obvious to all that he cared little for the petitioner. But, equally, this was to be his first act as king, and Ghast could not afford to trample too roughshod across the goodwill of his subjects. He turned, almost enquiringly, to Razzio, his neck stiffly soldered to his shoulders as if he feared to topple the crown from his fat head. With a wave of his long fingers Razzio signalled Oidos. She rose. 'It is the ancient custom of the Honourable Society that a king of wraiths should not refuse a petitioner in the Weave,' she said perfunctorily, and sat.

'Then anything that is mine to give,' Ghast replied, with a forced munificence and to all the company of the hall, 'upon the day of my coronation I shall bestow without stint.'

Ned More had neither flinched nor shaken, even for a moment, throughout this exchange, but still knelt, staring, at Ghast. 'I desire then that you should cause me to weep,' he said. Ghast stared at him. 'Or if not to weep, then to laugh. Or to fear, to joy, to sorrow, to suffer. Tell me some tale.'

Ghast, unnerved, looked again at Oidos, then over at Firedrake. With sudden resolution he said, 'I shall call one of my wraiths –'

'No,' said Ned More quietly but forcefully. 'I ask that it should be you.'

Ghast, who had already raised his arm as if to summon one of the lesser left-wraiths to him, slowly allowed it to fall. His face looked ashen. 'I will not,' he said.

'You must.'

Kay hadn't seen the curtains open for a final time. No one had. Nor did any wraith know the voice that spoke those commanding words – the clear and sonorous treble that sliced through the air like a sword at once rising and falling, striking and parrying; that both pierced the ear with its sudden violence and sheathed itself in the surety of its unimpeachable authority. But Kay knew that voice and, as she turned, tears had already begun to well in her exhausted eyes, and her hands, though she willed them to reach out, to clap, to fall upon that proud figure before her, only hung limp and paralysed by her sides.

It was her mother.

Oh my mother, oh my mother, cry, my wretched heart. Forgive me.

Clare Worth was dressed in the same long green cassock, trimmed with silver and studded with diamonds, that Phantastes wore. In her hands she held a rod of black forged iron. She held it like a bat, across her body, as if she had come to break with tradition and not to fulfil it – as if at any moment she might stalk down the hall with her rod ready and begin to swing it. She stared at the wraiths around her, turning her head with a measured sweep to take in first the assembled left-wraiths, then their antagonists across the aisle, the whole body

423

of right-wraiths, and at last the eleven knights assembled on the dais at the far end of the hall – and, last of all, Ghast upon his throne, and her husband, still patiently kneeling before him. Unlike everyone else in the hall, he had not turned round or even flinched at the sound of this new voice. Kay stared hard at his back, uncertain if it was tight with anger or loose with relief.

And then, with firm and unhurried steps, Clare Worth began to walk the length of the hall. The eye of every wraith followed her. Every breath drew even with her steps. Every heart sped to see the iron rod in her hands, that staff lost for a thousand years, for two thousand, for as long as a story can be told or a great imagining conjured. When she reached the hall's end, she hoisted the rod erect in her hands, holding it above her head – and then, with purpose, drove it home into its ancient slot at the head of the great wheel.

Kay lurched breaths. She had seen what she could not dare know, what she could not understand – the head of her mother's iron staff, unlike all the others in this, that it was tipped with gold.

It was you. All along, you. In the sewers at Alexandria. It was you with the kermes book. It was you in the catacombs. All along it was you.

Phantastes stood, and stepped forward from his throne.

My mother. You built the loom.

'My lady,' he said, and bowed. Even from where she sat, Kay could see the tears streaming down his suddenly haggard cheeks.

Clare ignored him. It was as if she hadn't even heard him. Her hands still grasped the iron rod where she had completed the circle. The room paused. The very air seemed unsure, and faltered. Her eyes were fixed on something distant, or something long ago, as if she were gathering her strength from a great afar.

Suddenly, with a heave and a terrible cry, Clare Worth pulled back with all her strength on the iron rod in her hands. Kay thought for a second that she had bent it – but no, it wasn't that. The rod, it appeared, was a kind of lever and, as her mother pulled on it, it declined from the centre of the circle with a hard grating sound, as of iron drawing against stone, or a plough cutting into rocky ground – and then rested, fixed and splayed. Clare Worth proceeded around the wheel, heaving on the rods one by one until they had all opened like petals, away from the centre of its circle. And with the last, almost like magic, the iron wheel opened at its hub, and from a circular boss she retrieved a huge, luminous dark-blue stone. Cupping it with both hands, she carried it down the length of the hall.

'Mum,' said Kay. 'It's Ell – they took her, I couldn't –'

'I love you,' said Clare to Kay, placing the stone in her outstretched palms. Their eyes met in a fathomless tenderness, but she did not smile. 'Don't go running off again.'

In the utter hush she re-crossed the length of the hall. The knights stood as she approached, making way for Clare Worth to assume the throne of honour at their centre, and then together the twelve of them took their seats. Ghast stared at them, at Kay, and with obvious terror at the heavy blue gem in her hands, which seemed to glow within its rounded surface with the white lines of a twelve-pointed star.

Stars were there.

Ghast had gone grey with fear. But that, Kay thought, was as nothing to the pallor that swept across his features as Will – without prologue or demonstration – slipped the pirn into the shuttle, then began to set the threads upon the loom. After so many years he would have a story at last.

'Tell your story, Ghast of the Bindery, King of Wraiths and Phantasms.' Clare Worth put her hands on the arms of her throne and closed her eyes. 'Tell your story and grant your boon.'

After a painfully protracted silence, during which not a single wraith so much as cleared her throat, Ghast began.

'There was once a man. All his desire was to be great. He would achieve great things, but he had neither skill nor knowledge. He had no aptitude, no opportunity. For years he woke, ate, did unmemorable things, repeated them, ate again, slept; and he hid his desire for greatness in the darkest corner of his awareness. He hid it because, as an ambition he could not fulfil, it was able to cause him only pain. The years accumulated and grew upon him like earth, weighing him down, driving ever further into the cold, airless, lightless past his sacred hunger. If he had recalled his youthful ambition, he would have found that his appetite for greatness had dulled with the gradual accomplishment of mean honours, with the acquisition of almost useless abilities – but he never had the leisure to consider himself, and ever less as his authority widened, the demands on his schedule multiplied and the number of his clients grew.'

The words were produced slowly, but not haltingly. Like them all, Kay could see that this kind of speaking did not come easily to Ghast, and yet his features and the tension in his frame as he spoke seemed to betray not only uneasiness, but a kind of contemptuous intensity. Before him, though completely disregarded, her father still knelt, impassive.

'The day came when other men might have crested that imperceptible ridge, passing from a life of industrious ineffectiveness to one of unremarkable incapacity. But this man discovered, to his surprise, that the world around him had shrunk, withered, decayed, lapsed. The skills he had once sought and failed to achieve; the knowledge he had once sought to master, but staggered in; the opportunities that he had once so fervently coveted, but missed – these now had vanished from the world. Little by little the ambition and hunger that had relentlessly dogged his youngest years fought their way to the surface of his being and his doing, and he began to discover – though only by glimpses at first – that all he required to differentiate himself from and, indeed, to prefer himself to the world was his pure ambition. The hunger alone would set him apart. In a very little time he was reputed the greatest man then living, and so achieved his desire.'

There Ghast ended, punctuating his speech with a defiant stare not only at Edward More, but at the assembled wraiths on both sides of the hall, whose expectation had demanded, and secured, this demeaning display from him. And well might he defy them, Kay thought, for his story had been awful, mean, pointless and empty; and as she followed his eyes to those of his audience, she saw in them the same distrust, the same dissatisfaction, the same contempt that he reflected back at them; nor was this among the right-wraiths only, but even the left-wraiths, and even those who only a short while before had chanted most enthusiastically, Ghast's brief, incompetent and vicious display met with less than a resigned disbelief. It had aroused their impatience, their shame and even (as Kay watched the faces, and the minds that made the faces) their hatred. Ghast had ended, and the hall fell not silent, but uncomfortably, simmeringly void. Rustling, stamping and the clearing of throats began menacingly to emanate from the right of the hall, and from its left a shamed defiance. Kay could sense the coming confrontation, though it was not yet clear whether it would conclude as cooperation or an outright brawl.

And then Ghast began again to speak – or so Kay thought, until, reverting to him, she found his lips still and his features verging on a poorly concealed rage. She couldn't see, couldn't hear whence the voice came, but it was scored and stippled out with the faint beat of a tapping drum – and though it rose and fell like a wave rolling (that both falls and rises only that it may go on rolling), or like a thread passing in and out of the texture of the weave, it always moved, was always there, full of forward motion. In a clap of stunned recognition, Kay realized that it was Will's voice, and that he had taken up the story while he worked at it himself upon the loom.

'This was the man of despair who, like Phaethon, child of Helios, attempted in his greed to seize and control that which lay beyond him – and, in reaching for it, destroyed it. Phaethon, disregarded boy, who was not content to remain one of the blessed children of the sun, to wear his father's livery on his cheek or upon his shoulders; Phaethon who could not rest in his thought until he had caught the very reins in his hand, until he had put the horses under his sole direction, until he had seized his father's chariot and driven the sun almost into the earth. Cruel and catastrophic ambition! The fertile vines of Italy and Greece burst into flame, and the vineyards, laid waste, became deserts; the sea like a pot set upon a stove bubbled and steamed, and then boiled dry; the trees grown torches, the fields grown sheets of fire, burned, and upon them the people ran like whole, searing blisters, their eyes frying in their sockets and their skin pouring from their charring bones like fast-melted wax. Who heard the cries of children among the bellowings of oxen and horses, among the screams of plummeting eagles? Happy then were those who chanced before the relentless ball of flame to fall into some deep pool or flooded cavern, where they might shelter a while from the blast! Happy then were the worms, the moles, the badgers and the foxes that by burrowing in the cool soil and clay seemed to evade the scorching flames that fell from the air! Happy then were all those towering birds of prey that in the high mountains sought out ice and snow in which to blanket themselves! But pools were blasted away, the very clay was baked into dust, and the mountains stood bare but for the drifting heaps of ash that once had been forests. Small wonder, then, that, while the world burned, the father of the gods whetted his titanic bolt and, hurling it, dashed Phaethon from the sky and scattered him in pieces upon the earth.

'So was the world and all that was in it brought to destruction by a childish overreaching, a greed born of despair that would rather kill the thing it covets than suffer others to enjoy it. It is a story as old as stories are, told by every people, a memory of the great cataclysms of the past and a prophecy of those to come. But it is not the last story; for always when the selfish appetite, overrunning everything, has consumed itself and fed at last upon its own ruin, then other voices, perhaps quiet at first, can be heard; then other feet, light steps though they may be, tread the embers and from them begin again to raise a harvest. The daughters of Helios, in grief for Phaethon, their brother, scoured the plains and shores of Italy looking for and collecting the pieces of his thunder-torn corpse. Piece by piece they composed him, a work of years, until they were able to give him burial, their brother, the companion of their mother's womb, their blood and their flesh, at last laid to rest. But in their mourning, in their sad and weary steps as they brought his body to the grave, they also created something new: no sooner had they poured funeral libations upon his scattered corpse, no sooner had they cast the dust upon his body, no sooner had they with tears and laments sounded the last of his days than the gods caused thin webs to spin along their palms and fingers, transforming them into leaves, while a crusty bark ramified each limb, stretching and branching it into a network of trunk, bough, twig and stem. From their feet, where they stood along the banks of the river Eridanus, roots crawled into the earth, binding them to the shore, while from their eyes tears like thick slugs of amber dropped into the water below, as still they do today.

'In the same way Isis, goddess of the moon, soaked all Egypt in her tears when, after the death of her husband Osiris, she roamed the valley of the Nile, seeking the scattered pieces of his body. With his death the great light of the sun had been extinguished; all Egypt surrendered to flood, to rot and to plague; and it seemed as if every good of the world would be drowned in the relentless waves of the spreading river. But in her grief Isis told another tale, and as she gathered here an arm, there a finger, here the hip of her beloved and there a rib, piecemeal she reconstructed her lord and husband, until the day when, through her devotion and determination, he sat again upon the royal throne at Abydos, dispensing justice. It is said that this queen of Egypt breathed life into her dead and dismembered lord not merely by her laments, her tears or her faith, but by her stories: myths of Osiris' great acts dropped from her mouth as she trod her pilgrim way; myths and legends, the histories of his ancestors, the tale of his miraculous birth, his attributes and his life, word after word knitted like the stitches wherewith surgeons bind flesh on flesh to heal the ragged wound. So by telling him over she gathered him together. So by telling over his story, even now, we too not only remember him and her, the tale together with its teller, but also breathe into them both new life, and renew our own.

'For which poet, which teller of stories, is not also a healer? Which ballad-maker is not likewise a priest, who in laying on the hands of a parable brings the dead again to life? To spin a yarn, as the singer Orpheus knew, is to go to hell for your bride – as Orpheus himself did when the gods moved the venomous snake to strike the heel of his beloved Eurydice. Orpheus braved the gods, charming the three-headed dog of the underworld, Cerberus, and seducing the ear of horrid Persephone, queen of Hades, before he might in triumph lead his bride again towards the light. So, even in death there is life, even in the end there lies a beginning, even from ashes a conquest may rise. Then let fall your tears of amber, O you daughters of Helios! Drop here and there your quickening stories, Isis, faithful queen! And you, Orpheus, great singer of tales, go you to hell and ransom the fair Eurydice – for while I weave, the Bride still whispers among the groves of old Bithynia!'

Kay knew as soon as the last word was pronounced that it had happened again: she must have slipped mesmerized into that same trance she had experienced in Paris three days before, because she now stood not before her chair or in the middle of the hall, but at its end, just before the dais and adjacent to the loom itself, which still worked quickly, weaving, under the hands of the First Wraith. In her cupped hands lay the Bridestone, faintly glowing, its star the quiet, still promise of a new birth; in Will's hands the shuttle, by contrast, moved like a wild and a live thing. He was nowhere near completion, but the beginnings of the tapestry had started to take colour under his hands as the shuttle wove through the threads with such speed that the air, rushing through it, created a low hum from every one of its tiny apertures: a quiet music, whistling and droning from Will's light grasp as he worked. Kay watched his delicate fingers threading in the total silence of the hall. She knew, this time, what had shocked the wraiths, and why they now sat so still. She knew what momentous heavings were stirring in their conscious thoughts, but strangely this understanding of their gravity seemed to free her from it, and she was all witness to Will's working, and she loved the dance of his hands among the thread, the way his fingers hardly touched the shuttle at all – as if they held, rather, all the air around its quick ovular sheen, and didn't so much push it through the warp as guide the places where it might no longer be. It was a negative moment, a play of space and gap, a dance between forms.

But the movement of the shuttle was not all; there was, too, the hard pressure of the bar, and the relentless closing up of space between the threads – and the bar worked like a lung, yawning open to free the hands, then slamming closed to build the weave, then open again, then closed. The voice of the shuttle moved murmuring in among these long breaths, with the lesser music of words weaving in the line, and Kay knew that the origin of the poetry she had been sung all her life lay in this two-plied weaving-up of depth, of motion, time, colour, as the shifting weight of recognition turned over, behind her, in hundreds on hundreds of minds, like the upending of some great mass in the sea. And she was conscious then of another sound, which was nearby and completely unlike the silence, completely unlike the blurred chaos of the shuttle; it pealed raspingly, like the death to which it was the prelude. Kay didn't need to look behind her to know that Ghast now lay upon the stone floor of the hall, or that the little rhythm of flecking hisses she heard was his last breath escaping between his foamy lips. Her father would be kneeling still at his side, trying to revive him; perhaps Kat, too, or another – but there would be no saving him. Kay felt neither sorry nor glad; she simply felt the open and closing of the bar as it moved across the gaps of threading fingers. Within the black border that would run all around the final work, she had known what the image would be, and she smiled now to see the face of Eurydice emerging, wreathed with serpents.

There was but one thing remaining. Kay knew just how it would be. She turned to face the silent hall, and the eyes of the whole Honourable Society of Wraiths and Phantasms settled upon her. She was still smiling. Almost as one, every wraith in the hall turned to follow her own gaze towards the far entrance, where Ell's face suddenly appeared, draped in the embroidered green velvet that still curtained her little body.

'Mum!' she shouted, and the peal of it rang across the ranks of wraiths as a ripple spreads on water, washing every face with the joy of return, of renewal, of rebirth. Ell broke through the curtains and ran the length of the hall, her feet stamping upon the mosaics – and, threading the rods, straight across the opened flower of the wheel. And the centuries of wraiths where she passed rose as one to their feet. And as she threw herself into her mother's outstretched arms, every one of their voices – with the very stones and glass, the wood and each painted ornament that decked the ancient hall, still rocking to the beat of the working loom – exploded into song.

Epilogue

The fingers moved across the piano keys like a rippling wave over pebbles. Kay watched them roll and then, by little leaps, spring up and down across the arpeggios, or fan to collect distributed chords. Her mother's hands were long and slender, with no apparent cast of muscle to them at all; and yet she could make the little room throb with the sound of a handgrip. Nor did she ever look down at them as they wheeled, eddied, pounced, twirled and wove across the keyboard, instead keeping her eyes firmly fixed on the score flung open on the rack before her. It was almost as if she were two people, and not one: a watcher with her eyes and a doer with her hands. As the long waltz fell into the last of its cadences, Kay bounced a little on to her toes and, from her patient stand next to the higher registers, cleared her throat.

'Mum?'

'Yes, Katharine.' Clare Worth placed her hands exactly on her thighs, and swivelled upon her stool so as to face her daughter.

'Do you ever look at your hands while you're playing the piano?'

'Not for a long time, Katharine. Why?'

'They remind me of something. Well, of a lot of things, actually.' Of a shuttle as white as the purest ivory, of the dark lamp-black of the plotting stone, of the hands that dance in the air, of an outstretched palm and of the cloth that sews the needle.

Clare Worth was silent, and Kay wasn't sure that she even took a breath. Outside a wood pigeon found its throat, but her mother just regarded her calmly, staring directly into her eyes; and for a moment Kay felt as if a hood had been drawn up over all the world but this one face, which lay revealed to her in all its simplicity and ancientness, its inarticulate kindness, its mathematical materiality.

'By the muses, they remind me of those things, too, Kay,' said Clare Worth at last. 'I'm so very, very glad that you are all home again.' Without another word she stood and lifted the cover of the huge piano, drawing up the prop to set the cover open. With the same quiet delicacy she removed the music stand and all its furniture. When she had exposed the sounding board, and above it all the instrument's strings and hammers, then she sat down and began again to play from the beginning – and while the music whorled and threaded, the two of them poured their mutual gaze upon her long, agile, harp-stringing, loom-building fingers.

Acknowledgements

Early readers – Jason Scott-Warren, Deborah Meyler, Jonathan Sissons, Adam Gauntlett and Davara Bennett – helped me to pull *Twelve Nights* out of its dusty shoebox and coax it into shape. I am so grateful for their encouragement!

Again and again Emily Sahakian has set me straight when I have lost the plot; she is that right *stedfast starre, in Ocean waues yet neuer wet.*

To Ruth Knowles at Penguin Random House, and all the team there, I can only imagine how much I owe.

To all of them, and to you, latest reader, with open arms, thanks.

About the Author

ANDREW ZURCHER is Director of Studies in English at Queen's College, Cambridge, and he writes widely on the works of Spenser, Sidney and Shakespeare. *Twelve Nights* is his debut novel.

@andrewzurcher